CORPSE ROADS

SABRE SECURITY BOOK ONE

J ROSE

For my fellow slow burn romance lovers,
I take zero liability for smashed kindles or angst-induced heart
attacks. Enjoy!

TRIGGER WARNING

Corpse Roads is a contemporary reverse harem romance, so the main character will have multiple love interests that she will not have to choose between.

This book is very dark and contains scenes that may be triggering for some readers. This includes physical and psychological abuse, torture, sexual assault and abuse, imprisonment, graphic violence, serial murder, PTSD and Trichotillomania.

If you are triggered by any of this content, please do not read this book.

This is a slow burn romance, so the relationships will develop over time, and the spice level will build up with each book.

"Beware that, when fighting monsters, you yourself do not become a monster… For when you gaze long into the abyss, the abyss gazes also into you."

- Friedrich Nietzsche

PROLOGUE

Harlow

White Noise – Badflower

f we confess our sins, he is faithful and just to forgive us, and to cleanse us from all unrighteousness.

Whispering the words in my hoarse voice, I link my shaking hands and squeeze my eyes shut. In these dark, desperate moments, I often feel like God is watching my suffering—laughing and thoroughly amused.

My prayers have never been answered.

No one is coming to save me.

Tipping my head upwards, I stick my tongue out and catch the falling water droplets leaking from the basement ceiling. It's rare that I'm brought food or water.

Good behaviour is rewarded in this paradise of darkness, but even after years of learned obedience, hunger is my constant companion. The devil whispers to me sometimes, telling me to fight back.

It never lasts. They beat the defiance from my bones with violent malice, breaking skin and bruising organs. I've been shattered a thousand times, then glued back together in a haphazard jigsaw puzzle just as many.

If I scream when told to and kneel as Pastor Michaels unlocks my cage, I'm awarded brief slivers of life. Enough to keep me alive. I fantasise about being bad most nights, certain it's the only way to escape this life of misery.

"P-Please... I w-want to go home," her broken voice whimpers.

"Shhhh," I hush.

Peering through the half-light, I find the curled-up ball of despair in the cramped cage adjacent to mine. Laura was so bright and full of life when she was dragged down here, unconscious and bleeding.

She's told me stories about her family and friends, tales of a world that I've never seen. Her dreams and hopes, regrets and wishes. She promised that we'd see it together one day. It was a pinkie promise agreed upon between our cages, borne of desperation and grief.

There's a heavy clank that sends dread spiking through my veins. Light floods into the dank basement, illuminating the steep, rotting staircase and a shining pair of boots. It's time for nightly prayers.

"No... p-please... let me go!" Laura shouts, backing into a tight corner for protection. "I want to go home!"

"Be quiet." I kneel before the cage door.

"I won't just lay there and play dead!"

"Stop talking, Laura! You'll get us both in trouble."

Lowering my head, I fix my gaze on my filthy hands. The right index finger is swollen and hot to the touch with a steady throb from my missing nail. Blood is still crusted around the infected digit.

Pastor Michaels ripped it out a few days ago when I dared to ask for a drink of water. On the rare occasions that I grow weak enough to beg for sustenance, my courage is swiftly punished.

In the dead of winter, my left arm still hurts. I asked to be freed once, too young and stupid to know better. The bone was shattered in two places with a steel-capped boot.

"Evenin', folks. Ain't this a fine day, eh?"

Pastor Michaels' greeting feels like razor blades slicing me into blood-slick ribbons. My entire body trembles, and my heart explodes in my chest. I bite my lip, trying to breathe through it.

It's worse if I pass out.

Far, far worse.

He draws to a halt outside my rusted cage, rapping on the bars until I lift my chin. Meeting Pastor Michaels' clear, green gaze, I swallow the vomit burning my throat.

"Done your nighttime prayers, sinner?"

I nod once.

"If I can't hear you, then the Lord Almighty certainly can't."

"Yes, s-sir," I murmur, barely above a whisper.

"Good little girl. Again."

Turning his broad back to me, I watch him approach Laura's cage next. My eyes fall shut as he unlocks the door with an ornate skeleton key. The words come to me without thinking.

"Lord have mercy on me, a sinner."

"Louder," he barks.

"Please Lord, have mercy. Free me from my sins and grant me your almighty forgiveness."

Laura's cries soon turn into agonised screams. The sound reverberates around me, deafening my empty prayers. Some of the girls before her screamed when Pastor Michaels knelt between their legs, unclipping his belt buckle. Others didn't.

I think I hear Laura trying to scramble away, followed by the crunch of her body being thrown into the metal bars. Peeking one eye open, I watch her crumple to the concrete, boneless and barely conscious.

"What happens to sinners, Harlow?" Pastor Michaels shouts.

"They burn in eternal damnation."

"You hear that, Laura? It's your fault that you're here. Selling your body is an unforgivable sin. *Unforgivable*."

Pastor Michaels likes to punish prostitutes the most. At least, I think that's what they're called. Mrs Michaels calls them that, or *sluts*. I don't know what that word means, but it sounds bad.

Her voice gets all low and hissy when she talks about some of the girls brought down here for their final judgement. She says they bring the devil out in Pastor Michaels.

The devil isn't inside of him though.

He *really is* the devil.

Grabbing Laura by the throat, he smashes his lips against her mouth, trapped open in a scream. My stomach threatens to revolt. I can't afford to throw up the meagre crust of bread I was rewarded with for being a good girl.

Laura jerks and wails as Pastor Michaels' hands roam over her naked body. When he pushes a thick finger inside of her, she screeches like she's being dipped in acid.

"I am a messenger of God, you filthy whore. You will submit to my will or burn for an eternity in hell."

"Get your fucking hands off me!"

Striking Laura across the face, Pastor Michaels' gold ring leaves a deep, oozing cut. He pins her against the bars, raising the heavy silver cross from his chest. The chanting begins.

I cower in the corner of my cage, my arms covering my head. It does nothing to eliminate the sound of sobbing and Pastor Michaels' pleasured grunts. He doesn't even remove his ceremonial robes to do it, though he always takes care to pull a little foil packet from his pocket.

This part always makes the girls beg for death. When he has growled out his release, the final steps of the ritual proceed. I keep my eyes tightly shut until it's all over. Pastor Michaels whispers a final, fervent prayer before leaving the basement.

Laura's blood seeps into my cage from the deep, vicious carvings in her skin. The Holy Trinity. Beautiful symbols that are desecrated as they're engraved with serrated steel.

Most girls die quickly. The ritual cleanses them of their sins, but they aren't forgiven. Not by this cruel God. They're freed into the punishing arms of the devil to escort them down to hell.

Pastor Michaels usually slashes the girls' throats or chokes them to death when he's had his fill, but not Laura. She's been trouble since the beginning, according to Mrs Michaels.

He leaves Laura barely clinging to life. It's a brutal game, and the final punishment for her relentless defiance is a slow, agonising death, with no choice but to bleed out until her last breath.

"H-Harlow…"

"No," I sob, clamping my hands over my ears.

Laura whispers into the dark, begging for relief. She tells me that it's going to be okay, and I'm strong enough to find my own way out of here without her. I don't believe a word of it. I'm nothing.

"Please… don't make me… d-die like this."

"You're the one that's leaving me. Like everyone else."

"Not… this… help me," she gurgles.

"I won't do it. No."

"P-Please… friend. My s-s-sister."

Peering through the gloom, I stare at her broken form. She's splayed out on the floor of her cage, unable to move as the slashes carved into her body slowly kill her.

Once bright, platinum-blonde hair is now a deep shade of crimson. I can't see her eyes, usually full of mischief. I'm glad.

"Help… me…"

"Don't make me do this," I plead.

"H-Harlow… it hurts… p-please…"

Covering my face with my hands, I feel my heart splinter into jagged shards of despair. It never gets easier, watching my friends die. No matter how hard I try to shut myself off from it.

"I d-don't want you to go… I'll be alone again."

Laura lets out a wet cough. "Never… a-alone. I'm h-here."

I won't tell you what happens next. God is listening to us, even now. If he hears, I'll be in even more trouble. In the silent aftermath, I curl back into a ball.

She's at peace now.

My torment, however, is just beginning.

Laura's fresh blood has flooded my cage, coating me in her warmth. I have no choice but to sleep in what's left of my friend. Her spirit has departed this world at my hand.

"Goodbye," I whisper to the dead silence.

Laura doesn't respond.

Now, I'm alone until the next girl arrives.

The cycle begins again.

This is my life. It has been for as long as I can remember. My parents—angry, terrifying Pastor Michaels and cruel, cold Mrs Michaels—tell me this is all I deserve.

This existence.

This pain.

This suffering.

I've learned to close off all thoughts of a world beyond these bars. The stories I'm told are just that—flights of fantasy, a taunting glimpse

of a world I'll never be allowed to see.
Lord, please forgive me.
All I wanted was to give her some peace.
Forgive me for what I've done.
Of course, there is no reply.

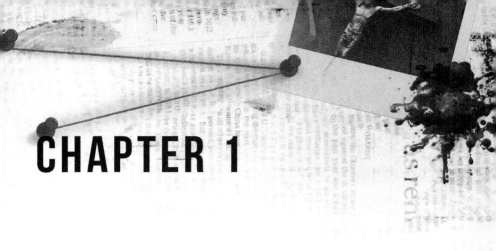

CHAPTER 1

Harlow

Holding Out For A Hero - Nothing But Thieves

"**N**o funny business," Mrs Michaels instructs.

Fighting off the shiver wracking my thin frame, I bite back a sob. She throws a scrap of bread across the stained concrete floor. Her lip is curled in a sneer beneath tangled grey hair and pronounced wrinkles.

I'm too weak and feverish to accept the gift, unable to even lift a finger. I should be kneeling in the prayer position, my hands clasped and head lowered.

"Take it or you won't eat for another week."

"I c-can't," I whisper, too dehydrated to cry.

"I said *take it*, devil child!"

Her foot connects with my ribs—once, twice, three times. I bite down hard on my tongue until blood floods my mouth. It silences my screams as the bones in my ribcage shatter spectacularly.

Mrs Michaels grabs me by the hair and drags my limp body across the cage. I can't stop her. This latest bout of sickness has stolen any remaining strength I possessed. I've barely moved for days.

"Do you know why God has made you sick?"

For what I did to Laura.

"Answer the question, whore!"

I'm smashed into the bars face first. Agony melts my flesh like unholy flames, igniting every shredded nerve within me. Hellfire is raining down on my unworthy soul.

"Because you're a filthy little bitch. You think I don't see the way you look at your father? He's saving your corrupted soul, yet all you can think about is spreading your fucking legs."

If he heard her use that word, he'd take the belt to her. I've seen it happen. Only once. Pastor Michaels whipped his wife until the milky flesh of her behind was dripping red. She could barely walk for days.

"Say thank you for the food," Mrs Michaels demands.

Swallowing hot, coppery blood, I let out a gargle. She drops me back down onto the floor with a final curse, then exits my cage. Lying on my back, I dip in and out of consciousness for what seems like forever.

The throaty growl of a car engine startles me awake sometime later. Terror and relief wash over me. My parents have left to find their next sinner, ready for punishment. Another girl.

They're gone again.

If I die down here in their absence, no one would notice.

Feeling around blindly, my fingertips scrape against the hunk of stale bread. For the first few days of this latest torment, I was starving. Enough to dominate my every thought.

But now... the thought of eating repulses me. The fever hit yesterday and there's nothing left in me to fight it off. I'm so tired of the constant cycle. Death is beckoning me.

"This is my punishment for what I did," I state, addressing the adjoining cage.

The pile of bones doesn't answer me, swimming in unidentifiable bodily matter and scraps of clothing. I don't know how long ago Laura was—her death, that is.

I've blocked it out of my memory, like so many other things. I still talk to her. She's alive somewhere in this room, a spirit lingering in the place between here and the afterlife, like layered sheets of wallpaper.

Her ghost is my only source of comfort. As her skin turned black and peeled away from her bones, revealing organs that soon liquified, Pastor Michaels grew apocalyptically angry.

His last voyage out to stalk his prey was unsuccessful, and he cursed Laura's remains for tempting him, just like the others. I still remember her wails of pain as he hurt her repeatedly in the weeks before her death.

He *touched* her. That always made Mrs Michaels mad. She would beat me afterwards to vent her hatred while Pastor Michaels' victims watched and bled from between their legs, helpless.

After forcing the bread down, I lie back and try to sleep. It doesn't come. Despite everything, I'm terrified of being alone here. What if they don't come back?

The unknown scares me so badly. My world spans the size of this basement, and my entire existence is dependent on the Michaels. I'll starve to death if they don't come back. Maybe that would be a good thing.

"Please... let me die," I sob.

You're so weak, Harlow.

Giving up so easily?

Ignoring my scathing inner voice, I scrub my aching eyes that refuse to cry any more tears. I haven't had a drink of water in far too long, my lips are cracked and dried out.

I want to scream and shatter into pieces that are sharp enough to rip a hole in the fabric of this world and escape into heaven's light. Surely, I've atoned enough. The price has been paid in my blood, time and time again.

They'll be gone for the rest of the night.

Why aren't you running?

"I can't run. The cage is locked," I scream uselessly.

Pull yourself together.

You are the darkness now.

Don't be afraid of it.

Time ticks by as my sanity spirals. The fever and dehydration are doing something to me. I'm hearing things that aren't here, taunting whispers and invisible voices.

I think about Laura. Abbie before her. Tia. Freya. Adelaide. Lucy. Countless others who, despite my best efforts, I can't remember anymore. Their faces are blank in my mind.

There have been so many lives lost in this dark place. I was so glad when the girls started to arrive after spending so long in the basement alone, my solitude only broken by daily beatings.

Then the violence began. The killings. Rituals. Prayers and slashed throats. Bloated corpses and blackened skin. Relief turned to horror, then numbness took over. It became a new normal to watch torture on a daily basis.

You're alive. They aren't.

Don't be ungrateful.

You still have a chance.

"Leave me alone. I can't do this anymore."

Get the hell up, Harlow.

Wrapping my shaking hands around the bars, I grit my teeth through the pain and drag myself up. The stubborn little voice inside of me refuses to give up, even as my body fails me.

Searching the basement, nothing has changed. It's still dank and empty, freezing cold and dark as night. The rusty, age-spotted cage door is still locked. There's nothing.

Laura didn't die for nothing.

Her blood is on your hands.

Make it count.

Acid rises from my empty stomach, but nothing comes out. I dry heave while clutching my aching midsection. When I'm done, I limp across the cage to reach between the bars, straining until I find the next cage.

You want to get out of here?

God isn't going to do it for you.

A fire burns beneath my skin. It's not the fever, but something else. A delicate, damaged butterfly of hope that has finally had enough. My fingers search through cold goo, wrapping around something hard.

It's a bone.

Laura's… arm.

I drag the prize back to my cage, silently crying as chunks of matted hair and rotting flesh smear across my palm.

"What now?"

This cage is rusted to hell.

Jam it in the door.

Use your strength.

"What strength? This is so stupid. He's going to kill me."

Jesus, Harlow.

You're arguing with yourself here.

Shaking my fuzzy head, I search the door's mechanism with my fingers and find the hinges. They're strong but old, corroded by the damp air.

Working with nothing but intuition, I jam Laura's brittle bone between the slices of metal, working it back and forth. I'm praying. Begging. Pleading for salvation.

The bone snaps.

Shards fall through my fingertips.

I scream in frustration, smashing my fists against the bars hard enough to jolt my broken ribs. Pain ripples through me so intensely, it blurs my vision. I fight to remain upright.

When the wave of agony dissipates enough for me to take a breath, I reach out for another bone. My fingers connect with something hard and textured in the dark.

I think it's her leg bone this time. Long and curved, it's crusted with dried blood. Returning to the cage door, the bone snaps again, too weak to withstand the lock.

Do you want to die here?

"No!" I shout back.

Then keep working.

Dripping with ice-cold sweat, I begin to lose energy. This will never work. I'm destined to die here, among the ghostly screams of the girls I failed to protect.

In many ways, I see the darkness into which I was born as a comforting absence of light. In these shadows, I learned to swallow my screams and play the obedient good girl.

A few desperate tears manage to escape my eyes, despite my dehydration. I lick the salty liquid away as it stings my sore lips. It isn't enough. If I don't get out, I'm going to die.

One more try. If this doesn't work, I'll accept my death. With a frantic scramble, I manage to seize Laura's other leg. Slotting the joint into place, I go slower this time, coaxing the groaning metal.

This cage has never changed. The hinges are old, weakened

by rust. A loud, metallic groan fills my ears. Then, *snap*. There's a frightening thunderclap of noise.

The door... *cracks open.*

It worked.

I'm paralysed, staring at the open doorway like a deer in headlights. I can't step through it. I haven't set foot outside this cage before, and even the rest of the shadowy basement feels terrifying.

Clutching my shirt tight to my emaciated body, I cuddle Laura's damaged leg bone even closer. She will never walk free, just like the others didn't. But... I could take her with me. If I can find the strength to do it.

"Move, Harlow," I order shakily. "Just move."

Each footstep outside the cage echoes like a gunshot going off. The floor is wet and slippery, laced with putrefied scents. Laura's body has long since melted into festering lumps of matter.

I'm glad I can no longer smell my own stench. Blood and dirt are crusted to me like a disgusting second skin. Crossing the basement, all I can hear is my pounding heartbeat.

The boards of the narrow staircase creak beneath my meagre weight as I dare to take a step upwards. I freeze, too scared to even blink. Pastor Michaels will break every last bone in my body.

But they aren't here.

Move, Harlow!

Reaching the top of the ancient staircase, I find the basement door unlocked. Why would Pastor Michaels lock it when his little pet is safely secured in her cage? He clearly never thought I'd try to run.

Feeling my way through the darkness, I emerge into a tight cupboard. Another door leads me into a wider space, the scent of mothballs and mildew heavy in the air.

It has a high ceiling, arched and adorned with empty candle

holders. Dirty stone floors are occupied by an audience of destroyed chairs. This place looks like… a chapel. I'm not sure how I know that.

There are no personal effects or ties to the monsters that inhabit this place. It's abandoned, the perfect killing field for their crimes. Silence wraps around me, deep and unnerving.

I am utterly, terrifyingly alone.

This is a mausoleum of my childhood.

Dragging my hand along the wall for guidance, I reach a wooden door. There are more empty rooms on the left, with the remains of a broken bed crumbling into ruin.

Past and present are superimposed over each other as I look around. Damp stone walls are replaced by peeling, rotten wallpaper, and empty candle holders rest within bronze chandeliers.

I know this place.

I've seen it before.

The cage is all I've ever known but that certainty is stripped away as I feel my scalp burning with the memory of being dragged through these rooms by my hair.

I shake the dark thoughts aside.

There isn't time for this.

Facing the door, it's littered with various locks and bolts. There's no way I will get out of here. No matter how many times I slam myself into the slab of wood, screaming as my broken ribs twist and splinter, it doesn't budge.

Sliding down the wall, I hug my knees to my chest, ready to succumb to death. It won't take long. If I'm still alive when my parents return, they'll reopen the healed scars on my body and let me bleed.

No, Harlow!

This isn't what Laura wanted.

"Laura isn't here!"

Yes, she is.

I look down at the bone in my arms. She's still with me, her essence distilled into blood-stained calcium. Laura died believing that I'd get out one day. I can't let her down.

Frantic, I search the chapel again. The stained-glass windows are high, and I'd certainly hurt myself trying to get through. If it buys my freedom, though, I'll walk through fire and offer my soul for the devil's fury.

I will do anything to feel the wind in my hair and finally see what the sun looks like. I've always wanted to know. Laura and the other girls told me such beautiful stories. I cried as they described the daylight.

Do something about it.

Let's get out of here.

Heaving the last unbroken chair nearly kills me. I have no strength. Throwing it with a furious scream, the flimsy structure hits a wall beneath the window and smashes into useless pieces.

Yanking handfuls of my brown, ragged hair, I scream again. I'm not strong enough to throw another. Grabbing an old candle holder instead, I tuck Laura's bone under my arm for safe keeping.

The altar is the last piece of furniture to remain standing. It barely registers my weight as I climb up, agonised tears soaking my cheeks. I can just reach the nearby arched window.

Smash it.

What have you got to lose?

"Everything," I reply to myself.

Or nothing.

Hit it, Harlow.

Crashing the candle holder into the window with everything I have left, satisfying cracks spread like cobwebs in the glass. Over and over, I scream and smash, letting the glass slice my exposed skin.

The pain doesn't stop me.

Fresh air does, though.

The freezing blast hits me straight in the face. I almost stumble backwards from the weight of it... pure, fresh air. So clean, it physically burns my lungs.

Dark, oppressive woodland stretches out in all directions I can see. The church is buried in trees, thick vines of ivy and dense shrubbery. Moonlight barely pierces the smothering sarcophagus.

Only someone who knows exactly where this is could find it. We're in the middle of no man's land. I could be the last human alive out here; reality is so removed.

Run, Harlow.

Run and don't look back.

"I... c-can't," I stutter.

This is your only chance.

"What if they catch me?"

What if you stay?

They will punish you for this.

Biting my lip, I excavate the truth. "I'm scared."

That's why you have to run.

You've survived much worse.

I tighten my grip on Laura and manoeuvre myself into the window frame. More shards of glass rip into my skin, but the splash of warm blood doesn't slow me down.

Taking a final deep breath, I launch myself into the dark. I'm airless for a brief, beautiful moment before my body smacks into the ground so hard, something inside me snaps. I scream myself hoarse.

Just a broken bone.

Run, Harlow.

I ignore the worsening pain that's flooding every inch of me, using Laura's leg to push myself up. My bare feet sink into the grass. It's wet, earthy, and feels like absolute heaven.

This is it.

With no time to waste, I begin limping away from the church. I'm so unsteady, I have to use the bone for balance. Sheer adrenaline pushes me forward.

I'm numb in the face of what lies ahead. Into the dark. Into the unknown. Into... the future. A world that scares me to death, but it can't be any worse than the life I'm leaving behind.

CHAPTER 2

Hunter

Natural Born Killer – Highly Suspect

Crunching the disposable coffee cup in my hand, I toss it into the bin and settle back in the leather chair. A steady thump behind my eyes threatens to distract me from filing this stupid incident report.

"That bad, huh?" Enzo chuckles.

"You could always file your own damn report."

"You're the bossman, not my area."

I stack the papers and crack my neck. "I seem to remember all of us raiding that warehouse, dickhead. Would it kill you guys to do some paperwork?"

"If we had some new leads, we could be doing more important things than filing paperwork."

I spread my hands, indicating to the walls of my office that are plastered with crime scene photographs, maps and reports.

"You know something I don't? We've been at a dead end for weeks. Until another victim turns up, we're screwed."

"Since when do we wait for the bodies to pile up?" Enzo frowns.

"Since we've been three steps behind Britain's most notorious serial killer for the last six months, and there is still no end in sight."

Abandoning my seat, I pace beside the lengthy conference table to expel some of my frustration. Enzo is my best friend and second in command, but he sure as hell knows how to get under my skin, even after a decade of working together.

"We have other clients to get on with."

"None more pressing than this," he points out, his boots propped up on the table. "The SCU is clueless, Hunter. They can't solve this without us."

"They can't solve this with us, dammit."

Joining me, Enzo lays a heavy hand on my shoulder. "We have a better shot at it together. Plus, the retainer fee is too good to give up. Let's go back to the evidence. Take another look."

I turn back to the master board we have set up on the back wall of my office, spiralling into organised chaos. Each victim in the last five years has their own place on the board with all of their information and autopsy reports spread out. Tiny red cord connects anything relevant.

"Eighteen girls in five years." Enzo runs a hand over the dark scruff on his chin.

At well over six foot six and two hundred pounds of pure muscle, he's the enforcer to my stratagem and planning. Enzo is a scary motherfucker to all but those who know him best—my team.

We're proudly known as the finest investigators and most prestigious private security firm in England. Sabre Security is a multi-million-pound success story, borne of determination and hard work.

After a tumultuous twelve years in the business and several high-profile cases in recent years, we've reached new heights. Everything changed after we took down Blackwood Institute and its parent company, Incendia Corporation.

Expanding into new premises was necessary as our team doubled in size with the influx of attention and new funding. While we run the main divisions, our trusted subordinates are working to build new areas of the firm.

"Too many lives," I agree, an unbearable weight on my shoulders.

We were drafted in last year by the Serious Crimes Unit. Despite undergoing a full reconstruction and new in-house regulations to protect against corruption, they're seriously slacking with this case.

Even after our work whipping them into shape, the fumbling fools took one look and swiftly surrendered all responsibility. That's where we stepped in.

The SCU prefers to sign extortionate cheques rather than continue wrestling with this impossible case. We take on government contracts regularly, but this has proven to be beyond anything we imagined.

The victims are all the same—young girls from working-class backgrounds, many of them living in poverty and forced into sex work as a result. All brutally murdered, raped and carved with religious iconography.

"You hear from Theo about those traffic reports?" Enzo muses.

"He's still working on it. The last girl went missing nearly two months ago and there's no body yet. Perhaps she's still alive."

"You really believe that?"

Meeting his intelligent amber eyes, I shake my head. This man knows my thought processes better than I do at times. We've worked together for so long, our minds and bodies are completely in tune.

Building Sabre up to the reputable firm that it is today has taken absolutely everything from us. Even loved ones. We sacrificed it all, but we never lost our love for each other.

"She's dead. But why is there no body?"

He tugs a photograph down from the wall to examine it closer. "Something's changed. Maybe the killer was spooked? Or they're dragging it out this time. Who knows?"

"She'll turn up eventually. They all do."

My blasé attitude when discussing death should disturb me, but honestly, it's self-preservation at this point. We've handled many messy cases since dismantling Incendia five years ago, though none quite on this scale.

I've seen things that I'll never forget and suffered for it, but I still go to sleep every night knowing we've done our best to make the world a safer place.

"Perhaps we should revisit the last victim. Maybe we missed something," Enzo suggests, replacing the photograph of the missing woman.

"We picked that crime scene apart, along with the SCU. There was nothing to report, clean as a fucking whistle. We're not dealing with an amateur here."

We lapse back into tense silence, studying various reports and brainstorming for new ideas. It isn't until the door to my office slams open that we startle back to the real world. We're both far too accustomed to losing ourselves in death and destruction.

The blur of blonde curls and bright-blue flannel reveals our techie and third team member, Theodore Young. He drops his laptop on the table and straightens his usual graphic t-shirt, this one depicting some complex mathematical symbol that worsens my headache. It's rare that he makes an appearance outside of his computer lab these days.

"It's a miracle." Enzo smirks.

"Are we sure he's real and not a mirage?"

"Throw something at him to check."

Frowning at us both, Theo slides his phone from his pocket and hands it over to me while mouthing the word *Sanderson.* Great, that's the last thing I need. The SCU is breathing down our necks for results they can't find themselves.

"Rodriguez," I greet.

"You're a hard man to track down, Hunter."

"Apologies. We were in a meeting."

Sanderson snorts like the annoying bastard he is. This man is the definition of a middle-aged pencil pusher, happy to dole out the dirty work while he keeps his hands clean.

"I got somethin' for ya."

Pinching the bridge of my nose, I force some patience. "Be more specific."

"Next victim has turned up. Meet me at the hospital, half an hour."

"Same MO? Body dumped and carved up?"

"Nah," Sanderson answers grimly. "She's alive."

The line goes dead. I toss Theo's phone back to him, my mind spinning with possibilities. Relaying the information to the others, they both look equally stunned. I refasten my tie and grab my car keys from the desk, already racing against the clock.

My desperation to get this fucking case behind us overrules any misgivings I may have about working with a man like Sanderson. We need results. I'm done facing victims' families with zero answers.

Enzo grabs his leather jacket as Theo's eyes bounce around the room, like he expects me to drag him along too. Field work is not his forte.

"Keep working on those camera feeds for the upcoming raid. We'll take care of the SCU."

"Call me if you need backup," he offers.

"We'll be fine. See you at home?"

He mumbles, refusing to agree with me. The bedroom we set up for him when we bought the luxurious townhouse in outer London remains untouched, even five years later.

Though, that wasn't when our problems started. Theo pulled away from our group the day he lost his reason for existing.

Meeting Enzo in the garage, we greet a handful of employees on the way to our blacked-out SUV. Everyone defers to us, their heads lowered with respect.

After dismissing them, we climb in and set the navigation for the hospital. It won't take long to get there from Sabre's HQ.

"We'll catch this sick bastard," Enzo states, mostly to himself.

"I hope you're right. This case is starting to get to me."

Both smoothing professional masks into place, we leave no room for weakness. It's a necessity in our line of work, something we aren't always the best at. Emotion comes with caring about what we do.

Enzo is far worse than me, a complete sucker for a sob story. He's adopted many strays into Sabre's ranks over the years.

Heading out, we prepare to face our first living victim.

Only this time, I hope it will be the last.

†

Sanderson doles out handshakes before leading us into a private meeting room. It's a small space down the corridor from the intensive care unit in London's biggest hospital.

I glare at his back, cloaked in an ill-fitting shirt that's stained with sweat marks. He loves to lord his authority over us, even though Sabre could reduce the SCU to rubble in a matter of hours.

"Take a seat, gentlemen."

Folding myself into one of the hospital chairs, Enzo lingers behind me. He always plays the watchful bodyguard. Even among government employees, he trusts no one but our team.

People always have hidden agendas in this business. Caution is necessary. We've learned to keep our cards very close to our chests or risk imminent death.

"Cut the shit. What happened?" I ask bluntly.

Sanderson looks between us. "One week ago, a stray kid was reported by a delivery driver. They found her holed up in the back of the truck, half frozen to death. She was admitted to intensive care."

Fiddling with my Armani watch beneath my shirt sleeve, I stifle an eye roll. He's grasping at straws, looking for his moment in the spotlight.

This doesn't fit our MO. We're looking for bodies, not teen runaways. Our killer would never leave one of his victims still breathing.

"This is a waste of time," Enzo grumbles.

"Just listen," Sanderson snaps. "It wasn't brought to my attention until the medics had her stabilised. She was a mess. They called the police first, so it took a while for us to catch wind of this. Trust me, you need to see this shit."

Snapping open a brown, battered briefcase, he pulls out a stack of glossy, full-page photographs. I take the bundle and quickly lose my train of thought as I spot the awaiting horror.

Despite months of working on this case, nothing could prepare me for this. The victim bears identical markings to every single female known to our investigation. Old, vicious scars that disfigure over half of her entire body.

I feel Enzo's breath on my neck as he leans in to inspect the gruesome evidence, growling out a curse. He's right to be alarmed. If the woman survived this, she's a seriously tough son of a bitch. And possibly our first real lead.

"Where is she?" I demand.

"Sedated and under our protection."

His protection means jack shit; we both know that. I'll have a full unit of our agents down here in under half an hour. Reading my mind without a word, Enzo steps outside to make the call.

"How bad is she?"

Sanderson sighs. "You want the short version?"

"I want everything."

"Sepsis nearly killed her. It was left untreated for a long time while she fled. Two broken ribs, shattered radius in her left arm, and severe dehydration. Plus years' worth of badly healed injuries that indicate a long history of abuse."

He gulps, oddly emotional.

"What else?" I prod.

"She's tiny and weak from malnourishment. Dunno how the fuck she made it out alive. Looks early to mid-twenties, I'd say."

I unclench my fists and glance back down at the photographs. The ugly scars cover her torso in harrowing detail. She should have died from these injuries alone. All the other victims did.

The religious symbolism of the Holy Trinity has tied every murder together, if nothing else. All of the women were carved up prior to death. Some were butchered like pieces of meat, the slices cutting down to the bone in places.

"These are old marks."

Sanderson shrugs. "Looks like she's been held captive."

"We weren't aware of any other victims, let alone hostages. Any idea how long she was held for?"

"She's being eased off sedation as we speak. I'll interrogate the victim and get us some answers."

I don't think so, dickhead.

This is a very delicate situation that could alter the course of our entire case. The girl doesn't need this wanker interrogating her.

"Our team is on the way. We'll take her into protective custody and handle questioning from there."

"You don't have the authority to do that," Sanderson blusters. "She's mine, Rodriguez."

"Your authority means fuck all to me. Back off or I'll give your boss a call. You'll be on your way to retirement in no time."

Sanderson's face turns purple with rage. "You wouldn't dare."

"Try me. I've worked closely with the superintendent over the years. She'll be happy to do me a favour."

Cursing me out, Sanderson takes a step back. "What exactly gives you the right to take jurisdiction here?"

"We have to assume the killer will come looking for the girl. Sabre is best equipped to deal with that eventuality. This is our case."

"I hope you know what you're doing, asshole."

"Stay out of my way or I'll bury you. Have a great afternoon."

Stacking the photographs to take with me, I exit into the corridor. Enzo is wrapping up a phone call, and his eyes connect with mine. I can spot the riot of tension and anger a mile off.

It takes a lot to rattle the big guy. He's used to wrapping himself in barbed wire to get through the hard cases, but those goddamn slashes are harrowing on a corpse, let alone a living person.

"The Anaconda team is coming."

"Keep this quiet until we know more. I'll deal with the SCU and get them to sign the girl over to us. We'll need to get forensics in there immediately."

"If she's been here for a week, a lot of the evidence will already be gone," Enzo points out.

"Just do it, for fuck's sake." I grab my phone to call the superintendent. "Sabre has a new client."

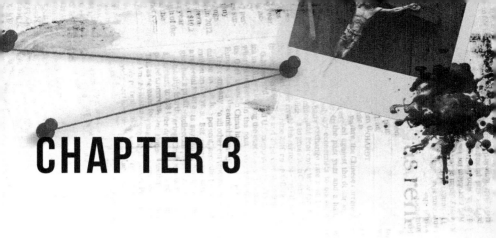

CHAPTER 3

Harlow

The Raging Sea – Broadside

A delaide's tear-stained face stares back at me from her cage. Blood is gushing from between her legs, creating a crimson tidal wave.

"You stupid little whore!"

Pastor Michaels' malicious scream cracks through the basement. He's staring at the mess inside the opposite cage, the keys dangling from his fist.

"You'll never have my baby," Adelaide says with a blood-stained smile. "My life isn't yours to take."

He shouts obscenities, fumbling to get the key into the cage door. I watch through my tears as Adelaide raises her hand, reaching for some invisible light that we can't see.

"No!" Pastor Michaels bellows. "You cannot die!"

Her hand drops, landing on the swell of her pregnant belly. I watch her mouth slacken as her soul departs from this mortal plane.

Adelaide is dead.

Pastor Michaels turns to me, his eyes dark with accusation. "You did this. I was going to save that baby from damnation! You'll pay for this, Harlow!"

†

With a scream lodged in my throat, I startle awake. For several disorientating seconds, I can still see Pastor Michaels striding towards me, removing his belt with threatening grace.

A frenetic beeping sound cuts through my terror, slamming me back into the painful husk of my body. Bright lights burn my retinas. I blink hard, my cheeks wet with streaming tears.

As my vision settles, I'm certain I've died. Everything around me is so clean. Light floods the white-dipped room, more than I've ever seen. The shadows that clung to my childhood are nonexistent.

Where am I?

Is this… heaven?

I search for the long-sought-after angels that blessed so many of Pastor Michaels' sermons. Every violent act he committed was supposed to bring him closer to his reward.

But he isn't here, and I was never destined to see God's light. How did I escape the basement? Is this real? It can't be.

Tendrils of truth seep beneath my skin, offering disjointed snippets. It's like staring into the bleak depths of a frozen lake, and the answers are trapped beneath the surface.

Trees. Stars. Biting wind. Exhaustion. Agony. Did I… run somewhere? I can feel the pain of sharp rocks slicing my bare feet to shreds. Knives tearing into my ribcage as broken bones were jolted around. The rest is a blur.

"Miss? Can you hear me?"

Someone is gently touching my arm. A woman, her smile wide and encouraging. I try to flinch back, but the layers of wires and needles wrapped around me are like a prison.

"Take a deep breath for me. I'll go and get the doctor."

She disappears from the room. I grab the line that's feeding air into my nostrils and yank it out. This isn't my home. I have no idea where I am. I need to leave, before he finds me.

More memories come as I fight to escape the bed. Towering trees. Soft, spongy moss beneath my bleeding feet. Icy water. Concrete. Old bricks. Lights. Engines. Cardboard and whistling wind.

"Hello?"

I'm slammed back to reality again. Someone else is staring down at me beneath a headful of greasy hair, with a rounded face that's lined with wrinkles.

"You got a name? I'm Sanderson."

Licking my dry lips, not a single sound escapes.

"You're in the hospital. We found you last week. You were pretty banged up. Care to explain what happened?"

He scans over me, cataloguing everything on display. My left arm is encased in thick plaster while the other is bandaged in places. Every inch of my skin is bruised and marked with deep scratches.

Sinners don't ask questions, Harlow.

They submit or pay the price.

Pastor Michaels' voice is so loud in my head, I jerk upright. The machine next to me explodes with a loud beeping as I pull at the wires across my chest. It sounds like a heartbeat, wild and out of control.

"Calm down or we will be forced to sedate you!"

My lungs stop functioning. It's like the devil is sitting on my chest, resolving to claim the pitiful remains of my life. The room is fading fast with each second that I can't breathe.

I'm too overwhelmed by the light, the voices, the sheer presence of real, living people. I can't trust them. Pastor Michaels is coming for me. He will torture me to the very last second of my life for running.

"What the *hell* is going on in here?"

This voice is harsh, barked, terrifying. A tall, muscled mountain slams through the door with an ominous crash. His broad shoulders brush the door frame as his two furious eyes eat up the room.

Everyone takes a collective step away from him. The giant's fearsome scowl sweeps over them all, condemning each person with a hate-filled glance.

"This is none of your concern," Sanderson says with a visible gulp. "I'm just doing my job."

"She's our client. You're out of bounds. The superintendent signed off on the order ten minutes ago."

"This is my jurisdiction!"

He takes a threatening step towards Sanderson. "I have the authority to toss you out and break your legs while doing it. This is your final chance to leave."

The deep, throaty boom of his voice fills the room with dread. With each person that's thrown out, the vice-like grip on my lungs eases. I take my first breath as the door slams shut on Sanderson's glare.

Smoothing a huge hand over his mop of glossy, black hair, the giant turns to meet my eyes from across the room. Brilliant orbs of raw amber stare back at me with curiosity.

The violent threat that hardened his voice isn't present in his gaze. I don't find evil or malice there. Beneath the obvious hardness, there's something... inexplicably soft.

"Hey there. Sorry about that. You should put the oxygen back in, it'll help with your breathing."

With trembling hands, I surrender. The wires won't let me out; there are too many of them. I grab the one I tore out and slot the two nozzles back into my nose.

I'm met by a flow of pure, clean air, and I force myself to take a breath. The giant inches even closer, stopping at the end of my bed. He's huge, an immovable boulder blocking my only exit.

"It's okay," he offers in a remarkably gentle voice. "No one is going to hurt you. Sanderson won't be back."

Nostrils flaring, he demonstrates breathing in, then blowing the air back out through his wide, chiselled lips. I follow his direction with well-practised obedience.

A small smile tugs at his mouth, but he doesn't allow himself to become distracted from instructing me until the beeping machine quietens. My heart stops hammering my painful ribs so hard.

"There you go. Better?"

I manage a small, timid nod.

"My name is Enzo Montpellier. I work for a private security firm, and we'll be keeping you safe from now on." He glances around the room. "Do you know where you are?"

All I can do is nod again.

"You've been in the hospital for over a week. Lucky to be alive, I hear. So, are you going to tell me your name?"

Pain is still screaming through me, despite the steady *drip, drip, drip* of fluids being fed into my body. My voice comes out in a raw gasp.

"H-H-Harlow."

"It's nice to meet you, Harlow. I'd like to help you, but I need you to answer a few questions."

Laura's face flashes into my mind. Spit bubbles escaping her slack mouth, joining the trails of blood as she slowly turned blue with my hands at her throat. Her tears falling in silent rivers, leading her into the arms of death.

"Can you tell me how you got here?" Enzo asks, his thick brows furrowed in a frown.

He's going to find out what I did and drag me back to Pastor Michaels' basement from hell. My parents will systematically break every last bone in my body until nothing but crumbs remain.

They'll slice the remaining unmarked places on my skin to remind me of the Lord Almighty and all he has done for me. Only when I've been thoroughly desecrated will my carcass be allowed to die.

"Breathe, Harlow. I'm losing you again."

My eyes are screwed tightly shut. All I can see is the walls of my cage closing in, inch by suffocating inch. As my surroundings melt away, the warmth of someone's hand on mine is like a punch to the chest.

Sometimes, the other girls would hold my hand, late at night. I fumble with my fingertips, snagging on a loose shirt sleeve. Is it Laura? Is she back? Have my sins been cleansed?

With the fabric bunched in my grip, I refocus on my breathing. In and out. The warmth is strangely comforting, like the softness of an invisible blanket draped over me.

"That's it, good girl."

The rough growl of a voice breaks my hazy dream. Laura isn't holding me. A stranger is. A man. He's going to kill me. Break me. Beat me. I have to start running.

"Deep breaths. Come on, like I showed you."

Silent minutes trickle by as I wrestle with myself. The giant's weight settling on my bed causes the springs to groan in protest. Rather than shuffling away, I grip his sleeve even tighter.

My legs curl closer to his body, seeking shelter from the biting chill of the basement in my head. It doesn't go unnoticed. Gentle fingers prise my hand from his sleeve, taking it in his calloused palm instead.

Maybe he isn't here to kill me.

Maybe… he's a friend.

"I'm here with you. Focus on my voice, nothing else."

"The l-l-light," I stutter out.

"Too bright?"

His weight disappears from the bed. The sharp pressure on my eyes vanishes as the fluorescent lighting winks out, draping the room in early evening shadows.

I manage to open my eyes, breathing evenly again. Enzo has settled back on the edge of the hospital bed, watching me closely.

"Thank you."

"Welcome back, little one."

His midnight-black hair is buzzed short on the sides and left long on top, adding to his edgy, aloof vibe. He wears a plain black t-shirt and worn leather jacket over some strange, dark-green trousers.

It's nothing like Pastor Michaels' processional robes or his wife's demure, floral frocks. The girls were always naked when brought down to join me, covered only by blood splatters.

"Where?" I manage to ask.

My throat aches with the single word. I'll soon lose my voice. It doesn't last long after so many years spent screaming into darkness.

"London," Enzo answers crisply. "The authorities transferred you to the intensive care unit. You were found in the back of a construction truck, looked like you'd been travelling for days"

"D-Days?"

"At least. Where did you come from? Did you hitchhike?"

I lose my breathing for a third time, spiralling back into panic. It's all too much. I'm glad I can only remember bits of how I got here. My bruised and beaten brain is keeping me safe.

"Listen to my voice, Harlow. I promise you that you're safe. Whoever is out there… they won't find you. I won't allow it."

"No… not safe. He's coming."

"Who's coming?"

I try to sit up and fail, pain lancing back through me as I slump against the pillows. "I need to pray. I'm dirty… bad, bad Harlow… he's coming…"

"Who? Tell me."

The warmth and tenderness drains from Enzo's voice. Staring up at him, his face transforms into someone else's. Strong angles and handsome smile lines dissolve into cold, righteous fury.

Grey hair supersedes his glossy, black locks. Enzo's tender, amber eyes dissipate, infected by ribbons of dark blue. So dark, it's like I'm looking into the void. I'm staring at my father.

"I'm s-so sorry," I whimper.

Pastor Michaels' lips remain tightly sealed. He doesn't need to speak. The sermons he espoused are forever scored into my brain.

Slamming my hands over my ears, I start screaming at full volume. Anything to get him away from me. The machines go crazy, adding to the chaos as I writhe and buck in the bed.

Loud voices sneak past the tight grip I hold on my imploding head, feeding into my sense of panic. Two hands grab my shoulders, pinning me down on the bed. The sharp scratch of a needle pierces my skin.

You evil little girl.

I'm going to find you, Harlow.

You'll regret ever running from me.

I fall back into my memories. Deeper and deeper, lost to the ravages of years spent in captivity. This was a mistake. I never should've left. Pastor Michaels will kill me when he finds me, far more brutally than any of the others.

Whatever they injected me with begins to kick in. My hands

slacken and fall to my sides while my head crashes against the soft pillow. Pain is fading back into numbness.

I try to keep my heavy eyelids open, but an almighty force is weighing them down. The last thing I see is Enzo, trapped behind a sea of frantic nurses, watching me with determination.

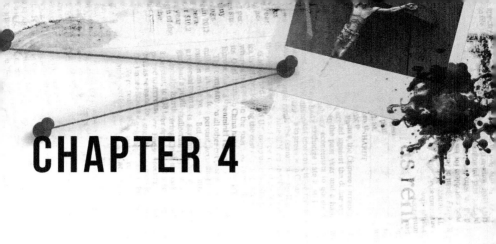

CHAPTER 4

Harlow

Dead Letter & The Infinite Yes – Wintersleep

"Recovery from sepsis can take a while," Doctor David explains. "We caught it just in time. It's a miracle that you travelled alone with such a severe infection."

"I was… h-hearing things," I admit, studying my nail-less index finger. "This voice was telling me to keep going, no matter what."

His blue eyes meet mine. "You were very brave, Harlow."

"No. I'm not brave."

"I wouldn't be so sure. You've survived something horrific. Give yourself some credit for getting this far."

He resumes taking notes of the latest readings on the array of machines surrounding my hospital bed. The other nurse hasn't returned after she forcibly sedated me.

I have a feeling that Enzo has something to do with her disappearance. The last thing I remember is the incandescent rage on his face as they pinned me down and slipped a needle in my arm.

"All looking good," Doctor David concludes.

He looks a few years younger than Pastor Michaels. I think I like him, but my trust is nonexistent. Monsters can wear many masks, and the kindest smiles often hide the sickest of souls.

"We need to discuss your recovery," he says, placing the clipboard down. "You're lucky to be alive with these injuries."

"Lucky," I repeat, the word alien on my tongue.

"The sepsis infection has been brought under control. You have two broken ribs, which will take time to heal. Keep them strapped with compression wraps, and I'd recommend lots of hot baths. You'll be given pain medication to take home."

"Home?"

"I understand arrangements are being made for you as we speak."

Worry settles over me. Pastor Michaels will be out there right now, burning the world to ash as he searches for me. There's a reason I was kept alive for all this time while others were murdered.

I'm his daughter. The beginning and end of the sick ritual that he's perfected over time, fine-tuning the art of brutalisation with each fresh kill. My body bears the same marks that killed each girl he stole.

"We performed surgery to set your broken arm," Doctor David continues, startling me back to the room. "You'll be in the cast for several weeks while it heals. Physiotherapy may be required."

Nodding, I pick at the sore flaps of skin around my missing nail. The sharp bite of pain grants me some clarity. Enzo said I was safe. Pastor Michaels can't get to me here, surely?

"Harlow?"

I startle as he rests a hand on my shoulder, quickly removing it when he spots the look on my face.

"We need to talk about your diet now that you're off the feeding tube. I understand the idea of eating may seem impossible, given all that's happened. Extended periods of malnourishment do that."

"I… f-feel sick just thinking about food," I concede, my voice strained. "They didn't feed me often… where I was held."

His gaze softens with sympathy. I hate the way that look makes me feel, my skin crawling with self-hatred. I don't want to be the broken person my parents made me.

"You need to stick to a strict, high-calorie diet to gain some weight. I'm concerned about your immune system. The infection nearly killed you, and in your current state, a common cold could wipe you out."

"Put some weight on." I clear the lump in my throat. "Got it. I'll try my best, Doctor David."

"Our nutritionist will write up a meal plan for you to take away. Lots of protein shakes for meal replacement, some light foods to try. You will need to take it slow, avoid anything rich or heavy."

A dull ache starts behind my eyes. Between the bright sunlight pulsing through the window and the doctor's information dump, I'm feeling overwhelmed. It's all so much.

"Do you have any questions for me, Harlow? I'm sure this all sounds like a lot. You'll return to me for regular checkups to keep your recovery on track in the coming months."

"How old am I?" I blurt out.

"You don't know?"

I avoid the concerned look on his face. Admitting it out loud makes me feel sick with vulnerability. My life before the confines of this clinical room feels so far away now. Like an endless nightmare from which I've finally awoken.

Part of me doesn't believe it. Everything I've grown up believing is being systematically dismantled with each passing second. The world isn't a fiery wasteland of sinners and angels, battling to reach the welcoming relief of God's light.

Running a hand over his face, Doctor David takes the empty seat at my bedside. "We're having difficulty tracking down your medical records. You're a ghost, Harlow. All I have are best guesses."

"Why can't you find them?"

"Your case is being treated as classified. There are some powerful people outside, arguing about what to do with you. We've tried to identify you based on our records… but there's nothing."

"You're saying… I'm n-not real?"

"That's not what I'm saying," he assures me. "I'm sure there's an explanation. I'll be discharging you into protective custody, and the right people are working on your case. They will get you answers."

Strands of dark-blonde hair cover his eyes as he writes some more notes. I stare down at my fingers, peeking out through the thick plaster encasing my broken arm.

They don't look like my fingers. This doesn't look like my body. Everything about this is wrong. Any moment now, I'll startle awake, trapped in the familiar imprisonment of my cage.

"Doctor?"

His head snaps up. "Yes, Harlow?"

"I d-don't… uh, feel real. Is that normal?"

Brows furrowing, he places his pen down. "What do you mean, exactly?"

Raising my hand, I touch the tender skin of my face. I caught a glimpse earlier when a different nurse gave me a sponge bath. There are two vertical stripes staining my skin in mottled shades of purple and green.

The marks perfectly match the bars that Mrs Michaels smashed me into on my last night. Her personal brand of evil has left an indelible mark on me, and in a twisted way, I'm relieved. I have proof.

"How old do you think I am?" I ask instead.

Doctor David sighs at my obvious topic change. "Early twenties.

May I ask when you got your first period?"

My mouth falls open. I know what that word means. Adelaide usually haunts my bad dreams, more than the others do. Her story is the most horrifying of all.

The other girls bled between their legs every now and then. I learned about periods from them. But Adelaide never did. Her belly was swollen when she arrived, begging for mercy.

Not for her own life—but for her baby's. Pastor Michaels broke her nose and called her a slut. He was determined to save the child's unborn soul. In his mind, she didn't deserve to be a mother because she survived by selling her body.

Adelaide died in excruciating pain.

I can still hear her screeching wails.

"I've n-n-nev…" I stammer. "Never… h-had it."

Doctor David's jaw hardens. I look away as anger flashes in his eyes. I'm not worthy of their care and attention, not after what I've done to get here. They should've let me die instead.

"Lunch time," he declares suddenly. "I'll send the nurse in with something suitable. Time to get better, eh?"

Patting my hand, he disappears with his note-clustered paperwork. I'm left staring up at the ceiling, blinking away tears.

The nurse bustles in shortly after, disconnecting the empty bag of medication flowing through the port in my arm.

"I'll get your protein shake," she offers, leaving the IV line unhooked. "How about some jelly, hmm? It'll be nice and light on your stomach."

"Okay… thank you."

Left alone again, I push back the bedcovers and attempt to move my legs. Every muscle screams in protest, and it takes several minutes to place my bandaged feet on the floor.

I blink away the rush of dizziness and manoeuvre myself up. The pain isn't so bad; I feel weak more than anything. How I made it here, I can't even begin to imagine.

I've heard the nurses gossiping outside my room, trading theories. If I ran, it must've been for miles. Beaten, broken and starved. The level of desperation that takes is unthinkable.

Limping over to the window, I take in the hospital grounds. Loud vehicles come and go beneath me, flashing with blue lights. I'm not sure where we are. London sounds vaguely familiar.

"Look who's up!"

The nurse walks back in, placing a plastic tray on the table over my bed. I quickly take her outstretched hand before my legs fold. She tucks me back into bed and bustles away.

The tray in front of me holds a cup of gloopy, sludge-like liquid. One sniff and nausea rushes over me. Instead, I pick up the clear pot filled with wiggling red stuff.

After managing two tiny spoonfuls, I feel painfully full. My stomach aches, threatening to revolt. Abandoning the food, I turn and stare out of the window again.

The day has slipped by. On the horizon, a fiery ball of light and heat is being swallowed by darkness. The colours fascinate me, like paint strokes brought to life on a giant canvas.

"You were right," I whisper to Laura's memory in my head. "The sunset is so beautiful. I wish you were here too."

There's a gentle knock at the door before it cracks open. Enzo peeks inside, his raven hair floppy and slightly damp, like he's freshly showered. It shows off his glowing, animal-like amber eyes.

Wearing a tight, short-sleeved black t-shirt, his rippling forearms and toned shoulders stretch the bounds of the fabric. There's a buttery leather harness strapped across his muscular back. My heart stutters at the gun tucked inside.

"Hey, Harlow. Can I come in?"

I pull the covers closer to my chest. "Um, sure."

His thick-soled army boots thud like thunderclaps as he stomps into the room. The ceiling almost brushes his head, he's so tall. Like the branches of a powerful, ancient oak tree.

Anxiety slithers down my spine, but it's tempered by the inexplicable sense of warmth that radiates from his gentle smile. It looks foreign on his face, softening features a little too hard and rough to be classically handsome.

"You're looking better," he comments softly.

"I guess."

"Have you been up long?"

"I slept most of the day, before I saw Doctor David." My eyes stray back to the window. "I wanted to go outside, but they wouldn't let me out alone."

"It's for your own protection," Enzo answers, a shoulder propped against the wall. "It's not much of a view, anyway. I'm not a huge fan of London myself."

"Do you live here?"

"On the outskirts, about an hour away." His intense gaze doesn't waver. "Our base of operations is more central. It's not far from here. We take contracts across the country though."

His phone buzzes, breaking our staring match. Enzo fishes it out of his pocket, and I watch his face darken as he notes the caller ID before answering.

I recognise the device—Mrs Michaels had one. She would play gospel songs on it as she cleaned blood and dead bodies in her husband's lair of death.

"Yeah, she's awake. Alright, understood." Enzo flashes me an apologetic smile as he ends the call. "Sorry, that was my... co-worker. He's coming to say hello."

I shuffle backwards on the bed, wincing as my ribs protest. What if this person wants to hurt me? What if they're all lying? What if I wake up back in my cage? These men could all work for Pastor Michaels.

"You can trust Hunter. We've known each other for our whole lives," Enzo states calmly. "I promised you that everything would be okay, and I meant it."

"Why?"

"Because we're good men, Harlow. You've been through a lot, and it's our job to make things easier for you from here on out. We're the best in the business."

"Do you help people?"

His gaze softens again. "Yeah, little one. We help people."

Creeping across the room like a stealthy jungle cat, Enzo outstretches a meaty palm. It's twice the size of my hands. I should be running as far away from this menacing giant as possible.

But when I look into his eyes, there's nothing but a soft concern that doesn't match his burly exterior. He moves slowly, giving me time to adjust to his presence, before taking the empty seat next to me.

"What h-happens n-now?" I whisper.

"We will take you somewhere safe. It's called protective custody. You'll be comfortable and we'll make sure you're looked after."

"You don't h-have questions? About where I was?"

His lips twist in another small smile. "You catch on quick. Our priority is making sure you're okay. We never expected to find you…"

"Alive?"

"Truthfully, we didn't even know about you. Another girl is missing, and we believe she's connected to your story too."

Pain crashes into me with the realisation that I am inarguably alone. Nobody was even trying to find me. It's a heavy blow.

"We're glad you're alive," Enzo adds with a meaningful look. "Our firm has been working on this case for over a year now. We're hoping you will be able to help us."

His words finally catch up to me, and I frantically look around the room, searching and finding nothing. Not even the threadbare shirt that I escaped in. How did I not notice before? She isn't here.

"What is it? What's wrong?" Enzo demands, reaching for his gun.

"I h-had... I'm looking…"

Tugging my long, brown hair until my eyes burn with tears, I realise how broken I am. Those endless miles of starlight and blood-stained footsteps were not travelled alone. The memories are becoming clearer with each breath I take.

"Harlow?" Enzo urges, still on high alert.

"Was I found with anything?"

Relaxing infinitesimally, he braces his elbows on his knees. "Not that I'm aware of. I can get someone to check, though, if you want. In the truck?"

Nodding, I want to thank him, but no words will come out. My throat is thick with bitter regret. I promised to myself that I'd get Laura out... the parts of her that remained anyway.

The thought of her remains being left behind to rot alone is unbearable. Tears start to stream down my cheeks, thick and fast. I can't hold them back any longer. I've failed her.

"What is it?" he asks.

"I… I shouldn't be here," I choke out.

Enzo reaches out, his thumb stroking over my cheek to catch my tears. I flinch at his touch, expecting pain instead of comfort. He freezes, horror filling his expression.

"I'm so sorry," Enzo rushes to apologise. "I didn't mean to scare you."

"You don't scare me," I answer quickly. "I just... I'm not used to... well, people."

"That's fine. I apologise again."

We lapse into awkward silence. Enzo stares at his feet, wearing a pained frown. I can tell that he's beating himself up. For such an imposing guy, he wears his heart fully on his sleeve.

There's a sharp rap on the door and he moves to answer it, exchanging hushed words with whoever's on the other side. When both men enter the room, I sit up ramrod straight.

"Easy, Harlow." Enzo raises his hands in a placating manner as he spots my panic. "This is the co-worker I mentioned."

Standing next to Enzo, an imposing figure drinks me in with his molten-chocolate eyes, framed by thick lashes. He's almost as tall as Enzo, but much trimmer, his body sculpted with lean muscle instead of bulk.

Wearing a pristine charcoal suit, his long, chestnut-brown hair is tied at the nape of his neck, highlighting his trimmed beard that covers the symmetrical lines of his picture-perfect looks.

He's very handsome, attractive in a model-like way that Enzo could never achieve with his terrifying exterior. Despite that, there's a veneer of coldness that seems to cloak his posture.

As he comes closer, I can see a sleek panel of black metal attached to his left ear. It's a hearing aid, partially covered by flyaway hair. There's an old scar bisecting his eyebrow too, the only blemish on his spotless appearance.

"It's a pleasure to meet you," he greets, his voice smooth like honey. "My name is Hunter Rodriguez."

"You too. I'm Harlow."

"Any last name?"

My mouth dries up. "Uh, no. Just Harlow."

Hunter nods, lacing his hands behind his back as he paces the room. "As Enzo has explained, we own a private security firm that has been put in charge of your care."

Leaning in the corner of the room, Enzo watches his friend closely. There's a weird tension between them that fuels my anxiety.

"We perform large-scale criminal investigations, among other things," Hunter continues brusquely. "You are a person of interest to one of our current cases."

"A p-person of interest?"

His cold eyes land on me. "We're investigating a spate of serial killings spanning the last five years. They appear to be motivated by religious ideology. Bodies carved with holy symbols and dumped."

"Hunt!" Enzo hisses.

He ignores Enzo completely. This slick businessman has an acid tongue. My cheeks burn hotter than hell as I stare down at the hospital gown I'm wearing.

Holy symbols.

I can see them; they're burned onto my retinas. The scars twist my flesh into ugly disfigurations. If they've seen the other bodies, they know what Pastor Michaels does.

"We're going to move you to a secure location and ensure you get the help you need to recover." Hunter halts, casting me an emotionless look. "You're going to help us with our investigation."

Enzo curses under his breath. He looks ready to use the gun strapped to his body with each harsh word that Hunter wields.

"Do you understand?" Hunter demands.

I nod, fear binding my tongue.

"Good. I have two agents stationed outside of your room for

protection. We intend to move you in a couple of days when your consultant signs off on the discharge."

I plaster a neutral expression into place. People lie, I know that. Like when Pastor Michaels stroked my sweaty hair and told me he loved me after beating me to a pulp with his belt.

It didn't stop him from breaking skin and bone. Like Hunter, he wielded his words as a weapon, only using his fists to deliver the final, back-breaking blows.

Hunter clears his throat. "You were found in the back of a construction truck heading south from Cambridge. My team has traced it back to a depot. It appears you hopped on from a lorry."

"Hunt," Enzo warns in a low voice.

"That lorry was traced back to a warehouse in Nottingham." Hunter ignores his friend's thunderous expression. "How far did you hitchhike? Were you being held nearby?"

Enzo marches up to him. "Enough! Jesus."

"It's a simple question."

"She is in no position to answer your fucking questions. Have some goddamn empathy."

They're almost nose to nose, the lash of anger slicing into me like a whip. I hate confrontation. Enzo glances at me and blanches, taking several steps back from Hunter with another curse.

The names and places he's thrown at me mean nothing. All I can remember are the jagged shards of broken memories. My mind checked out as I ran for my life.

"Fine," Hunter growls, flashing me a look. "We'll talk more in a couple of days. Be ready to leave then."

Turning on the heel of his luxurious leather shoe, Hunter storms from the room without another word. Enzo watches him go with a biting glare.

"He seems… um, nice," I say awkwardly.

Enzo's chest rumbles with a laugh. "No need to bullshit me. He's a miserable son of a bitch. Are you going to be okay?"

"I'll be fine."

"If you need anything, ask one of the men stationed outside. Becket and Ethan are both good agents. They'll protect you."

He stares at me from across the room, looking like he wants to say more. I'm hit by a wave of exhaustion that pulls at my already heavy eyelids. It's been an intense day.

"Rest, Harlow. We'll be back soon."

With a final, unhappy nod, Enzo sweeps from the room. The moment the door shuts, my throat aches with the force of emotion ramming into me. I feel like I've been deserted on an island.

The niggling voice of fear sneaks back in as the shadows in the room seem to grow without Enzo here to ward them off. He was the first warmth and real human contact I've experienced for a long time.

I survived the basement alone, but in this unknown place, I feel more afraid than ever before. All I want is for Enzo to come back and stand guard, his intimidating size scaring everyone else off.

Lord, I truly must be broken.

Pastor Michaels succeeded.

CHAPTER 5

Enzo

Even In The Dark — jxdn

My feet smack against the pavement in a rhythmic beat. I focus on the road ahead and crank my classic rock music up even louder. I like it high enough to hurt my eardrums when I'm feeling like this.

I've circled the suburbs of rural London twice, in all its luxurious, middle-class charm. The miles passed by quickly as I lost myself in the simple act of exercise.

It takes a lot to exhaust me. Years of suffering from insomnia have given me a superhuman ability to run on absolutely nothing. After tossing and turning in bed for an hour, I called it quits and pulled my running gear on.

I can't stop thinking about Harlow. Her wide, frightened blue eyes, bird-like features and gently curling brown hair have filled my mind since I left the hospital last night.

Finishing my tenth mile, I circle back home. Countless red-brick townhouses, fashionable apartments and closed cocktail bars frequented by the filthy rich pass me by.

After twelve years of running Sabre Security, we could afford to buy property somewhere more upmarket. This was supposed to be our family home when we bought it several years back.

In reality, the house is as empty as our lives. The family we once were shattered a long time ago. Hunter comes home just to pass out. Theo's room is untouched. I can't catch a single night's sleep without being haunted by the past.

The brick wall that encloses the property comes into view, topped with lacquered black spikes and concealed CCTV cameras. We live amongst normal society, but our home is a fortress of solitude.

With a generous garden and tall birch trees for privacy, you can just spot the painted pillars marking the entrance to our Victorian-style mansion. Red bricks are broken by generous windows, fitted with specially made bulletproof glass. We went all out.

I let myself through the electric gate, cursing the complicated security system that Theo had one of his techies install. Leaning in for a retinal scan when it's pitch-black is a feat, but it would take an army to break in.

Inside the house, I toe off my trainers and rest against the wall. My body is exhausted, but my mind still won't quiet. There's a thump of feet on wooden floors as Lucky comes padding over.

She licks my legs in greeting, and I bend down to scratch behind her ears. Her pearly-blonde fur practically gleams in the moonlight leaking through the window panes.

She's a golden Labrador retriever, and weighs a hell of a lot when she insists on climbing into bed for a cuddle. I'm the only one that lets her do it. We got her not long after we moved in.

"Good girl," I murmur.

We head into the kitchen together. The under-counter lights

are on, revealing Hunter sitting with his back to me at the kitchen island. He's shirtless, showing years of scars and the tattoos that cover everywhere from his throat down.

As usual, he's nursing a cup of tea, his dark-green sweatpants hanging low on his hips. I approach slowly, noting his hearing aid on the marble countertop. I'd like to avoid a broken nose if I startle him.

He's been known to take it out, preferring the silence his permanently damaged eardrums provide while deep in thought. Hunter's completely deaf in his right ear.

An explosion caused his hearing to decline over time. Only his left ear retains some functioning, so he relies on the hearing aid to live a somewhat normal life. It affects him a lot more than he lets on.

Offering him a wave, I grab a bottle of water from the fridge, draining it in three quick gulps. Hunter reattaches his hearing aid, switching it on so we can talk.

"Couldn't sleep?" he guesses.

"Something like that."

"Me neither. This case is fucked up, man."

I splash my face in the kitchen sink. "You're telling me. I'm ready to never look at a mutilated body again."

"Like anything is ever that easy."

"What about the girl?"

"She's been given medical clearance to leave in the morning. I'm sending Doctor Richards in for a full psych eval before we take her to the safe house. We can't have a messy suicide on our hands too."

Cringing at his words, my hands clench into tight fists. "She wouldn't. Harlow's a fighter. How else did she escape in such a state?"

Hunter studies me closely. I fucking hate it when he does that. I'm not a client, and he always sees far more than I'd like. He's fiercely intelligent and, sometimes, far too ruthless.

I'm the brawn to his brains, but my emotions get the better of me more than his do. I feel enough for both of us. It's why I stick to the physical side of the business—training recruits, running active operations, beating on the bad guys on occasion.

I couldn't do what Hunter does. My fists speak more than his fancy words ever could, but we need him to keep us afloat. He has the tongue of a politician and the stratagem of a military commander.

Hunter's intelligence does make him vulnerable. While his ability to get inside the heads of our perpetrators makes him so brilliant, it's also his greatest threat. He feels more than he lets on and bottles it up, ruling with an iron fist instead.

"Don't get attached, Enzo. She's a client."

"I'm aware," I growl back.

"Are you?" He drains the rest of his tea. "We will have to grill her hard to get the information we need to hunt this motherfucker down. There isn't time to be gentle."

"You said that more questions could wait. She's traumatised, Hunt. We have to give her time."

"As soon as she's in our custody, we need to get to work. This sick son of a bitch has evaded us for too long. I'm done playing games."

Fighting the urge to break his fucking face, I drag my sweaty shirt over my head while storming from the room. I need a shower and a few hours of sleep, but I know the latter won't come.

Hunter's warning infuriates me because it's true. Even if I don't want to admit it. I can't afford to get attached. Not after last time.

Love is a weakness.

In our world, love gets you killed.

†

68

The next morning, grumpy and sleep deprived, I camp out in the intensive care waiting area. Hunter is in the small meeting room down the corridor, ironing out the final details with Sanderson and another SCU representative.

We have a safe house lined up for Harlow in East London. It's a grey, faceless apartment, more of a prison than her first taste of freedom. Once she enters that place, she won't leave.

Not until this is all over and it's safe to do so. The thought of her—alone and scared with nobody to hold her close—is pushing me over the edge. I promised we'd keep her safe.

This is internment, not protection.

She will suffer for it.

The door to the meeting room opens. Hunter strides out, smoothing his designer, three-piece grey suit. Sanderson follows, his face red and eyes lowered as he quickly makes an excuse to leave.

The spineless worm has been making our lives difficult for months, angered by his department's decision to hire external help. It effectively removed this case from his control.

"All done?"

Hunter closes his briefcase, depositing it on the coffee table. "We're good. Is the doc out yet? I'd like to wrap this up fast."

"Not yet."

Sighing, Hunter takes a seat, scrubbing a hand over his beard. I don't think either of us slept last night. We lapse into silence and wait for the shrink to finish his assessment.

It takes another two hours before Doctor Richards emerges from the intensive care unit, pulling on an expensive wool coat to protect against the winter chill.

"Afternoon, gents."

Surging to his feet, Hunter offers a hand for him to shake. "Thanks for coming in, doc. We appreciate it."

We've worked with Lionel Richards for several years now, and he's assisted on many of our high-profile cases. The fame granted to us after Blackwood sent his career into the stratosphere too.

"So?" Hunter prompts.

"You do like to give me a challenge." Richards sighs, smoothing his wild bush of silver hair. "I'm not sure what to make of this one."

"What the hell does that mean?" I snap tiredly.

He spares me an assessing glance. "When was the last time you got some sleep, Enzo? You look dead on your feet."

"You're not here to assess me, doc. Just fucking spit it out already. We have places to be."

Raising his hands in surrender, he takes the seat opposite us. Richards is used to my attitude. He supported the entire team when we were on the verge of selling up.

We felt unable to go on after everything that happened back then, but with his help, we made our way through and rebuilt. Family and friends convinced us to keep working, despite our grief.

"Harlow is suffering from severe PTSD as a result of her imprisonment, extensive abuse and brutalisation." Richards adjusts his spectacles. "She will need to see me every week for the foreseeable future."

"How long was she held captive?" Hunter fires off.

"To her account, she has never seen the outside world. I am inclined to believe she is experiencing dissociative amnesia."

"What does that mean?" I ask next.

"It's a common response to very extreme cases of trauma. She can't recall a lot of her time spent in imprisonment, only flashes here and there."

Hunter swears under his breath. Harlow's memories are our best shot at tracking down the killer. Our case now lives and dies by the testimony she will provide.

"Oddly enough, she presents with a reasonable level of understanding and social development for her age." Richards shakes his head. "Only so much can be learned from others."

"You don't think she was held captive for her whole life?" Hunter guesses.

"I'd hesitate to speculate at this stage," he replies. "We need to take this very slow. Push too soon, and she will close down. Her mind is a puzzle that needs to be pieced back together."

"We don't have time, doc."

"Then interrogate her and watch that poor girl spiral. I don't need to tell you how trauma can affect a person. Her risk of suicide is already significant."

I shiver at his angered words. We've had enough experience with traumatised clients. Hunter deflates, taking a moment to reconsider.

"Is it the same perp?" I ask uneasily.

"I can't answer that," Richards responds. "She has been subjected to extreme psychological and physical torture, complete isolation, and emotional abuse."

"So?"

"Your killer rapes and butchers young women. It's not exactly the same kettle of fish. Serial killers don't tend to hold their victims for long."

"You've seen the marks," Hunter points out. "She bears the same scars that every dumped body had. Only they're old, healed. Why didn't he kill her as well?"

None of us has an answer. We've all suffered through studying the photographs of Harlow's body in further detail. The harrowing scars on her body match our morgue of dead bodies perfectly.

We had further analysis performed by forensics. Down to the symbolism of the Holy Trinity carved into Harlow, the knife patterns matched to a high degree. It was likely the same blade used.

"I'm not here to draw conclusions." Richards stares at Hunter. "I shall leave that to your team. Harlow is my patient now. I am more concerned for her mental stability."

"Should we be worried?" I frown at him. "Are we safe to move her?"

"I believe there is some cause for concern. Re-introducing Harlow to society needs to be handled with the utmost delicacy. That's why I'm not recommending an inpatient stay."

I breathe a sigh of relief.

"She needs to feel safe, supported," Richards outlines. "Isolating her in a hospital could exacerbate her symptoms and lead to further dissociation."

I cut Hunter a sharp look. He still won't admit that I'm right, despite the heated argument we had on the drive over. This safe house is a terrible fucking idea.

Ignoring me, he stares down at his phone. "She'll have a full team for security. I'll see to it that regular visits with yourself are arranged. We have questions that need answering, doc. I would appreciate your help."

"Harlow's been through something horrific," Richards says emphatically. "This needs to be handled with extreme care. That doesn't involve sticking her in some faceless apartment with a team of spooks."

I knew he'd be on my side. Richards is the best in the business. This is exactly why we pay him the big bucks to consult for us.

"So, what do we do with her then?" Hunter snaps.

Pulling a colourful scarf on, Richards inclines his head. "I trust you to think of the right thing. Set up a regular therapy slot for her with my secretary. I'll await your updates on her living arrangement."

Once Richards has breezed from the ward, Hunter's head falls into his hands. His long hair is in a bun today, exposing the thick muscles of his neck and the beginnings of his chest tattoo peeking under his shirt collar. I give him a moment to gather himself.

The distance between myself and Harlow's room feels like a whole goddamn ocean. I want nothing more than to stand between her and the rest of the world, whatever it takes to keep her safe.

Christ, this is bad.

We're in seriously hot water.

"This is turning into a clusterfuck." Hunter reads my mind with a sigh. "Clearly, the safe house isn't a good idea."

"Let's take her back to HQ. We can go from there."

Hunter nods. "Go get her."

Heading for Harlow's hospital room, I slide my best emotionless mask into place. I need to get my shields up before she worms her way any further under my skin.

She's our responsibility, but not one of us. The sooner I realise that, the better. Rapping on the door, I peek inside and find her bed deserted.

Reaching for my gun holster, I'm ready to tear the hospital apart to find her when the sound of running water draws my attention. Entering the room, I remain poised, ready to pounce.

A familiar pair of slender legs stands stiff before a mirror in the corner. Breathing hard, I force myself to relax. She's here.

"Harlow?"

She slowly turns around and her wide, cerulean eyes meet mine. Her right hand is tugging a nest of impossibly long hair over her shoulder, while her broken left arm is strapped to her chest.

"What are you up to?" I ask suspiciously.

Her teeth sink into her bottom lip. "Considering a haircut."

Inching into the room, I stop behind her. I can feel her body heat in the tiny gap between us. Another step, and her small, pert ass would be pressed right up against me.

Fucking dammit, Enzo. I can't be thinking shit like that around her. She's vulnerable and innocent. I'm supposed to be protecting her, not slavering over her like a fucking dog.

"The doc thought it would be a good idea."

"We can arrange a haircut. But for the record, I like your hair."

Limping past me, Harlow returns to her hospital bed and grabs the light-blue hoodie left for her to wear. She unclips the sling holding her broken arm, attempting to wrestle it over her head.

"Come here." I walk over, grabbing handfuls of fabric. "Let me help. Put your head through here, like this."

When her head pops through the hole, there's a ghost of a smile on her lips. She lets me pull it over her small body and I grab the sling, slipping it back over her head.

"Thank you," she says quietly, sliding her broken arm into place. "Guess I'm going to need a hand for a while."

"Nothing wrong with asking for help. Are you ready?"

"I... I think so."

Even in borrowed sweats that swamp her legs, she looks better for getting out of a hospital gown. The loose, V-necked shirt beneath her hoodie shows off her collarbones and a hint of scar tissue on her chest.

I don't point it out. The last thing I want is to embarrass her, and she doesn't need to know about the photographs. We've taken something from her, something irreplaceable. Her choice. If I could unsee those scars, I would.

Harlow sits down on the bed, staring at her feet. I realise that she's silently crying. Her shoulders are shaking with each sob. A pair of unlaced black Converse wait for her on the linoleum.

"What is it?"

"I don't know how to do it," she whispers.

Realisation dawns. I fight the urge to take her in my arms and hold her tight. There's a certain fire in her gaze, and I can't wait for her to realise that.

"Here, let me."

Sinking to one knee in front of her, I ease the Converse over the light bandages still on her feet and loosely tie the laces.

She watches with curiosity, her bright eyes analysing each movement. I have to force myself to look away as her teeth bite into her pink bottom lip.

"Thanks, Enzo. Could you show me again sometime? If that's not too much trouble."

Her soft request sends tingles down my spine. I nod, rising to my full height. Hesitating for a moment, her tiny palm slides into my outstretched hand.

"Got everything? You ready?"

Harlow quickly nods. "I have nothing to bring."

"Then let's move. Stick with me and don't speak to anyone apart from myself and Hunter. Got that?"

She gulps before nodding. Her fear hurts me on a bone-deep level. Unable to stop myself, I find my calloused fingers tilting her chin up so that her aquamarine eyes meet mine.

Wide, afraid, the endless blue depths of the ocean stare back at me. Her irises are flecked with the faintest shades of pale green, but it's the flames of courage that astound me.

"You're going to be okay."

"I don't think... I mean... I'm not sure what that means." Harlow chews her lip again. "To be okay or safe."

"Then allow me to show you."

Cursing myself, I can't take the words back. I really don't want to as the most beautiful smile twists her lips, all lit up with fragile hope just for me.

Her hand squeezes mine. "Lead the way."

Jesus fuck, I'm an idiot. Hunter is telling me not to get attached. Little does he know, it's already too late. She's under my skin.

That can only mean one thing.

Trouble.

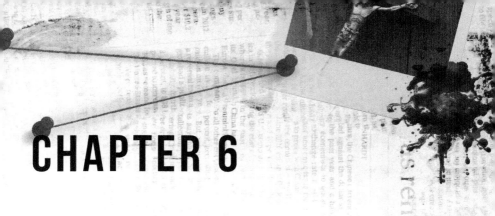

CHAPTER 6

Harlow

New Eyes – Echos

Keeping my hand tucked in Enzo's paw-like grip, I'm given a huge paper bag full of medications and instructions. The nurse's words wash over me, but Enzo nods, listening to it all and taking the bag for me.

I'm glad one of us is able to pay attention.

All I can focus on is my shallow breathing.

Out in the waiting area, I find a familiar face carved in frustrated lines as he peers down at his phone. Hunter's dressed smartly in another suit, his hair slicked into a neat bun and beard freshly trimmed.

He looks up as we enter, his eyes narrowing on my hand still clutched tight in Enzo's. Panicking, I try to let go. My cheeks are flaming, and I have no idea why.

These men are so confusing. Enzo tightens his grip, casting me a warning look that ends my futile attempts to escape his grasp.

"I really hate hospitals," Hunter declares darkly. "Let's get the hell out of here and never come back."

Enzo nods. "The car is parked downstairs."

I'm guided to an odd metal door in the wall. Hunter presses something and I gape in shock as the wall splits into two with a ding.

The slices of metal part to reveal a small room, built straight into the wall. It looks a lot like another cell to me. My eyes sink shut as I begin to panic all over again.

"Harlow? You good?"

I'm surprised to find Hunter peering down at me when my eyes peek open a fraction. There's a flash of concern on his face before it's wiped away.

"I'm not getting in there," I force out.

"The elevator? It won't hurt you."

"I'm not getting in."

His nostrils flare and he strides away, opening another door off to the side. It reveals a metal staircase leading down. We begin to descend the stairs in frigid silence.

When Hunter's phone rings, he answers it with a barked greeting. I feel sorry for whoever is on the end of the line. He suddenly raises a hand for Enzo to halt behind him.

I crash straight into Enzo's back, nearly losing my balance on the stairs. His strong, trunk-like arm wraps around my waist before I can fall, placing me back on my feet.

"Careful," he quips with a smile.

Before I can thank him, Hunter curses colourfully.

"Fucking hell. You've got to be kidding me."

"What is it?" Enzo immediately asks.

Listening to the urgent voice on the end of the phone, I find myself spiralling out of control. The simple curse word triggers something inside of me that I can't suppress.

It's another forgotten memory, wrapped in pain and misery. The darkness of the basement washes over me like a storm cloud, chilling me to the bone with the familiar scent of blood.

We don't use that word here, Christie.

Lay still or I'll slice your throat instead.

There's a good girl.

My mind is filled with the visual of Pastor Michaels pinning Christie's naked body to the floor of her cage. He carved the holy marks into her stomach while she sobbed uncontrollably.

I'd forgotten the sheer intensity of her wailing. She was younger than the others, less able to handle the torture. Her screams overwhelm me as I sink against the stairwell's wall.

"Shit!" Enzo swears, his hands landing on my shoulders. "Come on, Harlow. Stay with me."

I shove his hands away with a silent cry, unable to cope with the feel of someone touching me.

"What's happening?" Hunter barks.

"What does it look like, idiot?"

"Sort her out. We have a situation downstairs."

Hunter's words ignite something within me. The flare of anger catches alight and burns through my mind. Seizing the powerful emotion, I use it to pull myself out of the darkness.

Sweet, glorious air enters my lungs as I fight to retake control. When I manage to open my eyes, Hunter's watching me with mild astonishment.

"She can sort herself out," I reply shakily.

"So I can see."

It's my turn to be astonished as Hunter offers me a hand. Enzo watches us, open-mouthed. As I'm pulled up, my tightly wrapped ribs burn with pain. I bite down on my tongue to hold it in.

"What's the situation?" Enzo speaks up.

Hunter offers him a grim look. "The press are camped outside. They've caught wind of something and reckon we've found another body. They're fishing for an update."

"Goddammit. We can't let them see her."

"Why?" I ask cluelessly.

"The last thing we need is your face plastered all over the news when we're trying to keep you safe." Hunter runs a hand over his man bun. "Enzo, I need you to field questions. Tell them nothing."

He nods. "Get Harlow past while they're not looking. I'll meet you in the garage when the coast is clear."

Sparing me a final look, Enzo jogs ahead down the staircase. We follow behind him at a much slower pace. Hugging my broken arm to my chest, I feel a bit lost without his hand in mine.

"What happens if they see me?"

Hunter shrugs off his suit jacket at the bottom of the stairs. "The people we're keeping you from will know exactly where you are."

Short of breath, I press the still-sore wound where Pastor Michaels ripped the nail out. The burst of pain is immediate, slicing through my fear like a flash of lightning.

From outside, I can hear the greedy roar of voices. Shouting, heckling, demanding attention. The odd flash of light accompanies the chaos, even as Enzo's voice booms over them all.

"Put this over your head." Hunter pulls his jacket over me and wraps an arm around my shoulders. "Hold on to me and don't let go."

Fisting my hand in his pressed shirt, I shut my eyes, letting him guide me. Warmth radiates from Hunter's skin, seeping through the material of his shirt. It feels weirdly intimate to cling to it.

He smells peppery, like spices and exotic adventures. Pastor Michaels only ever smelled like blood. I want to bathe in this new, exciting scent. Let it wash over me, washing all the bad stuff away.

"You smell really good," I blurt without thinking.

Hunter stumbles before righting himself. "Huh?"

"Uh, n-nothing."

The shouting fades as we march ahead. His suit jacket is soon removed from my head, and I blink, looking around what seems to be a parking garage. There are cars everywhere.

Hunter's still holding me close as we walk up to a huge, blacked-out beast. The wheels are almost as big as me, and it's painted in a sleek, matte-black colour.

"Get in," Hunter orders, opening the back door.

Staring inside, I doubt my ability to climb in. My starved, tiny body betrays me. With a mutter, a pair of strong hands land on my hips. My breath catches in my throat.

Hunter doesn't apologise as he hoists me into the back of the car and slams the door in my face. I can still feel the burning heat where his hands squeezed my hips.

Impure sinner.

God does not condone pleasures of the flesh.

I will beat the devil from your bones.

Mrs Michaels always said that sinners make men stupid, steering them away from the path of God. My father never touched me as he touched the other girls. That did nothing to lessen her fury, though.

Hunter slides into the driver's seat and fires up the engine. It vibrates with a throaty, powerful purr, breaking the uncomfortable silence. The minutes trickle by until Enzo suddenly appears and clambers inside.

"How bad?" Hunter snaps impatiently.

"Someone from the hospital must have leaked the story. They know we have information that we're withholding. With our reputation, they've rolled out the live cameras."

"Goddammit," Hunter curses, throwing the car into reverse. "We'll be splashed over the fucking newspapers by morning."

"HQ is compromised. We can't take her there now that they've put the dots together. We need to give this time to blow over."

They share an intense conversation with lingering looks and frowns. It's fascinating to observe. They're almost like two halves of one person.

"You win." Hunter slides a dark pair of sunglasses into place. "This is a temporary measure. Don't make me regret this."

"Regret what?" I dare to ask.

Enzo's eyes meet mine in the rear-view mirror.

"You're coming home with us."

†

I'm woken up by someone shaking me. Hunter's familiar spicy scent hits my nostrils. After spending so long starved of all contact, it seems I've become sensitive to the slightest smells and tastes.

"Wake up, Harlow. We're here."

Blinking sleep from my eyes, I find his grumpy face softened with exhaustion. He offers me a hand, stepping back to give me space to stretch my limbs.

I accept the offer of help, but my entire body is throbbing with pain. My last pill was several hours ago. Hunter must read something on my face, and he leans in to scoop me out of the car.

I'm placed back on my feet in the middle of a circular driveway. Two other cars are parked nearby—a smaller, sportier model, and one with a soft-top roof painted a beautiful shade of red.

"Where are we?" I say around a yawn.

"Home."

Hunter helps me over to the massive house waiting for us. The open doorway is flanked by two stone pillars, stretching upwards into a brightly lit monster of a building.

It looks old, not that I know much about the real world, let alone buildings. I like the way these tiny vines seem to creep over the bricks. Dark, glossy leaves contrast against the rich-red brick.

"Your home?"

Hunter gestures inside. "Like I said, this is only a temporary measure while the vampires are chasing us for a story."

"What are vampires?"

Hunter sighs for the hundredth time. "Never mind."

We step into a large entrance painted in a crisp shade of grey. Sparkles reflect off the shining wooden floors from a jewelled light hanging high above us. The effect is mesmerising.

Easing my shoes off, I wince at the pain across the soles of my bandaged feet. I've barely taken a breath before the sound of footsteps against wood races towards us.

A blur of golden fur launches across the room with an excited yip. The toned body of an animal collides with my legs, and I nearly fall over from the sheer size and weight of my attacker.

"Down, Lucky!" Hunter shouts. "Fucking dog."

The creature doesn't listen to her owner. She wraps herself around me, preening as I bury my fingers in her velvet fur. She's a huge dog, reaching almost to my waist with strong, muscular limbs.

"Sorry." Hunter takes off his navy coat and hangs it up, his suit now rumpled. "She gets lonely when we work late."

"It's okay."

"Just push her away if you want."

Lucky seems to sense her owner's bad attitude. She snorts and disappears through a large archway where Enzo's voice greets her. I follow the sound, emerging into a kitchen.

The marble countertops are accentuated with stainless steel and several intimidating appliances. Modern amenities meet classic, expensive charm in a perfect blend of old and new.

Enzo waits for us, leaning against the vast oven top. "Are you thirsty? Hungry? We have some of that crappy protein powder from the hospital."

"Sounds delicious," Hunter mutters sarcastically. "I'd rather pluck out my eyeballs instead of drinking that, but thanks."

"Not for you, jackass. Harlow?"

Shifting my weight, I bite my lip. Will he strike me if I ask for a drink? Tell me that sinners don't deserve to be sated, and instead I must beg for God to forgive me if I want to live?

Enzo's gaze is scorching as he watches me deliberate. He loses patience before I summon the courage to speak. Opening the giant, gleaming fridge, he offers me a bottle of water.

I'm almost afraid to take it. My feet are rooted to the spot as new sights and smells overwhelm me. I recognise all of these objects, and I have no idea how.

"For you," Enzo prompts.

I reluctantly pull the bottle from his grasp. He gives me an encouraging nod and returns to the fridge, pulling two dark-brown bottles out and passing one to Hunter.

The pair of them settle against the kitchen island, taking long pulls from their drinks. Lucky is loudly scarfing her dinner in the corner of the room, her tail wagging happily.

It breaks the tense silence as I stare down at my bandaged feet. I'm searching for something to say and coming up empty. Unanswered questions lay heavy in the air between us.

Enzo clears his throat. "I'll get the guest room set up. We should have some clean sheets and towels after your folks stayed last month."

"Round up Leighton too," Hunter adds. "If he's in."

"Doubt it. Friday night; he'll be out until dawn."

Hunter tosses his empty bottle before loosening his tie. "One less thing to worry about. You hear from Theo?"

"He called to say the reporters have dissipated from the hospital. Probably returned home to write more shitty articles about us."

"Nothing new there."

Hunter absently fiddles with his hearing aid. It seems to be a nervous tick, his impenetrable mask showing a tiny crack of weakness. Enzo disappears upstairs with a tired smile.

"Tomorrow... we need to talk," Hunter finally says. "You should rest for tonight. It's been a long day."

"Talk?"

"We need to discuss what happened to you and where we go from here. I'm offering you our protection, Harlow. It isn't free."

Embarrassment stains my cheeks pink. I can feel the shame burning my insides. I would never take what they've done for me for granted, but the threat is clear, even unspoken.

Hunter is in charge.

I have to do what he says.

They could easily kick me out onto the street to fend for myself. I don't even know where we are, let alone how to function in the world alone. I don't trust them, but I trust the unknown even less.

"I'll tell you what I can. My memory is patchy. Doctor Richards says more of it will come back over time."

Hunter's hand brushes against my arm, startling me back to silence. An unnamed emotion dances in his dark eyes, showing another precious glimpse beneath his armour.

"We'll get them," he promises in a gruff whisper. "The people who hurt you. It's what we do."

His words strangle me to death.

"You c-can't. They're dangerous."

"So are we, Harlow."

I'm overcome by the image of their corpses splayed across the basement's floor, bloated with rot and their skin slowly sloughing off.

Perhaps Pastor Michaels will repeat Abbie's cruel death. He fancied an experiment one day and peeled the skin from her bones with his knife. She died before he got very far.

"This is what we do, what we're trained to do," Hunter reassures calmly. "You don't need to worry about us. Okay?"

"Who else will worry about you?"

My question takes him aback. Hunter stares at me for a moment longer, his lips parted, before he strides away without answering me. I'm left alone in their sparkling kitchen, feeling filthy and out of place.

Lucky returns, her wet nose nudging my belly for attention. While stroking her, I briefly consider grabbing my shoes and hightailing it out of here.

I don't belong somewhere like this, bruised and trembling amongst their expensive possessions. Truthfully... I don't know where I belong. At least in the basement, I knew the status quo.

"Harlow!" Enzo shouts down the stairs.

Shuddering, I fight the instinct to duck and hide. His raised voice tangles with Pastor Michaels' in my mind, and my skin breaks out in terrified gooseflesh.

"Come on up," he adds.

Steeling my spine, I make myself walk out of the kitchen. The curved staircase leading upwards is a challenge, and I'm panting by the time I finally reach the top.

On the second floor, carpets are lit by soft lamps, casting shadows against the cream walls. Everything about their space is masculine, but it still manages to be comfortable, albeit sparse.

"Enzo?" I ask uncertainly.

"I'm in here, little one."

I creep across the hallway towards the last door on the left, passing several others. The room beyond is cloaked in colourful light that beckons me inside with open arms.

Pale-blue walls meet grey carpets, contrasting the lines of dark, polished wood. The room is dominated by a large bed with two bright, multi-coloured lamps on either side.

They remind me of the stained-glass windows in the chapel, dappling coloured shadows across the walls. Huge windows have been cut into the ceiling, revealing the gleam of starlight.

I peek in the attached bathroom, finding even more luxury. Just the idea of running water and a real toilet makes my eyes burn with tears. I've gotten used to the degradation of a bucket.

"We don't have guests often," Enzo says as he finishes fluffing the pillows. "Hunter's parents come and visit sometimes."

Running a hand over the fluffy, grey bedspread, I feel even worse for disgracing this beautiful room. The sheets are crisp and smell like summer nights, full of floral blooms. It was a luxury when that rare scent filtered into the basement.

"I don't know what to say," I reply in a tiny voice.

"You don't need to say anything." He watches me take in the room, wearing another reluctant smile. "Make yourself at home."

I run my fingers over the smooth wood of the bedside table, marvelling at the softness of everything. There's no dripping water, mould or piles of bones. Nothing but clean lines and luxury.

Enzo ducks out, returning with my paper bag of medications and another bottle of water. I accept the pills he drops into my palm without question. I'm hurting too much to care.

"Do you need anything else? I'm no good at sponge baths, but I can show you how to use the shower."

The thought of anything else today makes me want to run and scream. It's all too much. My eyes are drooping with fatigue.

"I'm good, Nurse Enzo," I joke, pulling back the covers on the bed. "Do you mind if I go to sleep?"

"Of course not. My room is across the hall. If you need anything in the night, just shout. I don't sleep much, so I'll hear."

Enzo backtracks, flicking off flights on the way out. Before he disappears, I call his name, mustering a small smile.

"Yeah?"

"Thank you for… well, everything." I unclip my sling to avoid meeting his eyes. "I don't know what I would've done if you guys didn't find me."

"You don't need to thank me."

"Yes, I do. No one's ever looked out for me before."

Enzo rubs the back of his neck, his stubble-strewn cheeks heating up. The sight makes my toes curl in the most extraordinary way. I have no idea what this weird feeling in my belly means.

"You're welcome, Harlow. Get some sleep, alright?"

The door clicks shut behind him. I tentatively climb into the bed, keeping my borrowed clothes in place. The idea of being naked in an unknown place is not appealing.

Everything about this room is so wrong. Laying down, the bed cradles my battered body, and the pillows are softer than air. I'd be more comfortable sleeping in someone else's blood.

Sinners don't deserve clothes or food.

Stop your whining or I'll give you something to cry about.

I stare up at the ceiling. I'm too exhausted to even sleep, my senses on high alert despite my safe surroundings. It's all so new and unknown. I can't handle it.

Leaving the comfort of the bed, I curl up on the carpet in the furthermost corner, keeping a direct view of the door. My broken ribs hate the position, but the pain is a familiar comfort. It reminds me of home.

As sleepless hours pass, I let my flimsy pretence crumble into ruin. My sobs grow louder, more frantic, forcing me to bite down on my fist to remain silent. I don't want anyone to hear me.

I cry until nothing remains in me but broken pieces that I can never fix. I cry for the girl I used to be. I cry for the girl I am now. I cry for all those who lost their lives while I remained alive.

But most of all, I cry because I have no idea what lies ahead. For the first time in my life, I have a potential future. Hope. Maybe a fresh start. That's more terrifying than any punishment I've endured.

CHAPTER 7

Leighton

Conversations – Juice WRLD

T he bouncer gives me a rough shove. I sprawl across the pavement outside the nightclub, spitting blood. With an exasperated sneer, he leaves me to stumble to my feet.

My jeans are ripped from the fall. In my drunken haze, I can't feel the pain of my busted nose. Some dickhead clocked me right in the face for running my stupid mouth, like usual.

"Fighting again, stretch?"

Diablo smokes a cigarette, standing on the street corner. I stagger over, attempting to remain upright. The whole world is spinning with the litres of alcohol in my veins.

"You seem surprised," I drawl.

"You wanna watch yourself. They'll throw you back in the slammer for that shit." Diablo claps me on the shoulder. "You've only been out for a couple of months."

"Still doesn't feel like returning home."

"Never will again. You come to see those bars as more than brick and mortar," he says, blowing a smoke ring. "I did, anyway. Family means more on the inside than out. You feel me?"

"I have family out here. They don't give a damn whether I'm in or out of prison. Nobody wants to help the family fuck-up."

"Now that ain't true, is it?"

Diablo shouts a taxi down and shoves me in the back, handing off a stack of notes to the driver. He knows my address from previous drunken nights.

Hunter would hang, draw, and fucking quarter my delinquent ass if he knew that. Me and Diablo have become friends after we both got out of prison recently. He understands me a little too well.

I dip in and out as the miles race by. The imposing shadow of my new home welcomes me when the taxi pulls up on the curb. He keeps all of Diablo's money, shoving my drunken ass out with a curse.

By some miracle, I make it to the front gate without falling over and lean in for a retinal scan to allow me inside. Hunter has a stick up his pompous rear end about security.

The rising dawn offers some light as I scratch around, finally unlocking the front door. I have to abandon my beer-stained shoes before clambering upstairs. Everyone must be fast asleep.

Blindly heading for my bedroom, I undo my belt and rip my sweaty shirt over my head. I could sleep for a thousand years after far too many vodka shots and drunken dares. The last girl's lipstick is still smeared on my neck.

Fuck me, she was hot.

Almost worth the right hook.

Eyes already shut, I collapse on the bed with a groan. My head hurts something fierce. Rather than blissful silence, there's a strange squeak before the light slams on.

It quickly escalates into a full-blown, blood-curdling scream. The sound lances through my head like a fucking bayonet.

"ENZO!"

Rolling over, I faceplant on the floor with a grunt. The screaming gets louder and louder, reverberating around the room with soul-sucking terror.

"Harlow!"

There's a thud as the bedroom door slams back open and a bare-chested Enzo arrives like a bat out of hell. Lucky is hot on his heels, her teeth drawn back in a threatening grimace.

"Leighton!" he yells, spotting me on the floor. "What the fuck are you doing in here?"

"Trying to find my goddamn bed," I shout back.

"This isn't your room!"

He approaches the bed, his hands outstretched in a soothing manner. The screaming has died down into a gasping whimper that stabs me in the heart.

Managing to pull myself up, I realise what a mistake I've made. This is the spare room, and there's a shaking wreck in the bed I just tried to climb into. A fucking girl.

Her hazelnut-coloured hair stands up in all directions, like she was deep asleep before I stumbled in here. Beneath a sheet of tears, her sweetheart-shaped face is scrunched up, almost in pain.

Enzo approaches like he's stalking a deer, ready to pounce at any second. He sinks onto the bed, gently wrapping his arms around the sobbing woman.

"It's me, Harlow. Open those pretty eyes."

"Please... d-don't hurt me... I'm sorry for r-running," she stutters through her tears. "I'll pray, I will. Don't hurt me..."

"Come on, little one. Take a nice deep breath."

"I'm s-s-sorry, I'll pray harder..."

"Enzo? A little context would be nice," I complain, managing to find my feet. "Who the hell is this chick?"

"Shut up, Leigh. You're a fucking idiot."

The girl curls into Enzo's side without opening her eyes. Holding her in an intimate embrace, Enzo murmurs quiet instructions to ease her panic attack.

She looks to be in seriously rough shape. I've seen some shit in prison, and this girl's been beaten to within an inch of her damn life. She's covered in bruises, including two stripes down her face.

I've seen enough guys getting their skulls broken against bars to know what causes those marks.

Eventually, she falls silent. Tears cease to streak down her cheeks. Lucky jumps up on the bed, settling by her side. The girl's fingers bury in her fur before she passes out again.

"She's exhausted," Enzo comments. "I found her sleeping on the floor a few hours ago. She barely stirred as I put her back to bed."

Carefully extricating himself, he settles her tiny body back on the bed and pulls the sheets up to her chin. I frown at the alien creature in my friend's body.

Enzo is many things. Brutal. Violent. Unshakeable. Tender is not a word I'd use to describe this tough son of a bitch. I have no idea who's standing in front of me, but it isn't the man I know.

"As sweet as this is, an explanation would be awesome. Who is she, and why was she sleeping on the floor?"

"Call me sweet again and I will crush your skull with my fucking pinkie finger," Enzo warns, grabbing me in a headlock. "Get out."

I'm escorted downstairs, his arm wrapped around my throat like a steel noose. The kitchen lights are now on, sealing my death sentence. I never should've come home.

Hunter's fixing a cup of tea, dressed in a pair of sweats. He spares me an exasperated look as Enzo finally releases me.

"What time do you call this, Leigh?" Hunter's eyes narrow on me. "What happened to you?"

I briefly touch my face, feeling the tender skin around my nose and flecks of dried blood.

"I call this early, Hunt. Some asshole tried to steal my hookup, so I punched him. Turns out, she was his girlfriend. Whoopsie me."

"You're drunk," he deadpans.

"I sure as hell hope so after what I just saw. You seen Enzo around? Someone's hijacked his body and made him go fucking soft."

I'm delivered a smack on the head that makes my ears ring. Enzo's face is downright unnerving. He looks ready to serve my carved-out organs for breakfast.

Hunter takes a sip of tea as he considers me. "You know the rules. Stick to curfew. Keep your nose clean and out of trouble. You should not be stumbling in at five o'clock in the morning."

"Drunk and attacking our house guest," Enzo adds.

"I'm a grown man of twenty-four. I don't need a curfew." I give them my best shit-eating grin. "Since when do we have guests? Let alone hot, screaming ones."

Enzo tries to hit me again, but I dance back, easily dodging his next swing. He's big and strong, but that makes him slow. I'm quick on my feet and well accustomed to defending myself.

"You live under my roof, so you follow the rules," Hunter reminds me.

"Alright, *Dad*. If I mow the lawn, can I get my allowance?"

"Don't be a smartass," Enzo growls.

"You're not my father!"

Slamming his cup down, Hunter faces me with obvious weariness. He looks far older than his thirty-four years. There are ten years between us, but he's always shouldered the burden for us both.

The person I remembered before I was convicted wasn't here when I came out, three years later. A lot of shit went down in my absence. I lost more than just my freedom.

"I'm trying to help you," he spells out. "Giving you a job and a place to stay. Nowhere else would employ a convict. The least you can do is act like you give a damn and respect the house rules."

"You act like I'm some hardened criminal."

"You served time."

"And you love to remind me of that fact!" I shout back. "I'm your fucking brother, not some stranger!"

Enzo steps between us before I can wrap my hands around Hunter's throat. He shoots us both placating looks.

"Harlow is asleep upstairs. Let's not wake her, hmm?"

"Is anyone going to tell me why there's a kid sleeping upstairs?" I ask again.

"She's an adult, and a client," Hunter answers at last.

"A client? In the spare bed?"

"We're keeping her out of the spotlight," Enzo reveals.

"And between your sheets."

Stepping closer, Enzo pins me with an ice-cold glower. "You want to try that again, Leigh? Between what?"

Fearing the integrity of my skull if I push him again, I raise my hands and take a step back. I don't fancy getting squashed by the ogre anytime soon.

"Harlow is part of a case we're working on." Hunter doesn't lift his eyes from his phone. "If you bothered to turn up for work, you'd know all about it. Sleep it off, Leigh. We'll talk when you're sober."

"Yeah, I'll pass on the heart to heart. Thanks for the invite though, bro. Great catching up with you."

Flipping Hunter the bird, I storm from the kitchen, leaving them to bitch about me in peace. The frame rattles as I slam my bedroom door shut like a petulant child.

Fuck being an adult.

Those assholes aren't worth it.

CHAPTER 8

Harlow

Heart-Shaped Box - Ashton Irwin

M y entire body feels heavy as I creep downstairs without making
a sound. It's getting light outside. After almost two days in
bed, I feel slightly more ready to face the world.

I drank the protein shake left on my bedside table and swallowed
another handful of meds before going back to sleep yesterday. Nobody
disturbed me, but the food and medication had replaced itself when I
woke up to pee.

It felt good to sleep, knowing I was safe at last. As soon as I
surrendered to exhaustion, that was it. I couldn't move again, barely
able to limp to the bathroom before getting back into bed.

The kitchen is blessedly empty. I tip my mouth under the tap and
take several frenzied gulps of water. Dribbles run down my chin as I
fill my belly, wiping off my mouth when I'm done.

Water on tap. It's a crazy thought to me. I often had to lick droplets
from the walls of the basement, relying on leaks and the occasional
mercy of my tormentors.

These people have everything.

It reminds me of all I've lived without.

It's raining outside—slanted, silvery bullets that pelt the ground in a rhythmic shower. I trail over to the sliding door that leads to luscious greenery as far as the eye can see. The garden is beautiful.

Lucky trots to my side, her breath fogging up the glass. Petting her head, I twist the lock and step out into the cold air. She breaks into a run, bounding across the lawn with a yip.

My feet carry me into the falling rain. With my head tilted upwards, I can catch the droplets on my tongue. They taste sweet, unlike the putrid water that sustained me for so long.

Lucky finds me in the middle of the lawn, a ball locked between her drooling fangs. She drops it right at my feet.

"You're a real softie, you know that?"

Bending over with gritted teeth, I manage to pick up the ball and toss it across the grass. She chases, her satisfied barking disturbing a cluster of birds. I watch them take flight with awe.

Instead of returning inside, I ease myself down onto the wet grass to watch the world wake up. My bandages are already soaked through, but I tuck my plastered arm inside my hoodie for protection.

The rain is coming down thick and fast, hammering into me like the beat of fists on flesh. It feels exactly as I imagined. My skin is being sloughed off, stripped down layer by layer. I'm being cleansed.

There's this weird smell in the air that comes with a fresh rainfall. I can't get enough of the heady scent. If I could, I'd bottle it and keep it close so it can't be stolen from me again.

That's where Enzo finds me, what feels like hours later, drenched and shivering violently, but more content than I've ever felt. Even Lucky has abandoned me and gone back inside to get warm.

"Harlow? What on earth are you doing?"

His voice startles me from the meditative state I've slipped into. Looking up, I find his angry amber eyes staring down at me.

"Hey," I reply with a smile.

Enzo scans my sopping wet clothes and the tremor of my cold body. He's wearing a pair of loose pyjama bottoms and a tight tank top that exposes the chiselled expanse of his chest, covered in a smattering of dark hair.

"Hey," he echoes. "You're soaking wet."

"So?"

"I don't want you to get sick again. Come inside and warm up before I lose my mind."

"I'm fine out here. It's nice."

"Harlow, it's raining."

Sighing, I wiggle my toes in the wet grass. "I never saw the sky. Raining or not, it's beautiful. The wind makes me feel less alone."

"Why?" Enzo asks with interest.

"It's like the world is screaming along with me."

Sealing his lips, he crouches down and slides his hands underneath my arms. I'm too cold to protest as I'm cradled against his chest, our bodies pressed tightly together. He turns to head back inside.

"Are you hungry?"

I nuzzle his tank top, loving the blanket of warmth his skin provides. "No. I've been drinking the shakes you left for me."

"How do you know it was me?"

"Because Hunter would have woken me up and asked those questions he promised to hit me with."

"Damn, Harlow. You've got him nailed already."

His chest rumbles, vibrating against my cheek. I should be embarrassed, snuggling up to him like a baby bear. Now that we're inside, I can feel just how cold I am. He feels like a furnace.

"Shower," Enzo decides, carrying me upstairs. "You need to warm up. What the hell were you thinking?"

My teeth chatter against each other, silencing my answer. The shower looked so intimidating when I arrived; I don't know if I'll be able to work it. I'm afraid of breaking something.

"I like the cold."

"It isn't good for you though," he argues.

Carrying me back to the bedroom, Enzo shoves open the bathroom door with his shoulder. Inside, the slick, modern en-suite awaits. Dark-slate tiles are matched with silver finishings, the space revolving around a walk-in shower.

He places me down on the counter space next to the sink basin. Protests are lodged in my throat as Enzo begins to unwind the muddied bandages covering my feet, his jaw clenched tight.

The brush of his fingertips against my inner ankles causes a zip of electricity to race down my spine. I almost gasp out loud at the foreign sensation. It's like he's hitting me with tiny, delicious bolts of lightning.

"Your feet are healing well," he mumbles, inspecting the soles of my feet. "The water might sting some of the deeper cuts."

Tossing the dirty bandages, his eyes coast back up to meet mine. There's a hint of nervousness there, a perplexing contrast to the sheer gravity of his physical presence. I manage a shrug.

"The pain doesn't bother me."

"It bothers me." Enzo's hand skates up my leg before he realises and pulls it back.

At the last second, I grab his wrist. Enzo looks startled by my initiation of more contact. I feel comfortable around him in a way that I've never experienced before.

Subconsciously, I'm craving the closeness, desperate to avoid the crushing emptiness of being alone again. That's when the bad thoughts creep back in. I'll do anything to keep them at bay.

"I've survived much worse," I whisper, my thumb resting over the steady pulse of his heartbeat.

"That isn't the comfort you think it is, little one. Surviving is one thing. This is the start of your time to actually live."

Pulling his hand from mine, he clears his throat and moves to turn the shower on. Water cascades from a silver disc in the ceiling, the hot spray creating billowing clouds of steam in the bathroom.

"How do I work it?"

Enzo spares me a glance. "Pull this lever to adjust the temperature, and this one to turn it off. Don't burn yourself."

I'm mesmerised by the waterfall imprisoned in slices of frosted glass. It's like my very own rainstorm. I'd be quite happy to spend all day here.

"I'll find some fresh clothes." Enzo retreats to the doorway. "Leighton's should fit you until we go shopping."

"I'll be fine wearing whatever. No shopping required."

"You need clothes, toiletries, the works."

"I don't need anything," I try again.

"Why are you fighting me on this?"

"You've given me enough."

When I think Enzo is going to give in and return to the gentle giant I know, he closes the space between us again. His expression is stormy as he slowly, deliberately, trails his eyes over my entire trembling body.

"That was then, this is now. You need everything. I'll damn well get it for you, and you'll damn well wear it. Got that?"

I refuse to break eye contact.

"And if I don't?"

"I'm not accustomed to that word, Harlow. You'll learn soon enough. We take care of our own in this house."

With a final pointed look, he leaves me in peace. My heart threatens to break through my ribcage as I stare after his retreating back. Being bossed around by Enzo feels different from the orders I was forced to abide by before.

The ingrained need to obey is there, but without the all-consuming pull of fear. I know he won't hurt me. There's no darkness within him, spitting and writhing in its bid to escape. I've gotten good at sensing it.

Now Hunter, he's a whole other puzzle entirely. I'm fairly certain he hates my guts, even after the limited time we've spent together. I'm only good for one thing to him—information.

What happens when I give it to him?

When does their protection end?

These thoughts plague me as I hide in the shower, holding my plastered arm outside the door at an awkward angle to keep it dry. There are all kinds of bottles lined up, begging to be smelled.

I wash myself over and over again, testing each fragrance and savouring the scented steam. Washing shampoo from my hair is a challenge with only one hand. It brushes my lower back in snarled knots.

After spraining my arm trying to reach the ends, I give up. Washing my hair with bottled water was easier than this. Pastor Michaels would occasionally offer me the luxury of bathing, usually when he was disgusted by the scent emanating from my cage.

Avoiding the fogged-up mirror as I step out, I find a pair of dark-red sweatpants left on the bed. They're too long, bunching around my ankles as I slip on the oversized white t-shirt next.

My feet are sore, but well into the healing process, so I don't bother re-wrapping them. There's no hope for my bird's nest of hair. I try to untangle it with my fingers while trailing back downstairs.

It's still raining outside, obscuring the winter's day in fog and gloom through the large bay windows. After a tentative descent down the stairs, I'm hit by the sound of someone yelping.

"Shit, that's hot."

"You think? The toaster doesn't make it cold, genius."

"Fucking thanks, Hunt. Wanker."

"You're so welcome. Call me that again and I'll tell your parole officer you've been out drinking until sunrise most nights."

"Don't you dare. I'm not above murdering you in your sleep."

With his shirt-covered back to me, Hunter sits at the breakfast bar. For the first time, I notice dark swirls of ink peeking out around his neck. I didn't realise he had tattoos.

The intricate-looking designs are obscured through the blue fabric. His chestnut hair is hanging loose today in glossy waves, complementing his slate-coloured suit.

"Hi," I say awkwardly.

He startles as I limp in, surveying me with a lingering glance. There's a complicated sheet of paper in his hands. It takes a moment for the word to click into place. Newspaper. I know that one.

"Jesus Christ. Cereal it is."

Spinning on the spot, the newbie's eyes flare with surprise. He's dressed in tight sweatpants and a muscle t-shirt that shows off his tanned, lean body. He's shorter than the other two, but stocky and well-built.

I take note of the thick scarring across his knuckles, contrasting the child-like grin on his lips. His hair is shaggy and very overgrown, covering his ears with slight curls in the exact same shade as Hunter's waves.

Propping his elbow on the breakfast bar, he faces me with amusement dancing in his forest-green eyes.

"Well, if it isn't Goldilocks. Risen from the dead!"

Hunter snorts as he returns his attention to the newspaper, dismissing us both.

"I don't know what that means."

"She speaks!" He unleashes a megawatt smile. "I'm Leighton, Hunter's better-looking brother. Sorry for, erm… you know. The other night."

"Trying to get into bed with me?"

His easy grin widens. "Yeah, that."

"You're lucky Enzo didn't knock you out," Hunter comments. "Or worse. He was well within his right to shoot you."

Leighton proudly flexes his biceps. "I reckon I could take him. What say you, Harlow? I think I prefer Goldilocks. You know, the girl that breaks in and sleeps in the bears' beds?"

I choke on thin air. I've got no idea what he's ranting about. Leighton spares me a cheeky wink, returning to prepping his breakfast while humming under his breath.

Seeing no other option, I take the empty bar stool next to Hunter. I can tell he's studying me over his newspaper as I wince while sitting down. The meds I swallowed upstairs haven't kicked in yet.

"Breakfast, Goldilocks?"

Leighton plops a bowl down in front of me, tipping some golden clusters into it from a bright-yellow box.

"What… ah, what is this?"

Leighton's smile falters. "Huh? Cereal?"

"She's on a strict diet from the hospital," Hunter chips in sternly. "Protein shakes for weight gain and light foods only. Not your sugary crap."

Leighton rolls his eyes. "Nobody wants to drink that tasteless shit. Let the girl live a bit."

Staring down into the depths of the bowl, I watch him pour milk in and add a silver spoon. Mrs Michaels brought me milk once, when I helped clean up after a particularly messy night.

It was the only time she was remotely kind towards me. I think she was relieved to have some company in the dark hours after the ritual was complete. When I slipped on a puddle of urine, she soon lost her temper again.

"What are your plans today, Leigh?" Hunter fastens his collar, adding a silk tie. "I'm leaving for the office if you'd care to show your face at work."

Leighton wrinkles his nose in distaste. "It's far too early for the 'w' word. I'll be resuming my *Greys Anatomy* marathon."

"Great. Sounds real productive."

"Someone's gotta make the most of that fancy subscription you pay for. It's a hardship, but I'll shoulder the burden."

Hunter catches me staring as he stands and smooths his trousers, offering me a tiny frown. Panicking, I take a mouthful as a distraction.

My eyes almost roll back in my head. This stuff is insane. I've never tasted anything like it.

"Good?" Leighton smirks.

"It's so... so..."

I shrug, unable to explain the taste of something other than the most basic food to sustain life. Leighton's attention is firmly fixed on my mouth as I take another spoonful.

"Note to self. The girl likes sugar puffs. Very interesting."

I can't help but smile at Leighton's antics.

"I'm off," Hunter interrupts us. "I have an intelligence briefing in an hour." He casts me a look that kills my appetite. "We'll be having that talk later on."

I hug my aching arm to my chest, nodding silently. Leighton casts Hunter a sour look before filling his own bowl with cereal.

"You're killing the fun. Go play scary secret agent. I'll take good care of Harlow." Leighton's voice is light and teasing. "I'm sure we can find some trouble to get up to."

I can't hold in my squeak of shock as Hunter flashes across the kitchen. He grabs hold of Leighton's shirt and pins him against the fridge with a low hiss of fury.

"Keep your hands to yourself or find another place to live. Harlow's under my protection. She doesn't need you messing up what little life she has left."

Leighton shoves him back with significant strength. "Don't touch me. I'm not a child. I know how to conduct myself."

"Do you? Could've fooled me"

"Fuck you, Hunt."

Locked in a bubble of rage, they look ready to kill each other. I want to duck underneath the nearby table and hide from the confrontation.

As Hunter's words sink in, anger replaces my anxiety. Somehow, somewhere, I find the strength to squeeze out a furious sentence.

"My life isn't little."

Hunter gives me a side-look.

"Of course it isn't." Leighton breaks free, brushing his rumpled clothes off with a glower.

"Is that what you think of me?" I ask tearfully.

Looking between us both, Hunter looks lost for words. It's the first time I've seen him unsure of himself. Leaving him spluttering, I clamber down from the stool and walk out without looking back.

Neither of them follows me.

Shame weighs me down like lead.

If that's what Hunter thinks of me, I don't want to be around him. I'd crawl back into my cage if I could at this moment. In that hellish wasteland, I know the rules and expectations.

I can play the game, and play it well.

This place... it's too much.

I want my life to be big. Bigger than the whole world and every last monstrous person in it. The killer blow, though? Hunter's right.

I'll never be more than the pathetic person my parents made me. A broken doll, destined for little more than hell's final taste of oblivion.

He who be worthy shall find redemption.

Get on your knees and pray, Harlow.

Pray for the Lord to forgive you.

Running without seeing, I collapse in a darkened corner. The prayers are already rolling off my tongue on instinct. My fingers slot together as I struggle to kneel despite my injuries.

I recite my prayers for forgiveness four times. Just as I was taught, a lesson forged in the devil's punishing fires. The words are scorched on to the very fabric of my splintered mind.

It still isn't enough.

Nothing will ever be enough.

CHAPTER 9

Enzo

Come Undone – My Darkest Days

After another gruelling run, I pass Hunter leaving in the driveway. His expression is steely as he speeds away in the convertible Mercedes. My exhausted wave is unreturned. Charming.

He doesn't tend to use that car in the winter. We have the company SUV for cooler weather, and the convertible is more of a toy to satisfy his inner adrenaline junkie. Speed limits don't usually stop him.

My phone vibrates in my pocket as I step inside the house.

> **Brooklyn:** Saw you running just now. Talk to me, big guy.

I quickly tap out a response.

> **Me:** Stuff on my mind. Call you later.

Her response comes immediately.

> **Brooklyn:** You better. Don't make me come over there.

Tucking my phone away, I bypass the kitchen, needing to shower before dealing with Leighton's attitude. Under the spray, I set the temperature to cold.

It's a trick I've learned over the years. I've barely slept since Harlow came home with us. Her presence has me on high alert for any potential threats, even when I should be asleep.

In the privacy of my shower, she floats back into my mind. That tiny spitfire is never far from my thoughts at the moment. Her crystal-clear, innocent eyes, and the small curves that round her body.

I should be fucking ashamed as I wrap my hand around my cock. Head lowered beneath the spray, I work my shaft in fast pumps. All I can think about is the feel of her gripping my wrist earlier.

She's so small and delicate, even for a twenty-odd year old. I'd break her if I touched her. But that doesn't stop me from fantasising about a world where I could cross the professional boundary between us.

When I've grunted my release, I wash off and step out of the shower. Guilt twists in my gut. The last thing Harlow needs is me fucking up her life. She's facing enough shit as it is.

Scraping a hand through my wet hair, I bypass my work clothes and throw on a pair of ripped, black jeans with a plain tee. Hunter can take care of Sabre alone today; I've had enough of his foul mood.

My priority is Harlow. I won't leave her alone in a world that she has no knowledge of. Fuck the rules. Someone has to look after her. Why shouldn't that be me? I can keep things professional.

Lightly knocking on her bedroom door, I peek inside. Her bed has been neatly made and lies empty. She was still in the shower when I left to go running.

Heading downstairs, I find Leighton bustling around the kitchen. He's washing up empty bowls while cursing to himself, the ceramics clattering as they're tossed about.

"Are you cleaning?" I watch in disbelief.

He casts me a glare. "I'm not some uncivilised caveman."

"Isn't that what people go to prison to become?"

"Ha ha, fucking hilarious. Hunter upset your girlfriend."

"She's a client, not my girlfriend."

"Whatever, man. She's refusing to come out or speak to me, so I'm trying to do something useful here instead."

"Why didn't you call me?"

Leighton tosses the tea towel down with exasperation. "Not everything is my fault, you know? Fuck this. I'll be upstairs."

Leaving him to continue pouting, I tear through the house. Hunter's book-lined office is deserted, along with the formal dining room that we don't use, and the downstairs gym.

When I attempt to open the sliding door that leads into the den at the back of the house, it refuses to budge. Something's barricading it.

"Harlow? It's me. Can you let me in?"

"Go away, Enzo," her timid voice replies.

"Not a chance. You have ten seconds to open this door before I break it down."

After five seconds, my very limited patience expires. The chair she had propped under the handle splinters as I use my shoulder to smash the door open by force. It falls off its hinges with a pained groan.

Shoving the destroyed door aside, I squint to see into the pitch-black room. The navy-blue curtains are drawn against the rainy day, adding to the darkness. This room is where we spend most of our time together, limited as that may be these days.

It's a generous family space, lined with stained black flooring and light, panelled walls. There's a huge log burner in the centre of the room, surrounded by perfectly cut wooden logs packed into the sides of the fireplace.

Above it, we have a top-of-the-line flat screen television and sound system Hunter insisted on when movie nights used to be a common occurrence. Two dark-green, velvet sectionals fill the floor, with cosy cushions and blankets.

The thick, woven rug beneath my bare feet adds a final layer of warmth. Hunter and Leighton's mum used to work as an interior designer. She took one look at our sparse, lifeless house and insisted on making it a home.

"Harlow? I can't see a damn thing. Where are you?"

"Leave m-m-me alone," she hiccups.

I flick on a lamp and follow the sound of quiet sobbing until I find her. She's curled up in the furthermost corner, half hidden by a towering bookshelf that fills the back wall.

I'm afraid to even go near her for fear she'll splinter into a thousand pieces. I'm no shrink like Doctor Richards. Hell, I can hardly understand my own bloody head. This is all new territory for me, but I can't stand helpless as another person dies.

Not again.

"You want some company?"

Harlow stares blankly over my shoulder, tears running down her cheeks in thick rivulets. Crouching down, I join her on the floor, folding my body into the uncomfortable corner.

The little ballbreaker has staked a claim on me already. Each second I spend around her only cements that bond even more. Despite the past, I always help people in need. It's hardwired into my DNA to look after the vulnerable.

"Enzo... am I broken?"

Taking a leap of faith, I prise her hands away from her face, revealing devastating doe eyes that resemble the lightest tropical ocean.

"Broken? No. Perhaps a little damaged, but it's nothing we can't fix."

"You don't know me. I c-can't… be fixed."

Engulfing her hands in mine, I squeeze lightly. "You're still here, aren't you? That's one hell of an achievement."

"Is it, though?"

"Yes," I assure her. "You're doing better than you think."

She nods to herself. "Can we get out of here or something?"

I weigh up the risks, daggered by the desperate look in her eyes. She looks like she's going insane, trapped in this house with us.

"Please?"

Her final plea breaks my resolve.

"Hunter's going to fucking fire me for this." I offer her a hand. "Let's go. We can go somewhere out of the city to avoid the press."

Harlow lets me help her up, brushing off her oversized, borrowed clothes. I ignore the fact they belong to Leighton, and how much that annoys me. My possessive asshole is clearly in overdrive.

Throwing on my leather jacket in the entrance hall, I watch as Harlow shrugs on her hospital hoodie. She cringes at the sight of her unlaced Chucks on the shoe stand.

Grabbing the shoes, I gesture for her to take a seat on the stairs. Her mobility is still limited, but she seems to be moving with slightly less pain than when she first arrived.

"Foot," I demand.

"I can give it a go."

"Watch one more time, alright?"

Easing the shoe on her left foot, I take my time tying the laces, giving her a moment to observe. She reaches for the second shoe and awkwardly ties a bow, favouring her unbroken arm.

"Quick learner?"

Harlow stares at her feet. "Apparently."

"Sure you haven't done this before?"

"At this point? I don't know."

I plaster on a neutral expression to conceal my worry. The disturbing gaps in her memory are on the long list of issues we need to discuss now that she's awake.

Rifling in the cupboard under the stairs, I come up with a worn denim jacket that should fit over her hoodie. It smells like Leighton—the bitter tinge of cigarettes with a citrus undertone.

"Put this on, it's cold out."

Harlow accepts the jacket and slides one arm in, folding the other over her cast. "Thanks."

"That looks good on you!" a smug voice calls out.

Bounding down the staircase like an excited puppy, Leighton is dressed in faded blue jeans and an old band t-shirt, his shaggy hair still wet from the shower. He's an unashamed Aerosmith fan, courtesy of his obsession with nineties movies. He's made us watch *Armageddon* at least ten times.

The motherfucker must have overheard us talking in the den. He shoots me a bright grin, then offers Harlow a hand up before I can.

"Mind if I tag along?"

She looks uncertain. "Why are you asking me?"

"Because your voice is heavenly, kitten."

I choke on a barked laugh. Fuck me gently. Even Harlow cracks a smile. Rolling with the punches, Leighton mock-sighs as he steers her outside into the rain.

Kicking him out of the shotgun seat so Harlow can ride up front, I boost her into the SUV. The feel of her hips in my palms nearly breaks my resolve. I can't seem to keep my hands off her.

I have to grit my teeth as I slam her door and head for the driver's seat. Leighton has slipped into the back, his feet propped up as he scrolls on his phone with a half smile.

"Alright, rules." I pin him with a stare. "No funny business. Harlow shouldn't even be leaving the house. Don't make me regret letting you come along."

"What do you take me for?" He frowns.

"I mean it, Leigh."

"Yeah, I got it. Loud and clear. So, what are we doing?"

Stopping for a retinal scan to unlock the gate, I take a right towards the main road out of London. "Harlow needs some stuff."

"I don't," she replies shortly.

"You do. Don't argue with me, Harlow."

Lips pursed, she looks out of the window. "Someone's got to."

Leighton smirks at me. "Hah. Is this your first lovers' quarrel? That's cute. We should commemorate the occasion."

"Shut the fuck up before I leave you on the side of the road."

We head through the rainy suburbs, merging into the morning traffic. The city is the last place we should take Harlow. Anonymous or not, her safety is paramount.

"What kind of stuff are we getting?" Leighton breaks the silence.

"She has nothing."

"At all? How is that possible?"

Harlow's face empties of all emotion as she slips back into blank numbness. Leighton knows a little of our work from the first few weeks he bothered to turn up to HQ, before he got bored.

Prison changed him. He isn't the carefree kid I once knew. He was always troubled, growing up in Hunter's impressive shadow, but that place stole the last of his youthful innocence.

"Is this something to do with... *that* case?"

I glower at him in the mirror. "Yes."

"You mean the serial k—"

"Yes."

Leighton averts his eyes with a nod. The bright-red tinge that spreads over Harlow's cheeks is simultaneously adorable and infuriating. I hate that she feels ashamed.

"Could've told me," Leighton says under his breath.

"Could've asked."

"I hate that you guys keep secrets from me."

"Show any amount of interest in the life Hunter is trying to build for you, and you won't feel so left out."

"You're being unfair."

I stare at the road ahead. "Life isn't fair. I think you'll find there's more to the world than the bottom of a liquor bottle."

Leighton sulks until we pull into a quiet shopping centre nearly an hour later. Harlow wakes up from her nap as we park, her eyes lit with excitement at our new surroundings.

Leaving Leighton to retrieve a trolley, I help her down from the car and pull a purple beanie from my pocket. She lets me tug it over her long hair, then I add a spare pair of Hunter's aviators.

"I look ridiculous," she murmurs.

"Better to look ridiculous and stay safe."

"You think the reporters will be here?"

"They'll be camped outside of HQ. The press are looking for the other missing person. Like I said, we didn't know about you."

She seems to cave inwards, her shoulders hunching and chin dipped down. I can't protect her from the truth forever. She's in for a grilling when Hunter returns home anyway.

"How long has she been missing for?" Harlow asks.

"About two months."

"And you think it's the same people that held me?"

I catalogue her nervous twitching. "It fits the same MO. Our killer follows a pattern. We're certain he snatched this victim."

"Does she have a name?"

I decide to take a risk.

"Laura Whitcomb."

Harlow lurches to the side and promptly vomits across the car park. I spur into action, rubbing her back and shouting for Leighton to return. People are watching us with concern.

"You're okay," I whisper, shielding her from sight.

"Stop saying that! I'm n-not... nothing is... no."

It's the first time I've heard Harlow raise her wispy voice. Wiping her mouth, she pins me with a devastated look. I suddenly regret pushing too soon.

"She's dead. Laura's gone."

"How do you know?"

"I… watched him carve her into pieces. She died a long time ago. You won't ever find her."

Distraught tears are streaming down her cheeks, leaking pain and suffering that I can't take away. It only adds to the simmering anger that's kept me awake since we took on this fucking case.

"Who killed Laura? Tell me."

"I c-c-can't," she stammers.

"Why not?"

"He will k-kill all of you."

Leighton chooses that moment to reappear, plastering on a cheery smile that I'd love to wipe off with my fist. We haul Harlow up, her featherlight body balanced between us.

"Let's go home," I decide, unlocking the car. "This was a bad idea. It's too much for you."

Harlow yanks her hand from mine. "No, I want to do this. My life... it's not little. It can't be little."

I have no idea what she means. Leighton seems to understand and offers her a smile.

"You got it, Goldilocks. Come on, let's get you out of those sweats before you give Enzo an aneurysm. He's the jealous type."

He traps her in place with his arms braced on either side of the trolley. It's another invasion of her personal space, but Harlow doesn't seem to mind the closeness right now.

In fact, I'd argue her body is craving the familiarity of human touch while she's so lost and afraid. Blowing out a breath, she forces herself to calm down. Fuck if it doesn't take my breath away.

Letting them head inside, I retrieve my phone from the pocket of my leather jacket and hit Hunter's name. He answers on the second ring.

"Rodriguez."

"Hey, I've got something."

"Talk to me."

My sigh rattles down the line. "Whitcomb is already dead."

"Where did you get that from?"

"Harlow."

Hunter hollers at someone in the background, ordering them to clear the room. He should be in an intelligence meeting about our upcoming narcotics raid right about now.

We've been playing cat and mouse with a large crime syndicate for several months. The next two weeks will be crucial as we wrap the case up. When he comes back on the line, his voice is bleak.

"Not exactly unexpected. Did she witness it?"

"I think so. Richards needs to be there to take her full statement. I'm worried about how Harlow will react."

"If Whitcomb's dead and Harlow escaped, this son of a bitch will be out there right now, stalking his next victim."

"She's not ready," I reply softly.

"Fuck, Enz. We have the government breathing down our necks and more resources invested in this than I care to admit. I need results."

"Hunter, ease up. We have to do this right."

There's a long, pregnant pause.

"I'll speak to Richards about setting something up. He can be there to supervise. You can't protect her forever though."

"I'm just playing this smart." I rub the ache between my eyes. "She's no good to us rocking in a corner. We can't catch this guy without her help."

Theo's voice filters through from the background. As head of the intelligence department, he works closely with some of our best agents. The legwork behind this raid has kept him busy for months.

"I'm coming," Hunter replies to him. "Theo's traced Harlow hitchhiking on four different vehicles so far. I have samples from forensics to have a DNA test done for her."

"You think she has a family?" I guess, feeling sick at the thought.

"No one's looking for her. She's a ghost, but we have to be thorough. We need new leads to identify the killer."

"What about the raid this week? We've been planning it for months. Everything is in place."

"I need you here to run point," he answers firmly. "This operation requires our full attention. Theo will keep working on Harlow's case."

The line goes dead, and I stare at my phone for a few seconds. My loyalties should lie with my best friend, my company, and the ongoing investigation. Sabre matters above all else.

It's the family I've created for myself, one case at a time. Our ranks are made up of talented individuals, all let down by the world. I've found friends for life, family even, in the bleakness of my profession.

I can't let Harlow threaten our equilibrium. Regardless of the pathetic scrap of hope it offers to my cold heart to be needed by someone again.

CHAPTER 10

Harlow

Speaking Off The Record — Hotel Mira

The pen shakes in my hand as I'm overcome by trembling. Each word I manage to write is wobbly, like a child's love letter. Just recalling the names I can remember has exhausted me.

Little details come back to me with each word. Hair colours, broken smiles, heart-wrenching stories shared in the dead of night. All of the girls had someone they loved, even from afar.

He took that from them.

Worst of all, I know there are others. Their identities are blurred in my mind, like polaroid photos with the faces scratched out. It's killing me to know that I've forgotten them.

Slamming the pen down, I grab handfuls of my stupidly long hair. My heart is beating too fast. Pumping blood. Keeping my vital organs alive. Suspending me in life, when all I deserve is death.

Tugging on my hair, I gasp as a few strands come away in my hands. The sizzle of pain is a welcome distraction. Breathing deeply, I wrap a thin strand around my fingers.

Pain cleanses us of all our sins.

We suffer for him.

Fire races across my scalp as I pull again, harder this time. The strands rip away from my head with a faint pop. It hurts even more, and I nearly cry from the relief.

"God loves us for our labours," I whisper hoarsely.

Staring down at the list of girls that looked into my eyes before they took their last breath, I feel physically sick. None of them had to die. I scrawl another name at the bottom, biting back a sob.

Harlow Michaels.

I should've joined them on this deathly list. The night he carved his marks into my flesh, I saw the fabled light. It was so close, inches away. I could almost taste it on my tongue.

Why did I survive, when they didn't? For what purpose did God spare my life? There has to be a reason for all this pain and bloodshed. I can't live in a world where the darkness exists for no goddamn reason.

"Goldilocks? You awake?"

I'm still staring at the scrawled list when Leighton trails into my bedroom. He stops at the end of the bed, noting the paper clutched in my hands.

"Harlow?"

My eyes snap up to his. "Yes?"

"Are you… erm, alright?" His brows draw together in a worried frown. "I mean, you don't look alright. Like, at all."

My fist closes around the piece of paper before he can spot the names. Blood is pumping through me so fast, I feel dizzy with the steady, relentless throb. It's an endless taunt.

Alive.

Alive.

Alive.

A hand brushes my shoulder, startling me from my daze. I shoot upright so fast, my knees crumple. Leighton catches me halfway down to the thick carpet.

"Woah, easy."

My hand bunches in the soft material of his blue t-shirt. He wraps his arms around me as we both fall backwards onto the neatly made bed.

"Harlow?" Leighton repeats urgently.

"Sorry," I stumble out. "Lost m-my balance."

He doesn't loosen his grip on my body. "Don't scare me like that, Goldilocks. What's on the piece of paper?"

Forcing myself to relax, I lean into his embrace. He smells like a tantalising cocktail of lemon and lime, the fragrances clinging to his overgrown hair. I love the way it spills over his ears without a care in the world.

"The past," I answer quietly. "Are they back yet?"

"Nope." Leighton shifts, still keeping one arm around me. "Enzo texted to check in on us though."

"It's been days since Hunter left." I bite my lip so hard, blood leaks into my mouth. "What's he waiting for? I thought he wanted to… you know, interrogate me."

"They're snowed under with some urgent operation. I wouldn't worry. The longer Hunter's away, the better for all of us."

I glance up at him. "Why don't you two like each other?"

"It's complicated." He shrugs, his eyes straying away. "Shall we watch a movie or something? I'm bored."

"You're always bored."

Leighton smirks. "I spent all morning setting Hunter's stationary in jelly. The stapler's taking a while to set."

"Wait, what?"

He finally stands, stretching his arms up so high, his t-shirt rides up. My throat suddenly tightens. I can see a flash of his firm, washboard abs, covered by a carpet of soft fuzz.

"You know, like the scene in *The Office*? He's been a dick recently. It's only fair."

I make myself look away from the slither of skin that's setting my pulse rate high. Leighton's been my only company for the last few days as I've rested up, alternating between napping, showering, and choking down protein shakes with pain meds.

He loves physical affection, which took some getting used to. I wasn't prepared when he brought me a grilled cheese the other day and climbed into bed to chat while I ate.

The casual touches and whispers of motiveless affection were unnerving at first, but I'm slowly adjusting to Leighton's constant need for assurance and attention. He's a sweet person.

"I don't know what you're talking about, Leigh."

His nose crinkles with adoration at the offhand nickname. "You're kidding, right? You've never seen it?"

I shake my head.

"What about *Friends*?"

"Like, did I have any friends?"

"No." His expression grows even more horrified. "The show, Harlow. *Friends*? No?"

My cheeks burn. "Not a clue."

Cursing under his breath, Leighton snatches the screwed-up piece of paper from my hand before I can react. Panic rushes over me, but he simply tosses it onto the dresser and offers me his hand.

"We're rectifying this situation immediately. You're not going to sit here and wait for Hunter to come home. We've got catching up to do."

Gently pulling me up, he grabs the discarded mustard cardigan I left hanging on the wardrobe door and tucks it around me. My heart stutters at the thoughtful gesture.

"Enzo needs to buy you some more shit," he complains, taking my hand again. "Those bags we got the other day weren't enough."

I'm dragged out of the room, his skin burning into mine like a cattle brand. All I can smell is his citrusy shower gel, clinging to his skin in a delicious, inviting cloud.

"He bought way too much."

Leighton gives me a side look. "Yeah, that really wasn't a lot."

Making it downstairs with several aching ribs and a lot of controlled breathing, Leighton guides me into the den. I'm steered towards the huge sofa and dumped in a nest of cushions.

"Get comfy," he orders with a stern look. "Doctor's orders."

Taking the other corner, Leighton stretches his toned legs out. He's dressed for a rainy afternoon, his sweats well worn and fitted perfectly to his muscular frame.

Grabbing a knitted blanket, he covers me with it and fusses over me like a mother hen. His half smile is amused as I squirm and evade his touch-feely hands.

"We can't have you catching a cold on my watch," he explains. "Enzo threatened to mount my head on a spike outside the house if I don't keep you safe."

"Safe from what?" I gesture around the room. "This place is a fancy prison. There are even people guarding our cell."

"They're outside for security, apparently." Leighton settles in while flicking through channels. "Ever seen a movie?"

His questions are always subtle, slipped into casual conversation. Bit by bit, my secrets are being unravelled.

I hum a noncommittal response.

"That's a no then. Mystery girl, you're killing me here."

"Your indecision over my nickname is killing me," I reply without thinking.

Leighton barks a laugh. "What can I say? You're impossible to pin down, Goldilocks. I'll figure you out someday."

"Good luck with that."

"Is that a challenge?"

"Not in the slightest."

Settling on a movie, the screen erupts in an explosion of colour. Cars battle each other in the opening scenes, racing at breakneck speed through a flash of gunfire.

"Shit," Leighton curses. "Are you okay with an action movie? I didn't think."

I'm so entranced by the screen, I don't answer him. The scene changes, depicting a rich, vibrant city glittering with lights. I'm tempted to touch the TV, desperate to experience the alternate reality within its glass walls.

It doesn't matter how I know what the magical contraption is. Like most things, I'm learning not to question it. There are a lot of items in this house that are familiar, even if I can't remember why.

"Hunter hates these kinds of movies," Leighton reveals, his foot brushing mine. "He's a closeted rom-com lover."

"Rom-com?"

"Fluffy shit."

I snuggle into the soft blanket. "Hunter doesn't strike me as a... um, fluffy person."

Choking on a laugh, Leighton grins at me. "I love it when you say exactly what you're thinking."

"Is that a bad thing?"

"Hell no. You should do it more."

We refocus on the movie as a fight scene unfolds. I shock myself by watching the whole thing, repressing a shiver when blood sprays against the heavy beat of fists.

By the end of the movie, I'm hanging on to the edge of my seat and ready for more drama. Stories have always fascinated me. My world was so small for so long, I learned to cling to the scraps I received.

Most of the girls spoke to me. Some told me all about the intricate details of their lives. Hopes, dreams, passions. I lived vicariously through them, and it was the most freedom I ever felt.

Humming under his breath, Leighton flicks the TV over to something else. A group of friends are trading jokes over coffee—a black, sludge-like liquid in their cups.

"That looks so gross."

He collapses back into laughter. "Enzo drinks coffee like he's mainlining heroin. You should smell his breath."

"It smelled okay to me."

Rolling onto his side, Leighton ignores the TV and watches me instead. "You're a breath of fresh air."

"Huh?"

"We live in a world where everyone knows everything." His green eyes scour over me. "And in walks this gorgeous creature who can't name cereal brands or recognise a show like *Friends*."

We stare at each other, the show disregarded. There's something in the way that Leighton looks at me—an almost playful challenge, like he's daring me to prove him wrong.

He sees me differently than the others. I'm not treated like broken glass, a second away from implosion. Leighton is sensitive, but he still talks to me like we're two normal friends, hanging out.

"You're an enigma, Harlow."

"Well, I'm not sure I like that nickname."

Still chuckling, he bounces off the sofa in a blur of energy and disappears into the kitchen. When he returns, balancing two plastic bowls, I quickly grab one before he drops it on my head.

"What is this?" I ask quizzically.

Plonking himself down several inches closer to me, he indicates for me to help myself. I take a sniff of the contents, assaulted by sweet and salty scents. My mouth immediately waters.

"Popcorn," Leighton says around a mouthful.

"Pop...corn?"

"Like popped corn, mixed with butter and stuff."

"That makes no sense. Are you just making this up?"

Shaking his head, Leighton grabs a piece of popcorn and holds it in the air. His hand travels closer to my closed mouth. With the food pressing against my lips, he raises an eyebrow in challenge.

"Open up."

"No chance."

"Don't you trust me?" he asks simply.

Unable to resist the draw of his wide, impish smile, I relent and take a bite. Flavours burst across my tongue, causing me to moan before I can stop myself.

"Woah. S'good."

"Told you." Leighton nudges my shoulder playfully. "Have at it. Put some meat on those bones."

We lapse back into comfortable silence as the show plays. He's so relaxing to be around, more so than the others. Their intensity is a lot for me to handle, but Leighton's like a cool, welcome breeze on a blistering summer's day.

Stretching his legs back out, he sneaks underneath my blanket. With his knee brushing mine, I have to work on breathing through the automatic brush of anxiety. While he does make me feel at ease, the implicit trust I feel around him is even scarier.

"Harlow? Do you mind if I ask you a question?"

Leighton's voice is gentle and coaxing, tuned to melodic perfection. I'm unable to fight his siren's call.

"I guess so."

"I was wondering if you'd tell me about what happened to you?"

I choke on a mouthful of popcorn, chasing it down with a gulp of bottled water. Leighton looks contrite beneath his haphazard hair, dropping his eyes to our blanketed legs.

"I d-don't… ah, why?" I splutter.

"I'm not spying for Hunter, if that's what you're thinking," he answers sadly. "I just… I like spending time with you."

My voice catches. "I… like being with you too."

"Well, I wanted to know if there's anything I should be doing, or anything I *can* be doing, to help you. No matter how small."

His words make my stomach do this weird flippy thing that's usually reserved for Enzo's soft glances. I stuff the unknown feeling down to the depths of my heathen soul.

The guys said it themselves. This is only temporary. Once they have what they want—the sinister information buried deep in my brain—who knows where I'll be sent.

This little slice of respite is bound to expire. Letting them in will only make it hurt more. When I let the girls get close to me, it killed another fractured piece of my heart to watch them die.

"My, ah, the people that, erm… they are very religious. Where I came from, that is," I explain awkwardly.

"How so?"

I take a deep breath for courage. "Pastor Michaels' job is to punish the sinners. He calls it redemption, but it's not."

"Pastor Michaels? That's his name?"

Exhaustion has loosened my tongue. Despite getting more rest than I ever achieved in the freezing cold darkness, I feel more drained than ever. Lying is too hard.

"Yeah."

"And does he help many of these… sinners?"

Our eyes meet—cerulean on viridian, confidence on terror. His inner light is calling to my darkness, demanding the truth. I'm powerless to hide my internal torment.

"Yes, many," I choke out. "Too many."

"I'm so sorry, Goldilocks."

Leighton's scarred hand reaches out and takes mine. His skin is rough, calloused, contrasting with his endearing exterior. I'd love to know how he got his scars, and what anguish lies beyond his facade.

"But you know, you're free now," he adds.

"To do what?"

Leighton's sparkling smile isn't cocky or full of his usual swaggering confidence. It's simple, sweet. Like he's genuinely interested in helping me rebuild from the ruins of my life.

"Whatever you want. I can help you."

"For what possible reason?" Tears sear the backs of my eyes. "You don't know me. Hunter made it clear; I'm just another job."

"That isn't true."

"Yeah, it is. Once it's over, I'll be gone."

"What makes you think that?" Leighton snaps, his voice turning dark and dangerous.

It takes a moment for me to find the right words. I'm enraptured by the anger twisting in his irises, rising to the surface. The truth slips free.

"Because people don't like to look at broken things. Look at me, Leigh. Take a long, hard look. Nobody wants this weak, stupid person around forever."

His hand is still in mine, tightening like a noose. I don't pull away. His gaze is cutting into me, sharp and painful, burning with defiance.

"I'm looking, Harlow. I see you."

Warmth cradles my heart, beginning to thaw the icy edges. He sees me. Somebody actually sees me.

"You do?" I whisper back.

Leighton's lips twist in a tiny smile. "I do."

Giving my fingers one last squeeze, he releases my hand and looks back at the screen, his throat working up and down. What is he feeling? Thinking? Does he feel the same way I do? I can't decipher the emotion on his face.

I stare at him for a moment, contemplating. My fingertips still tingle from where they were wrapped around his, mourning the loss of touch. I decide to take a leap into the unknown.

"Leighton?"

"Yeah?" He spares me a hopeful glance.

Licking my dry lips, I try to find a smile just for him.

"Thank you for being here."

He reciprocates without a beat of hesitation, his smile far brighter and happier than mine. I'm dazzled by it, caught in the sun's devastating rays of pure light.

"Anytime, Goldilocks. I'll always be here."

CHAPTER 11

Harlow

Without You – PLTS

After more resting, recuperating and learning all about Gotham's eccentric conveyor belt of villains, Leighton is snoring his head off next to me. There's popcorn stuck to his face while three-day stubble is smattered across the strong line of his jaw.

Grabbing a blanket, I tuck him in and take the time to pick the kernels from his cheek. He shudders a little at my gentle touch, seeming to go on high alert.

I slow my movements, letting my fingers stroke against his skin. We've spent a lot of time together in the past week, our solitude broken by regular text messages from Enzo and his men patrolling outside the front gate.

A tiny, almost imperceptible whimper escapes Leighton's lips. His eyes are moving behind his shut lids, battling an invisible enemy. Waiting for him to drop back off, I untangle our entwined limbs.

There's more behind his carefree exterior.

I've seen darkness in him too.

Sneaking my way out of the den, I catch sight of the fading sun outside. Anticipation slips down my spine. Lucky is nipping at my heels as I sneak through the French doors without stopping to grab a coat.

I don't care about the cold. This has become our nightly routine in the last few days, come rain or shine. Once outside, icy air wraps me in its familiar embrace.

I begin the long, peaceful walk around the perimeter of the garden. It's huge, littered with shrubbery and twisted, gnarly trees. Lucky trots by my side, yipping occasionally.

We circle the garden, inspecting the falling leaves that paint the scene in orange and yellow. Autumn is surrendering itself to the harsh reality of winter in a riot of warm, burnished colours.

"Here we go," I whisper, sinking to the wet grass.

Lucky settles by my side, her strong body curled against mine. I stroke every part of her, from her velvet ears to her shimmering, golden coat. She licks my cheek in return.

Laura had a dog when she was a kid. Something called a Staffie. She talked to me a lot. I know she hated her job, using her body to make money. Her brother was the only family she had left.

Every night, she'd walk the streets, convincing herself to keep going in his name. Each penny she earned would free him from a life of poverty that didn't afford her the same opportunities.

Laura was smart and fiery. Unapologetically alive. She loved sunny days and hated snow—cold weather meant less work. Her entire existence revolved around the life she was determined to build for her sibling.

We're going to get out of here, Harlow.

I'll show you the sun.

I promise. Together.

With my eyes on the blazing horizon, I feel my tears flow again. After all these years, I finally see what I've been missing—the unparalleled beauty of the world as it falls asleep.

This is my new favourite time of day. I can almost feel Laura's ghost next to me. In my imagination, her bloodied hand rests on mine as she watches the sunset with me.

When I look to the side, I can see her flowing auburn hair and sweet, gentle gaze. She smiles, piercing the numbness that's wrapped around my bones. Reaching out, I try to cup her cheek, but my fingers pass straight through her, and she vanishes.

My hand hangs in the air, limp and useless. I'm staring at nothing. Laura isn't really here. I'm alone. Every step I've ever taken has been utterly alone. Laura is dead. She begged for the abyss and left me to face the devil without her by my side.

"I'm so scared, Lucky," I admit brokenly.

The dog butts my shoulder in response.

"What happens now? How am I supposed to... live?"

My aching eyes sink shut as the sun disappears, the final rays gone from sight. A sudden shiver rolls over me as feeling returns, but I don't move to return inside.

The numbness comes and goes every day. Sometimes it lasts for hours, and I stare at the TV screen, feeling detached and unreal. It makes me feel so lost and out of control.

Teeth gritted, I take a handful of hair and separate the individual strands. It burns as I pull them, one at a time, letting the hair fall to the grass. Each burst of pain punches through my numb shield.

Pull.

Pull.

Pull.

A small pile gathers. I feel sick with shame just looking at it. I don't need Doctor Richards to tell me this isn't normal. Sometimes, I catch myself doing it without realising, surrounded by torn-out hair.

It's all about pain.

Control.

Clarity.

This is the only thing that works.

Coming back to my senses, awareness slams into me like an avalanche. The numb sense of detachment slowly abates. Until next time, I'm back in my body.

"Harlow? Are you out here?"

Quickly blowing the hair away, I pull Lucky closer and remain tucked away from sight. There's a string of curses before silence resumes, an empty chorus to my never-ending supply of tears.

No matter how much I pull or make myself hurt, I can't remove the image of Laura's mouth foaming with blood from my memories. Her eyes connected with mine one final time between the bars as I sobbed uncontrollably.

Ignoring Lucky's whines, I painfully position myself on my knees, linking my stiff fingers together. The cast on my arm makes it difficult, but I've been in worse states.

When Mrs Michaels broke my other arm all those years ago, I could barely move. It must have been for months, because at least two girls came and went during that time.

"Please, forgive me of my sins," I recite shakily. "I don't know where I belong in this world. Show me the path of the righteous."

There's shouting from back inside the house, sounding far away with the sprawling gardens hiding me from sight. The bluster of loud, frantic voices threatens to distract me.

An argument is rumbling somewhere. I remain focused, reciting the words scored across my heart. I'm so wrapped up in the ritual, I don't notice the pad of tentative footsteps.

"For fuck's sake. Shouldn't have brought her home."

Startling, I peek open an eye. Hunter inches around the perimeter of the grounds, holding something in his hands. He looks rumpled, his blue shirt wrinkled and collar ripped open, while his loose hair stirs in the wind.

Before I can slink away, Lucky starts barking. *Traitor.* His head cocks, tracking the sound with the ease of a well-trained bloodhound.

"Shut up, damn dog," he curses.

There's a distinct, metallic click. I peer through my curtain of tears long enough to see Hunter tuck a gun back into the leather strap wrapped around his shoulders.

"Harlow?"

"Go away, Hunter," I plead.

"That's not gonna happen. Get your ass up right now."

His furious tone makes me flinch. I bite down on my inner cheeks hard enough to draw blood, bracing myself for the inevitable strike. I knew this was too good to last.

Maybe he'll beat me with his belt or lock me in some evil basement beneath their beautiful home. He has the devil in him. I can see it imprinted across his skin like a mirage.

"What are you doing?" he thunders.

I whimper in response, my eyes flinging open to meet his.

"Fuck, love." He looks mortified, his face paling. "I'm not going to hit you. Alright?"

With a shuffle, the terrifying pillar of power sits down opposite me, crossing his broad legs in the grass. Hunter's face is an open wound of guilt as he intently studies me.

"What are you doing out here?" he asks more gently.

"I l-like... watching the s-sunset."

"You do?"

I manage a timid nod. "It's… peaceful."

Hunter runs a hand over his messy hair. Chestnut flyways are pointing in every direction. He looks so tired, his beard less sculpted and more caveman-like as it grows out.

Part of me wants to take care of him and ensure he's okay. I've seen enough people suffer to build a hatred for the pain of others. He can't have slept much since I last saw him.

"I'm sorry I haven't been around," he offers, keeping his voice low. "There have been some complications back at HQ."

"To do with me?"

"No, we've been planning a raid for the last six months. Last night, we made our move. The case is being wrapped up as we speak."

Hugging myself tight, I wince at the twinge of my broken arm. Hunter notices, the brief flash of gentleness vanishing. He climbs to his feet and offers me a hand.

"Come inside. We should talk properly."

With reluctance, I let him help me back up. The feel of his fingers gripping mine is strangely soothing. I thought he would chew me out or drag me off to some lair to inflict his questioning.

Lucky sprints ahead when she spots Enzo waiting back inside the house. Too busy frowning at me with his huge arms crossed, he's unprepared for Lucky smashing straight into him.

Despite being the size of a mountain, Enzo falls under her weight and loses himself to a storm of excited licking. I can hear him cussing out the beast from here.

Hunter snorts. "Someone should've filmed that."

"I think he would kill you if you did," I murmur back.

"Worth it."

"What were you doing out there alone?" Enzo barks as we

approach, climbing back to his feet. "Dammit, Harlow. It isn't safe to wander around."

"Your people have been watching me this entire time." I gesture back outside. "I've been taking a walk every night."

He scrapes a hand through his tangled, raven locks. "We were worried. You weren't here when we got home."

Taking a chance, I reach up and briefly touch his bicep. "I'm sorry, Enzo."

"It's… fine." A heavy breath whooshes out of his nostrils. "Come inside. Get warm."

We pile around the marble breakfast bar as Hunter boils the kettle for several cups of tea. He seems to drink the stuff like water. It must flow in his veins instead of blood.

Enzo retrieves a thick, grey hoodie and drapes it over me. His woodsy scent clings to the material, and it reminds me of fallen leaves draped in the fragrance of pine trees.

"You been okay?" he asks quietly. "Sorry things took longer than we thought."

"Leighton's kept me company." I tighten the hoodie around me. "He's made me watch some terrible TV shows though."

Hunter scoffs while steeping his tea bag. "Sounds about right. Mr Slacker could be a professional couch potato."

"He has looked after me," I reply sharply before backtracking. "I mean… he, well, I don't know. He's nice."

"Nice?" Enzo repeats in confusion. "Our Leighton?"

I avoid both of them looking at me like I'm an alien and adjust my plastered arm for a distraction. The thud of half-awake footsteps approaches the kitchen to disrupt our awkward moment.

"Jesus." Leighton stumbles in, rubbing his eyes. "Are you two real or is this a bad dream?"

"Sit down, Leigh." Hunter sighs.

He tightens the blanket wrapped around him like a cape. "Sorry, who are you again?" His eyes meet mine. "Harlow, I rented us the extended edition of *Batman Begins*. Ready for a rewatch?"

There's still popcorn stuck to his face as he winks at me. The other two look more than a little confused.

I clear my throat. "Leighton made a list of his top-ten favourite movies. We're working through them all."

"Seriously? *Batman* made the top ten?" Enzo deadpans.

Leighton's mouth drops open. "Don't knock it, Enz. You know I'm wet for Christian Bale. What a man."

His eyes blow wide. "You're... wet for him? That's the word you're choosing? Seriously?"

"Dude, did you see him topless?"

Hunter slams several cups of tea down. "Focus, idiots. We're not debating fictional fucking characters right now. Jesus Christ."

Smirking, Leighton helps himself to Hunter's tea. Before he ends up with a broken nose, he retreats to the empty table on the other side of the room. Hunter's glower deepens with each step.

"You were saying?" Leighton slurps the tea. "Dang, bro. This is a mean cuppa. You've been holding out on me."

"Give it back before I come over there and rearrange your face."

"Didn't you know that sharing is caring?" Leighton singsongs.

Sliding his tea over to Hunter before a fight breaks out, Enzo braces his hands on the breakfast bar and turns to me.

"Drink up. Have you taken your pain meds?"

"Not yet," I admit, taking a sip of sweetened goodness.

Enzo makes everyone wait as he thumps back upstairs to retrieve my evening pills. I'm dying of embarrassment while the other two stifle the urge to kill each other.

When Enzo returns, he deposits the brightly coloured tablets in front of me. I shiver under the weight of his sharp gaze. He's seriously going to stand there and watch me swallow them.

"You don't need to watch," I whisper.

"You were outside without a coat again," he answers crisply. "Someone has to make sure you look after yourself."

Washing them down with a warm mouthful of tea, I stick my tongue out for him to inspect.

"Satisfied?" I ask him.

"Not in the slightest," he grumbles under his breath. "Let's get this over with. She needs to rest."

Rolling his eyes, Hunter returns his attention to me. "Harlow, I understand that Laura Whitcomb is deceased."

I manage a nod.

"We were expecting this news after nearly two months, but we still don't have a body. I need to take your statement. The killer is still out there, perhaps searching for his next victim."

All of them are studying me now, tearing apart my defences and stealing my secrets for their own satisfaction.

"What do you need me to do?" I ask wearily.

Hunter drains his cup in one long gulp. "The press have started to join up the dots. We need to release a statement before that happens, announcing that you're cooperating with the investigation."

"Fuck no," Enzo hisses. "We can't tell those assholes that Harlow's alive and helping us. It's too dangerous for her."

"We have to get out in front of this, Enz. We've been contracted by the SCU. That's public money. Transparency is our only option."

Anxiety brushes over me like a phantom's skeletal hand. "You w-want me to... s-speak to those people?"

Hunter shakes his head. "Forget them. We'll handle it. You need

147

to sit down with us and tell us everything you know."

There's no escaping me, sinner.

You thought you could be someone else.

Pathetic, soulless demon.

Shaking Pastor Michaels' voice from my mind, I look into Hunter's chocolatey irises. He's so hard to get a read on—passionate one moment and cold the next—but I think he wants to help.

If I can't trust him, I can at least trust his actions. They've kept me safe, given me clothes and a warm bed. It's more than anyone's ever done for me. I'm safe because of them.

"I'll tell you what you need to know," I finally say. "I can't remember everything. It's all so blurry still."

"Any information will help." Hunter glances up at Enzo. "I'll have Richards meet us at HQ tomorrow to supervise."

"You want to take her in?" Enzo asks in surprise.

Hunter shrugs, pulling his wild hair back. "We can do everything there where it's safe and secure. Theo needs to meet Harlow, and he's got some updates for the team."

Enzo falls quiet again. He's studying me with such intensity, I shift uncomfortably in my seat. There's raging fire and violence in his eyes. I've seen that look before.

It scares the living daylights out of me. Rage can corrupt even the gentlest of souls, and he's teetering on the edge of that dangerous fall.

Leighton claps his hands together. "Well, it looks like I'm returning to the office. Christian and his sexy body will have to wait."

I don't miss the way Hunter narrows his eyes at him.

CHAPTER 12

Harlow

Manic Memories – Des Rocs

A s we wind into Central London, a dark atmosphere descends. The streets and urban surroundings grow busier, with endless fancy cars and people rushing about.

I watch with my nose pressed against the tinted window. There are so many human beings, wearing different clothes and hairstyles, and no two people look alike.

Some are smiling and some not, some walk while others run. It's dizzying, the sheer variety of it all. I feel intimidated by the size of the world I've been locked away from.

"Why don't you live here?" I ask randomly.

"We like our privacy and quiet," Enzo answers from the passenger seat. "This place is a fucking cesspit."

"I don't mind the city," Hunter chimes in. "We have several spare apartments in HQ. I stay there sometimes."

Leighton is strapped in beside me, his hand wrapped around mine. I don't mind. The way his thumb strokes over my knuckles is reassuring, grounding me in the present.

"I spend more time here than with them and sleep wherever I pass out, princess."

"That's worse than Goldilocks."

"I will pin your nickname down eventually," he vows with a wink.

The buildings grow so high, they touch the dreary, cloud-covered sky. I study the glass monsters in awe and blanch a little at the one we head straight for.

The skyscraper is a towering, black monstrosity, cloaked in darkness and hard steel lines. The windows are tinted extra dark, concealing all activity inside. There's even a helicopter pad on the roof.

I'd imagine it's the closest thing to an evil lair in the real world, like Batman's cave. We finished the trilogy last night. It's now entered my top three, thanks to Leighton.

Batman reminds me of Enzo a little—a colossal beast, intense and deadly, but with hidden kindness that only certain people are allowed to see. I'm not sure he'd appreciate that comparison.

"Welcome to Sabre," Hunter says grandly.

Leaning out of the window for a retinal and fingerprint scan, he replaces his dark aviators and speeds into a busy parking garage. The city is swallowed by awaiting shadows.

I bite my lip, watching several armed guards press their hands to their foreheads before pushing them into the air. It seems to be a mark of respect that Hunter returns, his emotionless mask in place.

We park up in a bay with his surname printed in indelible ink. The others slide out of the car as Leighton helps me down. Enzo quickly muscles him out of the way and wraps an arm around my shoulders.

"Dickhead," Leighton mutters.

Enzo ignores him as he holds me close. "Everyone here works for us, so there's no need to be afraid. Don't wander off though. This building is massive."

Silently, all three of them move to block me in without a word to each other. Even Leighton is looking more subdued as we stop at a heavily armed entry door. Several guards greet Hunter and Enzo, stepping aside for them.

Escorted through a spotless corridor, we emerge into a glittering glass paradise. I have to suck in a deep breath. So many people are buzzing about, dressed in slick suits and smart dresses, talking on phones or to each other.

The ceiling is impossibly high, further than I can see. Giant lights stretch down in crystal droplets. Every surface is carved in glass or marble, sticking to clean, white lines that give a clinical feel.

Layers of beefed-up security guards line every corner of the cavernous reception. Ahead of me, moving metal teeth carry people upwards like stairs in motion.

"What is that thing?"

"Escalator," Leighton supplies.

I cast him a grateful nod. "Huh."

Several people stop and shake Hunter's hand or incline their heads towards Enzo with clenched jaws. No one dares to step near him. They're both treated with an air of superiority.

"Come on." Hunter sighs, seeming tired with the formalities. "Theo's waiting for us upstairs."

We pack into an elevator that awaits down another slick corridor. Hunter has to scan a special black pass, causing the doors to slide shut with a quiet beep.

I fist my good hand in Enzo's tight, black t-shirt, terrified by the odd sense of inertia in this tight space.

"You're okay," he comforts under his breath.

"I hate these things."

"Breathe. We'll be there soon."

When the elevator opens on a brightly lit floor, I rush out of the enclosed prison as fast as possible. Hunter escorts us into a nearby office, tapping in a code to open the frosted-glass door.

My breathing is shallow as I step inside the space. Light washes over me, blazing through a series of floor-to-ceiling windows. The vast expanse of London awaits in high-definition grandeur.

Trailing over, I rest my palm against the glass, greedily taking in the view. It's like we're in heaven looking down upon the world, safe and secure in our high-rise bubble. I feel invincible up here.

Leighton joins me. "Like the view?"

"It's so high."

"You scared?"

Shaking my head, I smile at the little ant people on the ground. I'm away from the clutches of anyone looking to hurt me. They can't penetrate this glass fortress wrapped in clouds and wealth.

In the corner, there's a glass desk situated before the windows with a stunning, panoramic view. Neat stacks of books sit on every available surface around the room, with framed photographs and odd trinkets.

Hunter drops his suit jacket and keys on the desk, seeming at ease. On the console next to him, I can see several framed photographs of him, Enzo, and even Leighton, smiling and posing.

"Hey, Hunt?" Leighton inspects the room. "Did you feng shui this place with a bloody ruler? This is some obsessive shit."

Hunter glares at him while straightening the stack of papers on his desk so they sit at a perfect right angle. Snorting, Leighton pulls out a chair at a long, dark-wood conference table.

Before I can sit down next to him, I glance around the rest of the spacious office. My heart immediately plummets as my extremities go numb with the wave of shock.

This can't be real.

Every inch of the back wall is plastered in thick layers of paperwork. There are more sheets of paper than I can count, typed lines of ink and endless photographs stuck on top with little pins.

Strands of red cord are wrapped around the pins, connecting different sections. Every inch of wall space is covered in a chaotic contrast to the ruthlessly organised office.

My feet carry me without thinking. I'm numb, helpless, pulled back into the embrace of detachment. Studying the walls, an awful weight curls in the pit of my stomach.

I count every photograph pinned in place. Altogether, there are eighteen girls staring back at me. I'm sickened as I check the various profiles. I recognise every single one of them—some made it on to my list.

Others could be complete strangers, but their faces resonate in the back of my mind. I know that I watched them die, even if I can't remember it.

"This c-can't be h-happening," I stammer.

"Sit back down, little one."

Enzo's hand lands on my arm. I jump so fast, I end up crashing into the wall in my haste to get away from him. Papers rain on my head as my healing arm flares with pain.

Panting hard, I stare up at the towering, black-haired beast above me. I don't recognise him anymore. The numbness has infected every part of me, metastasising, taking over everything.

"Stay away from me!"

"Harlow?" he asks, frowning. "It's me."

"N-No... I c-can't... stay back!"

His next words are drowned out by screaming, echoing on repeat in my head. Countless voices. Different tenors. Soft. Raspy. Feminine. Scratchy. Desperate. Pained. Hopeful. Pleading. Dying. Gone.

I'm drowning in glimpses of memories I'd compartmentalised. Their bloodstained words slide down my throat like swallowing bullets. Voices and faces are disjointed.

Please, just let me go.

I want to go home.

What do you want from me?

Let me out.

Don't touch me!

Scrambling up despite my throbbing body, I touch the nearest photograph. It's Tia. I remember her well. She has a beautiful, confident smile in the picture, with another woman's purple-painted lips sealed on her cheek.

Pastor Michaels had a special word for her, one that I refuse to repeat. Something to do with her kissing other girls. God doesn't like that. I can't imagine being capable of such mindless hatred.

God is supposed to love all of his creations. Why should it matter who kisses who? She talked about Kara, her girlfriend, a lot. The happiness she radiated, even in the basement, was heartwarming.

"I'm so sorry," I whisper, pulling the photograph down.

The strange men around me are deathly silent, watching me unravel while cataloguing every clue I give away. Pressing my lips to Tia's pixelated face, I reattach her to the wall.

Every other girl that I watched die waits for me to acknowledge them, all accusing me with their printed eyes. I wouldn't call them my friends, not in the conventional sense.

These brave human beings were all my sisters. I never had a family, but somehow, I found kindred spirits in the darkness of my captivity. We were bound by tragedy rather than blood.

I'm the only one that knows what happened to them. The weight of responsibility is crushing me to death. I have to remember all of them, even if it kills me.

"Do you know these women?"

I look up, and the world snaps back into focus. I know these people. Hunter. Enzo. Leighton. My brain stumbles, attempting to reorientate itself. It's excruciating, the way reality punches into me.

"Harlow?" Hunter repeats.

All I can do is nod.

"I'm sorry, but I need you to say it out loud for the record."

I stroke my fingertips over Christie's braid, her photograph pinned a few metres down from Tia's. She didn't like me much, preferring to shiver and weep alone in a curled-up ball.

I kept her company regardless, whispering whatever comfort I could. She died as silently as she lived. I hate myself for admitting that I was glad in some way. It made it easier to watch her violent death.

"Yes."

"How?" he demands.

Turning to face them all again, I gulp hard. "There was a cage next to mine in the basement where I was kept. It was rarely empty."

Hunter looks away, shuffling through papers on his desk with his scruff-covered jaw set in an unyielding line. Conversely, Enzo refuses to look anywhere but straight at me.

His expression is even more murderous than usual, borderline animalistic. He looks ready to tear the entire office apart with his bare hands. Seeming calmer, Leighton smooths his hair in an absent-minded fashion.

"All of them?" Hunter clarifies.

"Yes," I make myself say. "Some of them I recognise, but I don't remember exactly what happened. There were so many."

Hunter and Enzo take seats on the opposite side of the table. There's no sign of the doctor from the hospital or the mysterious Theo. I take my seat, feeling small beneath their brutal gazes.

Hunter places his phone in the middle of the table. It's already recording, but he repeats today's date and all of their names. I'm startled to find that it's nearly November.

"Introduce yourself," he orders firmly.

I clear my throat. "Harlow."

"Surname?"

The name Michaels doesn't fit, even if it's the name my parents used. If I prescribe it to myself, I will be nothing more than their daughter.

Just another cruel, malicious joke from God that inflicts misery on others. I have to be more than that. If I could strip my skin off and burn it to escape them, I would.

"I don't… ah, know. I can't remember."

Hunter nods, his pen poised. "Tell us everything."

CHAPTER 13

Theo

Scavengers (Acoustic) – Thrice

Fingertips flying across my keyboard, I squint at the breadcrumb trail I've been tracking for the past week. It's painstaking work, using a mixture of CCTV footage, private feeds and traffic cams.

I'm tracking the path of the victim to London—Harlow, I should say. She is a person, after all. I'm not great with those.

Silence and predictability are my companions, the controllable comfort of computers and code that lies within my manipulation. People? Not so easy to control.

I avoid other human beings out of sheer necessity. Even the guys— my teammates and supposed family—are intolerable to me. My social anxiety has always been bad. It's ruining my life now.

The woman in question dominates the huge screen stretched out across the wall of my office, playing a live feed of Hunter's interrogation. Rather than overwhelm her, we opted to play this another way.

Doctor Richards sits by my side, twirling his cufflinks as he listens intently while taking notes. He agreed to watch from here, on standby if needed.

"How long were you held captive?" Hunter asks.

"I don't remember a time when I wasn't held in a cage." Harlow stares past them all. "But I know things… stuff that I shouldn't. So I have no idea."

"Do you remember your childhood?"

She shrugs. "Beatings. Being starved and tormented. The girls didn't start showing up until later, when they got bored with hurting me. I was so happy to have some company."

"Nothing before that?" Hunter presses.

Harlow shakes her head. "Just the cage. When the girls started to come, they spoke to me, taught me things. Reminded me that I was real. It felt so good after being alone for so long."

"Jesus," Richards mutters. "Poor woman."

I press my lips together, glancing back down at my laptop screen. The last known sighting of the latest victim, Laura, was way up north. That's the direction from which Harlow hitchhiked.

I'm still working to pin down her exact route. She hopped across more than eight vehicles over several days, sneaking in undetected. She's damn lucky the journey didn't kill her.

"Still think this is amnesia?" I ask the shrink.

Richards nods, his eyes bleak. "She's disassociating. Fight-or-flight mode kicks in, changing how traumatic experiences are stored in the long-term memory. Unfortunately, memory loss is to be expected."

"Who held you, Harlow?" Hunter draws our attention back. "I want names."

Her fingers worry her hoodie sleeve. "Pastor Michaels and Mrs Michaels aren't good people. They like to hurt others. God sent them to punish the sinners and prepare for the rapture."

I can't help but wince. She's been indoctrinated, a warped reality bruised and beaten into her. The medics placed her age at approximately twenty-two. That's a long fucking time.

"Was it Pastor Michaels who hurt the other women?" Enzo asks gently. "Did he kill them?"

Harlow nods, biting her lip. "Mrs Michaels was in charge of cleanup. Pastor Michaels is God's servant. He does the Lord's bidding."

"Clean up?" Hunter repeats.

"The bodies." Harlow looks a little green. "They left a lot of mess. She'd sometimes make me help. If I refused, something was usually broken."

"And how did he kill these women?"

"You've seen the bodies, haven't you?" she replies numbly.

Hunter stares, demanding her answer. He's being pretty rough with her, despite the doctor's warnings. Anyone can see she is traumatised. I'm surprised by how well she's holding up.

I've witnessed plenty of people break down in Hunter's presence. He isn't one to mince his words or tread carefully through life. That's what Enzo's here for.

"Pastor Michaels punished them for their sins," Harlow whispers hoarsely. "To make them repent."

"How?" Hunter pushes. "Tell us."

"Ease up," Richards whispers.

Harlow stiffens, retreating inwards. "You know how."

"I want to hear it from you," Hunter prods further.

Shaking his head, Richards makes some more notes and shifts, seeming uncomfortable. I know he wanted to do things a different way. Enzo did too.

Neither of them wanted Harlow to be put in this position so soon, but what Hunter wants, Hunter gets. We're all beholden to his rules around here.

"Pastor Michaels beat them until they prayed," Harlow eventually answers. "Sometimes… he'd take his clothes off and… t-touch them. It usually got them to comply."

No one knows quite how to stomach that. I don't believe for a second that she's as naive as she's playing. Years of watching this abuse must have taught her some things.

"Did he… do these things to you?" Hunter asks carefully.

She shakes her head. Enzo relaxes a fraction, still holding himself as tight as a coiled spring, prepared to unleash hell at any moment. He'll be running tonight instead of sleeping, I'm sure of it.

"Before he… killed them, he had a special knife. From God, you see." Harlow grows increasingly pale. "He used it to carve holy symbols into their bodies. It cleansed them of all evil."

Disregarding another of Richards' warnings, Hunter retrieves a sealed folder. He pulls out a single, glossy photograph, then offers it to Harlow.

On it, the discarded body of Tia Jenkins has been captured in painstaking horror. The Holy Trinity is slashed into her skin, blackened and melted off with decay from the dump site.

"Like this?" he questions.

Harlow's hand covers her mouth, shaking badly. "She fought so hard. He strangled her in the end, tired of waiting for her to die."

Tia Jenkins' body was found sprawled out in a forest up north. She'd been there for weeks already, her skin feasted on by maggots and flies. Harlow can barely look at the horrifying picture.

"The bodies were left with me for a while," she reveals. "Sometimes for hours, sometimes days. Eventually, Mrs Michaels took them away."

"What?" Enzo's voice is razor sharp.

Harlow ducks her head, a waterfall of tears flowing freely. "He liked to make me sleep in their blood, to remind me. If I was bad, he left them for longer. Laura… she… he didn't…"

She chokes on a wet sob, like she needs to throw up but can't. Something is begging to be let free, but she's holding it back with all of her strength.

Leighton snarls at Hunter to stop, gathering Harlow in his arms. I've barely seen him since he was released from prison a few months ago. He looks so different.

"We need to stop here," Richards says.

"This has to be done," I remind him.

"Not so damn heavy-handedly."

"Do you want another girl to go missing?"

"I want to see my patient being cared for, Theo!"

He snaps his notepad shut with a frustrated sigh. It takes a lot to get under the shrink's thick skin. He's consulted for Sabre on many occasions, including cases as bloody as this.

But everything about this feels different somehow. We've become invested after months of failure. It's now personal, and hearing firsthand what this monster is capable of only makes it worse.

"You don't have to carry on," Leighton offers.

He's stroking Harlow's long hair. They seem friendly with each other. She's shaking violently in his arms, a bomb primed to explode.

"We can stop," he adds.

"I have to do this." Harlow pushes him away. "Laura… she… they kept her body for much longer, until there was nothing left. The smell was so bad, it made me pass out sometimes."

Hunter deliberately looks up at the camera where he knows I'm watching. I gather my laptop and the waiting evidence bag. Richards watches me go with reluctance.

Walking down the corridor, I let myself into Hunter's office.

Several heads snap in my direction.

"Take a seat, Theo."

Following Hunter's order, I place my belongings down next to Enzo. Harlow is looking at me, on the very edge of her seat. I can already tell that she doesn't like strangers, fear is written all over her.

I avoid her eyes, too socially anxious to make my own introduction. This is beyond my remit. I'm more accustomed to working behind the scenes than dealing with victims.

"This is Theo, head of intelligence," Hunter explains. "He has been tracking your route here."

She gives me a tiny nod in greeting. "Hi."

"At Enzo's request, we looked a little deeper into your last transportation and found something… unusual."

There's a flash of panic on Harlow's face. "You did?"

"Show her," Hunter instructs.

Without saying a word, I snap on a pair of latex gloves and reach for the evidence bag. Inside lies a bloodied, dirty lump of calcium—a bone, the femur, to be precise.

"You found her," Harlow keens. "Laura."

I place the item back in the bag. DNA evidence has already confirmed it belonged to the Whitcomb girl, but establishing Harlow's involvement was important. Now, we know she is who she says she is.

"Care to explain why you had this in your possession?" Hunter quips.

"I just wanted to get out… I didn't… I…"

Harlow drops Leighton's hand to fist her hair so tight, I'm worried she'll tear the whole lot from her scalp. Her eyes are blown wide and lit with fear as she rises.

The seat falls back with a bang, and Enzo follows, stalking her like an attentive predator. She's breathing hard through clenched teeth.

"Hold it together, Harlow," he advises.

"I had no other choice… I tried and tried, but the cage was locked. The only thing I could reach was… was… Laura's skeleton."

Stunned silence drapes over the room.

"I used it to break the door," she finishes, trembling all over. "It took so long, but the hinges snapped. I took all I could of her with me and left the rest."

Backing away from us all, Harlow retreats into the furthest corner. Enzo tries to approach, but each step in her direction increases her sobs, until he's forced to fall back. She doesn't respond to her name.

The door to the office slams open with a crash. Richards stalks in, his tweed coat flapping behind him, looking far angrier than I've seen him for a long time.

"I warned you about too much, too soon," he shouts angrily. "This is unprofessional and, frankly, unethical!"

Hunter doesn't flinch. "We have a job to do."

"Not at the expense of those you are supposed to protect. Dammit! I won't stand for this!"

Hunter looks away, rubbing a hand over his slicked-back ponytail. The silence is punctuated by Harlow's cries as she curls into herself. She still won't allow anyone to get close, completely unresponsive.

Leighton is frozen metres away from her, itching to move closer. Enzo looks ready to tear his own hair out at the root as he repeats her name, over and over.

Richards is right—she's lost in her head. I recognise the signs. Guilt gut-punches me at the mess we've made. She isn't a suspect here. Hunter's letting the case cloud his judgement.

Before I know what I'm doing, I've eased past the others with the evidence bag. Harlow's tear-filled eyes latch on to the plastic-wrapped body part in my hands.

"I think this is yours," I whisper shamefully. "I'm sorry for taking her away, Harlow. She was your friend."

"F-For me?" she stammers.

"You can have her back to say goodbye."

"Theo," Hunter warns darkly.

Ignoring him, I sink to my knees and hold out the bone as a peace offering. Harlow tentatively accepts it, her bottom lip wobbling. She studies the remaining piece of the last girl she saw alive.

"I'm so sorry, Laura. I thought… I just wanted to help you," she murmurs, stroking the femur. "I wish I could've taken all of you."

No one utters a single word, watching the devastating sight as Harlow holds her friend close. She spares me a quick look.

"Thank you for giving her back to me."

I sit back on my haunches, nodding. It's been a long time since anyone thanked me for… well, anything. Harlow's eyes are haunted as she holds my gaze for a moment.

"I lied to you all," she says, looking back at the others. "My name is Harlow Michaels. They're my parents."

"What the fuck?" Hunter curses loudly.

But Harlow's already gone, cradling the femur to her chest like it's a teddy bear. Her eyes are open, but empty. Unseeing.

"Hunter," Richards calls sternly. "A word, please."

Retreating to the other side of the office, Leighton stands and storms over to butt into their conversation. I can hear them arguing about suspending the rest of the interrogation.

"Harlow," Enzo begs, lingering behind me. "Why can't she hear me?"

"Careful," I advise. "Don't spook her."

Harlow's body is in our presence, but the essence of her has been scooped out. All we can do is wait for her to come back. Climbing to my feet, I gesture for Enzo to take my place.

He crawls closer to her, an impressive feat at his size. Slowly and carefully, he manages to ease the bone from her hands and pass it back to me. Harlow doesn't even notice, too spaced out.

I take the evidence and carefully repackage it. The Whitcomb family has something to bury now. Enzo takes his time lifting Harlow into his lap, and she soon collapses against his chest.

It triggers a barrage of memories that wash over me before I can clamp them down. Each one hits like a bullet between the eyes.

Bright-pink strands of hair sliding through my fingers. The love of my life's nose buried in Enzo's chest. His eyes squeezed tightly shut as insomnia surrendered its control.

We had someone before, what feels like a lifetime ago. She made us whole. Happy. Complete. I haven't felt that since the day we lost her.

"I'm gonna get Harlow out of here," Enzo rumbles.

I have to look away from them to conceal my grief. "Sure. Go before Hunter stops you."

Holding Harlow's trembling body like she weighs little more than air, Enzo strides from the room without another word. No one would dare stop him with the bone-chilling anger on his face.

"I'll see them out," Richards announces, his face grim.

Hunter watches him go with exasperation. Gathering my stuff, I straighten my plaid shirt, needing a moment to collect myself. It's been a long time since I thought of... *her*. Seeing Harlow has stirred all that shit back up again.

"You need to rush through her DNA profile," Hunter barks as I approach him. "I want dates, relatives, the works. If she had so much as a fucking cold as a kid, I want to know about it."

I clear my throat. "I'll see what I can do."

"No one passes completely under the radar for twenty-two years. I want this done quietly. Enzo and Richards clearly want to continue walking on eggshells."

"Got it, boss."

"We need to inform Whitcomb's family now that we have confirmation," Hunter adds. "Hudson can do it. He questioned the different victims' families earlier in the case."

"Thought you wanted to keep Harlow's presence between us?"

Hunter shakes his head. "We have to do a press announcement anyway. Get Kade to bring the whole team in to be briefed tomorrow. I'll speak to them myself."

With a final nod, I manage to break free from his office. Things are stepping up a gear if we're bringing in the Cobra team. They're our secret assets—ruthless and merciless in perfect measure.

I grab my phone and bring up the contacts with a sigh. I haven't called anyone for a long time.

"I was starting to wonder if you were dead," Hudson answers with a grunt. "Unless you're calling me from the afterlife, in which case, kudos."

"Hilarious," I return dryly. "Is this a bad time?"

"Gimme a sec."

The sound of fists meeting flesh rattles down the line, along with someone's yelping in the background. I hang tight as Hudson shouts at someone, the line muffled before he returns with a low growl.

He's been on clean-up duty all week after our successful narcotics raid. Enzo trained Hudson himself, breeding the perfect henchman to beat, break and bully his way to fast results.

"Free now. What's up, Theo?"

"Need you all to come in tomorrow."

"Got something for us?" he asks excitedly. "I'm tired of these lowlife gang bangers."

"You're not gonna like what we have instead. Hunter will brief you in the morning."

"Gotcha. Theo, why don't you come—"

"I have to go," I interrupt, hanging up.

Returning to my lonely office, I hit the coffee machine and settle in my desk chair. My phone vibrates with a text, but I don't bother checking it. Hudson needs to give up.

I'm not interested in playing happy families like the last five years have changed anything that happened back then.

I don't want their help.

I don't want their company.

All I want is the one fucking person I can't have… because she's dead.

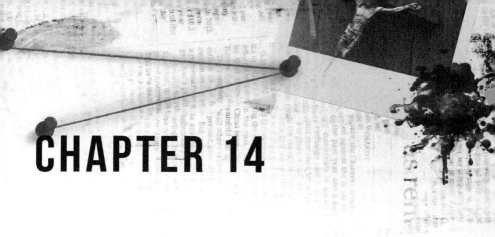

CHAPTER 14

Harlow

.haunted. — Dead Poet Society

The skittering of a pebble hitting my window startles me awake in a split second. The meaty tissue of my heart bruises itself against my rib cage, the fuel of terror pumping through my veins.

I was running through thick woodland in my dream, wracked by pain and desperation. The voices of eighteen ghosts followed my footsteps with wailing cries.

Crack.

Am I dreaming still?

Is someone… here?

A louder crack pierces the silence. It's pitch-black outside—I fell asleep with the blinds wide open, bathing me in moonlight. Falling asleep each night is proving difficult after the interrogation.

It's still playing on repeat in my mind, and has been ever since, no matter how hard I try to forget about it. Telling them everything felt like scooping out the innards from inside my empty carcass.

Crack.

Throwing back the covers, I hug my plastered arm and creep across the room to the source of the noise. From what I can see of the driveway, it's empty. Not a single soul in sight.

Leighton didn't go out drinking, and I heard the others come home from another long day of work several hours ago. It must be my imagination. Lying back down in my huge bed, I fight to go back to sleep, but it's no use.

I'm wide awake, as I have been every night this week. Absent-mindedly, my fingers twine with strands of my hair and begin pulling. I can't resist the compulsion.

It's becoming an addiction, tearing my hair out and revelling in the blissful familiarity of pain. Hiding it is becoming harder as the little voice infects every hour of my day, not just the moments I feel unreal.

Another half an hour of silence and I can't stand it anymore. Throwing on a loose pair of sweats to cover my bare legs, I sneak downstairs after cleaning the hair from my pillow.

Moonlight is dappled across the polished tiles, lighting my path to the fridge. I grab one of the glass bottles of milk that gets delivered to the front gate every day. I swear, the real world is so weird.

As I'm retrieving my warm milk from the microwave, there's another crash from behind me. The mug slips from my hands and shatters on the tiled floor, sending scalding hot liquid over my feet.

I yelp, slipping over and landing amongst the ceramic shards with a thud.

"You stupid, foolish child."

Dread slips beneath my skin and lances through my heart with its icy shards. I'd forgotten how malicious his voice sounds, filled with holy determination.

"I'm asleep," I whisper to myself. "This isn't real."

When I look down at my hands, blood is seeping from the slices that the mug inflicted. I absently smear the red spill, feeling its sticky warmth. It feels real. The pain is tangible. Do people bleed in dreams?

"Harlow. Kneel before your father."

Breath held, I make myself look up. In the doorway, Pastor Michaels is staring at me with a smarmy grin. His processional robes are in place—rich, crushed-red velvet and gold thread that contrasts his silvery coiffe of hair.

I blink repeatedly, hoping he'll vanish. How is he here? No. It can't be. Screwing my eyes shut, I rub them hard before reopening. He's still standing there.

"This isn't real."

His smile takes a violent edge. "I'm as real as you are."

"You're not here," I reassure myself.

"Aren't I? It was easy enough to break in."

As I stare up at my father, fear slamming into me like tumultuous ocean waves, the room goes wonky. Everything is warping and twisting, the air seeming to reform in new visions of horror.

Pastor Michaels inches closer, drawing a long, curved knife from his robes. It's still stained with Laura's blood.

Drip, drip, drip.

"Harlow," he repeats. "Kneel."

Drip, drip, drip.

"Kneel before your father."

Drip, drip, drip.

The blade glints in the moonlight, illuminating crimson stains. His footsteps approach. My heart somersaults, threatening to explode into pieces. Before his fists can meet my flesh, I scramble to my feet.

"I said kneel! Do what the Lord demands of you!"

Searching for something to protect myself with, my fingers wrap around the handle of a knife protruding from the kitchen block. It cuts the air with a metallic swoosh, thrust out in front of me.

Pastor Michaels' face darkens into an ugly shade of red. I can see the enraged fog perfusing his entire being, transforming the appearance of a normal, friendly man into a monster.

"Stay back!" I scream at him. "I won't kneel for you. I won't fucking kneel for anyone!"

"We don't use that kind of language here," he yells back, his spittle spreading across the floor. "Perhaps the time has come for you to move on, heathen child. I will free you from this sinful place."

Darkness oozes across the floor as he lunges towards me, like the devil himself is breaking free from Pastor Michaels' mortal shell. I scream and race across the kitchen, attempting to flee.

When his hand grabs my shoulder, I gather whatever scraps of courage I can find and grip the blade tighter.

"I'll kill you! Get away from me!" I threaten.

"Harlow! Stop!"

The words don't resonate, nor does the different voice throwing them at me. Spinning back around, I take advantage of the momentum and launch at Pastor Michaels.

We both tumble to the tiled floor, the impact jarring my broken arm. I grit my teeth through the pain. I won't die here.

"I hate you!" I shout, out of control. "You're a monster!"

"Harlow, it's me. Stop!"

"No!"

My one good hand sails into his face, and I savour the sharp crack of his nose. Slick blood coats my knuckle, spurring me into a frenzy. Each punch feels like salvation.

I'm breaking free, smashing the prison of my childhood to pieces. My punches rain down, albeit weak and feeble, but I don't stop.

"Harlow… please! Fuck, I can't hear anything."

This voice doesn't sound right. It's high and panicked, but underscored by a warm, honey-like quality. Pastor Michaels doesn't sound like that.

Snatching my knife back up from the floor, I ignore the niggle of anxiety at the back of my mind and press the blade against his throat.

One slash.

That's all it would take.

"I hate you," I repeat, sobbing.

"Harlow," the man beneath me repeats. "Drop the knife. It's okay. I've got you."

This isn't right. Pastor Michaels doesn't have a thick, chestnut beard, or glossy hair that tickles his shoulders. The processional robes on the chest I'm straddling disappear, leaving nothing but bare, tattooed skin behind.

Pastor Michaels' face morphs before my very eyes. Harsh lines and bitter hatred become wide eyes and plush, inviting lips that are stained bright red.

The knife is heavy in my grip, cutting skin to release more blood. The moment I realise who I'm pinning to the floor, I immediately toss it aside, terrified by the blood soaking into me.

"Oh my God," I exclaim in horror. "Hunter!"

His eyes pull me into their chocolate depths as he frantically searches for the hearing aid that fell from his ear during my attack. The longer he can't find it, the more panicked he becomes.

"Fuck," he curses. "Where is it?"

Spotting the tiny black device under a kitchen counter, I quickly pass it over to Hunter. He slots it back into place, and when it connects, the fear on his face dissipates.

"Okay," he says to himself. "Okay."

I want to drown in the molten pools of his eyes and never take another breath. I attacked Hunter. I… cut his throat. I nearly killed him! I'm no better than the monsters that birthed me.

"Harlow," he pleads, cupping my cheek with one hand. "I need you to take a breath for me. Everything is okay. You're safe."

"No! You're bleeding!"

"I'm fine, Harlow. Just startled, that's all."

"You c-couldn't hear… I did that to you."

"Breathe, sweetheart. It was an accident. Not the first time, and it won't be the last."

Despite his oddly gentle words, all I can do is stare at the blood dripping down his clavicle from his gushing nose. I did that. Me. It felt so good to fight back.

I hurt him.

I enjoyed it.

What does that make me?

Climbing off his body, I spiral deeper into despair. My back hits the marble breakfast bar until I can't run any further. Hunter ignores his injuries and pursues me.

He's a pillar of power and intimidation, but in this moment, his expression is broken. He looks indescribably sad. Does my pain entertain him? Am I nothing more than another fractured specimen for him to study?

"He was so real," I say, the words dark and ugly. "I could… f-feel him. His voice. The s-smell of his skin… everything. He was so real!"

"It was a dream," Hunter assures me. "You were sleepwalking or something. None of it was real."

"But I attacked you! I thought you were… my father."

"I'm not. Can you see me now?"

I stare into his coffee-coloured irises. "Yes."

"Do I look like him?"

"N-No."

Tentatively, Hunter reaches for my hand. I'm too stunned to protest. He raises it to his chest, placing it right above his pounding heartbeat. I can feel it hammering away.

His tattooed skin is hot to touch, softened by a patch of brown fuzz across his defined pectorals. His tongue darts out to clean the blood from his lips, still weeping from his nose.

"Look at me," he commands sternly.

I obey without hesitation, trapped in his gaze.

"He isn't here. Look at me, feel me. Know that I'm not him."

His voice is mesmerising, gliding over me like thick treacle. My hand moves of its own volition. I trace the hard planes of his chest, over the dark swirls of ink that mark his tattoo.

It wraps itself around his torso, sneaking up to the ropy muscles of his neck. I can pick out individual elements—an intricate tree, wrapped in beautiful vine leaves that spreads across his stomach.

Birds with vast, powerful wings fly across the slope of his ribcage to escape, blending into the path of shadowy storm clouds and strobes of white ink that paint individual raindrops.

It's a thunderstorm, painted on his body in a real-life canvas. Hunter is exactly that—deadly and mesmerising all at once.

"You're home with me," he murmurs, his voice growing throaty. "Nobody is ever going to touch you again. I won't let them."

A thick lump gathers in my throat. I let Hunter slide his arms under my legs, too numb to protest. He lifts me until I'm pressed against his bloodstained chest.

We head upstairs, where the distinct sound of Leighton's snoring can be heard. I expect Hunter to take me back to my bedroom, but he bypasses it and heads to the other end of the hallway.

I'm carried into a dark room, assaulted by masculine scents. Hunter's spicy aftershave, fresh linens, and the smell of rainfall from the open window. It's intoxicating, the essences that make up his persona.

"How you didn't wake Enzo up, I'll never know," he grumbles. "It's a miracle he didn't come down and shoot us both by accident."

I try for a joke. "Maybe there is a God."

Hunter's chest rumbles with an almost laugh that doesn't quite escape his lips. He steps into an en-suite, keeping the main light off and flicking on the mirror light instead.

It emanates a warm glow that reveals his neat, organised bathroom. It's identical to mine, but every single bottle is stacked in regimented lines, the labels all facing forward.

"Let's get you cleaned up."

"You're the one bleeding," I point out.

Hunter lifts me onto the bathroom counter, next to the sink basin. He cocks a sculpted eyebrow at me.

"Look at your hands, Harlow."

I glance down. The slices I felt from the broken mug were real, blood seeping down my arms in a warm, steady flow. I didn't even notice it amidst the madness.

"Oh."

"Oh," he echoes. "You did a good job there, didn't you?"

The accusation in his voice grates against me.

"It's not like I did this on purpose," I argue back. "It all felt... real. Everything I was seeing and hearing."

Hunter's attention doesn't waver from my face. "I can see that."

Reaching under the sink, he pulls out a small metal box. Inside, there's a basic first aid kit. I reluctantly hold out my hands, letting him clean the blood with a damp cotton pad.

He works in concentrated silence, cleaning and inspecting. My eyes begin to droop as the adrenaline pours out of me.

"Nearly done," Hunter whispers. "Rest on my shoulder if you need to."

I force my eyes back open. "No. I need to clean you up."

"I'm a big boy, Harlow. I can take care of myself."

"But… you shouldn't have to."

He halts, a bloodied cotton pad in hand. The air between us feels weird—almost like it's charged with electricity. I can feel the tension gliding across my sensitised skin.

Hunter's lips are parted, still stained with blood, his breath escaping in a low hiss. Almost in slow motion, his thumb skates along my jawline, up to my cheek, and down to the slope of my bottom lip.

I don't dare move as he traces it with a look of confusion, his eyes flitting up and down in rapid succession.

"I take care of myself," he repeats, his brows furrowed.

"Because there's no one else to do it?"

His head is moving closer, eating up the pitiful distance between us. My legs are parted, his body eased between them as he cleans me up. I can feel the heat of his pelvis against my thighs.

My legs tighten without my permission, squeezing his frame closer. I don't even realise I'm doing it until a low growl emanates from his chest.

"Harlow."

I quickly take control of myself, releasing his waist. "S-Sorry."

"Don't be."

His thumb is still on my bottom lip. With the care of a skilled warrior tracking down his prey to devour, Hunter slips the roughened digit between my lips. I hardly know how to react.

As the very tip of his thumb touches my tongue, a delicious, tingling warmth pools between my legs. I feel my cheeks flush at the sensation. It feels so good. What is he doing to me?

"Hunter," I whimper around his thumb.

He takes a huge step back, staring at me like he can't quite believe what just happened. I immediately feel cold. The distance between us is agonising. I can't breathe with him so far away from me.

"I'm being unprofessional," he curses himself. "Fuck, I'm so sorry. I don't know what I'm doing. This… we… us, it can't happen."

"What can't happen?" I ask cluelessly.

His eyes burn in low embers. "Jesus, Harlow. Never mind. Go back to bed. We can figure things out in the morning."

Snapping the first aid kit shut, he busies himself, shoving it away with a loud clatter. I gulp hard and slide down from the counter, feeling like I've been punched in the chest.

His dismissal hurts more than I thought it would. I leave Hunter washing the blood from his bruised face, still breathing hard as he tries not to look at me again.

"Sorry," I whisper before walking away.

His scent clings to the sheets of his unmade bed as I walk past. The urge to climb in and nestle down is so strong, my feet almost carry me over to it. All I can think about is his arms around me.

I have to make myself leave, escaping the lion's den before he swallows me whole. The walk back to my bedroom is marked by emptiness as tears threaten to spill down my cheeks.

Hunter really must hate me.

He doesn't want me—whatever it means to *be wanted*.

I wonder what that's like.

CHAPTER 15

Hunter

The Madness — Foreign Air

"**S**abre Security has confirmed that a living victim has come forward," the newscaster explains. "She is said to be in protective custody and cooperating with the investigation."

Watching the news coverage from behind my desk, I rub my aching temples. We're about to drop an atomic bomb. Our non-disclosure window has run out and we're shit out of luck.

A reporter taps the comms in his ear. "Sorry to interrupt, but we're receiving breaking news that another body has been found."

Chaos ensues as they read through the statement we released to the national news agency. We kept details to a minimum, confirming Whitcomb's death without giving any more information.

Her next of kin, a seventeen-year-old brother, has been informed. He was the one who raised the alarm when his sister and main caregiver didn't return home from work.

Now, he has nothing more than a bone to remember her by. They were dirt poor, living on the poverty line. I've already instructed one of our teams to arrange a funeral, courtesy of Sabre. It's the least we can do.

My phone buzzes on the desk.

"Rodriguez."

"Hunter," Lucas greets with a heavy sigh. "Well, it's going down as well as expected. Interview requests are flooding in already."

"Deny them all."

For a country terrorised by a serial killer that snatches women without leaving a trace and carves them into pretty pieces, this development is big news. My balls are on the line.

"They want a name."

"We're not fucking giving them one," I hiss into the phone. "Harlow has a right to anonymity. It's a matter of safety."

"I know that, but these people don't care. They'll hire private investigators and terrorise her unless we give more information."

"Let them fucking try."

"They know she's under Sabre's protection," he supplies. "With Whitcomb dead and no new leads, your reputation is going to take a battering for keeping this under wraps."

"Christ, I thought I paid you to help me with this shit."

"You do, which is why I'm telling you—be transparent. The SCU lost public confidence early on in this case and never recovered."

Tell me something I don't know. We intervened and helped to clear up their organisation following a corruption scandal, but even after all that, a lack of funding and budget cuts have worsened the situation.

"Levelling with them is your safest bet," Lucas concludes. "Put Harlow out there. Get her to give a statement."

I knock back the last of my tea. "Just deflect any questions about the Whitcomb girl and keep Harlow's name out of it."

Hanging up the call, I slam my phone down on the desk. Chewing out my own employees has never been my style, but this case is doing things to all of us.

I've been firefighting this escalating nightmare all week. We're being hounded for results in every direction possible. Harlow's testimony only created more unanswerable questions for us.

Every time I think about her, my heart squeezes in pain. It took everything in me to kick her out when I wanted nothing more than to take her to my bed and wipe the sadness from her face.

It's driving me insane to be here every day, unable to be close to her as I want to be. We bump into each other around the house in the evenings, and she can barely look at me after what happened.

I often catch myself staring into her hopeless gaze, searching for a glimmer of strength to ease my guilt. She has this powerful effect on me, sparking emotions that I haven't felt in a long time.

I don't want her to be strong. I want to keep her safe, secure and well out of reach until this madness ends. Last time I felt this way, we lost everything. I can't go through that again.

None of us can.

"Hunt?"

Theo's head pokes through my door.

"What's up?" I sigh.

"I need to speak to you. It's urgent."

My stomach somersaults. "Come in."

He steps into the room, his navy-blue flannel shirt rumpled. There's an old coffee stain down the front of his white tee, and his clear, blue eyes look tired behind glasses half covered by tight, blonde ringlets.

I've been pushing him like crazy, determined to get this case wrapped up as quickly as possible. We're throwing all of our resources at it, for better or for worse.

"I've tracked Harlow all the way to a tiny town near Northumberland." He leans against the wall. "She appears on a CCTV camera approaching from the east on foot."

"Where?" I demand excitedly.

"Seems to be a very rural area bordering a huge nature reserve. Remote, unpopulated. It's safe to assume she escaped from somewhere nearby."

My anticipation rises. This is the biggest breakthrough we've had since we took the case on and spent months trawling through evidence.

"Start scouting the area for potential locations," I rattle off. "Check for churches with the local parish. This bastard could be living right under our noses."

"Harlow's description said the chapel appeared to be abandoned in the middle of nowhere. It may not be registered."

"Goddammit. Fine, we can send some drones to scope out the land. Alert the local police department so we don't get shot down."

Theo nods, taking rapid notes. "The Cobra team has wrapped up their other assignments. I'll rope Kade into some reconnaissance."

"Good. Get it done."

Anxiety is still written across Theo's stony expression. He's generally an awkward person, always has been. His computer code and textbooks wrap him in a security blanket. He wasn't always this detached and lifeless, though.

"What is it?" I sit up in my chair. "Theo?"

"We need to talk about Harlow's identity." He opens a folder, rifling through paperwork. "We've confirmed that Pastor and Mrs Michaels do not exist."

"I see. Well, we know that serial killers use pseudonyms," I muse.

"It's hardly surprising they lied about their names."

"I've had the whole intelligence department scouring decades of records." Theo hands me a sheet of paper. "That's a list of ordained pastors in the last forty years. No Michaels."

"So he's a whack job who thinks that he's God's fucking gift."

"Something like that." His eyes dart around the room. "But there's more to it. I just got the report back from forensics."

"Harlow's DNA results?"

Theo nods tightly. "It took a while to compile everything against the national database and verify what we found."

"Just spit it out. What's going on?"

"Well... her name isn't Harlow Michaels, as we anticipated. They're not her parents, Hunt. They never were."

I stare up at Theo's apprehensive face. We tossed this theory around after taking her testimony last week. Having it confirmed means a shitstorm is about to blow up in my stupid face.

"Please tell me she doesn't have family," I blurt.

His blonde eyebrows knit together. "Why would you say that?"

I slam my hands down on the desk. "We've been living with her for weeks and if she has a fucking family out there, we're about to get dragged over the coals for not reuniting them sooner."

Theo's cheeks darken. "These tests take time."

"Like they're gonna give a shit about that!"

I straighten the loose stacks of paperwork I disturbed, internally hating myself for being so callous. Someone has to worry about this firm. No one else seems to give a damn right now.

"Her name is Leticia Kensington," Theo grinds out. "She has a real family. And if there's a single scrap of humanity left in you, then you will do the right thing and call them now."

"Just give me the report and get out of my office. I don't need a goddamn lecture about how to look after my client."

"I'm not done."

Stepping closer, Theo slams the remaining folder of paperwork down in front of me. It's thick, with years' worth of records spilling out. More than a simple DNA report.

"She's been missing for the past thirteen years," he reveals. "This isn't just a murder investigation anymore—she was kidnapped. Harlow wasn't born in that cage."

"Thirteen years? Is this a joke?"

Theo visibly gulps. "She went missing at nine years old. There were zero leads, and the investigation went cold. She was never to be seen again."

Fierce pain begins to pound behind my eyes. Every word that has left Harlow's mouth is either a lie, or a traumatised delusion. Either way, my life is about to get a hell of a lot harder.

"We're so fucking screwed," I mutter to myself.

Theo's eyes narrow. "No. You're fucking screwed."

"What exactly is your problem?"

"You're my problem, Hunt."

"Watch your tone," I warn him. "I'm still the boss around here."

"And that's exactly what's wrong with you! Do you even care anymore? Harlow genuinely needs our help, and all you can think about is closing this case."

"Says the man that abandoned his family! Since when do you care about any of us, including Harlow?"

I regret my harsh words almost immediately. His face shutters, moving back to familiar emptiness as he drops my eyes.

"I thought… you understood me," Theo chokes out. "You and Enzo both moved on like nothing happened to Alyssa. I can't live like that."

"If you think we're fine, you don't know us," I reply in a quieter voice.

"You could've fooled me. It was you who has moved Leighton into her old room, like she never existed."

"It's been five fucking years!" I shout again. "How long can I live in a graveyard? She's gone, Theo! We have to move on."

When I think he's finally going to grow some balls, Theo's mouth snaps shut again. He turns on his heel and strides from the room in a cloud of barely restrained anger, leaving the damned report with me.

I stare after him, feeling like the worst person in the entire world. That's the most he's said to me in a very long time. Losing our fourth team member nearly killed us all, in so many ugly and awful ways.

None of us knew how to deal with our grief; stuffing the skeletons into the closet was simpler and far less painful. But after that, Theo never came back to us.

Fuck!

I stare at the sealed report on my desk. What now? I have no choice but to tell Harlow... but this could very well break her. It will tear apart the fragile foundations of the life she's started to rebuild.

Everything she knows. All the progress we've made. It will all be gone. But as fucking usual, I have no choice but to hurt the people I care about. It always comes down to me.

Absently rubbing at the pain in my chest, I snatch up my phone to text Enzo. Harlow should be in her weekly therapy session with Richards right about now.

I'll go and pick her up myself. Before I unleash a new level of madness upon us with this revelation, I need to know if this was all some elaborate lie.

Would she really lie to us?

Is she protecting the monsters that kidnapped her?

Do I know her at all?

Not bothering to wait for Enzo's response, I toss my suit jacket back on and storm from my office. Her appointment is being held back at the hospital. Richards agreed to meet there after Harlow's check-up with her consultant.

After running every red light in a storm of impatience, I camp out in the waiting area upon arrival. I'm in a foul mood. Harlow would be better off with Enzo, but he's been compromised.

I can see it in his eyes, the way he looks at her like she's his goddamn saviour after years of emptiness. One of us has to remain objective and treat Harlow like the client she is.

Someone slides into the empty seat next to me, ignoring the handful of other chairs in favour of invading my personal space. I run a hand over my ponytail and straighten.

The redhead is a familiar nemesis. She wrote a hit piece about my hearing loss after we took down Incendia Corporation, and scored herself a promotion in the process.

They're lucky I was too busy dealing with my entire life falling apart to sue them for being so fucking heartless.

"Care to give me a statement, Mr Rodriguez? Your press release this morning was deliberately vague."

"Sally Moore." I cast her a frown. "Long time no see."

"You're a hard man to find."

"So I've been told. I have nothing further to add. Refer your questions to my PR agent, Lucas. I pay him enough for it."

"I don't want to speak to your spin doctor."

"Then feel free to sit here in silence. See if I care."

Reaching into her designer handbag, she slides a stack of photographs out and tosses them on the coffee table. The unspoken threat hangs in the air.

I clock the long-range shots of the hospital we're sat in, our tinted SUV coming and going. In one of the pictures, Harlow can be seen climbing out of the car, Enzo's arm wrapped around her waist.

"She's been here for a while," Sally reveals with a grin. "I'm looking forward to getting her statement when she comes out."

Snatching up the photographs, I tuck them into my suit jacket. "This really is scraping the barrel now. Are you that desperate for viewers? Is the network threatening to axe your shit gossip show?"

"I'm doing just fine," she defends hotly.

"Then get out of my face before I file an injunction and have you suspended. You're not getting a statement, and this is a gross invasion of my client's privacy."

She places her phone to her ear and pouts her lips at me. "Bring the cameras up, Jerry. We've got a live interview with Sabre's bossman. Yeah, that's right. I want them all."

Silently cursing, I stand and loom over her. I have enough connections in London to ensure she'll never work again, no matter how many favours it fucking costs me.

But right now, my priority is keeping Harlow as far away from this nightmare as possible. I'm not sacrificing her to the heartless media just to get them off our backs.

"Don't test me. We've played this game before."

"People just want the truth." Her shark-like smile makes my skin crawl. "This is the age of information. You can't keep any secrets."

Spitting with fury, I grab the phone from her hand before she can stop me. Sally shouts as I crush the device beneath my shoe, stamping it into useless shards for good measure.

"Hey! You can't do that!"

I kick it back towards her. "Fucking bill me."

She's still swearing up a storm as I stride away, taking the corridor to where Harlow is having her weekly therapy session. Barging in without knocking, I slam the door behind me to block anyone from seeing in.

The ward matron shouldn't let the vultures get past, but we still need to get the hell out of here. Someone's ass is going to be fired for not spotting the cameras hiding outside the hospital.

"Hunter?" Richards protests from his seat by the window. "This is a private session. You can't just walk in whenever you feel like it."

Harlow is huddled in a high-backed armchair, her trembling knees pulled up to her chest. She looks so fucking good, her bright, furtive eyes framed by curling hair that she hasn't cut yet.

I really need to get Enzo to buy her some warmer clothing; the low-cut tank top she's wearing with grey sweats and an oversized cardigan won't hold up against the cold weather coming.

"I understand, doc. Unfortunately, we have a situation outside. I need to get Harlow out of here."

Richards tucks his glasses into the collar of his pinstriped shirt. "It's always a damn situation with you people."

"You can continue this at another time. I apologise for the interruption."

He stands and gestures for Harlow to do the same. She's unsteady on her feet, struggling to straighten with her tightly wrapped ribs. I offer her a helping hand, which she eyes mistrustfully.

"Sorry, Harlow. I didn't mean to interrupt."

Nodding, she purses her lips and takes my hand. Her limbs are still quaking with fear. Whatever they were discussing, it's left her feeling vulnerable and exposed.

I'm not the right person to deal with her fragile state. Hell, I was intending to come over here and lay into her until she broke and gave up the truth. Being her fucking white knight was not on the agenda.

"I'll catch you up later, Richards."

"Please do," he says pointedly.

We exchange a rapid conversation through eye contact. I nod again, silently asking him to back down. Richards is more than my colleague—he's a friend. I don't have time for one of those today.

Harlow still can't look me in the eye as we creep over to the door. In the corridor, the matron and several nurses are dealing with a horde of cameramen flooding the department. Perfect.

"Goddamn reporters," I curse quietly. "We'll have to find another way out. Keep your head low. Don't let them see your face. Got it?"

She flinches at my barked order. I force myself to be calmer, holding my hand out again until she has the bravery to meet my eyes.

"I'm sorry. Take my hand, Harlow. I'll get us out of here, okay?"

She still doesn't budge. I fight the urge to throw her over my shoulder, kicking and screaming. We don't have time for this.

"Have I ever given you a reason not to trust me?"

Hesitantly, she shakes her head. "I guess not."

"Then there's your answer. I promise I'll look after you."

Her fingers hesitantly link with mine and I squeeze her hand tight. I'm an asshole, but I do care, regardless of what Theo thinks of the person I've become to survive.

Together, we slip out into the corridor and take a right, heading deeper into the bustling hospital. There's a chorus of shouts, followed by the sound of pursuing feet.

"Call security!" a nurse shouts.

"You can't go back there!"

"Stop them!"

Throwing an arm around Harlow, I try my best to conceal her face from the flashing cameras. We duck and weave through endless hallways, trying to lose the greedy mob at our heels.

I've got no clue where we're going. Sally and her soul-sucking cameramen are determined to get an exclusive. I refuse to let them humiliate Harlow the same way they did to me.

"Wait," Harlow blurts.

"There's no time. Move it."

"No, stop. In here."

She throws my arm off and opens a door on our left, leading into a maintenance cupboard. I'm dragged into the darkness as she closes the door behind us, keeping the lights off.

Thirty seconds later, we hear the horde of cameras and Sally's near-hysterical shouting pass by. The noise grows quieter as we huddle together in pitch-black darkness.

"Harlow?" I search around with my hands. "I can't see a thing. Where are you?"

The complete darkness, coupled with my one deaf ear, is disorientating. I can't see if she's okay. Her fingertips ghost over my arm in a hesitant caress that causes my pulse to spike.

"I'm here," she whispers back. "Careful, there's a bucket behind you."

"How the hell can you see anything?"

"I'm used to the dark."

Her hand bunches in my jacket, and I can feel the beckoning heat of her body. Grabbing her wrist, I drag her closer, our bodies colliding in the tight space.

"That was a close one."

"Good thinking there." Hesitantly, I slide an arm around her waist to hold her close. "You covered our asses."

Her small, pert breasts press against my torso. "Believe it or not, I can be useful."

"I never said that you aren't useful."

"You didn't have to."

Still clutching my jacket in a death grip, Harlow guides me back to the door. She opens it a crack to listen, allowing a thin sliver of light to illuminate the cramped cupboard.

"I think they're gone. Who were those people?"

"Reporters," I growl out. "Sally Moore's a soulless bitch. I know her editor, and he owes me a favour. She won't have a job by the end of the week."

The thin strip of light illuminates Harlow's face. I'm trapped by her brilliant blue eyes boring into me, nervous and afraid. Lower still, her glistening bottom lip is caught between her teeth.

"I won't let them hurt you," I find myself promising.

Her eye contact doesn't break. The tension is excruciating. She wears the same broken expression as the night I dismissed her, throwing up impenetrable walls between us.

I want to reach out and bite that lip, tasting her sweetness for myself. A second before giving in, the DNA report comes back to me, and all of its messy implications.

"Your session with Richards… was it good?"

Harlow quickly looks away as the moment passes.

"Fine."

"Did you get any more information we can use?"

The angry little spitfire inside of her rises to the surface, her eyes filling with annoyance. Goddamn me to hell, I'm fucking hard watching her expression darken and hands tighten into fists.

She doesn't look like someone who's deliberately misleading us all, lying her ass off while eating our food and abusing our trust. I just don't see it. My judgement is never wrong.

"I told you everything, Hunter."

"There are significant gaps in your memory," I point out. "We need to establish a reliable timeline."

Surprising me, Harlow places a hand on my chest and shoves me backwards. I nearly topple over a brush propped against the wall before righting myself.

"I was locked in a cage, starved, beaten, and neglected by monsters that enjoyed killing other girls. I can't remember shit because I don't *want* to remember. Get off my back."

Her chest rises and falls in a rapid rhythm. She looks like she wants to punch me in the nose again, but on purpose this time.

"I didn't mean it like that," I backtrack.

"Yeah. You did."

Through the slanted light, I can see her lips are twisted into a grimace. It hurts me to see the pain I'm causing. I don't usually give a fuck, but with her, I'm not in control of my feelings.

"Give me a break, Harlow." I attempt to approach her, my hands spread. "I'm trying to fix this mess. It's nothing personal."

"Well, I'm trying to figure out how to be alive in this crazy, confusing place. You're not making it any easier."

My hands hang mid-air as I wrestle with my need to touch, protect, and cherish her. Even if it goes against every last warning bell blaring inside me. Caring only equals heartache.

"You're right," I blurt.

She halts. "Huh?"

Blowing out a breath, I prepare to plunge into the deep end. "I want to chase down every last lead and make them talk. Not being in control is hard for me."

"That's not an apology."

I splutter a laugh. There's a hint of a smile pulling Harlow's mouth taut as she stares up at me, a challenge burning in her irises.

The others think she's just a precious wallflower that has to be protected and nourished, but I see the other side too. There's a caged lion beneath her skin, begging to be set free.

"I'm sorry, sweetheart." I run a hand over the rough scruff of hair covering my chin. "I was wrong to push you."

Despite every reason my obsessive mind has already considered, my fingers still twitch with need as I battle not to drag her closer, pin her against the fucking wall and show her exactly what I'm thinking.

"I never thought I'd hear you say that," she murmurs.

"Enjoy it while it lasts. It's not happening again."

Harlow stares at me with an adorable crease between her brows. Unable to stop myself, I reach out and run the tip of my finger over it.

"I thought you hated me."

Her words crash into me like a five-vehicle pileup.

"What on earth made you think that?"

"You barely speak to me. Not like the others do."

Struggling to find an explanation that won't make me sound like an egotistical asshole, I sigh heavily.

"My priority is to solve this case. It doesn't leave room for emotion. The work comes first, you see? Especially when lives are at stake."

"I understand." She looks down, fighting to keep the pain off her face. "As soon as this is over, I'll leave you in peace."

"Fuck, that's not what I meant."

"Isn't it?"

She inches backwards, anxiously fiddling with her hair. The distance growing between us again is strangling me. I don't want to leave this cupboard and go back to how things were.

"They should be gone by now."

Her voice is detached, robotic. Without waiting for my answer, she opens the door and steps out into the corridor, leaving the shadows of our intimate moment behind.

Cursing myself, I follow behind her, wrestling with the truth. We're not good enough for Harlow. She deserves the world, and I can't give it to her. Theo was right.

I have to call her family and share the good news, even if that means giving her up and breaking my teammates all over again. Another loss may be the final nail in the coffin.

I'm not naive enough to ignore the impact she's had on our family in a matter of weeks. Enzo, Leighton—they've accepted her into our family without hesitating. I knew this would happen.

Losing her may be the end of us.

But like usual, I have no fucking choice.

CHAPTER 16

Harlow

(If) You Are The Ocean (Then) I Would Like To
Drown — VIOLET NIGHT

"**I**s everything okay?" I ask for the third time.

Behind the wheel, Enzo is staring at the country road with a clenched jaw. He's been quiet ever since we left the house, without his usual softness and charm.

The bags beneath his amber eyes are more pronounced than usual, ageing him more than his thirty-two years. I couldn't believe it when I found out his age. Enzo doesn't sleep much anyway, but he looks dead on his feet today.

"Everything's fine, Harlow."

"How many times are you going to say that?"

"How many times are you going to ask?" he replies sharply.

My mouth clicks shut. They've all been acting strange for the last few days. I thought it must be something to do with the reporters that tracked us down in the hospital, but this feels like more.

Leighton barely spared me a glance this morning, preferring to go down to the gym in the basement of their home and blast aggressive music. Not even a wink or bad joke.

"Where are we going?" I try instead.

Taking a right, Enzo releases a sigh. "You need more clothes. We only got the basics last time. Hunter wants you to have a phone too, so we can contact you."

"Am I going somewhere?"

"Of course not." Enzo frowns at the road. "It's just a precaution."

His words don't quite ring true. Anxiety wraps around my windpipe as he speeds through the autumnal gloom.

"I still haven't paid you back for the last shopping trip," I worry aloud. "Maybe I should get a job or something. Start pulling my weight around here. I can't stay cooped up forever."

"You don't need a job."

"I can't keep taking handouts, Enzo."

He curses under his breath. "It isn't safe right now. Working is out of the question. If you want to do something in the future, we can discuss that another time."

"I'm an adult. I can make my own decisions."

"Not if those decisions put your life in danger. That's not happening, Harlow. Not on my watch."

I slump back in my seat. His overprotective nature is endearing, but after weeks of resting, attending therapy and taking medication like a good little prisoner, I'm tired of following orders without question.

Winding through the countryside doused in fallen leaves and golden sunshine, we eventually reach a small village. Traditional cottages with picket fences and painted doors line the winding streets.

Passing through the residential area, small shop fronts start to appear as the houses melt away. Enzo finds a tight parking spot, manoeuvring the SUV into it with wordless ease.

The minute the car is parked, I leap out and slam the door shut.

My ribs twinge from the sudden drop, but the pain is manageable. I'm not some invalid, no matter what he thinks.

At first, his possessive need to wrap me in cotton wool was appreciated. It's given me the confidence to face the world a little more each day. But with each step I take, I'm changing.

I want to be treated like everyone else.

I want to actually *live*.

Enzo circles the car, pulling on his usual leather jacket. With his ripped, black jeans and dark-green t-shirt, every inch of corded muscle that carves his monstrous frame is on display.

A shiver runs down my spine, but not from fear. I can't explain the way he makes me feel, even when he's being infuriating and suffocating me to death.

"Why are you looking at me like you want to deck me?" he asks with a hint of his usual tenderness.

I drag my purple beanie over my long hair. "Because I'm seriously thinking about it. Why can't I have more freedom?"

Propping his shoulder against the car, he levels me with a serious stare. "No progress with the case doesn't equate to safety. The threat is still real. Do you want to go back to where you came from?"

"N-No," I stutter, seized by panic.

"I will do everything in my power to keep you safe, Harlow. Even if you hate me for it. I won't see you get hurt."

Closing the space between us, I wrap my un-plastered arm around his waist. He engulfs me in a tight embrace, and I can feel his nose buried in my hair. We stand like that forever.

It's like being crushed against a boulder, but the way he holds me is gentle, reverent. He smells like the garden after it has rained— earthy, fresh, full of new beginnings and hope.

My forehead is pressed against the hard planes of his abdominals, and we don't speak for several moments, holding one another. This has been happening more often, but I don't mind.

Touching Enzo is like coming up for air, coughing and spluttering, but thankful to be alive. He makes me feel safe. Cherished. Wanted. Even with the pain and secrets dancing in his eyes.

"What's going on?" I whisper against his t-shirt.

His muscles tense beneath my touch. "I just need you to be okay, little one. Nothing else matters."

"I'm right here, Enzo." Looking up into his amber eyes, I squeeze his waist tight. "Can't you feel me?"

Enzo cups both of my cheeks in a tight, almost desperate grip. I have to fight not to pull away. It's a vulnerable position for me, utterly trapped by his strength, but I'm not afraid.

"I can feel you," he echoes softly. "Harlow, I…"

Waiting for him to finish, the words never come. I wait, beg, silently plead for more. I want him to touch me. Hold me. Claim every last broken piece of me.

The realisation is terrifying. I don't know what all these confusing feelings mean. They've been building for a while now. From the way he looks at me… I think he feels the same way.

"We should go inside," Enzo finishes.

Disappointment stabs me in the chest. His hands drop from my face, taking my hand instead. I'm towed along as we leave the car park, taking a cobbled street into town.

Enzo is a wall of tension next to me as clouds bubble overhead. The first spots of rain kiss my skin with cool relief, gradually picking up until the shower soaks our clothes.

"Put your sunglasses on," he instructs.

"It's literally raining. I'll look more suspicious wearing them."

"Just do it, Harlow. I'm not risking anyone spotting you, especially with those fucking reporters causing mayhem."

Huffing, I release his hand to slide the borrowed sunglasses into place. With my long hair and beanie, I'm as anonymous as a ghost. It's the only reason I haven't cut it yet.

Enzo folds an arm around my shoulders, pulling me close again. I bathe in his pillar of warmth as we walk quicker to escape the rain.

"This place has the best pancake house," he explains, guiding me down another street. "A friend of mine found it last year."

"You don't seem like a pancake kind of person."

"What's that supposed to mean?"

Raising an eyebrow, I take in his huge shoulders and arms, the rippling muscles pulling his leather jacket tight. It's like walking next to a grizzly bear.

People take one look at Enzo and scurry away, even his employees. They don't see what I do. To the world, his sheer physical power is a threat. No one bothers to see what's underneath it.

"You've got the whole Bruce Banner thing going on."

"How on earth do you know that reference?"

I shrug. "Leighton likes movies. I like learning."

"You should choose your own movies from now on. Leighton will melt your brain with that shit."

"I liked it," I defend.

We pass beneath a thick canopy of trees cloaked in twinkling lights. As the rain eases off, little shop fronts begin to throw open their doors and lay out fresh fruits and vegetables, muttering about the unpredictable winter weather.

"What else do you like?" Enzo asks.

Despite devouring knowledge and new experiences from within my comfortable prison, there's still so much about the world that I don't know. My life, despite my best efforts, is exactly as Hunter said.

Little.

More than anything, I'm beginning to feel suffocated rather than protected. In the basement, I couldn't see what I was missing. It was easier to accept my isolation.

"I don't know. I'd like to find out."

"There must be something," Enzo pushes. "Humour me."

"Well, I like to watch the sun rise and set."

He nods, studying me out of the corner of his eye. "Lucky's never had so much company outside. What else?"

"I like the feel of rain on my face and wet grass beneath my feet." I tighten my jacket around me, feeling exposed. "Boiling hot showers are the best, and sleeping with the window open so I can feel the air on my skin at night."

He listens intently, hanging on to every word.

"I like listening to your voice when you're happy. Leighton's laugh too, it's adorable. And don't tell him, but Hunter makes the best tea."

Clearing my throat, I feel heat rise to my cheeks.

"I like not being alone anymore."

Enzo suddenly draws us to a halt. Two calloused fingers lift my chin as he pulls the sunglasses aside. Our eyes collide. Blue on amber, nervous on certain, our lives couldn't be further apart.

"You never have to be alone ever again," he murmurs, searching my face.

"You guys can't look after me forever." I fight to keep my voice even, hoping to hide the fear that rises at the thought of leaving. "I'm a burden to you."

His hand travels along my jawline, exploring the gaunt lines of my face. I'm still struggling to put on weight, despite moving to solid foods a couple of weeks ago.

I hold my breath, unable to stop myself from leaning into his touch. Enzo musters a sweet, heartbreaking smile.

"You are not a burden, Harlow."

"Then what am I? A client?"

He licks his lips. "How about a friend?"

We remain frozen in the street, despite a trail of people passing us by. Enzo doesn't move his hand, staring deep into my eyes. I realise there are tiny stripes of silver in his irises.

"You want to be my friend?" I whisper nervously.

"If you'll allow me."

My voice comes out raspy. "I'd like a friend."

This time when he smiles, he flashes teeth. I think my heart actually stops for a moment. Seriously, what's with these butterflies in my stomach? I need to find a trustworthy female to ask.

"Come on, I'm hungry," he declares.

We resume our slow walk into town, stopping outside a bright-blue shop front with a striped overhang. The sign proclaims it to have the best pancakes in England inside.

Enzo has to duck low to fit through the door, locating a cracked vinyl booth in shades of bright pink and yellow. He looks ridiculous sliding into it.

"Could this get any smaller," he grumbles.

I stifle a laugh. "Please don't break it."

"If I do, it'll be the booth's fault."

A blonde-haired woman trails over, trying not to laugh when she spots his predicament. I tuck my chin low, averting my face before she can attempt to speak to me. Enzo quickly dismisses her and hands me a menu.

"What's good?"

He shifts, making the booth creak. "Everything."

"Not helpful."

"Want me to order for you?"

I breathe a sigh of relief. "Please."

When the waitress returns, Enzo fires off a huge order. Her eyes bulge with shock as she's forced to flip to another page on her little pad. I'm pretty sure he just ordered half the menu.

Once she scurries away, Enzo stretches his long legs out until they brush mine under the table. He still looks uncomfortable.

"Tell me something." I fiddle with the paper napkins on the table. "I want to know more about you guys. I feel like you know everything about me."

He folds his huge arms. "Not much to tell."

"I opened up. It's your turn."

"Fine," he concedes. "Let's see… well, me and Hunter grew up together. Our parents were neighbours. We've always been best friends. I couldn't have gotten through my parents' deaths without him."

"What happened?"

"They died in a mountaineering accident when I was a teenager. It was during a sponsored climb of Mount Everest for a leukaemia charity. Despite years of training, it all went wrong."

Reaching across the table, I take his clenched hand. Enzo's fingers tighten around mine.

"My sister was diagnosed with cancer as a toddler, so my folks did a lot of fundraising for the expedition. There was an avalanche before they could summit. We never recovered their bodies."

"I'm so sorry," I offer, hating his pain.

His hand squeezes mine. "My dad's sister, Hayley, is a saint. She was looking after us while they were away and ended up taking custody of me and my younger sister. She raised us like her own."

"She sounds pretty amazing."

"Yeah, she really is. When Paula got her terminal diagnosis, Hayley devoted everything to her. We practically lived in the paediatric ward until she died."

Enzo stares down at the tabletop, his throat bobbing. I had no idea he'd lost pretty much his whole family. The pain he has to feel is unimaginable. Abbie lost her brother in a motorcycle accident. She told me about it once.

Grief is an impenetrable, lonely prison.

I hate the thought of Enzo suffering alone.

"After Paula died, I dropped out of school. Hunter was already working as a personal trainer, but he was unhappy. We decided to go backpacking around South America for a year."

"So how did you end up founding Sabre?"

Enzo's thumb strokes over my knuckles. "Hunter's dad is a retired police officer, so he grew up around crime scenes. His parents told us to get our shit together and lent us the start-up cash to create the company."

"How old were you?"

"I was twenty at the time. Hunter's a couple of years older than me. Private security seemed like the most flexible and varied job we could find."

I watch the brief smile dancing across his lips. The sense of pride is obvious, from the light that sparks in his eyes as he recalls his humble roots, to the determined set of his shoulders that reflects the unshakeable faith that got him this far.

"It was just the two of us as we established ourselves," Enzo continues. "For several years, we focused on private security. Once we knew the business, we took on more criminal investigations."

"Like my case?"

"Sometimes. We usually get the hard ones that law enforcement can't crack. We're good at what we do. People started to notice, and an investor helped us expand more. Twelve years later, here we are."

"When did Theo join?"

"Around eight years ago. He was nineteen at the time. We got him off a hacking charge that would've resulted in prison time."

I gape at him. "Theo? Really?"

Enzo chuckles. "He has the least respect for the law out of us all, little one. There isn't a database he won't attempt to hack."

In the small amount of time I've spent with Theo, he was kind and thoughtful. I'm struggling to imagine him getting arrested.

"He built the intelligence department from the ground up and broke into a whole new side of the business. We've been very lucky."

"You're good at what you do, that's not luck."

"We've made our fair share of mistakes," Enzo mutters. "There was this case a few years back. We took on a corrupt medical corporation, running an empire of psychiatric institutes. It nearly destroyed the entire company."

His face changes—growing darker, shadowed by suffering and regret. I watch his throat bob with emotion.

"Hunter lost his hearing the year after, and we were grieving for… well, someone important. Getting through it all felt impossible."

"I'm sorry, Enz."

"It's alright. We figured things out."

The waitress reappears with a tray propped over her shoulder. Enzo's mouth slams shut as he accepts the drinks, taking a black coffee and a water for himself.

I don't miss the way she checks out his muscled chest while he's distracted. The urge to scratch her eyes out overwhelms me.

"These all for you, hun?" she asks with a wan smile.

My mouth hangs open, but no words come out. I just stare at

her, silently panicking. Her eyebrow raises as she looks at me like I'm stupid. I want to curl up under the table and hide.

"I'll take those," Enzo interrupts, snatching the tray from her. "That'll be all, thanks."

Dismissed, she leaves with a glare sent my way. I work on uncurling my clenched fist as Enzo drops three drinks in front of me. Why can't I be normal? I had to go and embarrass him.

"I thought you could choose."

"Thank you," I force out. "Sorry, I panicked."

"Stop apologising and drink up."

Sticking a straw in the cloudy juice in front of me, I take a long drag and hum in contentment. It's exotic and fruity, kinda like the smell of Leighton's citrus shampoo, but sweeter.

"This is good. What is it?"

"Pineapple juice."

"I have no idea what that is, but I like it."

His smile is toe-curling. Enzo loves pleasing me as much as Leighton enjoys teaching me new things. I watch him sip his steaming mug of coffee and decide to try my own.

Taking two sugars, I dump them in before having a sip. The richness of coffee beans clings to my tongue, offset by sweetness.

"This is good too. It's kinda strong, though."

"That's the point. It kicks your ass in the morning."

"Then why does Hunter drink tea?"

Enzo chuckles around a mouthful. "Because he's a psychopath, obviously. Who else drinks tea instead of coffee?"

"I really have no idea."

Drinking some more coffee, I wince and swallow it down. I won't tell Enzo, but Hunter's tea is far nicer. I'll join him as a psychopath if it means I can drink that instead of this sludge.

"So, what about Leighton?" I change the topic.

Enzo rests his chin on his laced fingers. "Leighton was a good kid. He idolised Hunter growing up, but they fought a lot too. Their folks adored Hunter. He was academic and scarily smart in school."

"Figures."

"Not much has changed. He still lives a whole fucking level above the rest of us peasants. I can't pretend to understand his nut-job brain."

We share a laugh and Enzo takes another sip, studying the pitch-black liquid.

"Leighton was often overlooked. Their dad's an interesting character. He worked a lot but still piled pressure on his kids to excel. Leighton began to act out and started to get in trouble with the law."

"How so?"

"Getting into fights, smoking at school. Going to older kids' parties and drinking. He's always been a bit of a wild child. It hit Hunter hard when Leighton was sent to prison."

I nearly drop my cup of coffee. "What now?"

"It's still a sensitive situation. Leighton's only been out a few months after serving three years. He's isolated himself from his family since getting out. Even their folks haven't seen him yet. They're devastated."

Blinking hard, I struggle to keep up. Part of me can't believe it. Leighton is the warmest, most carefree spirit I've ever met. He's everything that's good in the world, wrapped up in a soft exterior.

"Have I blown your mind?" Enzo laughs.

"Um, a little bit. Why was he in prison?"

"That's his story to tell, little one. Though I wouldn't recommend asking him about it."

Pushing the coffee aside, I return to the juice. The bitter drink is curdling in my stomach with the realisation that I don't know these people as well as I thought. I feel awful for never asking before.

"What about you?"

His thick eyebrows furrow. "Me?"

"Tell me something no one else knows."

He's clearly stumped as he frowns at his huge hands. The roughened skin over his knuckles is discoloured from layers of scar tissue, painting a violent picture of the gentle giant I know.

"I hate my job," he suddenly blurts.

"You're kidding? Why?"

"Every day... all I see is death and pain. We help a lot of people, but we also can't help just as many of them. Those are the cases that make me want to retire, open up a chop shop or something."

"Chop shop?" I repeat.

"Cars. My pops taught me a lot; I used to go to work with him. He owned a chain of mechanic shops in outer London."

"So what's stopping you?"

Enzo chews his lip as he stares at the table. I sense that I should stop prying about his past, but my curiosity is far stronger than my need to be polite.

I want to know everything about them, all the tiny, intimate details that nobody else is close enough to receive. I want to *be* close enough to know those things.

"This is Hunter's dream," he answers carefully. "Sabre wouldn't be a success without his leadership. My place is by his side."

"But... what about your dream?"

He shrugs again. "When our work is done, I'll have a quiet life. Until then, we have a job to do. That's enough for me."

Several steaming plates arrive from the kitchen, and enough food to feed an army clusters the table. The waitress slides a stack of pancakes over to me, covered in strawberries and syrup.

"How did you know what I like?" I grin at Enzo.

He smiles back. "Leighton told me about the pancake disaster the other morning. You know he can't cook for shit, right?"

"I know now. These actually look edible."

Enzo dives in and clears his plate in under a minute, moving on to the next. I've never seen anyone devour a stack of pancakes so fast. It's a wonder he isn't the size of a house.

"A quiet life?" I break the silence.

He wipes his chin. "Maybe a house in the countryside. Lots of land, trees, fields of corn. Some animals. A workshop and place to fix old cars without listening to sirens or gunshots. I hate London."

"That sounds peaceful."

"I like to think so. What about you?"

I swallow a bite of syrupy goodness, caught off guard by his question. "What about me?"

"You must have stuff that you want to do."

His gaze burrows beneath my skin like a laser pointer, challenging me to answer. The pancakes turn to stone in the pit of my stomach. I place my fork down, taking a long drink of juice.

"I'm just trying to survive from one day to the next."

"There's more to life than that, Harlow. We can figure out what you want to do. I said that I'd help you before, and I meant it."

"Really?"

His nod is firm, decisive. "That's what friends are for, right?"

"I have no clue. I haven't had many."

Enzo's hand takes mine again. "We'll muddle through together. Come on, eat up. We still need to go shopping. I'm not having any complaints this time."

CHAPTER 17

Harlow

Someone Somewhere Somehow – Super Whatevr

Facing the huge pile of bags, I give myself a little shake. I was too tired to unpack when we got back yesterday. Walking around and trying on clothes for so long exhausted me.

I'm still building up my strength, and until I can keep on the weight that I'm supposed to be gaining, I have to take lots of naps when my energy levels crash.

Enzo totally took advantage of my desire to cheer him up and filled countless baskets with winter clothes, accessories and random things that caught my eye. He was like a man possessed.

I now have a full wardrobe of sweaters, long-sleeved t-shirts, a thicker coat and leather-soled boots that keep my feet warm. In the other bag, there's a huge, back-breaking stack of books.

I've trained myself to focus for longer periods of time and can now read without getting a headache. As a result, I've become insatiable. Enzo let me go wild, picking up every single book I looked at.

There's a glossy, white box in the final bag that holds my new mobile phone. I'm pretty sure this goes beyond the essentials he convinced me we were shopping for.

I almost wanted to ask if they do this for all of their clients, but I bit my tongue to avoid an awkward conversation. Hunter ordered it, so we're bound to obey him.

"Lucky," I chastise as she curls up on my new sweater. "You're getting fur everywhere, girl."

Her big, pleading eyes blink up at me.

"Don't look at me like that. You'll get me in trouble for being in here, let alone on the bed."

Nuzzling into the new, turquoise bed sheets, she gets comfy and falls asleep. Hunter would kill me if he saw her in here. He's a stickler for pointless house rules. Anything that gives him control.

After packing my new clothes away, I stack the books on my bedside table and check the window. It's evening already; I've missed my usual sunset walk in the back garden.

Curling up around Lucky's warm, snoring body, I crack the pages of a new book and lose myself to the tale of magic and mystery. Enzo and Hunter won't be home for a while yet.

"Goldilocks?"

Looking up from the pages, I realise the room is cloaked in shadows. The evening has already slipped away. The book gripped me so hard, I don't think I've blinked at all while reading into the night.

"Yeah, I'm in here."

Leighton pops his head around the door, giving me a wave. He went out last night after an argument with Hunter about paying rent, and his door has been shut all day. I didn't want to disturb him.

Propping himself in the doorway, he pushes back his messy mop of brown hair. My heart leaps into my mouth. There's a huge black bruise marring his right eye, and it's swollen all the way shut.

"Oh my God, Leigh!"

"I'm fine," he rushes to explain. "I got into a stupid fight in the club last night. Some asshole was forcing himself on a girl. Serves me right for getting involved."

"So you hit him?"

He smiles broadly. "Obviously. I don't take shit like that. It was worth getting my ass kicked so she could slip away and get a taxi."

He flops down on the bed, disturbing Lucky, who growls her displeasure. Leighton's head lays across my blanketed legs as he snuggles closer to the dog.

"You shouldn't be out fighting." I fold a page corner in the book and set it down. "I don't like seeing you hurt."

His green eyes meet mine. "I'm alright. Did you just fold a page? Do you want Hunter to crucify you?"

"What?" I exclaim in panic.

"No, no," he splutters, reading my fear. "It was a joke, Harlow. He's just weird about books. Dusts them and everything."

Taking a deep breath, I pin Leighton with a glower. "Don't scare me like that. And don't change the topic. Your eye looks bad."

"Are you worried about me, princess?"

"Didn't we discuss the p-word?" I sigh.

"We discussed how much you love it, sure. Other nickname options include pumpkin, honey bunch, and babelicious."

"Ugh, pass on all three, thanks."

"Spoilsport."

With a wink, Leighton snatches up the white box laying unwrapped on my bedside table. It was far too complicated for me to even contemplate.

"Enzo texted and asked me to get you set up. He's stuck dealing with some work shit. Hunter too, I think."

"This late?"

"Apparently." Leighton avoids my eyes, seeming shifty. "Something at the office. I wouldn't worry."

"To do with the case? Or me?"

"Oh, look!" He opens the box and pulls out a sleek, rose-gold phone. "It's pink and everything. How girlie."

Clearing my throat, I watch him plug it in to charge, still avoiding my question. His fingers fly across the screen so fast, it's almost intimidating.

When he hands the phone over to me ten minutes later, I gingerly accept it. The screen glows with too many icons and different functions to process. I hate this thing already.

"I don't know how to use this."

Leighton snorts. "I'll show you. It's easy once you get the hang of it."

He spends half an hour showing me how to send text messages, call people, and search the internet. Man, that place is wild. There's so much to learn. My mind is already spinning with possibilities.

Clicking the camera icon, I lift the phone to capture Leighton in the frame. He sticks his tongue out like Lucky would do, letting me capture a silly picture.

"All four of us are saved on there," he explains, showing me the contacts. "I texted the guys so they will have your number saved."

"All f-four of y-you?" I stutter.

Leighton's eyes sparkle with amusement. "Why does that surprise you?"

"Even Hunter? Theo?"

He ignores the doubt in my voice. "Even them. Although you'll be lucky to get ahold of Theo in daylight hours. From what I hear, he's nocturnal. Sleeps at his desk and works through the night."

"Doesn't he have a room here?"

"Never uses it."

Filing that information away, I ditch the phone on top of my discarded book. The thought of Theo eating and sleeping alone in an office makes my heart ache. He seems like a good person.

"We could try to make a late dinner for everyone." I stroke Lucky's ears as she huffs in contentment. "I'm sure they'll be hungry."

Leighton grins, all mischief. "Sure, I'm up for that. No promises that we won't give them food poisoning with us working in the kitchen."

"Can't be worse than your pancakes."

"Ouch! You wound me. Alright, shift your ass, mystery girl. You won't like me when I'm hangry and hungover."

Safe to say, dinner is a disaster.

In our defence, Leighton is over-ambitious.

He pulls ingredients at random out of the fridge, covering the spotless kitchen in so much mess, it gives me heart palpitations. Hunter will murder the pair of us when he sees the state of it.

We discover that it is possible to burn pasta and still end up with crunchy strands of spaghetti. Apparently, this is a scientific achievement. Leighton says we should win an award for culinary masterminding.

"You really are a terrible cook," I say between belly-hurting fits of laughter. "We can't eat this."

"Aren't you hungry?" Leighton snickers.

It happens so fast, I can't stop myself from slipping into the past. Richards has been teaching me to breathe through the flashbacks, but when they're so intense, I'm left falling to my death.

Aren't you hungry, sinner?

Come here and kiss daddy's cheek.

Be a good girl and we'll give you some dinner.

The rush of memories lance into me with such intensity, I drop the vegetable knife I was slicing an onion with. The kitchen around me melts away with each stuttered breath I take.

It's too late to pull myself back.

The past swallows me whole.

All I can see is Mrs Michaels, an old belt in her hand, striking me over and over. Christie's blue corpse has been dragged out of the cage, left on a thick, plastic sheet to be dismantled.

You will help me, fucking bitch!

Strike.

You disobedient little swine.

Strike.

The pain is so real, I can feel it searing my shredded skin. My younger voice fills my ears, begging for mercy. I refused to help her saw my friend's limbs apart to get rid of.

"Harlow? Harlow?"

Someone's shaking me, repeating this name over and over again. I don't know why. Who am I? Who is Harlow? All I can see is the dark, cramped cell imprisoning me in hell.

Scents assault me.

Blood. Urine.

Filth. Mould.

Rotting corpses.

I'm back behind those bars, screaming for relief as time loses all meaning. Days, weeks, years. My hair grew and body weakened, but nothing else changed.

"Harlow! Talk to me, dammit."

Tears soak my cheeks. Ice invades my extremities, trapping me in a bubble. I'm drowning. Choking. Sinking further and further out of reach. I need to call for help, but nothing comes out.

Their faces are all there. Plastered on the walls of my mind, connected by the same red cord. Every single one of them that died in that Godless place. I can't escape them.

"I'm sorry," I scream at the ghosts.

It isn't enough. They don't want an apology. My words won't bring them back or undo the evil that stole their lives. These ghosts won't ever leave me. Not until justice is served.

Backing into a corner, I cover my ears and squeeze my head; it feels like it might explode. I can still see them, bleeding and gasping for air, begging me with their eyes.

I can't run.

I can't hide.

I'm alive… and they're not. My life isn't free. It doesn't belong to me anymore. The stolen futures of eighteen women live within me.

Someone grabs my shoulders and shakes so hard, my teeth snap together. It doesn't break the sarcophagus trapping me in my head. I'm being chased, the thud of dead feet hunting me down.

"No!" I shout, thrusting a fist outward.

It connects with something hard, eliciting a grunt. I can't see anything but blood. Everywhere. Coating everything. Dripping. Pooling. Congealing. It covers every inch of me.

"Harlow!"

The voice is warped and garbled. Pastor Michaels screamed my name at me when I made him mad, throwing it like a dagger to illicit my obedience. Hearing it now makes me sick.

All I can think about is hurting. Inflicting the pain that's scarred my skin. Peeling off the hands gripping my shoulders, I shove my captor backwards, throwing another punch.

We crash into each other, both grappling for control. I don't stop.

Not yet. My cowardice caused those girls to die alone. I can't be weak anymore; they won't let me forget.

"Harlow, stop! I won't fucking fight you!"

The cast encasing my arm cracks against the tiled floor as we both fall. Pain batters into me, over and over, but it isn't enough. I can still see them—their eyes wide, mouths parted, blood pouring out.

Lifting my head, I slam it back down onto the tiled floor. Excruciating pain explodes through my skull, over and over, my surroundings beginning to fuzz at the edges.

"Stop it!"

Thwack.

Thwack.

Thwack.

"I'm sorry," the person weighing me down growls. "You have to stop."

A pair of hands wrap around my throat in a vice-like grip. I'm being strangled by a viper, the oxygen sucked from my lungs.

"Stop… fighting!"

My nails scratch at his tightening hands, desperate for a sliver of air. But it's working. The harder my lungs battle for control, the faster my body is turning limp. I'm losing energy, fast.

Blood is slick against my fingertips as I scratch and battle, frantically attempting to escape. Just as my vision is threatening to darken into unconsciousness, blissful agony wracks over me.

His hands are gone.

My throat seizes and expands, dragging in the sweet nectar of air. I cough and splutter, clutching my throbbing neck. A crushing weight is still pinning me to the floor.

Emerald eyes the colour of fresh moss peer down at me. His terror is palpable, hanging in the air with such potency, I can taste it on my lips. Reality is a razor-sharp wire around my throat.

"Oh fuck, Harlow," Leighton keens, his gaze frantic. "Are you okay? I didn't know what else to do!"

I can't muster a single word. The adrenaline has rushed out of me in a powerful surge, leaving nothing but emptiness. All I can feel is his weight and the crushing beat of his heart against mine, demanding forgiveness.

"I had to stop you from hurting yourself." His hands hover over me, unsure where to begin. "Please… say something. Shit!"

My mouth hangs open, silent.

"Fucking hell. Please don't hate me for doing this."

Grasping my cheeks so tight, it's almost painful, his mouth crashes onto mine. I don't know how to react. Our lips are locked in a bruising collision, and Leighton's determined to win this war.

He's kissing me.

Over and over again.

Pausing, he pulls back and searches my face. Whatever he finds is enough for his lips to return to mine—softer, more hesitant, moving in a tender rhythm that would rival a well-orchestrated symphony.

My lips part, seeking something I can't fathom. His tongue slides into my mouth without hesitating, deepening the kiss until it feels like he's drinking the oxygen that's dared to enter my lungs.

I can't breathe. Can't think. Can't do anything but lie there, filled with delicious heat, letting Leighton chase away the darkness that's infected my mind. He's leaving no room for the bad thoughts.

Our tongues touch, dancing together like twin flames battling to consume the other's light. Fire is racing over my skin, setting my nerves alight, plunging me into a storm of sensation.

I have no idea what I'm doing. His hands are running over me, stroking down my body to cup my hips. Heat gathers between my thighs, stoked by the pressure of something hard pushing against me.

Breaking apart with a pained gasp, Leighton's forehead meets mine. "Jesus, Harlow. What the hell did we just do?"

"Leigh—"

"Don't say anything. This is my fault."

He stares down at me with such regret, I feel like I've been stamped on. My eyes shutter, recoiling from the sting of rejection.

"No!" He panics, grabbing my chin to pull my eyes back up to his. "I didn't mean it like that. I've wanted to kiss you for weeks."

"You… have?"

Noses brushing, his lips whisper over mine again. "Yeah. That's why I'm apologising. You don't need me fucking things up for you."

Gasping for each pained breath, I feel the tingle of my extremities. I'm back. My brain is determined to drown me, kicking and screaming, but he's brought me back to life.

"Please, Leigh." My voice is a raw rasp. "Kiss me again."

"What?"

I do the only thing I can to remain in control. My lips seek his out, harder and faster. I want to taste him again, feel our souls brush against each other in a passionate waltz.

I've never felt anything like the electrical current running beneath my skin right now. It's powerful, obliterating any doubt or fear in my mind. I don't want distance between us.

I need Leighton to hold me in this world, before I lose myself permanently. He's the only thing that's broken through the icy lake of my isolation. I can't do it alone. The voices are still there.

My cream sweater rides up as his hips press into me, rocking slightly. Each brush feels like a lightning bolt. I'm not naive; my harrowing past taught me the basics.

I know that he wants me, his body tells me enough. The thought of it sends fingertips of anxiety across my scalp, intermingling with the screams of countless bad memories.

But this isn't Pastor Michaels.

It's just… Leighton.

Sweet, loving Leighton. He would never hurt me… would he? There are shadows within him, carefully concealed behind a playful smirk. I've seen them. I want to trust him, but life has taught me to be wiser.

The whispers of doubt are eviscerated when his hand sneaks beneath my sweater, stroking over the slope of my exposed skin. His touch is magnetic, stealing my whole attention.

Teeth nipping my bottom lip, his hand travels higher, grazing over the lighter wrapping that I've recently swapped in to help my healing ribs. When his thumb caresses the underside of my breast, I can't help but whimper.

He's going to touch me there. I can feel my nipples stiffening into hard peaks. His index finger travels lower, down the slope of my stomach, and halts as it reaches a solid ridge.

My scars.

He can't see them.

I push him away, gulping down air as he hovers above me. His eyes are hooded with desire, pupils blown wide.

"Did I go too far?" he murmurs.

I attempt to catch my breath. "No… I just, well, the others will be home soon. We should… um, stop."

Leighton sighs, his head landing on my chest. "You're right. They'll fucking kill me if they knew we were… ahem, doing this."

"This?" I repeat with a tiny smile.

He breathes against my collarbones. "This. I don't have any fancier words right now."

Stupidly, we both burst into laughter. We're surrounded by mess, his hands look like he tried to pet a rabid kitten, and I've been choked half to death. This entire thing is an almighty chaos.

Rolling off me, Leighton offers a hand. I let him ease me up until we're both kneeling, staring at the other with curiosity.

"What does this mean?" I bite my lip.

His eyes are focused on my neck. It will bruise, I'm sure of it. My throat still feels sore. I can't believe he had to resort to that.

"You scared me," Leighton admits in a soft voice.

"I scared myself."

"My cellmate in prison used to have panic attacks. I could hardly reason with him when it happened. Sometimes, he'd lash out and start a fight. It was the only thing that made sense to him."

Leighton startles, seeming to realise what he's revealed. I take his hand and intertwine our fingers.

"Enzo told me about your prison sentence."

The fear on his face increases. "Of course, he did."

"Not the full story, don't worry. Just that you served time and came out recently. You can talk to me, if you want."

Shaking his head, Leighton stands and slides his hands under my arms to pull me up. Neither of us knows how to approach the madness that just unfolded, so we begin to clean up in silence.

I'm rinsing off a chopping board with one hand when he stops behind me, depositing several more dishes to be cleaned next. His breath is hot against my ear.

"Does that happen often?" he asks.

"What?"

"These… attacks. Losing yourself like that."

Gulping, I focus on washing the soapsuds from the board. "More than the others realise. I usually find my own way back."

"How?"

I clamp down on the sudden desire within me that wants to be honest. He deserves that much, but I can't admit it. The growing bald patch beneath my thick mane of hair is a dirty secret.

"I don't know. I just do."

The crash of the front door opening startles us both. Leighton leaps away from me, and I immediately mourn his body heat.

"Anyone home?"

"In here," Leighton calls back.

Striding into the kitchen, Hunter carries his charcoal suit jacket over one shoulder, ripping his blue tie off with his spare hand. My mouth goes dry at the sight.

Whatever Leighton's stirred in me... that hungry, wanton creature is refusing to return to her sinful locker. Hunter's tattoos are peeking out of his shirt, hinting at the beauty beneath.

"What are you two doing?" he asks suspiciously.

Leighton shrugs, his lips sealed tight.

"Ruining dinner," I blurt.

Hunter laughs. It's a deep, throaty sound that scares the living daylights out of me. I can't believe what I'm hearing. Leighton looks equally unnerved as we exchange glances.

"You tried to cook?" Hunter chuckles.

Leighton glares at him. "I was feeling optimistic. I'm not that bad, jeez. You ate enough of my grilled cheese growing up."

"We're lucky the house didn't burn down. And for the record, your grilled cheese sucked. I was usually too hungover to care."

"Sucked?" he repeats in outrage.

Hunter snorts as he deposits his jacket. "Just order takeout. We have enough problems without getting food poisoning."

Leighton claps his hands together and perches at the kitchen island while scrolling on his phone. He gives me a pointed look, trying hard not to smile. I drop his gaze before I embarrass myself.

Hunter definitely doesn't need to know what we were doing. I'm still not certain he isn't going to kick me out soon, and if he knows I've been kissing his brother, we're all in for a battering.

"How was work?" I ask awkwardly.

Fiddling with his hearing aid, Hunter seems apprehensive. When the tension reaches breaking point, he finally stops avoiding me.

"You're going to find out soon enough anyway." He folds his arms while sighing. "We've been passed a missing person's report. Could be nothing, but we're looking into it."

My entire body goes cold. "What? Is it him?"

"We don't know. She's younger than the other victims and comes from an affluent family. It seems a bit out of character."

"Where?"

Hunter studies me for a moment. "A university campus in Leeds. She was walking home from a late lecture and took a shortcut. We can't see past the CCTV blind spot."

"A student on campus?" Leighton chips in. "Doesn't sound like the same MO. This asshole wouldn't risk getting caught like that."

"I agree," Hunter answers, twisting the tie in his hands. "The whole country is on edge. The police could be jumping to conclusions."

Flicking off the tap, I attempt to dry the chopping board with one hand, but end up dropping it. Hunter plucks it from the air with ease, his frown trained on me.

"You don't need to worry about this, Harlow. We're only investigating as a precaution. I still think the suspect is in hiding. Losing you has spooked him for the time being."

Helping himself to a beer from the fridge, Hunter removes the cap with his teeth, taking several large gulps.

"Is Enzo eating?" Leighton hums from his phone.

"He's working late on some stuff. Order enough, we can set it aside for later on."

"Gotcha. Credit card, big bro."

"In my coat," Hunter grumbles under his breath.

Leighton leaves us in tense silence. I can tell Hunter is watching me again, even as I hide behind a curtain of hair.

"We need to go somewhere this weekend," he says abruptly. "It's a… uh, work thing. Need your help with something."

"M-Me?" I double-check.

"It's nothing to worry about. I'll explain more on Saturday."

Without another word, Hunter brushes past Leighton on his way back in and disappears upstairs. I stare after him, unsure what has pissed off our resident hurricane so bad.

One minute he's almost smiling, the next he can hardly look at me as he drops these bombshells. His hot and cold attitude is exhausting.

"Keep thinking so hard and your head will explode," Leighton comments, pocketing his phone. "Ignore Mr Happy. He needs to cool off after work."

"I think that was Hunter's head exploding, actually."

Leighton chokes on a laugh. "Believe it or not, Hunter does give a shit. That was as good as it gets with him. Takeout and a lecture."

We return to the den while we wait for the food to arrive. I can hear Hunter's footsteps as he slips downstairs into the gym before the boom of loud music echoes through the floor. He's clearly got stuff on his mind tonight.

We're halfway through *Friends* and watch several more episodes over cartons of noodles and Chinese chicken that Leighton fetches from outside the gate. Hunter's plate sits untouched.

"They were obviously on a break," he yells around a huge mouthful of food. "This is such bullshit."

I jab an elbow into his ribs. "You're the one that's full of shit, Leighton Rodriguez. That is not an excuse for Ross's behaviour."

"Woah!" He almost chokes on a noodle. "Potty mouth, Goldilocks. You spend too much time with me. I'm corrupting you."

"At least we know who's to blame."

"Go and wash your mouth out already."

Despite his teasing tone, I fall silent, struggling with the intense urge to do exactly as he asks. Pastor Michaels made me swallow soap once. I yelled obscenities at him that Adelaide taught me, the pair of us giggling in the dark.

"Harlow? Am I losing you again?"

Covering my eyes, I try to force the bloody images from my mind. She screamed so loud, sometimes at night I can still hear it. I can hear all of them, every last girl that bled out in that freezing wasteland.

"Open your eyes, beautiful."

"I… n-need a m-minute."

Leighton's fingers wrap around my wrist. "I'm here with you, okay? I'm not going anywhere. You're not alone this time."

His breath tickles me, laced with the scent of the beer he finished and the familiar citrusy scent clinging to his sweats and t-shirt. I drink in the reassurance.

"You're home, Harlow. Not there, home." Leighton tucks a piece of hair behind my ear. "No one here is going to hurt you."

"What if I deserve it?"

"Don't make me call bullshit again."

When I feel calm enough to open my eyes, his signature smile is in place. Leighton settles back, but this time, he beckons for me to join him. I deliberate for a second before crawling across the sofa.

He's grinning from ear to ear as I end up curled against his side, my ear resting over his pounding heartbeat.

"Eat up," he orders, banding an arm around me. "No more yelling at Ross. We all know Rachel will forgive him."

"If she does, she's a moron."

"I'm loving his newfound sharp tongue of yours, mystery girl."

"Well, don't get used to it."

Leighton's chest rumbles with a contented noise. "I think I already am."

He refocuses on the TV screen, scarfing down great mouthfuls of food, but I set mine aside. I'm glad he can't see inside my head. No one else needs to know that we're not alone in here. The ghosts are never far away.

In the corner, spilling blood and decaying skin across the hardwood floors, Laura waits in my traumatised imagination. The blood drains from my face as she raises a single finger.

It's pointed straight at me.

The person who killed her.

CHAPTER 18

Enzo

Midnight Demon Club - Highly Suspect

Splashing my face in the bathroom sink, I savour the cool shock of water. My eyes are gritty and sore from another sleepless night. That's three in a row, and I'm paying the price.

No amount of cold showers or triple-shot coffees can compete against the smothering grasp of exhaustion. I tried to run last night to wear myself out, but it did nothing to quell my anxiety.

I've been restless ever since Harlow's DNA results came in. Keeping them from her feels wrong after all she's been through, but we have to play this right. I want to research her family first.

We can't gamble with her safety.

Nobody can be trusted right now.

Scraping back my messy, black hair, I leave the bathroom and return to Hunter's office. Tea and coffee have been set up for our meeting, and Theo's already downing his third cup.

He doesn't bother looking up from his laptop as I help myself to more caffeine. This little ray of sunshine has been my constant company this week as we deal with the aftermath of that damned DNA report.

"Where's Hunter?" I rub my eyes again.

"On his way in, I presume," he answers absently. "I'm not his fucking keeper, Enz."

"You're particularly cheery today."

Theo's ice-cold blue eyes meet mine. His scruff of blonde ringlets hangs across his face, messy and tousled. There's a ramen stain on his chest, and his clothes are heavily slept in. We're a mess.

"I have barely slept for weeks." Theo's gaze hardens. "We've had the whole intelligence team assigned to Harlow's case, and I've got three team members off with the flu. Leave me alone."

Sitting down, I take a swig of coffee. "Have you tried yoga? Meditation? Bit of Pilates? Gotta work out that frustration somehow, man. I can't have you hulking out on me."

"Fuck you," he mutters darkly.

"Hard pass. Your sparkling company is enough."

Glaring daggers at his laptop screen, Theo ignores me completely. This is the most time we've spent together in years. I wish it was under better circumstances, but there's nothing like a tragedy to bring a team together.

"You should come home and sleep in a real bed," I add more seriously. "Eat a hot meal, take a day off. Your room is still there. Untouched."

"I'm fine," Theo insists, his eyelids drooping.

"How much longer is this going to go on?"

"I'm the only one qualified to operate the drones scouting for abandoned churches. I can't take a day off."

"You know full well that Kade got his licence two years ago. Don't give me that shit."

"He's busy."

"Braiding Brooklyn's fucking hair and playing happy families?" I snort, swigging more coffee. "Give it up already."

"I am home," Theo snaps. "This is it, right here. The house has nothing but bad memories and people I have no interest in seeing."

The truth is a bitter pill to swallow. I stare into the depths of my black coffee, trying to remember a time when Theo last smiled.

"Including me?" I ask pointedly.

The harsh bark of my voice causes him to wince. I'm so sick of being treated like a stranger by someone I once considered my brother. This has gone on for too long.

We've fought together. Lost together. Grieved together. Does our history mean nothing to him? He abandoned the family we spilled blood to protect.

"This isn't what Alyssa would've wanted," I add, too tired to dance around it any longer. "You know that."

"How would I know that?" He slams a hand down. "She's dead, Enz. Alyssa can't give a fuck about us anymore. She's gone."

"You have to let go. We can't live in the past." My voice catches. "It won't bring her back to us."

"I'll do whatever the hell I want."

"And how's that working for you?"

"Better than this crappy act you're all putting on," he lashes out. "It's pathetic. Did you even care about her at all?"

"Enough!"

Hunter's furious growl stops us both as he strides into the office. He looks rested, his clothes clean and ironed. Fucking asshole.

"What are you two doing?" he demands, pouring himself the world's largest cup of tea. "Bickering like children when we have more important matters to discuss. What's gotten into you?"

I jab a finger at him. "Don't act all clueless, Hunt. We've been sat in this office for days, doing all the goddamn legwork."

"Leave it," Theo mumbles. "It's not worth it."

"No, I won't. He needs to take some responsibility for the state you're in, Theo."

"If you have a problem, tell me." Hunter levels me a glare over his cup. "We're all adults here. I can't run a business if the pair of you aren't on point."

Slamming his laptop shut, Theo stands and attempts to leave the room. Hunter grabs his shoulder before he can flee, as he always does.

"Where do you think you're going? We have work to do."

Theo grits his teeth. "I'm leaving."

"This is your department." Hunter gestures around the office. "Look how far we've come. We finally have leads."

"Leads?" Theo scoffs. "Fucking leads? We have nothing! An office full of dead girls and a traumatised witness with no memories. This case has taken everything out of us."

Pausing, Hunter looks at him. Actually looks. Not a cursory glance, or his usual emotionless dismissal. Theo stares back—drained, exhausted and at the end of his tether.

"We can't let Harlow down," Hunter says, shocking the hell out of me. "She needs us to catch these bastards. I won't break my promise."

Theo deflates. "I want to help her, Hunt. I really do. But we need more time, more resources. Hell, more evidence. This dickhead is a ghost. He's too good."

"More evidence? A girl is missing! We have eighteen dead bodies and firsthand fucking testimony. What more do you want?"

"I want my family back!" he explodes.

Grabbing fistfuls of Hunter's shirt, Theo's inches from his face. I don't step in. He needs to work through this, once and for all.

"We never left." Hunter pushes the hands off his shirt. "You're the one that checked out, Theo. Your family has always been here."

Gutted and alone, Theo looks around the room. Months of reconnaissance, gathering evidence, working himself to the bone. Harlow doesn't know it, but Theo has done most of the work here. This case has consumed his life.

He's been obsessed with finding the killer, even before we met her. Harlow doesn't even know this man, not really, but he's been fighting her corner since day one, and he's taken no recognition for all his hard work.

"I can't do this anymore." Theo backtracks, hugging his laptop close. "Tell Harlow I'm sorry."

"What does that mean?" Hunter snarls.

I approach them both. "Talk to us, Theo."

"No more talking. You're right. I'm not part of your family, not anymore. You're better without me."

"You are our family," Hunter insists. "That's not what I meant, and you know it. We're going nowhere."

"My family died along with Alyssa." Theo shakes his head. "It's never coming back. I can't stay here for a second longer, trying to fill that void."

"Don't do this," I plead with him.

He can barely look at me. "You told me to stop pretending like I'm okay. You got your wish. I am not okay."

Hunter's expression turns thunderous as he loses patience. "Walk out that door and we're done. That's it."

"Hunter!" I shout at him. "He's trying to ask for help, for fuck's sake. Don't be such a wanker."

Theo snorts, his eyes red. "He doesn't care about us, Enz. He never did. We've bled for this company. Suffered for it, time and time again. Where's the appreciation?"

"You're the one threatening to walk," Hunter supplies.

"Because I'm sick of being a stranger in my own goddamn life!" Theo yells. "You know what? Have it your way. Good luck with the investigation."

Before storming out, he stops and looks at his work laptop. It's an extension of him at this point, a physical manifestation of his brilliant mind. His tech gives him comfort in a cold, cruel world.

Theo drops it on the console so hard, it rattles several framed photographs that Hunter keeps displayed. One of them holds our last picture together. The people we used to be.

Alyssa is in the middle of us, grinning like a maniac. She was so beautiful, confident and sassy, with an acid tongue that kept us all in line. Everything about her was incredible.

Our relationship wasn't normal, not by a long stretch. We fell into sharing her by accident, swept up in the tornado of desire and first love that sucked us all into its destructive path. We loved her so fucking much.

"No," I croak, as the frame wobbles.

Falling from the console, the sound of glass smashing fills the suffocating silence. Pain rolls over Theo's face, matching the blast of agony tearing me up inside.

That was the last photo we dared to display of her. The others were boxed up along with her stuff, tucked into a quiet corner of the attic where none of us could stumble upon them again.

Leaving us with nothing but our memories and grief, Theo storms from the office without stopping. Both of us stare, open-mouthed. Part of me believes he'll come back.

He doesn't.

Theo is gone.

Striding over to the window, Hunter braces his hands on the glass, his head lowered in defeat. I leave him be and kneel beside the mess that Theo left behind.

The frame is ruined, and I slide the photo from it, making myself look at the memory in my hands. Alyssa's arms are wrapped around Theo's neck, her pink hair stirring in the breeze.

His lips are pressed against her cheek, while Hunter stares down at them with a look of happiness. I'm cuddling her from behind, content to share my soulmate with the people I loved most in the world.

My two brothers.

My best fucking friends.

The four of us were a messy, imperfect family, but we made it work. She brought life out in Hunter's weary soul, forced Theo from his anxious shell and quieted my mind enough for me to sleep.

"I'm sorry, Lys," I whisper to her memory. "We've fucked everything up. You'd kick all of our asses."

Her eyes stare back at me, radiating love and acceptance. She didn't give a damn about our sharp edges, the quirks and flaws that made us ruthless enough to run a company like Sabre.

Alyssa was our partner. The glue that bound us together, making us equals. Without her... we're nothing. Like Theo, I've been filling the void with whatever I could to survive.

"Theo will come back."

"I highly doubt it," Hunter replies from the window.

"He didn't mean what he said."

"Yeah, Enz. He did."

Placing the photograph on the console, I make it to the conference table and collapse into an empty chair. Hunter's gaze is fixed on the heavy rain clouds outside.

"I should go after him," I finally say.

"Don't." His forehead rests against the glass. "I'm not going to force him to stay. This is his decision. We have to respect it."

"This isn't right."

"Nothing is right anymore," he snaps, turning to face me. "Nothing has been right for a very long time. The one good thing in our lives right now… and we have to give her up."

I stare at him, disbelieving. "Wait, Harlow?"

"You know who I'm talking about, alright? I won't say it again."

"Jesus. You need to get over yourself."

Scoffing, he fists his long hair. "You think I don't know that? Goddammit, Enz. We all figured out our own ways to survive."

Sighing, I walk over to him, throwing an arm around his tense shoulders. We face the sprawling expanse of London together.

"We have to do this, Hunt. Harlow has a whole other life that she knows nothing about."

"What if it breaks her?" he asks, biting his lip. "All that time she spent suffering and being tortured… she has no idea that those monsters weren't her real parents."

"We will keep her safe, even from herself."

"Just like that?"

"Just like that." I squeeze his shoulders. "We can win this fight. The answers are there. We just have to find them."

Hunter watches the flash of ambulance lights passing on the busy road below us. Several police cars follow, parting the morning traffic.

"You want to reopen her old case," he guesses.

"Nobody gets kidnapped without someone noticing. It's been thirteen years, things have changed."

Considering, he nods. "We can recall the evidence, maybe get in touch with the old investigators. See what they missed."

"We already have the evidence here."

"What?" Hunter frowns at me.

"Theo told me he got the team to collect it a few weeks ago. The boxes are in storage, waiting for us."

He looks mildly stunned. It would be entertaining if we weren't a man down and left to pick up the pieces he left behind.

"Why?" Hunter wonders aloud.

"Fuck knows what goes on in Theo's mind. Come on." I clap him on the shoulder. "Let's lay it out and see what we've got."

Waving off several offers of help, we retrieve the evidence boxes from the locked storeroom down the corridor and bring them back to the office. They fill almost half the table.

It must've taken Theo countless nights to organise all this paperwork, trawling through old police files and filing the important stuff. We didn't even request this. He's done it all himself. It's further proof of how much he really cares.

"That her?" Hunter asks grimly.

I pick up a photograph and nod. The brown-haired, blue-eyed angel staring back at me doesn't look like the woman I know. There's a lightness to her, shining through a wide, toothy grin.

The person I know is hollow-eyed, empty at times, but a golden thread still runs through Harlow. Defiance steels her spine and sass rolls off her sharp tongue without her realising.

She's changing, growing, becoming more comfortable with challenging us and questioning the world around her. Freedom has given Harlow her life back.

"Leticia Kensington," I read, the name still sounding wrong. "This corresponds with the report from forensics. We pulled her school records too."

"That place was a disgrace. How on earth was she allowed to walk home alone when Giana Kensington was running late?"

"You know how it is." Swapping papers, I scan over an evidence log. "Underfunded state school, disillusioned staff. No one gives a fuck when the bell rings and they get to say goodbye to the little shits."

Hunter shakes his head with a chuckle. "Not feeling paternal, Enz? I figured you'd want your own little shit one day."

"We have a Leighton. That's enough."

"I say we put him up for adoption."

Opening another ring binder, Hunter checks the details we've nailed down so far. Our list of information is sparse at best.

"Leticia's been missing for thirteen years and was presumed dead after a year-long investigation turned up no leads." He drops the file with a sigh. "Classic cold case. No evidence, no witnesses."

"Another CCTV blind spot?"

"They lived in a shitty area. Rural, poverty-stricken. No infrastructure or spots for surveillance footage. Looks like she cut across a farmer's field to get home."

We pour more hot drinks, gulping them down in silence. Being surrounded by fragments of Harlow's life is surreal. It feels wrong to have access to all this information while she sits at home, none the wiser.

"Hang on." Hunter snatches up a printed report. "Harlow's family sued the school and won fifty grand in damages."

"Fifty grand?" I repeat.

"Negligence, open and shut case. The school was shut down by the council."

"That's a lot of money."

Hunter nods. "Looks like Theo got a hit on the prison system. Harlow's father was convicted for identity fraud. He went to prison and Giana got all the money."

"Jesus fuck."

"Funnily enough, she didn't mention it."

"Wait, you've spoken to Giana?" I snarl at him.

"I had to break the news. The media are determined to uncover Harlow's identity. I didn't want her to hear from anyone but us."

"Hunt!" I smash a fist against the table. "We have no idea who the fuck these people are. I don't trust them. You shouldn't have just told her that Harlow's alive."

"She's her mother," Hunter defends.

"I don't give a rat's ass who Giana is. We have to keep Harlow safe, even if that means keeping her family from her until we know more. Goddammit."

His eyes narrow. "If Giana found this out from anyone but us, our reputation would have been shattered. She could sue our stupid asses for keeping her daughter from her."

"Reputation, again? Do you care about anything else?"

"Of course, I do," he snaps angrily. "But someone has to think about the bigger picture. You're incapable of being impartial."

"Yeah, well, fuck you too."

Throwing my handful of papers down, I step outside to take some calming breaths. Hunter is the most infuriating, cold-hearted bastard at times. Even if everything he does is for the good of our family. His constant need for logic and order drives me up the wall.

But we're all under pressure.

I can't afford to break like Theo.

Returning to the office, I sit back down and pour some more coffee. Hunter barely spares me a glance. It's rare he knows when to shut the hell up, but he doesn't break the silence first.

"What did Giana say then?" I sigh.

"She was hysterical when I broke the news. We didn't have much time to compare notes."

"We have some more information here. According to public records, she remarried six years ago."

"What about the ex-husband?"

"Oliver Kensington's location is unknown. He was released from prison after serving a seven-year sentence and dropped off the grid. Hasn't been seen since."

"Motherfucker," Hunter curses.

Unease twists in my gut. Harlow deserves the chance to have a real family, but the idea of letting these strangers anywhere near her makes me want to beat the shit out of someone. Something doesn't sit right with this narrative.

I reach for my coffee. "What now?"

"I have to take Harlow to meet her mother." Hunter crosses his arms. "Giana's been calling every hour, asking when we're coming."

"Has Richards agreed to this?"

"Hardly. You know he wouldn't approve."

"Maybe he has a point," I suggest. "We don't want to push Harlow over the edge. She doesn't remember any of this."

"What else can I do, Enz?" Hunter drops his head into his hands. "Harlow can't get better until she knows the truth."

"Then I want to be there."

"Not this time," he snips back. "I need you here now that Theo's fucked off. We still have a missing girl to find, and the intelligence team needs managing."

"Get Kade to do it."

"He's running point on the reconnaissance op in Northumberland. We have to find that damn chapel."

Frustrated, I fight the urge to bang my head against the table. The distance between here and home where we left Harlow asleep this morning is too much. This trip will be even further, and I fucking hate it.

"I won't release her from protective custody until it's safe," Hunter answers my biggest fear. "Regardless of what Giana wants."

"And if Harlow wants to be with her family?"

I can see his reluctance and conflict, no matter the pointless games he plays. Gone is the man that wanted to pack Harlow off to a safe house and never deal with her again.

He's seen what the rest of us are so desperate to protect. She's a butterfly emerging from its chrysalis, beautiful and fragile in the trauma of rebirth.

I will do anything to watch Harlow spread her wings and become the person I know she is inside. Nobody on this damned earth is going to take that pleasure away from me.

"It's our job to protect her," Hunter decides. "Whether she likes it or not, we're her home until these monsters are caught."

I nod at him from across the table. We live and die by the sword, and our family is what keeps us alive. Harlow belongs with us. She's more than a client now.

Not even Theo can walk away from us without a fight. I'll get him back, no matter what it takes. His place is here, by our side. I'm going to get him back and I know exactly the person to help.

"You good here? I need to make a phone call."

Hunter waves me away, his attention caught by another police report. I slip out of the office and into the quiet corridor, reaching a tinted window concealing London's vast horizon.

We saved a family before. Maybe they can be the ones to fix us this time around. No one is more qualified than them.

Holding the phone to my ear, I call the only person left on the planet that I trust with my innermost thoughts. She earned that privilege in a war zone, and our friendship has only grown in the tumultuous years since.

When she answers with a half-awake groan, I can't help but smile. Her voice is heavy with sleep after the team took a few days to recover from their latest assignment.

"Hey, big guy. I've been waiting for you to call me back."

"Brooke." I breathe out a sigh. "It's been a hell of a month."

"You're telling me. The news has been dragging your asses over the coals for the entire country to see every night."

"You sound like you're enjoying it."

Her laugh is exasperated. "Hardly. Kade won't tell me shit about the case. Kindly remove the stick from his ass so we can talk about work at mealtimes."

"He put that stick up there, he can take it out."

"Dammit," she growls, disturbing someone napping in the background. "I was hoping you'd put a gag order on him."

"Afraid not, wildfire. He's your mess to sort out, last time I checked."

"Fucking great. Tell me something I don't know."

"Speaking of messes… I need your help. Things have gotten a little fucked up here. Well, more than a little."

I can hear the smile in Brooklyn's voice.

"I'll be there in half an hour."

CHAPTER 19

Harlow

Bad Place – The Hunna

S taring out of the window at the twisting country lane hugging Hunter's beast of a car, I watch the empty fields melt away. We've been driving all afternoon, only stopping to fuel up and grab some late lunch.

Hunter's being even more tight-lipped than usual. He's barely spoken a word to me since we left Leighton still asleep back home. I'm not stupid. This trip isn't for fun. I have a bad feeling about wherever we're going.

"Nearly there," he mumbles.

"Where are we going?"

"Croyde is up ahead. You'll like Devon. It's nice and quiet compared to London."

"Will we see the sea?" I ask excitedly.

His chocolatey eyes slide over to me. "Yeah. I've booked us a hotel on the coast for the night."

As anxious as I am to find out what on earth we're doing here, the idea of seeing the ocean has my fingers spasming with anticipation. This is exactly the change of scenery I've been craving.

Tia loved the beach; it was her happy place. She grew up in Skegness, amongst slot machines and arcade games. Her stories were the best—summer holidays spent touring the pier's attractions.

Remembering her late-night tales whispered between bars, a muddled, dream-like memory slips into my mind. I can see it so clearly as the hum of the car engine fades into the background.

There's soft, golden sand between my little toes. The summer sun beats down on me, carried by the whip of strong, coastal winds. Saltwater washes over my skin with a slight sting, filling the bright-pink bucket I've dipped into the sea.

Where am I?

Is this place… real?

The car jolts as we hit a pothole, slamming me back down to reality. I have to suppress a gasp. The clinging embrace of my fantasy remains, taunting me with images of a place I've never seen.

I shake the cobwebs from my head. A dream—that's all it was. More and more, these disjointed images appear at random moments. I dream about places I've never seen, conversations I've never had, nonexistent relatives that cuddled me close.

None of it is real.

With Hunter's eyes focused on the road, I can turn towards the door and begin to pull at my hair. Each snapped follicle lances me with relief. More. More. The pain brings me back to the present.

My motto accompanies each sharp tug.

Just a dream.

Just a dream.

Just a dream.

"Here we are," Hunter declares, turning into a tiny town centre.

"This is Croyde. It'll be dead in the winter months."

Releasing my hair, I plaster on an award-winning smile. No one would ever know that I'm being eaten alive by doubt. At least, that's what I tell myself each day.

With the winter temperature setting in and thick, swirling clouds covering the skyline, there's nobody on the roads. We pass thatched cottages and slick cobblestone roads that rise and fall with the cliffs.

It's beautiful. Deserted and quaint, like the traditional English villages you see in movies. Hunter navigates the tight roads as we begin to descend, winding through a cluster of closed shop fronts.

"Where is everybody?"

"There's a winter storm blowing in." He glances in the rearview mirror, noting an estate car several yards back. "Not much appeal for tourists, especially this time of year."

"Do you think it will snow?"

"Possibly. It's pretty rare on the coast, but the forecast said to prepare. I'd like to get this wrapped up as fast as possible."

I bite my lip. "Why the urgency? Couldn't it wait until after the storm, whatever this thing is?"

"No." He refocuses on the road, the nerve in his neck twitching. "It couldn't wait."

Leaving the main stretch of the town, we climb a steep hill that leads to a proud, three-story building overlooking the shoreline. Peeling white paint and wide bay windows are battered by the rising wind. It looks alone, isolated on a deserted cliff.

"This is the hotel." Hunter pulls into a half-empty car park, studying the building area. "It's the best I could do."

"I like it."

He's too busy studying the road behind us, where the blue estate car has passed the turn and carried on down to the coast. Hunter seems to deflate a little.

"Everything okay?"

"Yeah," he answers. "It's nothing."

Climbing out of the car together, he grabs our overnight bags and gestures for me to go ahead. We approach the hotel, our bodies swaying in the high winds. It's even colder than it was back home.

"Go sit down." Hunter points to a plush chair in the window, half hidden by potted plants and curtains. "I'll check us in."

My leg jiggles nervously as he approaches the front desk, handing off our overnight bags to the awaiting staff. They seem slightly startled to have a guest at this time of year.

Outside, rain is beginning to fall. It's thicker, mixed with snow to form a blanket of sleet. I don't realise my feet are moving until it's too late. They carry me out into the rising storm, desperate to taste the first winter snow.

It whips my face in ice-cold lashings, cutting through the haze that accompanies every second of my days. I feel like I can breathe easier in the midst of the storm, surrendering to a force bigger than myself.

"Harlow! Get back here!"

I ignore Hunter's yelling and carry on walking towards the sound of roaring waves. I'm being pulled towards the water, dragged by a soundless chorus of whispers. Tia's living inside of me, ready to be reunited with the sea.

"Harlow, wait up." A hand snatches mine, pulling me to a halt. "We're in the middle of a fucking storm."

I push Hunter away. "I'm fine. I have to see it."

"See what?" he shouts above the wind.

My eyes are locked on the dark horizon. "The sea. She wants me to see it."

"Who?"

He curses colourfully as I take off, following the descending path that cuts into the side of the cliff. Rather than turn back, he follows, tightening his pea coat and chequered scarf around him.

"Catch a cold and you'll only have yourself to blame," Hunter smarts, but he doesn't sound angry. "Jesus, Harlow."

"I have to see it," I repeat.

"Why? What's gotten into you?"

The flash of images slices into my brain again. Sand. Water. Giggling. Ice lollies and high-pitched squeals. I need to know what it means, why this place is tugging at something buried inside of me.

"I've never been here before, and even though it's impossible, I feel like I have."

Hunter tries to grab me again, digging his heels in. "We can't do this here, sweetheart. Let's go back inside."

"No. We're so close."

Darkness is descending quickly, but the glow of streetlights marks our path down the hill. The tang of salt in the air increases until I can smell the freshness of water, tantalisingly close.

Ahead of us, the cliffs finally give way to nature's unspeakable violence. Undulating waves of grey and dark blue beat the coastline into submission, roaring so loudly, it almost deafens me.

I stop at the sand's edge, staring into inky blackness. There's no light out here, just God's raw, ephemeral beauty in the crash of waves.

"It's beautiful."

Hunter stops by my side. "And cold."

Ignoring him, I hop down onto the sand before he can protest again. The promise of water calls to me, beckoning through the loud gale. It's like the wind is screaming my name, welcoming me home.

"Harlow!" Hunter shouts.

Stopping to toe off my leather boots and socks, I sprint straight into the sea without a care for the falling snow. Freezing cold water soaks into my cuffs, burning layers of skin until my bones ache.

I'm being cleansed in fire and ice.

The sea is setting me free.

My senses feel alive for the first time in years. Sloshing my bare feet around, I marvel at the touch of stones beneath the water. Their sharp corners cut into me, breaking through the numbness.

Wild wind sears my cheeks, whipping strands of hair out from my beanie. The taste of salt and ozone from the arriving storm are welcome reminders of nature's callous touch.

Splashing marks Hunter's arrival in the water. I spin around to find him sloshing closer towards me, his tailored charcoal trousers getting soaked. He doesn't look mad, somehow.

"Mind if I join you?"

I gesture around the deserted beach. "We have the place to ourselves."

Standing together in the darkness, shoulder to shoulder, we're both shivering all over. The storm clouds roll ever closer, begging to unleash their destructive force.

"Do you recognise this place?" Hunter shuffles closer to take my frozen hand.

It feels so natural to curl our fingers together. He's the single source of gravity in this lawless place. We could drown in the tide, but I know he'd still save me.

Not even God could avoid Hunter's wrath. He wouldn't allow me to die without his signed approval, and even then, I'd be beholden to his rules and regulations.

"Yes," I admit, catching wet snow on my tongue. "I've been here before. I know I have. Why did you bring me?"

His grip tightens. "I have a story to tell you, Harlow. It isn't a pleasant one, but you need to hear it regardless."

It feels like we're the last two people alive out here—trapped in a bubble of cold air and secrets, far from the chaos of criminal investigations and obligations.

And still, the past clings.

"I'm scared," I make myself admit.

Grasping my chin, Hunter raises my eyes to his. They look black in the darkness of the storm, but warmer than ever before. Emotion stares back at me for the first time.

"I know you are, sweetheart." His thumb strokes over my parted lips. "Come inside. Please."

Nodding, I let him tow me back to shore. The cold sinks deep into my core as we hobble back up the sand in sodden clothes. Relentless wind bruises us, angry and out of control, until we reach the hotel.

"You should warm up," Hunter worries, still holding me close. "I think I saw a fire in the bar area."

We pass the reception staff's gaping stares, dripping water through clusters of chairs and tables. Firelight fills the quiet bar, with only a small handful of people sipping wine and talking in low whispers.

"Want a drink?" Hunter asks.

I slide into a plaid armchair next to the open fireplace. "Do I need one to hear this?"

He hesitates. "Yes."

"Then I'll have a drink."

Disappearing and returning with two glasses, he takes the seat next to me. I eye the measure of dark-amber liquid.

"What is it?"

Hunter takes a mouthful, wincing slightly at the burn. "Try it and find out. Go easy, though."

"Am I even allowed to drink?"

"You're an adult. Decide for yourself."

Hunter watches as I take a sip, letting the fiery mouthful slip down my throat and warm my belly. It tastes awful, but I kinda like it.

"I didn't think you'd actually do it."

I cough and manage another mouthful. "People can surprise you. I'm not a kid you have to look after."

"I'm aware."

"So talk to me like an adult."

Sitting back in my armchair, I stare straight into Hunter's perceptive orbs. He holds my gaze without attempting to hide it.

"You have been here before," he reveals.

I take another sip of liquor, despite feeling sick at his words. Deep down, it isn't a surprise. I've felt the impending doom for a while now.

"When?"

The fire dapples light across his symmetrical features. "When you were a child. Your name isn't Harlow Michaels."

The bar falls away until it's just us, stargazers chasing the next meteor shower, now caught in the path of imminent destruction.

"Pastor and Mrs Michaels aren't your parents. They don't actually exist. Those are pseudonyms your kidnappers chose."

My heart shatters against my ribcage. "So, I don't exist?"

"Your name was Leticia Kensington. Who you choose to be now is up to you." His brows are furrowed. "Harlow is the name they gave you when you were taken from your family, thirteen years ago."

All I can do is stare blankly as my entire world burns to ashes around me. I should feel something, anything, but my body is numb. I can't find it in me to shed a single tear.

"It was all a lie," I say in a dead voice.

"I'm sorry, Harlow."

From the pocket of his wet coat, Hunter retrieves a white envelope. He hesitates before pulling out a small stack of photographs and placing them on my trembling leg.

"Leticia loved to draw," he says quietly. "She was a keen reader, well above her age range. Her mum had to ban her from staying up late, hiding under her duvet with a torch and a book."

He turns the first photograph over. Two adults stand on a beach not unlike the one we just found, a wrapped-up toddler swinging between them.

"She enjoyed playing on the beach," he continues, his irises poisoned by emotion. "Her grandma lived nearby. She'd take Leticia to feed the seagulls and get ice cream, even in the winter."

The next photograph shows a wizened, silver-haired woman with a little girl bouncing on her knee. Her loving smile strikes the killer blow.

"I know her." I pick it up and run a finger over her face. "She smelled like gingerbread biscuits and loose-leaf tea."

When I found the courage to look in the mirror a couple of weeks ago, it was hard to face the grief staring back at me in hollow-eyed brutality. The little girl cuddling her grandmother is still me, but younger, healthier.

"Why now?" I choke out.

He clasps my shaking leg. "We've found your real mum. You're not related to those monsters, and you never were."

I swallow my remaining drink in three quick gulps. It doesn't help the rising magma of rage seeping into my veins.

"Did she even look for me?"

Hunter rubs the back of his neck. "The police investigation fizzled out. Not enough evidence or resources."

"So the police gave up. Did she do the same?"

"Harlow, it isn't that simple."

I throw his hand aside. "Isn't it? Where is she, Hunter? What has my mother spent the last thirteen years doing?"

"She remarried," he admits. "Your dad went to prison for identity fraud and Giana met someone new. They have a five-year-old son."

Standing up in a rush, I'm still holding the empty glass. Hunter doesn't even flinch as it smashes into the exposed brick of the fireplace, sending shards flying into the air.

It isn't enough to calm me down. I want to break every single piece of furniture here, over and over again. My knees are knocking together with the strength of emotion pulsing through me.

"Upstairs." Hunter grabs me by the elbow, waving off the startled shouts of outraged bar staff. "Put it on my room bill, alright?"

"Let go of me," I growl, attempting to escape him.

"Not another fucking word," he orders.

Strong-arming me past the gossiping staff, I'm pushed into the awaiting elevator outside the bar. His painful grip on my elbow doesn't relent until we reach the second floor and find our room.

"We need to keep a low profile," he hisses in my ear. "I know you're upset, but it isn't safe to make a scene in front of people."

"Get your hands off me!"

He manages to scan the key card to unlock the door. "I said I'd keep you safe. Let me do my goddamn job."

"Because that's all I am, right? A job."

The insecurity slips out before I can clamp my mouth shut. Hurt spreads across Hunter's face, and it feels so good. I don't want to be the only one suffering. He should feel it too.

Inside the room, our overnight bags await on a double bed. I stare at it, every inch of me shaking with fury.

"Do you often share beds with your clients?"

He storms past me to inspect the mini bar. "It's obviously a mistake. You need to calm down."

"Calm down? I just found out my entire life is a lie, I've forgotten the only family I ever had and my mum wasted no time replacing me. Don't tell me to calm down."

Slamming the tiny fridge shut, Hunter rounds on me. He doesn't even look mad, more like weary with the world.

"You're hurting," he deadpans. "If you need to take it out on me, that's fine. But if you don't lower your voice, someone will come knocking."

Marching up to him, I grab a handful of his still-damp shirt. Deep down, I know that none of this is his fault. He's delivering the news that I'm sure they've long suspected.

I knew something was coming. I've had all these weeks to prepare, knowing that my life was going to be blown up when the pieces fell together, but it's done nothing to lessen the all-consuming pain.

"When Pastor Michaels was angry, he hurt others." I breathe in his familiar spicy scent. "I want to hurt you right now."

"If that's what you need to do, go ahead."

"Why?" I almost sob.

Reaching out to cup my cheek, Hunter closes the small space left between us. His chest is pressed against my breasts, and the tips of our noses touch. I can't move a single inch.

"Because I'm not a good person," he rasps. "I've dedicated my life to helping people, but it doesn't cancel out all the pain I've inflicted."

"I… I don't believe that."

"It's true." His eyes bore into me, intense and relentless. "In twelve years, I've killed two hundred and fifteen people. Bombings, assassinations, executions. Sabre benefitted from every kill."

I can taste his torment. It wraps around me, a familiar blanket of anguish, matching the festering pit of darkness where my heart used to be.

"I counted them all," Hunter whispers. "Every last one. Names, faces, dates. I won't let myself forget how we got here."

Releasing his shirt, I slip my fingers inside his open collar, stroking the tendrils of dark ink rising from his torso.

"Why do you count them?"

"Because the day I stop caring, I become a monster." He releases a long-held breath. "That's who I save people like you from. And it's exactly who I should've saved Alyssa from."

"Alyssa?" I repeat cluelessly.

His eyes squeeze shut. "The last woman I loved died in my fucking arms. She bled out, and I couldn't do a thing to stop it."

Someone, as Enzo said. She has a name, after all—the one who left such a gaping hole in their hearts.

"Is she why you can't stand to be around me?"

Hunter looks like I've slapped him. "What on earth are you talking about? Harlow, fuck. Why do you think I'm here?"

"To do your job?"

He starts to walk me backwards until my legs hit the bed. Hunter pushes me back onto the mattress and covers my body with his. Any signs of hesitation have evaporated.

"I have wanted to touch you since the moment I laid eyes on you," he says with fire. "Every time Leighton made you smile, or Enzo held your hand, I wanted to put a bullet in their skulls and take their place."

His hips pin me to the bed, pressing into me in a slow, seductive grind. Each movement causes these stupid little whimpers to escape my mouth. I feel like I'm on fire.

"Tell me to stop," he pleads.

Brushing loose hair from his face, I smash my mouth against his instead. Hunter's lips part, moving in a feverish dance. He doesn't run or plaster on a mask like every other time I've imagined this.

I'm trapped in a hurricane of calculation and precision, surrendering to Hunter's will. His lips are like fists beating me black and blue. I can't run from the onslaught, and I don't want to.

My legs slide open without being told, letting him settle between them. The new position causes a throbbing pressure to explode in the slick space between my thighs.

I can feel his hardness pushing against me, hot and demanding. The fear I thought I'd feel isn't there. After all I've learned, and with the terror of what's to come, I want to mean something to someone. Even if it's just for a moment.

"Fuck, Harlow," he breaks the kiss to gasp. "We can't do this right now. You're not ready."

"Please," I moan, writhing on the bed.

"Shhh." He kisses along my jawline, throat, clavicle. "I'll make you feel good. Just not that."

Hovering over me, he unbuttons his shirt and tosses it aside. I drink in the hard planes of his chest—defined pectorals, a fuzz of light-brown hair covering the gorgeous ink I glimpsed before.

"This wasn't how I expected this conversation to go."

"Hunt," I whine. "I don't want to think about that right now. Or ever again. Just... make me forget. Please."

He strips off his trousers, leaving only a skin-tight pair of black boxers. His legs are powerful, tanned, and my eyes bulge at the lump straining to escape its fabric prison between them.

"Eyes up here," he scolds, flexing countless rippling muscles. "If I make you uncomfortable, tell me to stop. Promise?"

Nodding fast, I bite my lip as his hand sneaks beneath my sweater. My breasts are small enough that I don't have to wear a bra, and the moment he realises, his throat bobs.

"Answer me," he demands, his fingers wrapping around a hardened nipple. "I want to hear you say it."

"Promise," I moan in pleasure.

Kneading my breast with one hand, he traces the seam of my jeans, reaching the button. My pulse skips as he unzips them and begins to ease the fabric over my hips.

That's when I freak out.

Bolting upright so fast, I gasp at the pain lancing through my ribs, I shove his hands away from me. Terror is constricting my lungs.

"I can't… I…"

"Shit," Hunter curses, his face pale. "This was a bad idea."

"No!" I rush to explain. "It's not you. I… well, it's hard to explain. I don't want to scare you with what's underneath."

Hunter rolls onto his side and tugs me against his chest. I nuzzle into his neck, revelling in the closeness I've wanted for so long. If he sees my scars, he'll run away screaming. That would kill me.

"Harlow, I know what's underneath."

My head snaps up. "What?"

"The police took pictures while you were unconscious in the hospital. I saw everything before we even met."

Clinging shame settles over me. I feel physically sick. Shuddering, I try to pull away, but his arms band around me.

"Don't you dare hide from me. I won't take that shit. You have nothing at all to be ashamed of."

Stupid, embarrassed tears begin to roll down my cheeks. I can't believe he's seen the real me, and yet, he's still here. Any sane person would've run away screaming by now.

"I look disgusting," I whisper through my tears. "The scars… they're everywhere. I don't want you to see me like that."

Hunter holds me tight and starts kissing the tears away, one at a time. Not a single droplet escapes his attention.

"Let me see," he murmurs.

"You don't want to do that."

"Yeah, I do."

I'm desperate to feel whole again. All I want is a moment, a glimpse. I can settle for being someone else tonight. A person worthy of his care and attention.

Gently unfastening the Velcro sling holding my plastered arm in place, he sets it aside and kisses my fingertips, halting at the edge of my cast. The sweater is pulled off, inch by inch, as I hold my breath. He won't let me cower or hide, holding eye contact the whole time.

My jeans are stripped off next, unveiling every gnarly inch of skin I'm so desperate to hide. I lie there in my plain white panties, wearing a mosaic of bruises across my ribs. The doctor said I could stop using the wrap now.

I know what I look like.

It's an ugly sight.

Intricate scarring covers most of my thin torso. Scars stretch down from the underside of my breasts, over my ribcage, and across the entirety of my stomach.

It begins with a perfect circle above my belly button, sliced deep enough to leave horrendous marks, even now. The knife lines branch out into three curved domes, connected by a central triangle.

The Holy Trinity.

Father, Son, and Holy Spirit.

I should have died that night. It was before Pastor Michaels perfected his ritual. He came at me in a state of animalistic blood lust, tired of coaxing my compliance with scraps of food and beatings.

The knife cuts are so deep, I can't feel anything over some patches of skin. The damage is permanent. He worked in methodical silence, creating a piece of art for the Lord's approval. I came so close to walking into the light.

Something in me refused to let go. I was tired, starved, desperate for a reprieve from the violence. God took one look at his offering and cast me out, back into the darkness of the cage.

I survived.

That was only the beginning.

"Please don't look," I beg him, biting back a sob.

His eyes refuse to look away.

"Harlow, you're beautiful inside and out," Hunter proclaims softly. "These marks are part of you. They tell me how strong, brave and fucking formidable you are. All I see here is proof of that."

His mouth crushes back on mine, cementing his words. Heat pulsates through the grip of anxiety holding me prisoner. Hunter pins my broken arm over my head, exposing my breasts.

Lips trailing down my neck, he sucks and nibbles on the sensitive slope of skin. The light bruises from the incident with Leighton have faded, leaving no evidence of our collision.

Does it matter that I kissed him too?

What would he say if he saw this?

Tiny bites and open-mouthed kisses force me to cast all thoughts of Leighton aside as his brother takes my nipple back in his mouth. Excitement zips down my spine. It feels so good to be touched.

Thumbs stroking over the tender skin of my ribcage, Hunter kisses all the way down to my belly button. I hate that he's seeing my scars up close, but when his tongue flicks around a gruesome lump of skin, I see stars.

"You're so fucking beautiful," he repeats, kissing each violent slash of the knife.

Reaching the edge of my panties, his fingers hook underneath the elastic. That's when I realise how damp the material is. I panic, closing my thighs around his head.

"What is it?" he demands.

"N-Nothing," I stammer.

Pushing my thighs back open, he looks at the wet cotton as his smile turns devilish. I have to cover my mouth as he takes a deep, unapologetic inhale of my panties.

"Little Harlow is so wet," he muses. "You're dripping, sweetheart. I can see your thighs glistening. Is that all for me?"

His beard is so rough against my skin. Back arching, I silently plead for relief. I don't know how to do it myself. Cold air meets my most private area as he tosses the panties aside.

"Hunt," I gasp again. "Please…"

"Please what?"

"I don't… I… ah…"

As he leans in, the rough scruff of his beard brushes over my folds. The combination of sensations almost sets off an explosion inside of me. I've felt around while showering, and I know the basics.

He easily finds the bud of nerves that I haven't dared to touch before. Rolling it between his fingers, Hunter smirks up at me.

"Look at this perfect pussy, untouched and waiting for me. Do you want me to taste you, Harlow?"

Tongue flicking against my sensitive bud, he sets off that internal wave of pleasure again, hitting me harder this time. I moan as my eyes squeeze tightly shut.

The warmth of Hunter's tongue flicks between my folds. He licks and sucks at my core, each stroke reminiscent of an expert violinist playing his favourite instrument.

"I want to see how tight you are," he says.

Gasping loudly, my legs spread further as his finger drags over my entrance. I'm so wet and feverish, I can't stop the tiny trembles that wrack over me at his touch.

"Have you ever fingered yourself?"

"I don't know what that means," I pant.

"Dammit, Harlow. You're really pushing my self-control right now. I'm going to touch you. If it hurts, I'll stop."

A scream of pleasure pours out of me as he begins to push his finger into my slick opening. The pressure is intense at first, causing anxiety to trickle down my spine, but I trust him.

Rubbing his thumb over my bundle of nerves, Hunter slides his finger out, gathering more moisture before he pushes it back inside. He goes deeper this time, reaching a part of me that feels like pure bliss.

Each time he pushes in and out, the feeling overwhelming my entire body intensifies. Something is building up, spiralling higher and higher, a volcano of rapture preparing to explode.

"That's it, beautiful," Hunter encourages. "You look so good, spreadeagled and crying out for me. I want to see you come."

"See me what?"

I scream out a curse as he thrusts a second finger inside me, working them both in perfect synchronisation. It feels like heaven and hell are battling each other beneath my skin.

I open my eyes long enough to meet his gaze—dark and wicked. The Hunter I know has gone. A sinful demon has taken his place, and I'll happily sell my soul to him.

"Like this," Hunter says huskily. "Let go."

His movements speed up, thrusting and teasing, pushing me closer to the edge with each rotation. My body takes over as ecstasy engulfs me. I cry out again, louder, like a wounded animal.

Warmth spreads between my thighs, coating his hand in fluids. I flush with embarrassment. Is that normal? Hunter pulls his fingers out and checks I'm watching as he raises them to his mouth.

I gape, watching him lick the glistening moisture from each digit. When he's finished, he ducks back between my legs. His mouth returns to my pussy, licking every last drop of moisture up.

"Hunter," I say dreamily. "Stop."

"Not a chance. You taste like fucking heaven."

Looking up at me beneath a mop of tousled hair, his eyes are twinkling with satisfaction. There's still stickiness smeared across his lips as he licks them clean.

Lord above, I've never seen the devil so clearly in real life. Not even in the harrowing stare of my supposed parent. This man walks in another sinful realm entirely.

"Are you okay?" he asks worriedly.

"Okay? After that?"

Hunter nods frantically.

"I'm not sure I can form words yet."

His lips spread in a smirk that screams of mischief. It's like I'm staring down at Leighton, dimples and all. Jesus Christ.

I shouldn't be thinking about Hunter's brother after that, but it doesn't stop me from wondering what it would be like to do this with him too. I can't get that kiss off my mind.

"Come here," he commands.

Carefully lifting my arm, I crawl across the mattress until I'm in Hunter's lap. My legs wrap around his waist, pinning us flush together. He's pressed up against my bare pussy, hard and throbbing.

"Should I be doing... erm, something about that?" I stumble out. "I want to make you feel good too."

Hunter nuzzles my throat, his beard scratching my sweat-covered skin. "Not tonight. Let me hold you instead."

Positioning me on his chest like I'm a tiny baby, I curl closer, oddly unafraid of my nakedness. He's seen it all now, and he didn't run.

I'm safe here. No demons can come to claim my soul while Hunter's fending them off. They wouldn't dare challenge him. I'm certain the devil would take one look and run from this man, screaming and promising never to return.

Tomorrow, I must reckon with the past.

But for tonight, I can rest.

Nothing can hurt me here.

CHAPTER 20

Leighton

The Search – NF

My feet thump against the treadmill in a steady, brutal rhythm.

Thump, thump, thump.

I picture Harlow—asleep and at peace next to me on the sofa, her thumb wrapped between her lips in a child-like gesture that reveals her vulnerability. But she's so much more than that.

Thump, thump, thump.

I hate her little whimpers of pain as she battles invisible demons, thrashing in her sleep, running from my touch when I try to help. Even unconscious, she doesn't trust the unknown.

Thump, thump, thump.

Fuck, I hope she's okay right now. Hunter's a drill sergeant. He'll keep her safe and secure. This entire trip is a terrible idea, but Giana insisted on meeting her daughter in person.

They've already been gone for two days. Apparently, a storm rolled in, so they've holed up in the hotel to let it pass over. The idea of Hunter and Harlow stuck in close quarters is laughable.

Enzo will riot and tear the country to shreds if this Giana woman even thinks about taking Harlow from us. She belongs right here, far from anyone that would dare hurt her.

I run until I feel like I'm gonna puke. Falling off the treadmill in a sweaty heap, I stare up at the ceiling of the basement gym. Exercise is what kept me alive in prison.

It provided a brief solace from the chaos of living with thousands of angry, trapped men. That place broke something in me that can't be fixed. But since Harlow, I've been feeling more like my old self.

After catching my breath, I rest against the wall and knock back a bottle of water. My workout shorts are drenched with sweat. I've been at it for over an hour, too restless to sit around.

Enzo should be home from the office soon, but fuck knows. He's been a miserable, sleepless bastard since they left. I fucking miss Harlow. She sweetens him up.

Cleaning the equipment in silence, I nearly drop the towel when a deafening crash reverberates down the stairs. The sound of smashed glass and someone shouting is unmistakable.

Fuck!

No one else is home.

Reaching under the weight bench, I grab the gun that Hunter taped into place. Checking the chamber, it's fully loaded. You don't grow up around our old man without learning to shoot.

Creeping upstairs, more crashing sounds echo through the empty house. It sounds like someone is beating the shit out of some china plates. I cock the gun in front of me, ready to shoot.

If that psycho bastard has come looking for Harlow, I'll put a bullet between his eyes, and then in his dick. The others can have what's left of him to finish off.

"Enzo?" I shout. "Is that you, man?"

Someone gasps in pain from inside the kitchen. Keeping the gun positioned, I creep through the hallway and into the dimly lit room.

"Theo? What the fuck?"

Every single glass, bowl and plate we own is smashed into pathetic pieces across the marble floor. Sitting cross-legged amongst the carnage is a sweating, bleeding moron.

"Leigh," he slurs.

Theo's glasses are crooked on his reddened face, and his usually neat curls are sticking up like he's been electrocuted. I can smell the vodka and beer rolling off him from here.

"Damn, buddy." I lower the gun. "This is impressive for you. Did you have to break the whole kitchen?"

"Yes!" Theo shouts drunkenly. "Tell Hunter to fucking f-fuck himself." He picks up a discarded spoon from the floor. "Here, g-give him this to help."

I accept the spoon while smothering a laugh. "You're bleeding. Christ, did you have to pull this shit when I'm home alone? I already get blamed for everything around here."

Picking my way through the debris, I grab a cloth and soak it with water. Theo's staring up at the ceiling with half-open eyes, clutching his sliced left hand.

I sink down next to him, our shoulders brushing. "Come on, give it up. If you need stitches, you're screwed with me here."

Wrapping his hand, I check there's no embedded glass and apply pressure to halt the bleeding. He's lucky it's nothing major.

Hunter really would kill me if I let one of his best friends die on the kitchen floor. They could bury us in matching graves.

"What happened?"

Theo groans in pain. "I found the local pub."

"That good, huh? I'm impressed."

"My head hurts."

"Serves you right." I check his hand and nod. "You're good, drunkard. Doesn't need stitches."

"Awesome," he drawls.

"We wouldn't want to fuck up your perfect office hands, would we? Look, not a single mark or scar."

"Fuck you, Leighton."

Snorting, I grab a brush from under the sink. "Is that any way to speak to your saviour? I should've let you bleed out instead."

He clutches his head as I clean up, getting all the broken crockery hidden in the bin. Enzo will have to make an Ikea trip before Hunter returns. I ain't shouldering the blame this time around.

Hooking my hands underneath Theo's armpits, I haul him into a barstool. "That's it, bud. Let's get you cleaned up."

"Don't need your help," he grumbles.

"Sure you don't. I'll make coffee, but please don't throw up. I draw the line at cleaning your vomit."

"If I do, it'll be on your head."

Flicking Hunter's fancy espresso machine on, I locate some painkillers and dump them in front of Theo with some water. He missed a few glasses and cups in his destructive stupor.

He can't even muster a thank you. By the looks of him, he's had an absolute skinful. The stench of liquor is clinging to his flannel shirt and rumpled jeans.

"I heard you had a fight with the terrible twosome the other day and stormed out. Didn't think we'd see you again."

"Where'd you hear that?" Theo guzzles the water.

"Enzo was beating the shit out of the punching bag downstairs. I managed to get a few words out of him before he went all caveman."

"Yeah, well, he deserves it."

With two coffees made, I fall into the seat next to him. Theo's far from my favourite person, but I can extend enough empathy to help the poor guy.

Dealing with Hunter and Enzo for years on end is bound to drive anyone to drink, let alone with the pressure of this fucked up case on top of that.

"They said you walked out," I push again.

Theo removes his dirty glasses and tosses them aside to rub his temples. "I did. Waste of fucking space."

"Hunter is?"

"No, me," he clarifies. "Things were supposed to get easier with time, you know? This grief stuff. Richards said… time."

Sipping my coffee, I watch the emotions cycle through him. Alyssa's death messed them all up. She was an awesome person. I was behind bars when she passed, but it still hurt. We were friends, but she was their everything.

"It's been years," Theo admits roughly. "Why hasn't it gotten easier, huh? I'm so tired of hurting. I can't do it anymore."

"Do you really want to know what I think?"

"Why not? Nobody else is listening to me."

"Well, I think you're waiting for things to go back to how they were. You know, before."

Theo nods. "Perhaps."

"You're holding out for something that isn't going to happen. How can you be happy, living in the past like that?"

"Fuck, Leigh," he curses. "When you put it like that, I sound dumb as hell. I know she's dead."

I rest a hand on his hunched shoulder. "You're still grieving. You think I didn't spend three years behind bars wanting to go back and make a different choice? It's human instinct."

Gulping the coffee down, Theo replaces his glasses. They're slightly crooked and still dirty, but he looks more like himself when his blue eyes meet mine.

"So how do I turn off human instinct?"

"You don't. Follow it somewhere else instead."

"Somewhere else?" he repeats, nose wrinkled.

"Anywhere's better than the hell you're in, right?"

Theo barks a bitter laugh. "When did you get so smart?"

I knock my cup into his. "Plenty of time to practise my wise buddha skills in the slammer. That and years of drunken conversations with strangers. It's good for the soul."

His head slumps and hits the breakfast bar. "Christ, I've been such a dickhead. I said some shitty stuff to Hunter and Enzo."

"You put up with them for all these years. That's earned you some leeway to be a dickhead, in my opinion."

"Jeez, how comforting."

Headlights suddenly light up the house as the security gate slides shut. A car parks, and we both watch as four figures step out. His monstrous frame betrays Enzo's presence. He disengages the security system before unlocking the front door.

"Leighton!"

"This'll be good," I mutter to Theo's slumped head. "In here, Enz."

Halting in the doorway, Enzo takes one look around the half-destroyed room and spots us both. His face hardens.

"Theo, I have been looking all over the city for you," he shouts. "You couldn't even answer your goddamn phone?"

His head doesn't lift. "Thought you'd take the hint three days ago, Enz. I don't wanna talk."

"We have bigger problems than your temper tantrum."

The front door closes as Enzo's three passengers enter the house.

I straighten, pushing the gun underneath a discarded newspaper that Hunter left behind.

"Theodore Young!" a familiar voice yells. "I'm going to kill you in your sleep and piss on your fucking corpse for good measure."

Tall, wiry, and wrapped in a leather jacket, Brooklyn West strides into the room with the confidence of a trained killer. Her ash-white hair brushes her shoulders these days, choppy and wild, highlighting her pierced nose.

Pert lips turned up in a fearsome scowl, she trains her silver-grey eyes right on me. Hell, I didn't need to hide the gun after all. She never leaves the house without one.

"Howdy, Brooke." I wave playfully. "Can you leave my corpse piss free, please? I didn't come home drunk. Well, this time."

Her mouth drops. "Leighton! Son of a bitch."

Behind her, two slabs of authority and power stomp into the room. With hair the colour of midnight, enough dark tattoos to reach his throat and several black eyebrow piercings, Hudson Knight is an unnerving sight.

He's dressed in his usual ripped jeans and black t-shirt, showcasing more tattoos that drench his generous biceps in darkness. Every inch of him is covered. I'd cross the damn road to get away from this motherfucker.

"Baby Rodriguez," he drawls. "Long time no see."

Yanked from my bar stool, he traps me in a painful headlock and scrubs my hair. Fuck me, it's like being body rolled by a crocodile.

"Can't breathe," I croak.

"Don't kill the little asshole yet." Enzo sighs from across the kitchen. "He has his uses."

Hudson snorts as he releases me. "Yet."

Brushing myself off, I'm hit by another tornado as Brooklyn pulls me into a suffocating hug. I swear, my ribs actually creak.

"Leigh," she whispers in my ear. "Fuck, man. Where have you been? We've been calling and texting non-stop."

"Sorry, B. Things have been hectic."

"We live a mile away, you asshole." She shoves me backwards and pins me with a glare. "You could've come over when you got out."

"Yeah… I know."

I brace myself to face the final pillar of intimidation. Hudson's older brother, Kade Knight, is more beefed up and sinewy than I remember him. He doesn't look like a geeky Clark Kent wannabe anymore.

Wearing his usual open-necked dress shirt and pressed trousers, the spotless fabric perfectly matches his slicked-back, golden-blonde hair and sharp hazel eyes.

"Leighton." He nods tightly. "You're looking good."

I stifle an eye roll. "Come here, idiot."

He chuckles and pulls me into a tight embrace. Before I went to prison, I got to know their ragtag group pretty well. They crashed into our lives without warning after Blackwood Institute was shut down.

The other guys—Eli, Phoenix, and Jude—aren't usually far away. This dysfunctional family is joined at the hip. They moved down the road after Hunter bought this place, keeping close relationships with the whole team.

"As charming as this little reunion is," Enzo interrupts, "we have an emergency here."

"What's going on?" I quickly ask. "Harlow?"

"No, she's still safe with Hunter." He jabs a thumb at Theo. "If this one bothered to turn on his phone, he would know what's going on. Our missing girl turned up."

"What?" Theo stiffens.

"The intelligence team has carried on searching," Kade answers grimly. "They spotted a suspicious vehicle leaving the abduction area using false plates."

"You found the bastard's car?" I gape at them.

Enzo braces his hands on the breakfast bar. "I traced it myself using ANPR cameras. Dispatched local police to an industrial site and found the van burnt out, no sight of the perp."

"Girl's body was left inside," Hudson says with a shrug. "No carvings, as far as we can tell. Autopsy will confirm."

"So it's not our killer," Theo surmises.

"Doesn't look like it." Enzo shakes his head. "That's not the reason we've been searching the streets of London for you."

Stepping forward, Kade pulls an iPad from his leather satchel and places it in front of us. I lean closer. There's a photo of a printed note on the screen.

Harlow,

'Let him know that whoever brings back a sinner from his wandering will save his soul from death and will cover a multitude of sins.' James 5:20.

Come home.

With love,

Your father.

I fight the urge to smash Kade's iPad to smithereens. "What the fuck is wrong with this sick son of a bitch?"

"That was delivered to HQ, which as we know, is publicly listed property registered to Sabre."

"Pastor Michaels knows Harlow is with you," Kade highlights.

Enzo's expression is dark. "Exactly. It was posted so we can't trace it. No fingerprints or DNA."

"A dead end then," I grit out.

Enzo replies with a stony nod.

"Why would he break his silence now?" Theo asks.

"He's been laying low, waiting to see if Harlow would lead you straight back to him," Brooklyn guesses with a shrug. "Now, he's ready to play again."

"I should've found him." Theo stands and almost falls over in his drunken state. "Now he's coming for Harlow. It's my fault."

The coffee has done little to sober him up. Before anyone can answer, Brooklyn storms straight up to him and smacks him around the head hard enough to send his glasses flying.

"You are the most frustrating genius I have ever met, and I agreed to marry that work in progress over there." She gestures towards Kade, exchanging grins with his tattooed brother.

"Hey, you're marrying me too." Hudson sticks his hand in the air like a school kid. "I earned the title of favourite fiancé fair and square, blackbird. Don't fucking leave me out like that."

"Hud," she growls at him. "Shut up. One infuriating male bastard at a time, please."

"Jesus Christ," Kade curses as he packs his iPad away. "We're doomed at this rate."

Wading through the thicket of disgruntlement, Enzo turns on Theo. The pair stare at each other for several loaded seconds.

"You've been working this investigation for months, alongside every other job we threw at you." Enzo looks exasperated. "No one has tried harder than you."

"Not hard enough."

"Killing yourself won't catch this killer," he offers, lowering his voice. "And it won't bring her back."

Theo looks away. "I know. I'm sorry for what I said."

"Yeah," Enzo echoes. "Me too."

Brooklyn steps between them with her hands on her hips. "Does that mean you've kissed and made up? We have actual work to do."

I pull her close and kiss her blonde hair. "Damn, I've missed you keeping these morons in line."

She elbows me in the ribs. "You could've enjoyed my charm a long time ago if you bothered to call. When I'm done beating the stupid out of Theo, you're next on my shit list. Better run."

"Nah. I reckon I can take you on."

Hudson cracks his knuckles from behind me. "Try it, pal. Prison or not, I can still turn your skull into a fucking hat."

"Hunter can always find a new brother," Kade chimes in.

I have no doubt they mean it. Murder is a very small price to pay when it comes to their girl. To buy a temporary peace, Enzo hands out a round of beers. We crowd around the breakfast bar, disregarding the mess in the kitchen.

Kade raises an eyebrow when he discovers the gun under the newspaper, but Brooklyn gives me a proud fist bump.

"No beer for you." Enzo makes Theo another coffee instead. "We need you back in the lab."

Theo rubs his bloodshot eyes. "I'll go when I can stop seeing three of you. One Enzo is enough for anybody."

"I'll join you," Kade offers. "I've narrowed down the search zone for the chapel in Northumberland, but the forest is too thick. The drone was damaged."

"Not the P300?" Theo winces.

I fight the urge to facepalm. Those drones are nothing more than hunks of soulless metal, not his prized possessions.

"Has anyone heard from Hunter?" I change the topic.

Draining his beer, Enzo's face is stony. "He's taking Harlow to meet Giana in the morning."

"How did she take the news?"

"He didn't say in his text message."

Rolling the bottle in my hands, I wrestle with the inexplicable sense of unease that's keeping me on edge. The sooner Harlow comes home, the better we'll all feel.

Pastor Michaels is alive and kicking.

That means she's in imminent danger.

CHAPTER 21

Harlow

Family — Badflower

He who be worthy shall reach the kingdom of God.
      That isn't you, sinner.
      You will never be worthy of the Lord's love.

Parked up on the curb a stone's throw from a neat row of cottages, Pastor Michaels' voice taunts me. He's louder than usual, rising from the mist of his shallow grave.

I stare at the red door of number thirty-five on Terrence Avenue. It's a small house, basic, entirely unsuspecting.

Almost too normal.

This could have been my life.

Clusters of hibernating blackberry bushes wind around the white picket fence. A tall apple tree dominates the garden, casting shadows as snowflakes continue to fall.

No flowers are blooming at this time of year. The fruit growing has been stripped from its brambles, consumed and tossed aside. It's like the whole garden is trapped in a deathly state of stasis.

I wonder how many times I crossed their minds. Did Giana see my face the day her second child was born? Was I even an afterthought?

"We can go in when you're ready." Hunter fastens his silver-grey tie in the driver's seat. "I'd like to set off this afternoon though."

I lick my cracked lips. "Sure."

His ringtone pierces the tension between us. With a quick glance at the screen, Hunter ignores the third call this morning.

He's been dodging calls all weekend since we stayed for an extra couple of days. I needed time to think and come to terms with my entire life being ripped apart overnight.

It wasn't so bad, sharing a cramped hotel room with Hunter in the dead of winter. Things feel different now. He actually sees me for who I am, and we've talked through the news until I felt able to face Giana myself.

His phone rings again.

"Answer if you need to."

"They're all adults," he says, switching it off. "I run that company all year round. They can cope for another day on their own."

"I really don't mind."

He reaches out to take my hand over the console. "Well, I do mind. You need me more right now."

The feel of his fingers clasping mine makes my pulse skip a beat. I'm still not used to the casual affection he's started to give. I half expect him to throw me out of the car and tell me this whole thing was a dumb mistake.

"Do I look alright?" I ask apprehensively.

"You look fine, sweetheart."

Dressed in plain blue jeans and a loose linen shirt, my parka keeps me warm against the early December chill. I've left my mousy-brown hair loose and natural, spilling down my back.

"What if she doesn't remember me?" I slip a hand into my hair and pull sharply. "What if I don't recognise her?"

"Harlow."

I stare ahead, gripping a strand of hair.

"Harlow, look at me."

Hunter's coffee-coloured eyes stare into mine when I muster the courage to look. He strokes his thumb over my cheek with a smile.

"It's going to be okay. I'm here and we can leave at any time. You don't owe her anything, alright?"

I make myself nod. "Alright."

Exiting the car, he circles around to let me out. I leave my phone and small handbag behind. The only person who needs to know where I am is right here, pulling me into his arms.

Hunter is dressed in his usual battle armour—a blue dress shirt and matching navy pea coat that complements his still-tanned skin. He's cleaned up his beard and pulled his hair into a neat bun, highlighting the old scar that bisects his eyebrow.

"I told her to make sure the kid wasn't home," he explains as we approach the cottage. "Figured that would be too much."

"Thank you."

The red door stands out against the snow-covered garden. It's stark, a violent shade of crimson, spilling blood across the lawn in a curtain of mortality. I'm almost afraid to touch it.

There's a car covered up in the driveway, and Hunter takes a quick glance under the plastic sheet.

"What are you doing?" I hiss at him.

"Checking her story out," he replies with a whistle under his breath. "That's one piece-of-shit old Beamer. Interesting."

"Why?"

He glances at me. "She kept the money when your dad got

convicted. What happened to it all?"

"Well… I don't know."

"Maybe we'll find out." Hunter rests a hand on the door. "Ready for this?"

"As I'll ever be."

I shrink into his side as he raps three times. Seconds later, the lock snicks and the door cracks open. Two green eyes run over Hunter, already sparkling with tears.

"Giana?" he prompts.

"Mr Rodriguez," she rushes out.

Holding the door open, Giana Kensington steps out onto the cluttered porch. She's short and slim—not much taller than me—but she wears her miniature-sized look with elegance.

Her silky, off-white blouse is tucked into her skinny jeans while her nutty-brown hair is pulled back in a loose knot that frames her middle-aged features.

Taking a deep breath, I step forward from behind Hunter. The moment she spots me, the tears begin to fall. Her hands clamp over her mouth as she takes thirty seconds to study every inch of me.

"Um, hi," I say awkwardly.

"Leticia?" Giana whimpers from behind her hands. "My God, you're so… so big."

"It's Harlow now. Not… that."

Hand flicking to her throat, she fingers a delicate silver locket as we stare at each other. I desperately try and fail to recognise her. Her hair is lighter than mine, our eyes are different colours.

She could be a stranger.

This person isn't my mum.

That title belongs to another woman, cruel and careless, beating my little body until her fists cracked and bled. Mrs Michaels has stolen the right to a loving parent from me. I can't get that back.

"Come in," Giana blurts, backtracking inside her home. "Gosh, don't stand out in the snow. I'm so sorry."

I let Hunter take the lead. He pulls off his coat and turns to me, an eyebrow raised. When I don't move, he gently pulls me inside and eases the parka from my shoulders. I can't lift a finger.

"Breathe," he whispers.

Pushing me in front of him, I catch the moment Giana sees my broken arm. The colour drains from her face.

"What happened?"

"As I said on the phone, Harlow is still recovering," Hunter answers diplomatically. "She contracted sepsis and underwent surgery for her broken arm around two months ago. She's due to have the cast off next week."

Giana can make all sorts of deductions from those brief slivers of information. I'm not sure I want her to know so much about me.

"How are you feeling, Letty?" she asks with a forced smile.

"Harlow," Hunter reminds her.

"Right." She ducks her head, flushing again. "I'm sorry... shall we make some tea? My husband, Foster, should be home soon with the dog."

We follow her through a narrow hallway into the kitchen out back. Her home is comfortable, albeit cramped, painted in muted tones. I resolutely ignore the kid-sized shoes scattered next to the staircase.

In the farmhouse-style kitchen, I study the spread that Giana's laid out. Sandwiches, biscuits and miniature cakes. She hums nervously while filling two tea pots, casting me looks every other second.

The room is warm, inviting, fit for a family. I can't help but notice the cluster of framed photos on the windowsill. The news still hasn't sunk in, and I'm desperate for proof.

"Can I?"

Giana nearly drops the teapot she's holding. "Oh, well, um… help yourself. Do you… remember her?"

Picking up the first frame, I hug my grandma to my chest. I can't believe she was actually real. Sitting on a picnic blanket, she's building a sandcastle with a miniature shovel and bucket.

"A little," I admit. "She's been popping up in my dreams for a while. I had no idea she was real, let alone family."

Giana remains at a safe distance, but she looks desperate to cross the kitchen. Whether to hug me or hurt me, I don't know. I can't trust her. Not after Mrs Michaels.

"She always took you to the beach when you went to stay. No matter how many times I told her it's illegal to feed those damn seagulls. You were the shining light in her whole world."

My finger traces her silk-spun hair.

She was real.

Maybe, all my dreams are.

"Grandma Sylvie," I whisper.

Placing the frame down before I drop it, I take the empty seat next to Hunter. Giana sits opposite, clocking the way he takes my hand in his. Her eyebrows pull together.

"As I explained on the phone, the current situation is a little delicate," Hunter begins, taking a sip of tea.

The cup shakes in Giana's hand. "I saw the press announcement. I'm glad you kept Let—ah, Harlow's identity private."

"I'm afraid to say that it won't be long before the media connect the dots. Secrets have a way of getting out. We've had some issues with reporters tracking Harlow's movements."

"That cannot be allowed to happen," she gasps.

"We will keep Harlow safe, no matter what. I can also confirm that we have reopened the case into her abduction. You'll need to be interviewed again, by my team this time."

"Oh, of course," Giana agrees uneasily.

"We will continue to dedicate our entire company to this case until all is said and done."

"What if it doesn't work?" I croak. "We can't fight this forever. Other people need your help too."

"Harlow," Hunter snaps. "We're not having this discussion."

When Giana attempts to pat my arm, I shift backwards, out of her reach. She pales even further. Tension is carving her entire frame into a marble statue.

Clearing his throat, Hunter refills his teacup. "I need to ask you about your ex-husband. We have some questions for him."

"I haven't seen him for over a decade," she replies in a sharp voice. "Our marriage ended when he was convicted. I moved here to be closer to my mother before she passed."

"You haven't heard from him since he was released?"

Hesitating, she touches the locket around her neck again. "There was a letter. It arrived on the tenth anniversary of the abduction."

"We'll need to take that into evidence."

"Well, if I can find it… um, we've moved since then."

"What did he say?" I fire at her.

Giana bites her lip. "Harlow… he wasn't a good man. In some ways, I'm glad you can't remember what he put us through."

"You don't get to say that." I hold back the tears threatening to spill. "My memories were stolen. I lost everything."

"And I didn't?" she counters.

Wiping her cheeks, she looks to Hunter for help. He's too busy guzzling his hourly dose of tea to pull her out of the hole she's dug.

"What happens now?" Giana clears her throat.

"Harlow will remain in protective custody until the threat has been dealt with."

She looks crestfallen. I hate that I want to wipe that look off her face with my fist. Violence isn't in my nature, but she doesn't get to sit here and cry for a girl that died a long time ago.

I'm not going to be her happy ending. Giana wants a daughter, a second chance. Like she hasn't been given that privilege already.

"I suppose that makes sense." She looks over to me. "But there is a bed for you here. I know you don't remember me, but I'd like the chance for us to be friends."

"Friends?" I repeat incredulously.

"If you'd like."

"But… I don't understand. You thought I was dead."

"Letty—"

"Stop calling me that! Letty is dead!" I shout, losing my temper. "She was killed a long time ago. You weren't there."

"Harlow," Hunter warns.

"No! She needs to hear what happened to me while she sat here with her new hus—"

My mouth clicks shut as the front door slams. Heavy footsteps thud down the hallway, and Giana scrubs her tears away as a tall, dark-haired man freezes in the doorway.

He's middle-aged, trim and smartly dressed in a quilted jacket over his dark-green sweater. Pale eyes are framed by thick, black glasses.

"Foster." Giana smiles weakly. "Come in, meet our guests. We were just catching up."

Hunter stands, clasping Foster's outstretched hand. "Hunter Rodriguez. Director of Sabre Security."

"Good to meet you," Foster greets, appearing nervous. "My wife has told me about you. Hope I'm not interrupting."

His gaze strays over to me. I can't bring myself to shake his hand. I'm sure he's comparing me to the little girl he's seen pictures of all these years.

"Hey there." He smiles brightly. "I'm Foster. You must be Letty."

"Harlow," Giana says in a panic. "It's Harlow now."

Foster quickly recovers. "Oh right, of course. I apologise. How are you, Harlow?"

"You know," I answer vaguely. "Bearing up."

He takes a seat as Giana busies herself pouring more tea. The tension is suffocating. I still want to shout and rave, throw my pain at these strangers and force them to drink it like poison.

"So," Foster prompts. "What were you talking about?"

Giana's eyes widen. "Well, uh. We… Harlow… I mean, Hunter was just telling us a bit more about himself."

Without hesitating, Hunter fills the awkward silence. Foster enquires about Sabre's expansion plans, seeming a little starstruck. He knows a hell of a lot about the company that's taken me in.

Giana can't tear her eyes away from me. There's something intense in her gaze, a secret message that I can't decipher. I don't know what the hell she expects me to say now.

I'm not her daughter.

That person died.

I wonder how she felt when they discovered I was gone. It's any mother's worst nightmare. Did she run around, screaming and demanding help? Did they put up posters? Knock on doors? I'm not sure she did.

My morbid thoughts take an even darker turn. How did she live with the guilt? Rebuild her life without wanting to end it all? I spent years praying for death. Was she doing the same thing? Part of me wishes she was.

My chair scraping back startles them all.

"I need the bathroom," I rush to explain.

She forces a smile. "Of course, darling. It's down the hall, on the left. Do you need me to show you?"

"I'll be fine."

Their voices pick up the moment I leave the room, urgent and worried. I walk even faster to reach the bathroom. I'm not sure I can trust myself to sit there without flipping out.

While they were getting married, having a baby and tending the damn rose bushes outside, I was being beaten to a pulp, starved and carved up like a hunk of meat for slaughter.

I want to know if they suffered. Grieved. Sobbed and begged God for the slightest glimmer of remorse. Locking the bathroom door behind me, I slump against it.

My breathing is shallow and pained. Hunter won't let me hide for long, but I don't want to see him either. All of them look like one person in my mind—laughing, covered in blood, a belt snapping against his palm.

Come along now, Harlow.

Kneel by the door, there's a good girl.

Ready for your nighttime prayers?

I obeyed Pastor Michaels. For years, I fought. When my strength ran dry, compliance was the only thing that kept me alive. I surrendered so much of myself for one reason.

I actually believed that he was my father. He convinced me it was true, chipping away at my memories with his torture and beatings until I forgot those monsters ever stole me.

Staring into the mirror, soulless eyes look back at me beneath silvery hair and blood-flecked skin. I see him in every part of myself, even my physical appearance. Pastor Michaels is always there.

Even if I wanted a real family, my mind holds no space for them. It's a sinking ship, water spilling in through traumatised holes.

I am your father.

You will obey me or face the consequences.

Don't you want to go to heaven?

"No," I reply to my reflection. "I don't want to go to heaven. I want to go to the depths of hell and see you there."

I'm coming for you, little girl.

Sinners don't get second chances.

You must repent in blood or die trying.

As I stare at the figment of my imagination, it changes. Pastor Michaels' hair grows, becoming white with age and soft like cotton candy. In a second, Grandma Sylvie stares back at me.

"Why did you have to die?" I whisper tearfully. "I don't even know you, but it hurts that I'll never get the chance to."

One blink and she's gone. I'm left staring at an unfamiliar face. Mine. I've managed to put on a few pounds, but my face is still too thin. Pale. Shadowed. Broken. The little girl they remember is dead.

Another thick scar peeks out the collar of my linen shirt. It's fresher than the others, stretching all the way down to my ribcage, twisted and puckered.

When Adelaide and her unborn baby died, the final piece of me broke. That's when I gave up on ever escaping my cage. I stopped fighting, stopped caring, stopped breathing.

All while Giana lived.

It isn't fair.

Unable to suck in a breath, I search for an escape on instinct. I can't go back in there and pretend everything's okay. Opening the small window, I stand on the toilet to climb through it.

You did this, bitch!

It's your fault that baby is dead.

You didn't pray hard enough, you filthy sinner.

My feet hit the lawn and I break into a run without thinking about the people I'm leaving behind. I'm back in that church graveyard, the stretch of desolate woodland ahead of me.

Run, Harlow.

Before it's too late.

Nowhere is safe for you.

Time has rewound. I have to run for my life again. My surroundings pass in a blur, reality drags to a halt and I leave the ruins of Leticia's life behind.

All I've got left is Harlow. The splintered fragments of a person that nobody could ever love. Not even Hunter. They're better off without me here.

CHAPTER 22

Theo

Won't Stand Down — Muse

From the private helicopter, I should have the perfect view of the shoreline that carves the expanse of Devon. Croyde in particular is deserted, whipped by wind and snow, obscuring anything from sight.

If Harlow's down there, she'll be dead from hypothermia by morning. After spending the past two months staying as far away from her as possible, I'm no better than the others.

I've grown close to the idea of her. This case has consumed my whole life for so long, and I've poured more into it than I realised. Harlow has dominated my thoughts every night for months, demanding justice.

"This is a waste of time," Hudson says into his headset. "We can't see shit up here. I doubt she's still in the area."

"What's that supposed to mean?"

His crystal-clear blue eyes meet mine. "She's been gone for twelve hours. We both know the statistics. We're running out of time."

Hudson couldn't mince his words, even if he tried. The guy's a walking offence to civilised society. He's exactly the person we need to cut through the bullshit of organising a wide-scale search party.

"You think he's found her?" he asks gruffly.

I shake my head. "She ran. This is something else. But if we don't find her soon, that sicko may very well take advantage of this opportunity and snatch her again."

"She could be hiding out somewhere. That buys us some time." He scans the misty skyline. "I just have a bad feeling."

"We should have divers looking in the sea."

"Huh?"

"If she jumped… her body will need to be recovered before it's swept away. Or maybe she's out there, waiting for her moment."

Hudson's expression hardens. "Jesus, Theo. You know Hunter won't want to hear that shit."

"His feelings are irrelevant. She ran for a reason."

"You're sure that she's a danger to herself?"

I stare at him, unblinking. "Did you think that Brooke was before she hurt herself? It isn't always obvious."

The vein in his neck throbs. Hudson is an excellent spook— ruthless, violent, an expert manipulator. He's also calm and controlled when a crisis arises.

All except when it comes to his girl. I've seen him butcher men and break necks without blinking for Brooklyn West, usually with a smirk on his face.

"We'll keep looking," he decides. "But doing it from up here is no good. Let's join the others on the ground and regroup."

We ride back down in silence. Hunter has commandeered the hotel they were staying at, paying off the owners as he shipped in a miniature army from Sabre HQ.

The helicopter lands on the hillside, and Hudson offers me a hand as we jump out. Back in the nearby hotel, chaos has broken out. We fight through the rush of people to find the bar.

Inside, the Anaconda team has set up, pouring over ordinance maps and surveillance footage. They've already sent a scouting party out that swept the town centre and surrounding farmers' fields.

"Someone better get me some results, or I'll be mounting your fucking heads outside HQ on a spike."

Commanding over the room, Enzo screams in the faces of everyone shrivelling away from him. Grown men I've worked with for years look petrified in his presence.

"Sir, we swept everywhere in a ten-mile radius," Becket protests, wet blonde hair coated to his neck. "There was nothing. She couldn't have run farther than that on foot."

With a snarl, Enzo grabs a handful of Becket's standard-issue black shirt. He pins him against the wall so high, his feet hang off the floor.

"I'm telling you to go back out there," Enzo shouts at him. "Check dumpsters, old barns, public bathrooms. Fucking libraries! Anywhere she could be hiding."

"We already did," Becket struggles to say, his face turning blue. "She's gone."

"Get back out there or find another goddamn job. Don't come back without the girl! You hear me?"

Hunter usually intervenes and calms his hot-tempered partner. Instead, our team leader inhabits the dark shadows of the room. He's propped up in the corner, an invisible wall of isolation warning everyone off. Desperation leaks off him in tidal waves.

Becket dusts himself off and storms away with a curse that makes my ears burn. His small team follows—a tight-knit group of three men and one woman—heading back out into the falling snow.

They're good operatives, second best behind the Cobra team. If they didn't find her out there, Harlow's already gone. Whether Enzo can admit it or not.

"Well, that was an encouraging pep talk," Hudson quips as he strolls in behind me. "Real calm and inspirational."

Enzo glowers at him. "You're a fine one to talk about being calm."

"When I threaten people, I do it properly. Some knives, a bit of blood, couple of broken bones, perhaps. You've really got to commit."

He's going to get his nose pulverised at this rate. Then Brooklyn will gut Enzo for laying a damn finger on her favourite psychopath.

"Can't see a thing up there." I meet Hunter's frozen gaze. "We need more people on the ground. Any forensic evidence will be deteriorating with each day that she's gone."

"Forensic evidence," Hunter repeats, his voice flat and unyielding. "What are you saying, Theodore?"

Sighing, I take a seat at the cluttered table. "It's just a suggestion."

"And here I was thinking your time at Sabre had come to an end."

"Hunt," Leighton warns from his perch at the table. "Theo came with us as soon as we heard. Lay off him."

I incline my head in thanks. The younger Rodriguez brother is far too loud and dramatic for my social anxiety to tolerate, but I've started to make peace with his place in our lives.

Pacing the room, Hunter dismisses me with a glower. He has ditched his suit jacket in favour of a rumpled shirt and loaded gun holster. Everyone else looks equally dishevelled.

"I never should've brought her here." Hunter fists his loose hair with another curse. "This was a huge mistake."

"You did what you thought was best," I point out.

He scoffs. "How many times can I use that excuse? My best

judgement has caused us enough casualties over the years."

Powering up my laptop, I hammer the keys hard. Sabre has extracted a very heavy toll on us all. Casualties have paid for the luxury our team lives in. Luxury I cannot fucking stand.

The hum of an engine outside the hotel causes our remaining staff to scatter, taking handfuls of paperwork and laptops elsewhere. I know who it is without looking up. Hudson's 1967 Mustang GT has a very specific growl.

"Took them long enough," Hudson complains.

Enzo scrubs a hand over his face. "I told Brooklyn to grab the other three. We need all hands on deck for this."

"You dragged them back in from retirement?" Hunter frowns at his teammate. "Why?"

"Because they're the only ones that can think like Harlow," I answer for him. "None of us can begin to understand."

There are worse people to enrol than the infamous inmates that turned our company upside down. Enzo's right. Only Brooklyn and her men can fathom what Harlow's been through.

"Enzo, sit down." Hunter slumps into a chair. "We've got our best people out there."

"Sit down?" Enzo's face darkens. "Sit down?!"

"Lower your damn voice."

"Fuck you, Hunt." He points an accusing finger. "Harlow's out there and it's your fault for not keeping her safe. I will not sit down and wait for that bastard to find our girl."

Snatching up his leather jacket and gun holster, Enzo brushes straight past Brooklyn in the hotel entrance as she yells his name. Hunter's fist crashes against the table.

"Our girl," he mutters. "I warned him. I fucking warned him and now look at us."

"Did you warn yourself too?"

Hunter bares his teeth at me. "You're one to talk. I've seen the whole bloody cupboard of evidence you've collected on Harlow. How long's that collection been going on?"

"It's my job."

"Bullshit. It's bordering on obsessive."

"I'm trying to help her!" I raise my voice.

Leighton's forehead thumps against the table in frustration. Before Hunter can hit back, we're joined by our latest arrivals, sliding the panelled doors shut against the rest of the hotel.

Hudson straightens from his casual lean against the wall. "Who drove then? Keys. Now."

Pouting, Phoenix tosses them through the air. His shaggy, chin-length hair is currently a lurid red colour, compared to the lime green it was when I saw him last.

With impish features, a shining nose ring, and tight black jeans that show off his toned legs, he's the resident wind-up in their team and an all-round pain in our asses.

"Sorry, Hud. I dented the bonnet."

"Not funny." Hudson narrows his eyes. "If there's so much as a scratch on my baby, I'll run over your video games. No more GTA for you."

Phoenix's lips curl into a grin. "Who needs games? That was a sweet as hell ride. I'll steal your baby myself and live out my real-life gangster fantasy."

"Fucking try it," Hudson invites.

"Behave, the pair of you," Kade warns, combing his blonde hair back. "We've got our baby right here. I'm sure she'll take great pleasure in castrating you with a rusty knife."

Ignoring the testosterone-fuelled entourage, Brooklyn rolls her eyes as she strips off her leather jacket, revealing jeans and her usual obscure band t-shirt.

"Too busy for any castrations tonight," she answers. "Put it in my diary for tomorrow. And I'm not your fucking baby, alright?"

Phoenix fist bumps the air. "Score. I'm off the hook."

Growing serious, the three of them take their seats, but not before Hudson drags Brooklyn in for a lip-smacking kiss that leaves her cheeks pink.

Both silent and apprehensive, the other two people to reject a job offer from Hunter step forward. I greet Eli with a nod that he silently returns. His brown ringlets are messy, hanging over vivid-green eyes and sharp cheekbones.

He's the most reserved member of their rowdy bunch. For several years, Eli struggled with selective mutism. When we met almost six years ago, he couldn't speak a single word.

It took long-term speech therapy and a lot of expensive cheques for him to regain his tongue. In the aftermath, he opted to pursue a career in academia rather than join Sabre's ranks.

"Eli," Hunter greets with a sigh. "Thanks for coming."

He takes the seat next to Kade. "Of course."

The last man lingers by the closed doors, observing us all. Jude is still dressed in his work clothes—a smart shirt and black trousers, his lanyard hanging from his neck.

Working with Sabre wasn't on Jude's list of priorities after years of being imprisoned and tortured, but that's a whole other story. He took a few years to recover before returning to his old profession as a psychologist.

Jude now works in a local rebab centre alongside Phoenix, who runs a recovery group for addicts. The latter worked his way up using nothing but determination and repurposed shitty life experiences.

"Theo," he greets, his light-brown hair cropped close to his head. "It's been a while."

"It has. How's the centre?" I ask him.

Jude shrugs, pulling off his lanyard. "I'm still looking for an excuse to get Phoenix locked up to give us some peace and quiet."

"Hey," Phoenix exclaims. "I got you that job, dickhead."

He winks at him. "Sorry, Nix."

With everyone seated, we all look at Hunter. He's staring at a full-page shot of Harlow that's been printed for reference. It's a selfie she took with Leighton during one of their late-night movie marathons. Their grins are wide.

"Hunt?" Kade prompts.

Still, he doesn't move an inch. That damned photograph has him in a grief-stricken trance. When we lost Alyssa, Hunter checked out on us. It got worse when he lost his hearing. We came close to losing him forever.

He carries this entire company on his back, even as it slowly crushes him to death. That man's a bloody martyr if I ever saw one.

Shoving aside my anxiety, I stand up. "Harlow's been gone for over twelve hours. We've combed the surrounding area, as she escaped on foot. No sign of her."

"We also searched the coastline," Hudson adds, an unlit cigarette hanging from his lips. "Our next move would be to bring in divers."

Hunter shakes himself, taking the photograph and turning it over so he can't meet Harlow's blue eyes.

"Why would divers be necessary?" he asks cooly.

Hudson stares straight ahead. "If she's gone in…"

"No," Hunter thunders. "I don't believe that's a scenario we need to explore."

"Why not?" Jude asks while taking a seat.

Out of them all, he knows exactly what Harlow's going through. This man has nerves of steel, borne from the darkest of evils that a human can endure.

"Harlow is recovering," Hunter grinds out.

"From long-term imprisonment, abuse and psychological torture. I know, I'm familiar with it."

"She wouldn't hurt herself."

Jude rests his elbow on the table, unveiling the stump where his left hand should be. "I understand that you care about her. Denial won't help you."

"I am not in denial, Jude."

"Is that why your agents are out there looking for her while you sit here, staring at photographs?"

"Careful." Hunter's tone grows frigid. "You may not work for me, but I will still throw you out of this hotel with my bare hands."

Jude's mouth turns up with amusement. I think he'd shatter Hunter's spine with his pinkie finger and not break a sweat.

"Richards sent me her notes," he continues, unfazed. "Harlow is suffering from dissociative amnesia and severe PTSD. She presents a huge risk to herself."

"I said she's recovering. End of discussion."

"Harlow might not even know that she's lost. Reality can twist and turn in cases of extreme trauma. Accidents happen."

"Jude! Enough!" Hunter yells at him. "You think I don't feel bad enough? Fuck! This happened on my goddamn watch!"

Grabbing his chair, he smashes it to pieces in a silent storm of rage. None of us flinch. With a shout of fury, he braces his hands on the wall and lets his head fall.

"There's something else." Leighton frowns at his laced fingers. "I've spent a lot of time with Harlow. She's been… hurting herself."

"What? Since when?" I cut the silence.

He shrugs. "I don't know when it started, but I've caught her pulling her own hair out several times. She doesn't even know she's doing it half of the time."

Jude raises an eyebrow. "Self-harm can take many forms. We all know that."

Lips pursed, Brooklyn stands up and dares to approach Hunter. I doubt anyone else would have the courage to right now. She bends down to whisper in his ear, somehow coaxing him to come back to the table.

"Do you think this is a cry for help?" he asks with a sigh.

"People don't always want to end their lives." Jude spares his family a quick glance. "They just want the pain to stop."

"To what end?"

"The world's a scary place when you've been kept from it for so long. I think Harlow may be looking for an out."

"Is that your professional opinion?" I ask next.

"It's what I know, Theo. I've been where she is."

Looking back down at my laptop, I churn his words over. Harlow didn't survive thirteen years of sheer hell to go and do something like that. I've seen the determination in her.

"Kade, laptop." I load my TOR browser to access the dark web. "I want to see every surveillance feed in Devon. Domestic and commercial. She has to be somewhere."

"You want to use the new AI program?" He grabs his satchel to start unloading. "We're still awaiting approval from the Ministry of Defence."

"Do I look like I care about the law right now? The Prime Minister can pull his finger out of his ass another time to get us security clearance."

He begins setting up cables and screens. "Alright, then. Let's give this baby a whirl."

CHAPTER 23

Harlow

Pray - jxdn

Mrs Michaels stands in the gloomy shadows of the basement, watching silently. She refuses to take her eyes off her husband. He says that he's my father, but really, he's the monster beneath the bed.

I've read books I'm not supposed to about bad people before. They always pretend to be angels, but they're the ones that hurt you most. God's worst devils in their perfect disguise.

He invades my cell, a black belt in his hand. The smooth leather thwacks against his palm, over and over. Each strike makes me scoot backwards in the cage I've inhabited for what feels like weeks now.

"Why do you continue to defy me, sinner?"

"I'm not a sinner," I argue back. "Grandma says that I'm a good girl. That's why she gives me ice cream every day. And Mummy gave me a gold star for moving up another reading grade."

"We're trying to save you. Your soul will face damnation without my help. Yet, every day you've spent here, you continue to defy us. Your parents. Why is that?"

Wiping snot from my face, I scream at him. "I want to go home."

"You are home. We're your parents now."

"No! You're bad people."

"The unholy always condemn those who threaten their indecent pleasures."

Pastor Michaels loves to rant about obscure Bible verses that I don't understand. For days, I've covered my ears and blocked him out. When I dared to try to escape, he hit me in the face.

I heard something crunch, and my face is hot and swollen. It hurts when I breathe now. I want my mummy to come and kiss it better.

"It's time. Bend over, there's a good girl."

"No!" I shout, clutching my baggy shirt. "You can't make me."

He stalks towards me, grabbing my child-sized body and pinning me against the metal bars. With his spare hand, he raises the filthy t-shirt I was given to wear, exposing my bare behind. They took my pink panties a while ago.

"Count with me, sinner."

His strength forces my back to bend. I scream as the leather connects with my butt cheeks, the buckle biting into my flesh.

"I said count!"

One.

Two.

Three.

"He who be worthy shall rejoice in the kingdom of paradise," Pastor Michaels chants.

Four.

Five.

Six.

"Pray for forgiveness and the Lord shall be merciful."

Seven.

Eight.

Nine.

"You will obey your parents, or we'll take the shirt away too."

It hurts so bad, I can't hold on to the meagre contents of my stomach. He hits me over and over again until I stop crying and lie empty in my own blood and vomit. Mrs Michaels doesn't say a word, watching from her perch in the corner.

"I am your father now."

I find the strength to look up at him.

"Say it," he warns, holding the belt at the ready. "Say it!"

"You're m-m-my father," I sob blindly. "I'm s-sorry."

"There, there, child. That wasn't so hard now, was it?"

His weathered hand strokes over my hair, sticky with blood and sweat. The tenderness of his touch is petrifying after so many awful beatings.

"I have to hurt you, Harlow," Pastor Michaels whispers. "It's the only way to save you. But don't worry, you're almost there. This next bit will be easy."

I'm too tired to repeat that Harlow isn't my name. I can't remember why. What is my name? Isn't it Harlow? I don't know why that doesn't feel right.

It doesn't matter anymore. I just want the pain to stop. If playing along and calling myself Harlow does that, then I'll be the good girl he's hoping for.

"Lay down," he instructs. "Time to pray."

All I can see is the glinting of the knife in his hands, inching closer to me. I'm too weak to fight back as he slices my t-shirt into dirty ribbons.

Mrs Michaels joins him in my cell, the sleeves of her floral dress rolled up. If she hits me again, I'm not sure I'll survive it. Her anger is raw and brutal.

"We must purge the demons from your soul," Pastor Michaels recites, kneeling over me.

"P-Please… don't hurt m-me."

"Hold her down."

Following orders, Mrs Michaels kneels behind me. She pins my thin wrists above my head, using her knees to weigh me down.

I try to buck my legs, but every part of my body is screaming at me to stop fighting back. They planned it perfectly, wore me down, stole my strength.

Now, I can't stop it.

Evil is coming for me.

"In the name of the Father, the Son, and the Holy Spirit, I purge thee of your sins. You may ascend to the kingdom of the Almighty. Lord, have mercy on Harlow's soul."

I don't feel the knife slicing deep into my torso. I don't feel the blood pouring out of me with each intricate cut, carving some kind of pattern. My mind detaches, letting me roam freely in the darkness.

I'm not Letty anymore.

I'm just… Harlow.

†

I never meant for any of this to happen.

All I wanted was to be free.

After running from Hunter and a house full of painful secrets, my feet lead me in one direction. Somehow, I knew that she'd be here.

I find her at the back of the deserted graveyard, with her headstone covered in frost-bitten vines. The little girl that haunts the eyes of my long-lost family.

Leticia Kensington.

Beloved Daughter.

Gone, but not forgotten.

They buried me. Wept. Prayed. Mourned an empty, child-sized coffin. My own family gave up on the hope of ever finding me alive. It feels like they never cared at all.

Ignoring the wail of distant police sirens and helicopter rotors beating through the stormy air, I curl into a ball next to my own grave. Six feet lower, the box I belong in lies untouched.

I should dig through the frozen ground and crawl into it. I'm desecrating the earth I lie on, infecting it with the evil sins bursting out of my pores. The world has forsaken me.

"Harlow!" someone shouts.

I cover my head with my arms, hiding from sight. The sunlight is fading, and the graveyard's shadows conceal me from sight, but I know that won't stop them from hunting me down.

"Harlow? There you are."

His booted feet stop a few inches away. My teeth are chattering together, I'm so cold. Exhaustion has set in after hours of lying on the cold, hard ground, letting the snow settle on my body.

Squatting down, he pulls my arms aside to check my face. Hysteria climbs up my throat, begging for an exit, but no scream comes out. I don't recognise him.

"You must be Hunter's whore." The man chortles as he studies me. "Nice of you to slip away from your guard dog. You did my job for me."

"You're n-not one of the guys," I garble out.

His thin lips pull into a grin. "I'm a friend. Come along, we need to get out of here before that helicopter lands."

I wish I could say that I fought. Screamed. Bucked and thrashed. The stranger wraps his strong arms around me and I'm weightless, tossed over his shoulder as a needle slides into my neck.

Perhaps I was always born to be captive, like those animals in the zoo that can't breathe fresh air without having a heart attack. They need four walls of impenetrable bars to survive.

"That's it," he coaxes, stroking my mane of soaking-wet hair. "Go to sleep, Harlow. Sabre can't save you now."

The afterlife beckons me with open arms as I slip unconscious. Ghosts welcome me home. Familiar faces, screams, pleas for help. One heart-shaped face stands out.

Laura.

This is your punishment.

You never deserved to escape.

I'll be seeing you soon.

Far-off shouting and the blare of a ringing phone cuts through the fog engulfing me. Laura smiles, slow and lazy, before she's swallowed whole by the light burning my retinas.

Agony lances through my temples as I lift my head. Shadows fade, and a dimly lit room settles around me. The curved walls are made of bare, roughened stone. Cobwebs. Discarded needles. Ashes and cigarette butts.

This isn't the basement.

Pastor Michaels hasn't found me.

Dragging myself up, my knees knock together as I fight to remain upright without passing back out. I'm dressed in my jeans and the ripped linen shirt, stained with blood and filth.

Gritting my teeth, I search the strangely shaped room. There's a small window that's been boarded over with wood. I can hear the wind whistling through it. We must be near the sea.

The arched door in the corner is locked. I press my ear against the rotting wood, straining to hear something. I'm met with silence. Based on the light streaming through the boarded-up window, it's the next day at least.

How long was I unconscious for? The guys must be out there right now, burning the country to ashes in search of me. I was so stupid to run away like that.

Foolish Harlow.

They don't care about you.

No one is coming to save you this time.

Desperation takes hold. I hammer my fist on the door, screaming for someone to let me out. When that fails, I growl and lift the sling over my shoulder, freeing my plastered arm.

"Hello? Please... let me out!"

Using my hand to beat on the door even louder, a shout of annoyance answers me. Footsteps draw closer on the other side, and I shuffle backwards as the lock clicks.

At the last second, I grab one of the used needles from the floor and hold it behind my back. The needle still looks sharp. Door creaking open, a short, heavily muscled man wearing a blue baseball cap steps inside.

"Who are you?" I scream at him.

Glazed-over eyes study me. Inching back further, I grip the needle tight. I can stab it into his eye if I have to. With a snarl, he flashes across the room, his arms banding around me.

"No! Let me go!"

I'm lifted into the air.

"Shut the fuck up, little bitch," he orders.

"I said let go!"

Growling under his breath, he runs straight at the curved wall. I'm smashed into the stone so hard, I see stars. His arms are the only thing keeping me upright, and I'm forced to drop the needle.

"P-Please..."

"Jesus. Do you ever shut up?" he hisses, the scent of tobacco washing over me. "Let's see if we can silence that tongue of yours, before I cut it out."

Tossed over his shoulder, we wind down a spiral staircase that's carved from more stone. At the bottom there's a circular room, strewn with empty beer bottles and piles of rubbish.

"Where are we?" I gasp.

He jolts me on his shoulder. "Silence, whore. I don't want to hear a damn word out of you."

Ducking into a smaller room, full of broken furniture, I'm dumped into a sagging chair with a thud. His fist slams into my jaw before I can ask any more questions.

My head snaps to the side, ringing with pain. I lick my split lip, a hot dribble of blood running down my chin.

"No funny business," he scolds.

Another figure steps into the empty doorway. "Now now, calm down, Jace. No need to scare our guest of honour."

Boasting scarred knuckles and a fearsome expression, the man that snatched me from the graveyard offers me a sleazy smile. He's older, wrapped in bronze skin that's lined with wrinkles.

"I was wondering when you'd wake up." He saunters into the room, a gun in hand. "That dose of ketamine was a bit excessive, I know."

Dismissing his lackey, he pulls up another chair closer to me. I can smell the stench of alcohol and cigarettes on his dark clothing.

"The name's Diablo. I'm a friend of Leighton's."

The way he's looking at me is sickeningly familiar. Hungry and curious, his lips are lifted upwards with amusement.

"Leighton?" I repeat.

"Who do you think he goes out drinking with? The kid's got some serious shit going on, you know." He taps his temple. "All up here."

"What d-do you w-want with me?"

"I've been getting close to Leighton for months now." His smile takes a sharp, dangerous edge. "He loves to talk after a few drinks. That boy needs to learn how to keep his mouth shut."

Flipping open his jacket, Diablo pulls out a long, sharpened hunting knife. My heart somersaults. The blade is glinting with menace in Diablo's hands as he uses it to clean his nails.

"Sabre's operations have caused some problems for my organisation, Harlow. London is my city. Their jurisdiction means nothing to me."

"Operations?"

Diablo narrows his eyes. "They raided our biggest warehouse and took something that belonged to us. I want it back. This is a trade, plain and simple. I planned to use Leighton, but you'll do nicely."

Fear pounds through me. "You followed us here?"

"It was easy enough once you left the big city. Now, what should we send them? Perhaps one of your fingers?"

I shrivel back into the chair. "I won't help you to lure Sabre in. No way. You'll have to kill me first."

"So eager to die, are we?" He leans closer, licking his lips. "I've heard all about you. Tell me, did daddy touch his baby girl like he did those other women? Did you like it, Harlow?"

My eyes flit around the room, searching for an escape route. I need to get out of here right now. He knows too much.

"The windows are boarded up and the doors are locked," Diablo supplies. "Do I look like an amateur? This place is a dump, I know. You can thank your boyfriend for that."

"You're w-wrong about them," I stutter out. "They don't care about me. I'm nothing to them. Holding me as bait won't work."

He reaches out and strokes his calloused hand along my jawline. Sickness rises up my throat, forcing me to clamp my mouth shut rather than throw up on him.

My fear of touch comes roaring back so fast, it's disorientating. Living with the guys has desensitised me. I don't want this disgusting snake touching me, though.

"Of course, they care," he says simply. "We've seen the helicopters. The town is crawling with assholes in black, tearing the place apart."

Hunter. Enzo.

Leighton. Theo.

Please, come find me.

"Don't worry." He breaks my silent prayers with a wink. "They won't find you until I want them to."

Pulling his phone out, Diablo shows me a grainy camera feed. It's the rugged, snow-swept coastline of rural Devon, but Croyde is nowhere in sight.

"Say hello to Paulo. He's keeping an eye on our perimeter. We sent your friends a nice little video to get them riled up."

Panning the camera to the left, a huge, decrepit lighthouse comes into view. It's high above the craggy cliffs, isolated from the clustered houses and town centre in the distance.

We're inside.

The guys will never find me.

Tucking his phone away, Diablo shifts even closer. His hand strokes over my throat, teasing my pulse point with a single finger.

I fight to keep still as he caresses my collarbones next, gently tracing the edge of the scar peeking out of my shirt. His breath is hot on my skin.

"Hunter, Enzo and Theodore wiped out our business overnight," he utters in a whisper. "They stole two million pounds in cash and butchered my men with machine guns."

"I c-c-can't help you."

"That's where you're wrong. I know what kind of men run Sabre Security. They won't give up their latest prize without a fight."

Tears spill down my cheeks as he cups my left breast through my shirt. Humiliation settles over me in a clinging cloud.

"They have to choose." He snickers. "Their fucked up little freak or two million pounds. I'm leaving with one."

"I told you. I'm nothing to them."

Diablo's hand slides inside my shirt and pushes the cup of my bra aside. I bite down on a whimper as his fingers pinch my nipple.

"You're living with them, eating their food, wearing their clothes. I don't like being lied to, Harlow. You're one of them."

As his hand sneaks lower, touching the scars that wrap around my torso, I lose it. Obeying won't save me. I know that now. The past has taught me something.

Seething, I lunge from my chair and collide with him. Diablo shouts, grabbing me by the hair and smashing my face into the nearby wall. My vision blackens for a stomach-churning second.

"Bad move," he jeers.

Pinned against the wall, his nails dig into my throat. My windpipe is crushed in his strong hand, tightening, wringing, twisting.

"I'll send them your fucking corpse if I have to." Diablo spits in my face. "But not until I've had my fun with you. I want to see those scars for myself."

Leaning close, his tongue flicks across the steady stream of blood soaking my face. I can't even scream. The violation breaks something in me—a flimsy barrier holding my rabid side back.

Managing to lift my knee, I smash it between his slightly spread legs. Diablo curses, his grip on my throat slackening enough for me to draw in a breath and kick his ball sack again.

"Argh!" he bellows.

Swallowing the blood pooling in my mouth, I advance before he can straighten. My plastered arm collides with his face, his nose exploding with a glorious crack.

I don't stop. It isn't enough to satisfy the monster baying for blood inside of me. Diablo's cupping his broken nose, falling onto his back. I leap on him and straddle his waist.

"I'll f-fucking kill you," he garbles.

I hit him again, spraying his blood across my face. "People worse than you have tried and failed."

Reaching for the knife he dropped on his way down, I hold it over his torso. His life is in my hands, ripe for the taking. I don't have to let him walk away from this.

I'm the girl that left the darkness behind. The girl who survived the devil himself. I've got nothing left to lose and no amount of pain will scare me back into the cage I escaped.

"I don't need anyone to come and save me," I spit at him.

"You w-won't do it."

His eyes widen through a curtain of blood. Whatever he sees on my face, it unnerves him. I'm not alone. The ghosts of the girls are here, seething and writhing at the back of my mind.

"I'm done spending my life afraid of men like you."

Time flashes in blinding snapshots. Diablo screams as the knife buries in his stomach, slicing through fat and muscle like butter.

Teeth bared, I twist the blade inside of him, soaking in the spray of blood. His wails of pain are music to my ears.

"Diablo!"

A cigarette hanging from his mouth, Jace steps back inside, paling when he sees the bleeding mess trapped beneath me. He reaches for the gun tucked into his jeans as I wrench the knife out of Diablo.

Plaster shatters above my head as he fires the first shot. I duck and slide through the expanding pool of blood, avoiding the next bullet. As he runs into the room, I dive to the left, letting the knife sail.

The world narrows as it parts the air, slashing into Jace's left arm before hitting the floor. He screeches, dropping the gun in the confusion.

I don't wait to see him fall. The lighthouse blurs around me. They're screaming in my ears—the ghosts fuelling my rage.

Run.

Run.

Run.

Bursting outside, I'm nearly swept off my feet by the wind. The snow has stopped, settling along the cliffs while the raging torrent of the ocean sweeps into shore.

I can't run down the hillside with the path obscured by snow and frozen ice. All around me, there's nothing but sheer drops and a frozen wasteland.

"You fucking cunt! Get back here!"

Limping into the snow, I scan for an escape route. A sudden crack breaks through the air as something whizzes past me. Jace is in the doorway, the gun in his blood-slicked hand.

"There's nowhere to run, bitch!"

Another crack.

I duck again, sliding over a huge patch of ice. The bullet barely misses me. The only way out is straight ahead where the cliff ends, leaving nothing but thin air.

Dark, foreboding waves await nearly a hundred feet down. The drop is huge, but adrenaline is forcing me forward, closer to oblivion.

"You're gonna pay for stabbing him!" Jace yells, attempting to pick his way across the ice field. "There's nowhere to run!"

"Fuck you," I shout back.

Crack.

Fierce pain tears through my thigh, a burning laser point melting flesh and bone. The bullet passes straight through me, tearing a deep, oozing hole.

"Next bullet's going in your head!"

Reaching the edge, I face the sheer drop. The ledge I threw myself off months ago was nothing compared to this suicide mission.

I'd rather die for my freedom.

Drowning isn't a bad way to go.

"Please," I whisper to God. "Please."

Eyes shut, I leave myself to his heavenly mercy. Plummeting hard and fast, wind tears into my hair and clothes, the roar of waves growing closer with each millisecond.

All my pain and fear are obliterated as I surrender to fate. Water rushes up to meet me, pouring into my throat and lungs as I'm swallowed by ocean waves.

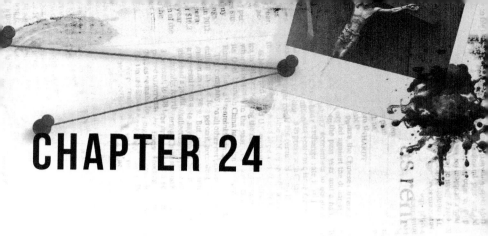

CHAPTER 24

Hunter

Keeper — Reignwolf

I must've watched the video a thousand times in the hour since it came in. Harlow looks so small, so broken, her unconscious body crumpled on the floor of some shithole.

"I want my money, Rodriguez," the voiceover croons. "You're going to put the cash back where you found it and I'll let the girl go."

Drawing his foot back, he boots Harlow straight in the stomach. Her mouth lolls open, but she doesn't wake up. They've pumped her full of something.

"My men are waiting in London. You have one hour before I start cutting pieces off your pretty girlfriend."

The video feed cuts. I shove the laptop back, twitching with the need to smash it to pieces. We cleaned that damn warehouse out during our latest raid. The cash was turned over to law enforcement.

It's gone, and we're out of time.

I'm going to break every single bone in this asshole's body, grind his organs into a paste and gouge his eyeballs out with my bare fucking hands when I find him. Death would be too bloody kind.

"It's been thirty hours." Enzo blinks, his eyes sagging with exhaustion. "What is she thinking? Has she given up on us?"

"Don't fucking say that. Harlow knows we would never leave her behind. We're going to find her."

"Hunter!" Theo shouts from across the room.

Surrounded by paperwork, wires, and countless computer screens, he signals me and Enzo over. Theo's working almost head-to-head with Kade, taking three laptops each.

"What is it?" I sigh.

"This guy sent the video from a smartphone, using a burner app to anonymise his number. But it doesn't encrypt the file itself."

Kade turns his closest screen. "We've decoded the metadata to triangulate a rough GPS location. Two other phone signals have moved between the cellular towers in the last twenty-four hours."

"Are they traceable?" Enzo demands.

"Already on it."

Theo studies lines of complex computer script, twitching with adrenaline as he jumps over the code. We're going to need a better lawyer. He's hacking into the national prison system before my eyes.

"Jesus, Theo," I curse.

"We don't have time to issue a warrant for information," he mutters, disabling their security software. "These pieces of shit have to be known to law enforcement."

Enzo nods, watching over his shoulder. "Most of the cartel we dismantled was made up of old-timers."

"I'm in." Theo flicks between several screens, plugging the number into the system and searching.

We all lean closer.

"There." I point a finger at the top search result. "Released from prison earlier this year, still open to the parole board."

Theo clicks on the profile. "Diablo Ramirez."

"Son of a bitch," Enzo breathes. "This bastard was on our hit list for the raid. He was mid-level, responsible for funnelling cash up to the big guy."

Loading the prison record, Theo magnifies the attached mugshot. We all study the face of the man that's holding a gun to our heads.

"We found no trace of him last month." I shake my head. "He's a fucking foot soldier. A nobody."

"That nobody is beating the shit out of Harlow." Enzo glowers at me. "Take this seriously, Hunt. We brought this on her."

"You think I don't know that?" I growl at him.

Leighton rises from his seat at the table next to Brooklyn and her men. His face is whiter than the frosting of snow outside.

"I didn't know who he worked for," he whispers, unable to look at us. "I swear, I didn't fucking know."

"What the hell are you talking about?"

When he refuses to look up from the mugshot on Theo's screen, I roughly grab him. He's wearing the same damned expression as the day he got convicted—a stupid, ashamed child, running from the responsibility.

"What did you do?" I bark in his face.

"I had no idea," he mumbles back.

"Goddammit, Leigh. Do you know this scumbag?'

He bites his lip. "We drink together."

Enzo steps up behind him, causing Leighton to startle when he collides with his barrel chest. There's no running away this time.

"We invited you into our home," Enzo says, seizing his shoulders. "Gave you a fucking job. Money. Anything you needed. One rule, that's all we asked."

"No breaking the law," I finish flatly. "What the fuck are you doing fraternising with this asshole?"

Everyone in the room is watching us with laser eyes, but they don't intervene. This is family business.

"Not all criminals are bad people," Leighton tries to argue. "The pair of you have dodged prison a million times."

"We protect people by any means necessary," I spell out. "You broke some poor fucker's vertebrae over a girl and earned yourself a prison sentence!"

"And clearly, Diablo Ramirez is an exception to that rule," Enzo adds in a thunderous tone. "He works for the damn cartel."

Leighton swallows hard. "He was the only one who knew how hard it was to come home. Do you have any idea how lonely I've been? My own family doesn't recognise me."

"So you became friends with a convicted drug dealer to feel less alone?" I shout furiously. "I've never heard such shit in my life."

"Enough! All of you!"

Slamming her hands on the table, Brooklyn sends papers and empty coffee cups flying. Eli visibly recoils. He still hates loud noises.

"You're all idiots!" She points between us. "Stop arguing about who is to blame. It doesn't fucking matter! What's so special about this girl that she has you at each other's throats?"

"Because she belongs with us!" Enzo booms, shoving Leighton so hard, he falls to his knees with a huff.

Lips spreading in a smile, Brooklyn looks pleased with herself. Enzo realises he's fallen straight into her trap and glances away.

"At last," she comments softly. "Took you all long enough to move on. I didn't think you'd admit it though."

Bracing my hands on my hips, I let my head fall. This shouldn't feel like a defeat. I've spent the last five years battling tooth and nail, keeping the company alive… keeping our family alive.

But accepting Harlow is a defeat. The best fucking defeat I've ever conceded. I'm laying down my arms and surrendering to the truth that I care about her. A hell of a lot.

More than I've cared about anyone since Alyssa passed. Harlow hit our home like a lightning bolt. None of us were prepared for the destruction of the suffocating prison we'd built for ourselves.

Her desolate smiles and unbreakable strength have reminded us of the power of living. Even Theo's coming around, bit by bit, no matter how hard he battles against it. We're all changing.

"Plug Diablo Ramirez into your new software," I order them. "If he's appeared on any CCTV feed in Devon, public or private, I want to know."

"You think he'd be stupid enough to stick around?" Hudson asks, smoking a cigarette in the corner despite the hotel signs.

Plucking the cigarette from his fingers, Jude stabs it out on the table. "Ramirez could be anywhere in the country by now."

"What about the exchange?" Leighton asks as he stands up. "He promised to return Harlow, so he must still be here."

Glowering at Jude, Hudson shakes his head. "You'll be lucky if she isn't dead already. He has no intention of trading."

"Hud!" Brooklyn exclaims.

"Just saying it how it is," he mutters.

"Well, keep your fucking opinions to yourself," Enzo yells at him.

Lapsing back into a ticking time bomb of tense silence, we let Theo and Kade go to work with their very much illegal software. They talk in low, urgent whispers.

Within half an hour, we've got a series of hits on private CCTV footage they've extracted from hacked cameras. Facial recognition software catches our perp right in the act.

"There he is." Kade zooms in the footage and sharpens it with a few lines of code. "He caught up with her just outside of Croyde. She zig-zagged through town on foot towards the graveyard."

"How did she get through town without our scouts picking her up?" Enzo seethes.

Theo studies another frame of camera footage, where Harlow's ducked behind a dumpster to hide and catch her breath.

"She's small, fast and determined," he observes. "By the time our helicopters arrived, she was already at the graveyard with him."

"How did he know we were here?" Hunter asks.

Swiftly sliding past the hotel's flimsy security, Theo runs his facial recognition programme on top of their CCTV camera. It dings with a hit almost immediately.

"Motherfucker," I bark angrily.

Diablo walked past our hotel on the day we arrived, pausing to glance up at the camera before shuffling back into the darkness. He's been here this whole time, waiting and biding his time.

"He followed us."

"Looks like it," Theo confirms. "Traffic cams place him half an hour behind you on the road down to Devon."

Enzo looks ready to explode. "Leigh, did you tell this wanker where Hunter and Harlow were going?"

"No!" Leighton blusters. "Of course not."

"Frankly, I don't believe a word that comes out of your mouth anymore." I pin him with an arctic glower. "Diablo has clearly been running surveillance on the team. You put us all in danger."

"Guys," Theo draws our attention back. "Look at this. He walked past Giana Kensington's house after you entered and tailed Harlow when she left. This was unplanned, but it worked perfectly for him."

"Fuck!" Enzo swears, snatching up his gun holster. "Where's the

GPS location for that video? I'm going to rip him a new asshole."

"We're all going," I assure him.

Hudson stands up. "I'll fire up the helicopter."

Quickly packing up and grabbing weapons, we begin to file out of the hotel. Eli and Phoenix opt to hang back, running comms with our team as Theo and Kade track our location from here.

Brooklyn checks the gun in place beneath her leather jacket. "Jude, Hudson and I will follow in the car. Take the helicopter."

Pulling her into a side hug, Enzo nods. "We can scout out the rough area of the GPS location from the air."

"Exactly. You'll find her, big guy." She smiles up at her closest friend and confidante. "Have a little faith."

Eyes connecting with mine, I nod in agreement. In many ways, Brooklyn has become the one constant in all of our lives.

She's spent hours listening to us, cooked us dinner, washed our clothes when grief made it too hard to even lift a finger. The broken phantom of a human we first met has transformed into an incredible person.

Piling out of the hotel, the Cobra team plus Jude load into Hudson's Mustang, speeding off in a spray of gravel. We take the helicopter, with Leighton quietly slipping in the back as I rush through pre-flight checks.

Within minutes, we're gliding through the air. The snow clouds are beginning to clear, unveiling Devon's long, rugged coastline.

"We're gonna get slapped with a fine for flying without a permit," Enzo complains into his headset.

"I couldn't care less about a permit right now."

Steering the glossy, black beast through the wind with ease, we follow the GPS location that Theo's transmitted to the built-in computer. It's a coastal location, deserted on a quiet hillside.

"There's nothing here," Leighton says, frustrated. "The town is miles back. I can't see anyone on the beach."

Dropping down a little, we scan the cliff more closely. Still nothing. They could be speeding down the motorway by now, leaving us to embark on a wild goose chase.

"Let's go down," Enzo decides. "We need to search on foot. There's nothing to see up here."

As we touch down on a quiet stretch of the beach, we leap out onto the wet sand. Devon is touristy in the summer, but in the dead of winter, there's nothing but wind and crashing waves.

"Where do we begin?" Leighton asks anxiously.

"You can stay here." I cut him a hateful look. "I don't need your fucking feelings getting in the way of finding Harlow."

"That isn't fair. Let me help."

"You aren't trained for active operations."

"I care about her too, asshole!"

Enzo grabs Leighton and pushes him forward. "You're coming. Call this lesson number one. Make a mess, and it's your responsibility to clear it up."

Storming past them, I jog towards the pavement winding through the clusters of locked-up houses. We haven't got time for this bullshit. Cold sweat drips down my spine as we go door to door, checking for signs of life.

The GPS was a rough estimate. They could be anywhere in this quiet borough. Brooklyn calls in to say they're combing the housing estate for abandoned properties a mile or so further on.

"There's nothing here!" I yell at them.

Enzo taps the comms in his ear. "Theo, we're getting nowhere. Can you give us any more information?"

Nodding, he spins on the spot, scanning our surroundings again.

I battle to keep my nerve. Fear and panic aren't emotions I've handled in a very long time. Not since I lost my hearing.

My phone blares, and I almost drop it in my haste to answer.

"Yeah?"

"Hunter!" Brooklyn screeches down the line. "There's an abandoned lighthouse on the cliff. Hudson and Jude are running up, but we heard gunshots."

Sprinting away, the other two battle to keep up as we return to the beach. It's huge, stretching out towards the next town. Craggy cliffs box in the ocean, with dangerous waves battering the rocks.

Crack.

Up the steep cliff, a decrepit lighthouse looks ready to collapse into ruin. I can just make out specks of people at the very top. If Jude and Hudson are running, it's going to take a while to summit that cliff.

"We need to take the helicopter!" Enzo shouts.

Something's happening. There are several more gunshots, and my heart leaps into my mouth as someone stops at the cliff's edge.

"Oh my God," Leighton exclaims.

All I can see is flowing, brown hair and a white, bloodstained shirt. Harlow stares out at the sea as she inches closer to oblivion.

The wind drowns out our yelling. She's teetering on the verge of a hundred-foot drop, her body swaying in the strong breeze.

We won't get there in time. She's being pursued as more gunshots crack through the air. My vision narrows as the seconds crawl by.

Gunshots.

Spraying blood.

Snow drifts.

Dark, thunderous clouds.

Reality ends as the blur of blood and brown hair plummets over the edge. I'm watching a movie, hammering my fists against the glass as characters take wrong turns and fall victim to the writer's brutality.

She's airborne.

I don't think before throwing myself into the sea. When the water gets too high to wade through, I dive beneath the next wave. The current is violent, battering and bruising me with stormy fury.

I don't know if Harlow can swim.

If she even survives the fall.

The world falls utterly silent as my hearing aid fails in the water. It doesn't stop me from frantically slicing through the sea, my arms powered by a pleading mantra.

I can't lose someone else.

I can't lose someone else.

I can't lose someone else.

In the icy darkness of the water, memories are painted in swirls of sediment. Past and present are entangled as that fateful day washes over me.

Alyssa is cradled in my arms, blood spilling from her mouth. Glassy eyes stare up at me. Her fingertips leave a red stain on my cheek as they fall away.

It's happening again.

Coming up for air, I search the water. It's so wild, I can't see anything. The cliff is a few hundred metres ahead, but Harlow jumped far into the air.

She must be here unless she's slipped beneath the water. Diving back in, I push my exhausted body to move. Each metre of progress takes great effort against the current.

More. More. More.

Lungs burning, my legs and arms beg for relief. Popping up for a breath, the silence is disconcerting in such a lawless place. She could be screaming, and I'd never hear it.

"Harlow! Harlow!"

There.

I squint through the burn of salt water. There's a head bobbing in the relentless waves, being pushed underwater over and over again.

With renewed determination, I dive back down and manage to grab hold of her arm. Kicking hard to get above water, we break the surface together.

I cough and splutter, waiting for her lips to move. She's barely clinging to consciousness, her lips blue and head hanging limp.

"Wake up, sweetheart."

Nothing.

"Wake up!"

There are streaks of dissolving blood on her skin, and a necklace of dark bruising circles her throat. All of this blood is coming from somewhere, but I can't find it in the choppy water.

Holding her afloat with all of the energy I have left, I bob in the water. Everything has drained out of me. I can't get us back to shore.

The helicopter is back in the air, silently flying towards us. I can't hear a single thing without my hearing aid. With rescue in sight, despair still swallows me whole.

Harlow is unresponsive, a dead weight in my arms. My vision is blurry from the salt water, morphing her familiar face into one I haven't seen for nearly six years.

Alyssa stares back at me.

Limp. Lifeless. Dead.

CHAPTER 25

Leighton

How – Marcus Mumford & Brandi Carlile

I'm the first one there when Harlow wakes up. I've been sleeping on her bedroom floor, dodging Sabre medics, IV drips and hired nurses. They pass me in a blur as I stare at her bed, unblinking.

After everything that happened, Hunter wasn't willing to let her out of his sight. The hospital released her for home treatment when he threatened to shut down the department.

Propped up on my elbow, I'm half-heartedly watching my laptop while lost in thought. I've never felt so fucking alone. None of the others will speak to me, and Harlow nearly died.

It's all my fault.

Every bit of it.

My life has been a series of shitty decisions and fatal mistakes. I'm the family screw-up; nobody expects much from me. Even growing up, my father never gave me a second thought.

The night I lost control and broke Thomas Green's back for sleeping with my girlfriend, I lost any chance of ever proving myself.

He will never walk again. I did that, accidental or not.

My anger is well concealed, but it's always been there. The indignation of a kid overlooked and pushed aside. I play a good game, but not many people know the real me.

Diablo was the only one that seemed to understand. The world inside prison is a completely warped reality. Coming home was like being set adrift, without a lifeboat, into the Atlantic Ocean.

"Did Rachel s-seriously f-forgive Ross again?"

Her raspy voice scares the shit out of me. Looking up from my uncomfortable nest on the carpet, I find Harlow watching me through half-lidded eyes.

"Goldilocks?"

"Hey, Leigh."

Her thin smile allows breath to enter my lungs for the first time since she was dragged from the sea. It's fucking dizzying.

"You said it first, Rachel's an idiot," I force out.

"You better not have skipped ahead without me."

I scramble to my feet, stretching sore muscles from camping out on the bare carpet. "I wouldn't dream of it."

Harlow lifts her hand and strokes it over Lucky's ears. The dog hasn't left her side, and not even Hunter had the heart to kick Lucky out of bed. She wanted to be with Harlow.

"I missed you," she whispers weakly.

My feet are rooted on the spot. I can't find it in myself to move any closer to her. People get hurt when I grow close to them. They suffer because of me. I can't do that to her.

"I missed you more."

Wincing when she tries to move, Harlow's eyes dart around the bedroom. It's late at night, the others are all downstairs. Hunter was taking another hysterical call from Giana when I last went down.

We've been taking turns watching Harlow, waiting for the moment her eyes would open. Nobody has slept a wink, and after the madness of the search party, we're all ready to crash.

"What happened?" Harlow murmurs.

A lump gathers in my throat. I have to look away from her before I can answer.

"We all flew back here last night. You were shot, princess. You're lucky it went straight through your thigh. No surgery required."

She tests her arm, the wet plaster cut away and replaced with a brace now that the fracture has healed.

"Diablo?"

I stare at the wall, silent.

"Leigh? Please talk to me."

"Enzo dealt with him," I answer emotionlessly. "The rest of his men are being rounded up by another team as we speak."

"He's... dead?"

"Yeah. Look, I should go. You need to rest and get better."

As I turn to leave the room, my heart seizing painfully, her high-pitched voice stops me in my tracks.

"Please," she whimpers. "Don't go."

"Harlow... I can't stay."

The soft, agonising sound of her crying knifes me straight in the gut. She may as well cut my heart from my chest and crush it. That would hurt less.

With every instinct screaming at me to walk away, I turn around and return to her bedside. The moment I'm close enough, she grabs a handful of my t-shirt in a death grip.

"Stay," she insists.

"The others... it should be them here, not me." I dare to meet her tear-logged eyes. "I trusted Diablo, and he hurt you."

Pulling me closer, the needle taped to her pale skin pulls taut. I peel her hand from my t-shirt before she hurts herself.

"None of this would've happened if I didn't let Diablo get close." I stroke her bluish veins. "I allowed him to manipulate me."

"Nobody allows anyone to manipulate them," Harlow whispers. "You wanted a friend. There's no harm in that."

"Well, my desperate fucking need to feel less alone put you in danger. All for what? A drinking buddy?"

"Leigh, stop."

"No. I don't even deserve to be in this room with you."

Gritting her teeth, Harlow wrestles aside wires and IV lines to free up a space next to her on the mattress. She pins me with a fiery look.

"Get in. No more arguments."

My heart threatens to shatter and slice us both to shreds. All I want is to feel her warmth wrapped around me, to be whole and content. She's reminded me of what it means to belong to someone.

Too bone tired to fight for a single second longer, I slide into the empty spot. Harlow burrows closer, her nose nudging against mine.

"I'm so sorry," she whispers, our lips a breath apart. "I never should've run. It was stupid and reckless."

I stroke her matted hair. "You've got nothing to apologise for. Apart from drooling on Hunter while unconscious, I suppose."

"What?"

"You ruined his favourite shirt."

"You're kidding?" Her voice rises.

"Easy, Goldilocks. I'm joking."

She relaxes against my chest with a sigh. We lie in silence, holding each other so close, it's a wonder either of us can breathe.

I memorise every inch of her. The expanse of her bruised and scarred skin, the tiny blemishes and freckles across her slightly crooked nose. Her thick lashes dappled over dark splotches of exhaustion ringing her crystalline eyes.

She's so fucking beautiful.

I need to remember this moment, capture it in mental ink and hang it on the battered walls of my soul. After prison, I vowed to never again give someone access to the most vulnerable part of myself.

No matter how alone that left me.

But with Harlow, I want to try.

"Please… don't run away again," I plead in a soft whisper. "If you need space, that's fine. Tell someone and we'll make it work."

"I'm sorry," she repeats tiredly.

"Stop apologising. Just don't walk out without saying goodbye. It may not seem like it, but I have… feelings. We all do."

"Feelings?" Harlow echoes.

"The world is a better place with you in it, believe it or not. I don't want to be here if you're not with me."

Seeing her bandaged and bruised after so much progress is excruciating, but I know she'll rise again. The frightened girl that arrived here has blossomed into someone else.

"I think… I have feelings too," she whispers back.

"You do?"

"I didn't want to leave, but seeing Giana was too much. I spent my entire life thinking I was someone else. Now, I don't know who I am."

I press a gentle kiss to her temple. "You're my Harlow."

Her head tilts up so she can look at me. She's breathing hard, and I can feel the pounding of the organ behind her ribcage.

Letting my eyes close, I press my lips to hers. No matter how stupid and downright fucking selfish it is. I want her. I need her. I can't spend another second in this house without her.

The kiss is featherlight, a tender, apologetic brush. We drink each other in with nothing but charged air between us. Running the tip of my tongue over her lower lip, she relents and allows me in.

It's the most subdued kiss of my life, and it may well get me burned alive if the others knew what we were doing up here. I can't find it in myself to care. I'll risk the punishment.

Nothing matters but the feel of her breath tangling with mine, infusing the very essences of our beings into one chaotic, destined knot. Kissing her is the biggest mistake of my life.

She's going to create a war within this family. I know it. I'm running into battle, blinded and unafraid. I'll fight the only family I've ever had if that's what it takes to walk away with her.

When we separate, neither one of us speaks for a long time, until the sound of arguing from downstairs breaks the daze.

"I should go and let them know you're awake." I sigh, brushing the hair back from her face. "Rest, Goldilocks."

She's asleep in an instant. Tangling my fingers in her soft, brown locks, I sift through the layers, afraid of what I'll find. There's a significant bald patch spanning the left side of her crown.

It's uneven and sore, the scalp reddened where she's ripped whole clumps of hair out over time. Gulping hard, I smooth her remaining hair back down.

Fuck.

This is such a mess.

She doesn't stir as I sneak out of bed and back downstairs. I can hear the others in Hunter's office, bickering again. We seem to be lurching from one disaster to another.

In the kitchen, the mess from Theo's drunken brawl last week still remains. None of us have stopped to shower or sleep, let alone clean up. I feel like I've been living on a razor's edge.

As I'm putting the finishing touches on a tray of sandwiches for everyone to eat, footsteps join me in the kitchen. Enzo silently steals one and retreats to inhale his food at the breakfast bar.

"Food?" I ask Hunter.

He shakes his head, hitting the kettle to make another extra-large batch of tea. Pulling out a fresh mug, he leans against the countertop and lets his head fall into his hands.

"What is it?"

Enzo drops his sandwich, seeming to lose his appetite. "Another letter was delivered to HQ while we were away."

Stepping into the room, Theo lingers awkwardly. It's only the second time I've seen him in this house since I've been home.

"It was a warning note," he supplies, his glasses tucked into his ringlets. "Delivered along with three dismembered fingers."

"What the fuck?" I exclaim.

Hunter slams the fridge door as he retrieves the milk. "DNA analysis got a match. Felicity Tate. No known address and not reported missing. She's been admitted into the hospital for several drug overdoses over the years."

"What the hell is this sicko thinking?" Enzo scrubs his face. "This doesn't fit his MO. Serial killers don't break their patterns."

"What did the note say?" I glance between them.

Pulling out his phone, Theo hands it over for me to inspect. I feel like I'm going to puke as I scan over the scrawled writing.

The longer you keep her from me, the more death there will be.
Harlow belongs with her family.
Patience is a gift from God.
Mine is running very short.

"What are these?" I frown at the lines of random numbers. "Coordinates?"

"We've sent Hudson and Kade to check it out." Hunter adjusts his new hearing aid. "They left a few hours ago."

"I have a bad feeling about this," Enzo complains as he retrieves some headache pills. "This bastard is taunting us."

"Let him play his stupid games. Harlow is staying right here, and we're going to hang him from a damn noose when we find him."

Grabbing some bottled water, I inch out of the kitchen. All of them are staring into space while eating the sandwiches I made. It's a start. They're not giving me death glares anymore, at least.

"Harlow's awake," I declare.

Their eyes snap to me, filtering between excitement and trepidation.

"Did she say anything?" Hunter demands.

Pushing aside the memory of her sweet lips on mine, I shrug. "Not much. She's gone back to sleep for now."

He strides from the room without another word. Theo watches him go while Enzo hesitates. If he chews his lip any harder, it'll bleed.

"She'll want to see you."

Enzo looks stricken. "I don't… I can't. We did this to her."

"Just get up there, Enz. Worry about everything else tomorrow. I feel the same, but she needs us more than she needs our guilt right now."

With a tight nod, Enzo follows in his best friend's steps. I'm left with the chatterbox staring at his battered Converse as he deliberates.

"Are you coming up?"

"M-Me?" Theo stutters. "Ah, I don't think so."

"Come on, man. You're here, aren't you?"

"I'm not sure why."

"Because… this is your home."

"I should go." Theo glosses over my words. "Kade and Hudson

will call to check in soon. Tell Harlow… tell her…" He lets out a heavy sigh. "Forget it."

I place a hand on his slumped shoulder. The ghost that haunts this house is so often unspoken, existing only in the empty space she left behind. No one feels that more acutely than Theo.

"You're allowed to want something *more*," I offer plainly. "No matter the voice inside your head screaming that you shouldn't. Alyssa would want you to find some happiness."

"What if… we don't deserve it?" he worries.

"We don't." I backtrack, gesturing upstairs. "But regardless, we're all she's got. I won't abandon her like the world did."

Shoving several bottles of water into his empty hands, I grab his flannel shirt and drag him upstairs. In Harlow's room, the awaiting puppy pile is laughable.

Enzo is curled up in the crater I left behind, a tree-like arm holding Harlow against his chest. He's… actually snoring.

"Is he asleep?" I laugh quietly.

Hunter's splayed out in the armchair next to the bed, his bare feet propped up on the mattress. He's staring at the IV line.

"Passed out the moment his head hit the pillow."

Placing the bottled water down, I search for a space to squeeze into. Hunter growls as I dislodge his feet and crawl in on Harlow's other side, so she's sandwiched between me and Enzo.

"You could've taken the floor," Hunter grumbles.

"And miss out on cuddles? No way."

"If the bed breaks, you're fixing it."

"Whatever you say."

Theo hasn't moved from the doorway, watching us all with palpable terror, like he's faced with shark-infested waters rather than a sleepover. He tentatively inches into the room.

Hunter's mouth is hanging open slightly, until I nudge him so he looks away. We don't want to scare Theo off now. This is the closest he's been to us in years.

"We should get a TV in here," I observe, snuggling against Harlow's chest.

Hunter's eyes are already shut. "Are you planning to do this often, Leigh?"

"Aren't you?"

Clicking the light off, Theo takes a fortifying breath before curling up at the end of the bed. It's big enough that he has space to sleep, pulling his legs up to his chest so he's tucked into a tight ball.

"Maybe a bigger bed too," Hunter adds sleepily.

I nearly die when Theo chimes in.

"Agreed."

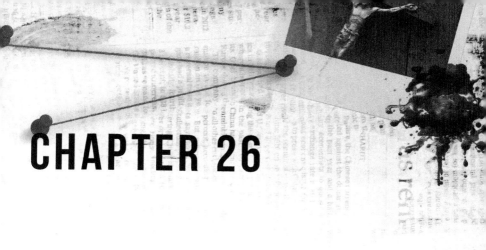

CHAPTER 26

Harlow

Last Night I Watched Myself Sleep And Saw Things That I Wish I Could Forget - Aurora View

startle awake, fisting the oversized black t-shirt I stole from Hunter's wardrobe. My bed is empty for the first time in a whole week. Breathing hard, I force myself to calm down.

I'm home.

I'm safe.

I'm alive.

The sound of someone's snoring penetrates my panicked brain. In the corner, curled into himself like a sleeping baby, Theo is dead to the world. I can't believe he stayed overnight.

The stack of books on my bedside table is a fresh selection from his wealth of literary goodness. I've been going stir-crazy on bedrest, but his daily visits to talk and discuss book theories have kept me sane.

I've seen a new side to him this week. Beneath the palpable anxiety, stone-cold detachment and awkward charm, there's a kind, caring and thoughtful person.

Easing out of bed without moving my bandaged leg too quickly, I pad over to him. The armchair can't be comfortable. Theo moans in his sleep as I brush tangled, blonde curls from his face.

Without his glasses, he looks so young. I can't believe someone so sweet and compassionate has experienced so much pain. You can see it written in every frown line etched around his eyes.

Slipping on a loose pair of sweats and my favourite cardigan, I silently slip downstairs. Snow is falling outside in thick curtains, dousing the world in a blanket of silence.

Lucky perks up from her bed as I walk into the kitchen. Padding over, she butts her head against my belly, her tongue lolling out.

"Hey, girl," I whisper. "You don't have to sleep down here just because Hunter tells you to, you know."

There hasn't been a whole lot of space in my bed. Enzo's taken to crawling in late at night when he's given up working or running for hours on end. He never speaks, just pulls me against his chest and passes out for four or five hours.

Making myself a cup of tea, I blow the steaming liquid while standing at the sink. The snow looks so beautiful, pristine and glistening like miniature diamonds on the front lawn.

"Got some more tea going, by any chance?"

Stifling a scream, I nearly drop my mug. "Hunt!"

Propped in the doorway, he watches me with a lazy half smile. My mouth dries up in an instant. He hasn't bothered to put a shirt on, wearing only a pair of low-slung, grey pyjama bottoms.

His whole chest is on display, every tanned, chiselled inch. The dark swirls of ink that paint his torso are stark in the early morning daylight.

"Sorry." He snickers. "Couldn't resist. You're up early."

"Yeah. I'll make you some tea."

His smile widens. "Sit down, sweetheart. I've got it."

"No, no. Allow me."

Grabbing another mug, I set to making him a cuppa. My heart is still pounding hard. I'm struggling with my anxiety at the moment, with every creaking floorboard and slammed door causing me to spiral.

"Sleep well?" Hunter asks as he takes a seat.

I open the fridge to grab the milk. "Yeah, not bad. I decided to get up before I become one with the furniture and never walk again."

"You've earned the time to rest."

I hand him the cup of tea with an eye roll. "You don't need to coddle me; I'm not going to run away again. No more lazing around doing nothing. It isn't helping."

"Coddling?" He raises a thick eyebrow.

"You heard me."

Walking over to the French doors, I stare out at the crisp snowflakes while finishing my tea. When Hunter's warmth meets my back, I let myself relax into his embrace as his chin rests on my head.

"What are you doing?" I breathe out.

His chest rumbles with a contented noise. "Isn't this okay? I've hated leaving you to go to the office this week."

"Theo's been dropping by to keep me company." My chest aches with sadness. "Although Leighton still won't talk to me. He's been drinking again."

"I know. I'm dealing with it. Enzo's going to take him to HQ today, get him assigned to some work. He'll be alright."

I turn in Hunter's arms. "You're helping him?"

"He's my brother, Harlow."

"I just thought... well, I didn't think you cared about him." I wince at my own words. "Sorry, that sounds crappy."

Sighing, his hands land on my hips as he pulls me flush against his bare chest. "I get it. We have a complicated relationship. But that doesn't mean I'll watch him beat himself up about Diablo."

"He's lucky to have you."

Hunter chuckles. "Not sure he sees it that way. I've always tried to look after him, even when he didn't want it."

His long hair is damp, spilling over his broad shoulders in dark, slightly curling waves. I play with a strand, biting my lip.

"What is it?" he rumbles.

"Do the others know about… us?"

"Us?"

"Don't play games, Hunt. You know what I mean."

He smirks down at me. My lungs seize up as he drags a single finger along my jawline, his thumb tracing my parted lips like usual.

I silently beg for him to keep touching me. Even if I've spent every night wrapped up in Enzo's arms, and the first thing I did when I woke up was lock lips with Leighton, I need Hunter as well.

"Is there something you want?"

"Yes," I mewl.

His lips brush across my forehead in a torturous tickle.

"And what is that?"

My thighs press together. Heat is pooling in between my legs, building in low, tantalising embers. I can still feel his lips against my pussy in that hotel room.

"Please touch me."

His touch vanishes, and I almost cry out in agony. Hunter's staring at me, a ferocious emotion writhing in his irises.

"You're going to be the death of me," he whispers. "And I couldn't care less. I'm done pretending I don't want you."

His lips smash against mine, so hard that our teeth clang together from the sudden movement. My back meets the French doors as he slides a leg between mine to pin me in place.

The delicious hardness pressing against my core sparks my fervent need to be touched and tasted again. He made me feel things I never imagined. Just thinking about it makes me wet down there.

"Come and buy a Christmas tree with me before I fuck you right here, right now, in the middle of the goddamn kitchen where everyone can hear us."

I choke on thin air. "Excuse me?"

"You heard me."

Trying hard not to pant as his hips rock into mine, I fight to straighten my lust-filled thoughts. "A tree? Now?"

Hunter's beard tickles my neck as he kisses his way down, his hot tongue flicking across my collarbones. Every place he touches feels like it's on fire, searing me down to the bare bones of my skeleton.

"Christmas is next weekend, Harlow."

"Seriously?" I gape at him.

"We've been busy with all the craziness."

"Don't you have to work? Enzo's been running himself ragged. He won't tell me what's going on with the investigation. I know something's happened, but—"

"Harlow," he scolds sharply. "I told you not to worry about it right now. You were kidnapped, threatened and shot. We're big boys, and we will take care of the investigation while you recover."

"We agreed you'd be more honest with me."

"You need to rest," he insists.

"I need you to tell me the truth!"

Defeated, Hunter releases his grip on my hips. "Another body turned up this week. We've been receiving... letters."

I stare at him wordlessly for several awful seconds. Part of me is horrified. Another part is surprised it took this long.

"Letters?"

"Threats, mostly," Hunter explains reluctantly. "The latest one had coordinates. We sent two agents, and they found a body waiting."

Stepping out of his embrace, I rest a hand on the door to stop myself from falling over. Everything is spinning all around me.

"How long ago?"

"Sweetheart—"

"How long, Hunter?!"

He sighs again. "Five days ago. We've identified the victim, no family. Nobody reported her missing. He could've had her for weeks."

Hanging my head, I bite back the furious sob that threatens to tear out of me. That woman doesn't need my tears. None of them did. They needed someone to save them.

"What kind of threats?" I ask in a strained voice.

"We're taking care of it."

"Hunter, if you don't tell me right now, I will walk out of that front door and never look back. I deserve to be treated as an adult."

Taking a seat at the empty table that we never use, Hunter shakes his head. "You're right. I just want to keep you safe, and I thought keeping this under wraps for now was the right call."

"It wasn't."

"Yeah, I see that now."

Softening, I wrap my arms around his lowered head. His nose buries in my stomach as he hides there, breathing deeply.

"I don't always get things right," Hunter admits, his voice muffled by my stolen t-shirt. "Especially when it comes to you."

We cling to each other for a moment. It's strange to see Hunter so vulnerable. He never admits to weakness or mistakes, nor does he let anyone close enough to comfort him.

"It's okay," I murmur back. "None of this is easy or straightforward. You're doing the best you can."

His head lifts. "You don't have to forgive me."

"No, but I am."

His smile is far more devastating than any near-death beating or badly placed knife wound. It slashes against my throat and steals the air from my lungs without a single warning.

"Pastor Michaels wants you back," Hunter explains. "He's threatening to kill more girls if we don't release you from protective custody, presumably so he can snatch you up."

"He s-said that?" I stammer.

Hunter grabs my wrist, his thumb stroking against my pulse point. "We're close, sweetheart. I've got drones and scouting parties searching for the chapel where you were held. We'll get him."

"They've been searching for weeks!"

"And that's why we can't give up now. Once we find this place, we'll raze it to the fucking ground. He can't hide forever."

Trying hard not to fall apart, I focus on each stroke of his skin on mine. I don't want to go back. I'd rather die than live a life of captivity, especially now I've tasted what it means to be alive.

"When you find it, I'm coming with you."

"Not a chance in hell," Hunter growls.

I pull his fingers from my wrist. "This isn't up for discussion. You want me to sit here while he's out there, hunting more women. I need to know that when the time comes, I'll be allowed to help."

"It is far too dangerous."

"You asked me to trust you." Staring into his eyes, I let him see the guilt eating me up inside. "I'm asking you to do the same."

Hunter seems to deflate. "Fuck, Harlow."

"Is that a yes?"

"You're not giving me much of a choice."

Standing up, he crushes me against him in a back-breaking hug. I hold him tight, my eyes stinging. It feels good to finally be accepted into the family and be trusted, like an equal.

"Come on," he says gruffly. "Let's go get this fucking tree."

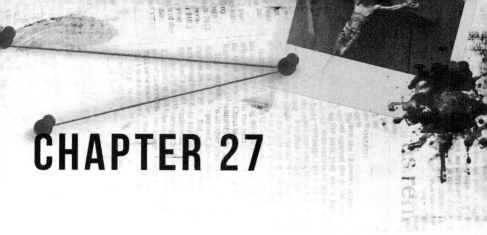

CHAPTER 27

Harlow

I Never Loved Myself Like I Love You — Dead Poet Society

"**W**hat is this place?"

I stare at the sprawling farm with two huge wooden barns and a queue of people marking the entrance. It's busy, despite the steadily falling snow and frigid temperature.

In the distance, several fields of pointy trees stretch as far as the eye can see. Little dots of people duck and weave through the thicket, children squealing with excitement as they find the perfect tree.

"Christmas tree farm." Hunter pulls a scarf and leather gloves on. "I haven't been here in years. It used to be a tradition... before we stopped celebrating."

The shadows are back on his face, and I hate it. Leaning across the console, I press my lips to his stubbly cheek.

"It's beautiful."

The corner of his mouth lifts. "You ready?"

"Hell yeah."

He walks around the car and opens my door for me, offering two large hands to help me down. I'm enveloped in the scent of his spicy aftershave as he reaches for my beanie and tugs it over my hair.

"Perfect."

"I don't think so," I say shakily.

"I wouldn't be so sure. Come on, let's do this."

We queue with the other locals, holding hands in the swirling snow. This place is in the middle of nowhere. We set off after scarfing down breakfast, leaving before the others woke up for work.

With our entry fee paid, Hunter guides me into the first field. I stare open-mouthed at the rolling hills, scattered with different sizes of Christmas trees. Every inch of it is crammed with luscious green pine.

"Oh my God! Look at them all!"

I take off as fast as my stiff leg will allow. The bullet wound is bandaged up and healing well, but it still hurts when I walk. The doctor dropped by for another check-up yesterday.

"Harlow," he yells after me.

I dive into the tightly packed rows of trees. I've never seen anything like this. Fishing out my phone, I snap a picture and send it to Leighton. This will cheer him up.

My phone buzzes with his response.

> **Leigh:** You went without me? :(
>
> **Me:** I'll bring you a Christmas tree back <3
>
> **Leigh:** You better. Enzo is making me go to the office. If I'm arrested for murder, please bail me out.

I'm still laughing when a red-faced Hunter manages to catch up to me, yelling his head off.

"What have I told you about running off?"

I show him my phone. "Leighton isn't loving office life."

Hunter rolls his eyes. "Enzo's going to enjoy punishing him with stacks of paperwork. I caught him sneaking a red sock into Leighton's washing the other morning."

"What? Why?"

"He's still pissed at him, but I've told him to back off. This is quiet revenge. Half of Leighton's wardrobe is now pink."

"No wonder he's been in a foul mood."

I turn to face the various sized trees. They're all gorgeous. We walk slowly around the whole field, taking it all in as the snow continues to fall. All of the trees are taller than me.

Hunter intervenes when I can't make up my mind and picks the most monstrous tree possible. It's easily twice my size. I doubt it'll fit in his car, let alone the house.

With our tree chopped, wrapped and transported by a friendly man in thermals, Hunter links his hand with mine and takes me to the onsite coffee shop.

We slip into a smaller barn that's been converted, blasted by warmth from the roaring fire in the back corner. Panelled in dark wood and decorated with wreaths of holly, several trees are dotted about.

Their twinkling lights add to the cosy, comforting atmosphere. The scents of baked cookies, fresh coffee and pine needles wash over me in a mouth-watering cloud.

"This is awesome."

Hunter peers down at me. "I like seeing you happy."

His words turn my insides to mush. I look away from his watchful gaze so he can't see me blushing for the thousandth time.

"I like being happy," I reply honestly.

We find two bright-red armchairs next to the fire. I let Hunter order for me, too mesmerised by the open flames dancing against the bricks. Despite the noise of people around us, I don't feel on edge or afraid.

Everything about this place screams of comfort and familiarity. I thought leaving the house after everything that happened in Devon would be hard, but my curiosity to see the world is stronger.

I refuse to be a victim again.

My life is mine to live.

Hunter returns, sliding off his jacket and gloves as he takes the seat next to me. He looks so handsome, dressed down in jeans and a t-shirt. It's a welcome change from his usual office wear.

"So… how does it work? Christmas?"

"We'll celebrate at home." Hunter stares at the fire. "Mine and Leighton's parents will probably come. Enzo's aunt sometimes makes an appearance. We haven't done this for a long time."

"Why did you stop?"

His throat bobs. "When Alyssa died, being together as a family was too painful. We stopped celebrating and never looked back."

"What about your friends? The ones that helped find me?"

"I'm sure they'll come by. Brooklyn's been bugging me all week about meeting you. They were there while you were unconscious, but you deserve a proper introduction."

Our drinks are plonked down by a friendly waitress, breaking the bubble of privacy encapsulating us. I often forget that anyone else exists when I'm in Hunter's magnetic presence.

He slides a reindeer-themed mug over to me, watching closely for my reaction. It's overflowing with whipped cream and giant, fluffy things covered in chocolate sauce.

"What is it?

"A hot chocolate."

I cast him a glare. "I know what that is. But this thing…"

Selecting one of the fluffy things, I place it on my tongue and almost groan. Hunter smothers a grin, looking beyond cute as he sips his drink.

"Marshmallow," he supplies.

"Yum. I think I've found my new favourite thing."

"Even above popcorn?"

"Nothing is above popcorn," I defend hotly. "Leighton always puts extra butter and salt on it for me. Delicious."

"He's determined to fatten you up."

Hunter moves his chair so it's closer to mine. The rest of the coffee shop is blocked out, leaving us in our own little world. We're both facing the fire, sipping our drinks in companionable silence.

"Hunter?"

He hums a response, his eyes nearly shut.

"Why do you think they took me?"

The question startles him from his fire-induced sleepiness.

"What do you mean?" he asks.

"The Michaels. Why me?"

He takes a sip of hot chocolate. "Well… I don't know, sweetheart. He has a pattern, but the victims are randomly selected."

"They could've chosen anyone." I fiddle with the Velcro on my arm brace. "I'm not wishing what I went through on someone else; I just need to know if there was a reason for it all."

"Does it matter?"

"I think… it does. I'm not sure why."

Licking cream from his lips, Hunter looks thoughtful. "Have you spoken to Doctor Richards about this?"

"Every week. He always says I need to focus on the future instead of trying to make sense of it all. That's what drives people crazy, looking for order in the madness."

"Well, he knows what he's talking about."

Hunter's studying me again in the way that I hate. I don't think he even realises he's doing it. I'm not an exhibit for his portfolio, another chip on Sabre's long record of successes.

"I always thought that everything happens for a reason," I try to explain. "I have to know why this happened to me before I can move on. That's what is holding me back."

Hunter shrugs. "Sometimes there isn't a reason for these things. I've seen a lot of shit. Good people that have suffered. I stopped looking for any sense of order in it all a long time ago."

"But… it isn't fair."

"Life never is. Why did Alyssa die? Why did Leighton go off the rails? Why did I lose my hearing? Why isn't the world fair and equal?"

Anger brews within me. I was looking for an answer, but I'm realising that nobody truly knows how the world works. It's an unknown force that washes our lives to shore, some harder than others.

I spent years praying to a God that didn't listen, being beaten to the rhythm of his sermon while countless twisted Bible stories were etched into my skin with blood and sweat.

"Why?" he repeats sadly. "There isn't an answer."

"Maybe we have to make our own answer in this life," I say slowly. "I don't need to make sense of the madness. Living in it… I think that's enough for me."

His eyes meet mine. "Then I'll hold your hand in the madness. Fuck God and his stupid why. This is our path to forge."

"You will?"

Smiling again, Hunter reaches out to clasp my fingers. "Yeah, I fucking will. I meant what I said about us."

I shuffle closer to press my lips to his. Initiating the kiss feels like a bold move, but he reciprocates without hesitating. This powerful, foreboding man is ready to bow before me.

Somehow, I have to tell him that I have feelings. Strong, complicated ones. And not just for him. All of them mean so much to me. I know it's not normal to feel like this for more than one person.

If I tell Hunter, will he make me leave? Will I lose them all? Because I can't fathom a world where I'm not surrounded by all four of these guys—the people that saved my life before they even knew who I was.

I can't give them up.

I don't want to.

I want... to be theirs.

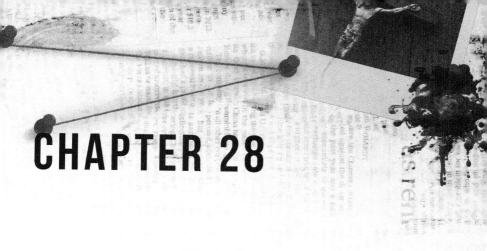

CHAPTER 28

Harlow

Sunny Side Down — Sad Heroes

"**H**oly shit. That's a fucking Christmas tree."

I smack Leighton's arm. "Language."

"Sorry, Goldilocks. But seriously, you couldn't find a smaller one? I knew I should've gone with you two yesterday."

He flops down on the sofa with a tired huff, leaving me to continue sorting through a dusty box of decorations. Hunter dragged it in before disappearing into his office to make some phone calls.

It doesn't look like anyone has touched the box in a long time. Whoever last packed everything away was methodical. Each package is labelled in neat, feminine handwriting.

I trace the curling script, imagining the woman that once sat in my place. I finally have a name for the ghostly presence that hangs over this family. *Alyssa.* I feel like I know her, somehow.

"When are we decorating?" Leighton breaks my thoughts.

"Just waiting on Enzo and Theo, I think."

"Snacks? I haven't eaten since second lunch."

I cast him a frown. "Second lunch?"

He winks at me. "I'm a growing boy, you know."

"Keep eating for three people and you'll need to go on a diet. I won't have you breaking my bed with that ass, Leigh."

His mouth drops open so fast, I swear his jaw might break. I'm too slow to scurry backwards as he throws himself at me, shoving the box aside to lean over me and start tickling my ribs.

"Apologise, princess. I am not fat!"

Gasping for air, I writhe on the carpet. "I'm sorry! Parlay!"

"We're not fucking pirates. Parlay doesn't count."

The way he's smiling down at me is a huge relief after his silence this week. I know he's still struggling with what happened, no matter how many times I've told him not to blame himself.

I want my buddy back.

He isn't allowed to self-destruct.

Disappearing to find food, Leighton returns with a doughnut crammed in his mouth, and three more stuck on his fingers. He wiggles a finger to offer me one.

"Yeah, I'll pass." I snicker.

"What?" he says around a mouthful.

"That doesn't look particularly appealing."

Snorting, he stuffs a second doughnut down his throat and collapses onto the sofa. Hunter's still wrapped up with his phone call, and Enzo went out for an after-work run to decompress.

Clicking my tongue, I join Leighton on the sofa and beckon for Lucky to follow. She ends up sprawled out across both of our laps, sneaking bites of doughnut Leighton feeds her when I'm not looking.

"We need a cheesy Christmas movie," Leighton suggests as he grabs the remote. "That'll get us in the spirit."

"Why cheesy?"

"Uh, because all Christmas movies are. I dare you to find a single one that doesn't make you cringe."

I shake my head at him. "Then why do you watch them?"

"It's traditional! The cheesier, the better! That's it. We're starting with the best, and we'll work our way down."

An hour later, I'm laughing so hard, I think I'll pee myself. Who knew that a pair of house robbers could almost die so many times, in so many creative ways? Cringy is definitely the right word, but I secretly love it.

"*Home Alone*? Seriously?" Hunter interrupts.

He walks into the den, carrying armfuls of snacks as he frowns at the TV. Leighton whoops in excitement, spreading his arms to receive the food.

"Harlow hadn't seen it."

"So you figured you'd torture her with this shit, huh?" Hunter slumps onto the sofa, opening a bag of peanuts.

"Shut up, you loved it when you were younger," Leighton bickers.

"I was a kid."

"Your point being? We're starting with the best."

"*Home Alone* isn't the best Christmas movie." Hunter stretches his legs out. "It's over-commercialised and pure fantasy. Nobody survives a brick to the head."

"You take that back." Leighton steals the bag of peanuts from his hands and adds it to his pile of food. "*Home Alone* is awesome."

"Want me to hit you in the face with a brick to check? I'm more than willing to perform an experiment. Give me those back."

"Only if I can return the favour, big bro. And no, they're mine now. You'll have to earn them."

While the brothers agree to arm wrestle for the bag of peanuts, the front door slams shut. Enzo's standing in the entrance, breathing hard and sweating. He gives me a wave before disappearing to shower.

Snuggling into Leighton's side, I open my mouth for him to put a chocolate-covered pretzel inside. Hunter munches on his peanuts triumphantly, the pair exchanging sour barbs.

When Enzo comes back, he's dressed down in sweats and a muscle tee, his black hair like spilled ink against his skin. Dislodging Lucky, he sits down next to me and slings an arm over the back of the sofa to ensconce me in his body heat.

"Hey there, little one."

I smile up at him. "Hi, Enz. Good run?"

"Cold. The roads are icy. Nearly broke an ankle a few times."

"You need to be careful out there."

The secret smile he shoots me makes my heart stutter.

"Are you worried about me, Harlow?"

I look back at the TV, stealing another handful of pretzels to busy my hands. "Nope. Not at all."

"Ouch."

We watch the movie, sharing snacks and laughing as the robbers return for round two. They still get their asses handed to them, and some imaginative use of swinging paint cans later, our second movie is done.

"*It's A Wonderful Life* next," Hunter declares, snatching the remote from Leighton. "Now that's a real Christmas movie."

"It's so depressing," Leighton groans.

"I'm counting on you going into a diabetic coma pretty soon, based on how much sugary crap you just ate."

He rubs his belly. "That was just a starter. We should totally order pizza. I'm still hungry."

Before we can start Hunter's movie, the security system in the entrance way beeps before the door clicks open. Excitement prickles across my skin as Theo calls out.

"Am I late?"

Pulling off a snow-dusted denim jacket, he wipes his glasses on the soft fabric of his flannel shirt. Clumps of snow are sticking to his blonde curls, but the smile on his lips is genuine.

"About two hours late," Hunter drones. "What took you so long? I told Fox and Rayna to cover for you tonight."

Theo meanders into the room. "Yeah, they are. Phoenix rocked up to drag the two brothers home for dinner. He stole my laptop and blackmailed me into eating with them."

Leighton chokes on a bite of chocolate as he laughs. Enzo reaches over me to hammer him on the back, also grinning.

"You went over there?" Hunter asks in surprise.

"Brooklyn cooked. Burnt lasagne."

"Nice." Enzo chuckles. "She brought some to the office for us last week and watched as we ate it. I gave an Oscar-worthy performance."

"Brooke brings in lunch now too?" Theo raises an eyebrow. "Huh. I placed bets on them calling the engagement off in the first three months. Dammit."

"You owe me twenty quid," Hunter points out. "I have more faith in them. We'll get her married off to the lot of them yet."

Toeing off his wet shoes, Theo tentatively pads into the living room. When his blue eyes brush over me, his smile brightens.

"Hey, Harlow. How're you feeling?"

"Good, thanks. I finished *The Picture of Dorian Grey* last night, so we need to discuss."

"I'll dig my spare copy out," he says happily. "It's been a few years. Go for *Frankenstein* next. You'll love it."

"Jesus Christ," Leighton curses. "Fucking nerds everywhere. Someone kill me."

"Careful what you wish for," Enzo threatens. "Nice pink t-shirt, by the way. Very masculine."

"I'm fully in touch with my masculinity, thank you very much. Mess with my laundry again and I'll shave your eyebrows while you're asleep."

"Children, now now." Hunter stands up and stretches. "I'm going to get a beer and dig out the pizza menus."

As he vanishes, I wriggle my way out between the arguing pair of idiots and approach Theo. He's standing awkwardly, seemingly too nervous to sit down with us.

"I'll go grab the books I need to give back to you."

"Harlow, wait." Returning to his coat, he slides something out of the pocket. "I found this on my lunch break the other day."

He holds out a slim, leather-bound volume to me. I tentatively take the old book and flip it over, tracing the title with my fingers.

"*The Grimm Tales*?" I exclaim.

Theo's cheeks flush. "I know it's your favourite of the books I lent you. This is an illustrated edition."

Thumbing through the book, the beautiful, hand-drawn pictures take my breath away. It's beautiful.

"Thank you so much."

"It's nothing," he rushes out.

Before he can run away screaming, I gently wrap my arms around his waist. Theo freezes like a pillar of ice, and I can feel the rapid pumping of his chest with each panicked breath.

It takes a full thirty seconds for his arms to band around me, but when they do, he pulls me close against his narrow waist. The scent of spearmint and old books clings to him like a second skin. It's so soothing.

"No, thank you," I repeat.

"You're welcome."

His voice is light and melodic, so far from the lifeless drone he's spoken with in the past. Offering him a smile, he hesitantly returns it, unleashing two perfect dimples.

"We're going to decorate the tree."

His face drains of all colour. "I, uh. I'm not su—"

I drag him over to the space we cleared in the corner of the room before he can run off. The boxes of decorations are still waiting, and the massive tree dominates the entire corner.

Hunter trails back in with a pack of beers, handing them out to everyone. I eagerly accept mine. With drinks opened and snacks spilling everywhere, we face the towering tree.

"Ready?" Hunter smiles at me.

I glance at Theo instead. His eyes are trained on the labelled box of decorations. The tension builds as we all wait for him to speak.

"Let's do this," he eventually says.

"How about some music, then?" Leighton suggests.

Breaking the silence, he turns the TV channel, and some crazy song begins to blast from the speakers. It's all tinkling bells and terrible singing that sets my teeth on edge.

We string the tree with lights first. Hunter meticulously spreads them amongst the branches, but his ruthless attention to detail becomes even more apparent when it's time for the ornaments.

"Just watch, he'll be getting a tape measure out in a moment," Leighton mock-whispers.

Enzo takes a swig of beer. "Remember the year we snuck downstairs and messed the tree up? He didn't speak to us until New Year's Eve."

"I thought his head was going to explode when he saw it." Leighton snorts. "It was worth the sulking though."

Theo smiles as he listens, sitting cross-legged on the floor. He's put himself in charge of the decorations box. With each memory he unwraps, his posture becomes more relaxed.

It's like he's opening himself up to the pain of being around his family again, but something so simple as decorating a tree is making the grief easier to handle. Not even Alyssa's handwriting slows him down.

Hunter glowers at the tree as Leighton deliberately places the ornaments too closely together or at odd angles, intent on pissing his brother off spectacularly.

"For fuck's sake, Leigh! Are you blind?"

"Nope." Leighton grins at him.

"Then stop messing with my organisation!"

Leaving them to it, I search the room for Enzo. He's leaning against the wall, watching them spar while drinking his second beer. They all fit together so perfectly.

He's got his family back.

I'm the one intruding here.

Swallowing hard, I lie about needing a drink and escape. This is exactly what I wanted—getting them all together, seeing the guys back as a family unit for the first time in so long.

I just didn't expect it to hurt, the realisation that I'll never be one of them. They're good people who deserve to be happy. I can never give them that, no matter how much I want to.

Slipping into the empty kitchen, I hop up onto the counter and wait for the kettle to boil. Tears are prickling the backs of my eyes and I feel stupid for letting the feelings overwhelm me.

I should appreciate what I have right now, not waste my time longing for something that will never be mine. It doesn't matter that the woman they loved is gone, and these four men are screaming out for someone to bring them back together.

"Harlow? Everything okay?"

Swiping under my eyes, I plaster a smile on as Enzo trails into the room and shuts the door.

"Are you okay?" I counter instead.

"I'm fine."

"Well, I'm fine too."

Sighing, he places his beer down. "I really hate that word."

"Then don't use it."

"You started it," he says, moving closer. "Look, this is hard. We haven't done Christmas in a long time. I thought I'd forget, but seeing everything laid out brings the memories back."

Making myself some green tea to avoid looking at him, I sense his imposing frame approaching me. Enzo is a physical presence, an unmovable mountain in an ever-changing landscape.

There's nothing impermanent about him, and I love that. He's the certainty I never had growing up. I know he'll always be here, no matter what, picking up the broken pieces of the people he loves.

"I keep getting snippets of memories after Devon," I admit quietly. "Glimpses, here and there. It's coming back quicker now."

"Your childhood?" Enzo guesses.

"Yeah. I remember more about my parents. The memories don't feel real though; it's more like remembering a story someone told me."

Enzo stops in front of me, his huge hands engulfing my legs. Unable to put it off any longer, I look up at his sad, accepting smile.

"We've been trying to find your dad this week," he reveals. "We need to question him now that we've reopened your old case."

"What? Did you find anything?"

"Not yet. The guy doesn't want to be found. He stopped checking in with his parole officer after a couple of months and vanished.

Probably abroad."

"Because he doesn't care," I snap angrily. "None of them do. Even Giana moved on and found a new family."

Enzo squeezes my knee. "Or he cares too much. People don't leave their lives for no reason. Either losing you broke your dad so much that he couldn't stay, or there's something we don't know."

"Like what?" I frown.

"That's what I'm going to find out."

Looking back down at the floor, I feel my throat catch. "What if you find him… and he doesn't want to know me? You said it yourself. He doesn't want to be found."

"Harlow, look at me."

I stare down at my sock-covered feet.

"Come on, little one."

When I finally manage to look up, Enzo's face is soft. He takes a strand of my hair, twirling the length around his index finger and absently studying it.

"How could anyone not want to know you? Fuck, Harlow. You're strong. Beautiful. Intelligent. So goddamn kind and giving, it puts the rest of us to shame."

"Just stop."

"Why should I?"

"Because it isn't true." I push his hands away. "I am none of those things. Do you have any idea what I've done? Who I really am?"

When I try to push Enzo backwards to escape, he steps between my spread legs and plants his feet. I can feel the smooth planes of muscle that make up his torso against my thighs, holding me trapped.

"Those girls' deaths were not your fault," he insists fiercely. "Is that what this is about? You can't keep blaming yourself."

"How do you know it wasn't my fault?"

"I know you."

My laugh is bitter. "That isn't enough."

"It is. You did nothing wrong."

His unwavering faith in me is a guilt-inducing knife twisting in my heathen heart. I don't deserve Enzo's trust or admiration. If he knew the truth, he would cast me out to die alone.

Laura's blood is on my hands.

She died because of me.

Despite feeling like the worst person in the world, my legs tense around him. I can't help it; my body won't listen to me. It wants nothing more than to be touched and worshipped in the darkness of sin.

That's the only revenge I can take on Pastor Michaels. I want to do every twisted, dirty thing he accused other people of. He told me I was a sinner, destined for hell. I want to earn that title.

Enzo's eyes narrow on me. My heart is racing so hard, I can hardly see the room around us. Ever so gently, he cups my cheek in his big, scarred hand. I feel so small and helpless in comparison to him.

"I know you," he repeats bluntly.

"You don't."

"Bullshit, Harlow. Say that crap again and we're going to have a problem. I won't hear it."

Burying my fingers in the length of overgrown hair at the top of his head, I stroke the shaved sides that reveal lumps and bumps in his skull, before moving down to his face.

Smile lines and a five o'clock shadow mark his skin, interrupted by the odd, faded scar. Enzo's eyes slide shut, his chest vibrating with a contended purr.

My friendship with him has always been different from the others, but after everything that's happened, he's been touching me more freely. Sharing a bed is so intimate, more than what mere friends do.

"Enzo?"

His eyes flutter open, revealing amber jewels.

"Yeah?"

"I just wanted to say… I'm sorry for leaving you all."

We stare deep into each other's eyes. I can see the imagined boundaries between us melting away like morning mist. It's all there on display—his hope, fear, the crushing loneliness and forever-present exhaustion.

He sees my anxiety and despair, the desperate need to fix the pain I've caused. Both of us are broken in different ways, but those shattered pieces are calling to each other, magnetised by hope.

"Harlow… the things I want to say to you… do to you… well, you're not ready for it. Do you understand what I mean?"

"Who are you to say I'm not ready?"

His eyes flash into dark, black pinpricks of desire. "You're not."

"Tell me what you want to do, and I'll tell you what I'm ready for."

"Are you bargaining with me, little one?"

I offer him an innocent smile. "What if I am?"

The heat from his body is burning through my clothing. I squirm on the countertop, needing some kind of relief from this relentless tension between us.

I want him to kiss me. Touch me. Worship me like Hunter did, claiming me for his entire team to hear. But I can't do this anymore. They have to know what's going on.

"Is this normal?" I breathe.

"What do you mean?"

"The way you make me feel. All of you, at the same time. I should tell you that Leighton has kissed me. And in Croyde, Hunter, um, he… we—"

"Slept together?" Enzo hisses.

"No! We just kissed and… he touched me. I liked it."

"He was the one who told me to stay away from you!" Enzo's face flushes as he takes a big step back. "That son of a bitch. I can't believe it."

"It wasn't like that, Enz. It just happened."

"With him and not me?" he deadpans.

I should fall to my knees before him or pray for forgiveness from the Lord Almighty. Pastor Michaels would beat me black and blue if he heard any of this. I hate how that makes me want to do this even more.

"You're right to be upset with me," I whisper sadly. "This is all my fault. Sins corrupt a holy man's soul. I've been corrupted. I'm evil."

Before my tears can fall, Enzo rushes back to me. I'm swept into his arms and lifted off the countertop. My back crashes into the nearby cupboard as he pins me against it, his lips seeking out mine.

In a moment I've dreamed about for months, our mouths frantically meet. Fireworks explode within me—bursts of heat and excitement, my nervous system becoming awash with pure sensation.

Enzo's lips are like velvet, teasing my compliance as he takes exactly what he wants without coming up for air. It's not like when the others kissed me. This is ravenous, infuriated.

I feel like I'm being punished, but the twisted voice in my head gladly accepts the beating his hungry lips bring. I'll surrender and take my sentence if it means he will spend forever kissing me just like this. I feel like a missing puzzle piece has slipped into place.

"Fuck the pastor," he hisses against my lips. "Fuck him and everything he has taught you. There isn't an evil bone in your body, Harlow Michaels."

Enzo kisses me again—harder, faster, his entire body rocking into me. The pressure is intoxicating. All I want is to crawl inside his body and hide there, curled around his heart like a cancerous parasite he can never escape from.

He shifts back slightly to let his hand skate down the length of my frame until he's teasing the waistband of my soft yoga pants. My heart rate triples with anticipation.

"Do you want this?" he growls out.

"Y-Yes... I want you, Enz."

Giving me time to change my mind, Enzo eases his hand inside. I'm pinned against the cupboard, a willing victim to his exploration. His teeth nip at my bottom lip as he pulls aside the material of my panties.

I can feel the wetness soaking into them from between my legs. It's embarrassing, but having him dominate me like this is heart-pounding. I feel so special under his attention.

"Did Hunter touch you like this?"

"What?" I refocus on him.

Enzo's fingers gently pinch my bundle of nerves, sending tremors through my body. He buries his face in my neck, his voice strained.

"Or was it more like this?"

He pushes a finger deep inside of my slick opening, causing me to moan out loud. I'm so worked up and wet, it didn't even hurt this time. Bliss pulsates through me.

"Answer me, little one. I want to know why my best friend tasted your sweet pussy before me. I've been waiting very patiently."

"I d-don't..."

Squeezing my eyes shut, I see stars behind my lids as his finger moves in and out of me with confident ease. When he thrusts another finger inside, I'm stretched even wider. I feel so full, ready to burst.

I'm not completely clueless. I know there's more than this to being with someone physically. The thought of sleeping with any of them is petrifying. I've seen how painful and awful it is.

All of the girls that Pastor Michaels touched were left broken, empty shells torn apart by the torture. I can't imagine any of the guys hurting me like that, but it's all I know.

"You're tensing up, baby," Enzo murmurs. "Do you want me to stop?"

While my brain is screaming at me to escape, I clamp down on the flow of bad thoughts. This is exactly what Pastor Michaels wants. I refuse to let him dictate my future any longer.

"No… don't stop," I moan loudly.

"Be quiet, then. I don't want those robbing bastards coming in here and seeing what's mine. They've already had their paws all over you, by the sounds of it."

I can't argue as he slams his lips back down on mine, moving in time to each thrust of his fingers. I know what's coming after the night with Hunter. Tension is pooling in my lower belly, churning with heat and excitement.

As my release builds up, I find myself wondering what it would be like to sleep with Enzo. The movies and TV shows have taught me enough. It doesn't have to be all blood and pain.

I want to be that close to someone, to have their entire world narrow until it's just you. It's the highest form of intimacy. I long for the guarantee that you will become someone's whole world. Nobody can take that away.

"There's my pretty girl. Come for me, Harlow."

Clasping Enzo's shoulders, I dig my nails into his shirt as the feeling bubbling inside of me erupts. Each wave of pleasure is melting me into a boneless puddle.

"So perfect," Enzo whispers in awe.

If anyone walked in right now, there would be no denying what just happened between us. That doesn't seem to bother Enzo as he pulls his hand out, raising two glistening fingers to my parted lips.

"Suck."

"M-Me?" I stutter.

"Do you see anyone else here? Your mess, little one. Clean it up."

His demand has heat flooding my body all over again. I wrap my lips around his wet digits, using my tongue to clean them. Salty fluid bursts in my mouth. I don't love it, but it's not disgusting either.

"Does it taste good?" Enzo asks wickedly.

Giving his fingers one last lick, I wipe my mouth. "It doesn't taste bad."

Pulling me close again, I cuddle his barrel chest. It feels so good to have Enzo's arms around me, my nerves still twitching with the aftershocks of him touching me. I wonder what Hunter or Leighton would think if they knew.

"What happens now?" I ask nervously.

Enzo squeezes me tighter. "I won't let you go for their sake. We've shared before, and we can do it again. It might take some convincing, though, after last time."

"Because of Alyssa?"

He flinches. "You know about her?"

"Not much," I admit, flushing. "Just what I've pieced together. Hunter told me some stuff as well. Did you... um, share her?"

His lips purse as pain is scored across his face. I can see it so clearly in his eyes—the gaping black hole that sucks in all hope and light. I've watched enough people die to know what grief feels like.

"Alyssa gave herself to us, and in turn, we did the same. She became more than a co-worker or a friend." Enzo's throat bobs tellingly. "She was our everything. Losing her tore us apart."

Reaching up, I rest a hand on his stubble-strewn jawline. Enzo's eyes flutter shut as he leans into my touch, placing his huge hand over mine.

"I'm not here to replace anyone," I whisper hoarsely. "I'll never be good enough for you guys, no matter what you think. I wish I didn't want you all, but I do."

His eyes open and lock on mine.

"I'm selfish. After losing so much, I want something good."

"That isn't being selfish," he argues.

"Isn't it?"

Enzo's nose brushes against mine. "No, Harlow. You deserve to be happy. I just don't know if we're the right people to give you that."

The truth stings, but I don't disagree. They're not the right people. Everything they think about me is a lie, and my presence in their lives only sentences them to an eternity of damnation.

Peeling Enzo's hand from my skin, I force my feet to move. Each step feels like the crack of fists breaking my bones, blow after blow. Enzo doesn't stop me from walking away, but I can hear his sigh of defeat as I do.

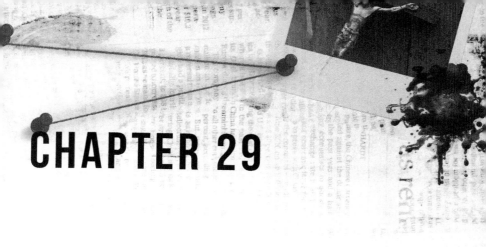

CHAPTER 29

Enzo

Vaccine – hometown & young

"Alright, listen up."

Staring out at the packed room in HQ, I clock the various teams. After a breakthrough in the past few days, we're closer than ever to ending this. Hunter's throwing every single resource Sabre has into a final push for results.

On the left table, the whole intelligence department has been dragged from their dark, antisocial caves to experience the light of day. Theo is chugging an extra-large coffee while his staff—Liam, Rayna and Fox—are all glued to their open laptops.

Opposite them sits the Cobra team—Brooklyn, Hudson and Kade. The Anaconda team, in charge of backup operations, is spread out in a rowdy group next to them.

Warner and Tara are breaking open the energy drinks already. Becket glares at his number two, Ethan, urging him to stop arm wrestling with Hudson before any bones are broken. I trained both teams myself. They're the best of the best.

Hunter clears his throat. "Let's recap."

Behind me, five full-size whiteboards display every bit of horror. All the photographs of mutilated bodies spill across the surface in violent detail, and a high-definition map of the country marks each dump site.

"Eighteen girls in five years, one who was pregnant at the time of death, and another body dumped last week." Hunter steps up beside me. "All victims are aged between teens to late twenties, with mixed ethnicities and impoverished backgrounds."

I gesture to several of the familiar faces. "Some of these women were sex workers operating across several different cities up north. They were all taken in public, taking care to avoid being spotted on CCTV. Most of them had no families to bother looking for them."

Hunter strolls past each photograph—blue, lifeless, their flesh carved like prime cuts of meat—until he stops at the whole board dedicated to Harlow.

Her younger self, Leticia Kensington, was a bright-eyed, angelic wisp of a child. Her hair was the colour of melted caramel, long and slightly curling at the ends, matching her impish smile.

Next to that, the comparison photo is stark. Only her brilliant-blue eyes and hair colour are the same. Leighton provided the picture, snapped as Harlow decorated the Christmas tree last weekend.

She has some more meat on her bones now after the past few months, but the childlike innocence and curiosity of her younger self is long gone. Pain intermingled with strength stares back at us.

"Harlow Michaels is our only living witness," Hunter explains. "Assisted in his crimes by his wife, the suspect held Harlow captive while indoctrinating and abusing her."

Theo knocks back the rest of his coffee and brushes tight ringlets from his face before coming to the front of the room.

"Harlow fled captivity on foot," he addresses the room. "We tracked her back to Northumberland. She travelled for nearly a week, hopping from one truck to another, contracting sepsis in the process."

Fishing a remote out of his jeans, he clicks the projector on. It splashes a satellite image on the wall, showing a stretch of woodland in rural Northumberland.

He uses the laser pointer to highlight a deep section of forest, far from the nearest town and inaccessible by any vehicle. It spans a good ten-mile radius in all directions.

"Using drones, we have narrowed down the search zone and used public records to find our target. Rayna, would you mind updating everyone on what you've found?"

Standing up, Rayna flicks purple hair over her shoulder. "We've identified the Mary Magdalene Chapel. Decommissioned for public use in 1936. Over time, the woodland grew and swallowed it whole. No one's seen the place in years."

Staring at the tiny region that could represent our first real breakthrough in months, I feel sick. This might be a turning point, the beginning of the end.

I should be relieved, but this case is the only thing keeping Harlow with us. A sick, broken part of me isn't ready for that obstacle to be removed. No matter how many lives it saves.

"Any signs of activity?" Hunter asks crisply.

Theo shakes his head. "No immediate signs of movement or inhabitation, but the drones can't get through the woods. We need to send a full reconnaissance team."

Nodding, Hunter glances around the room. "This is our first lead in months. We can't afford to screw this up. A team will find the church and check all the surrounding land for evidence."

"Are we expecting to find another prisoner?" Kade flicks through his paperwork. "If so, we'll need forensics and a medical team on site. Whitcomb's corpse is also still unaccounted for."

"As far as we're aware, there haven't been any more victims snatched." Theo looks grim. "But as we know, he has a type. These women aren't always on the police's radar when they vanish."

Hunter looks thoughtful for a moment. "We should be prepared for all possibilities. Make the arrangements just in case."

Kade takes notes and sets to work on his laptop. It will take a lot of coordination, but we have the infrastructure to pull it off.

"There's something else." Hunter clears his throat. "I agreed with Harlow that she could come with us for this bit."

"What?" I blurt incredulously.

Levelling us with a stare, Hunter doesn't appear fazed by the nuclear bomb he's dropped. It's preposterous. After years of fighting, he's finally lost his fucking mind.

"Why on earth would we risk Harlow's safety after everything that's happened?" I ask with a scoff. "Was one near-death experience not enough for you?"

"She asked me herself," Hunter explains. "She knows this sick fuck is out there, threatening to rain shit and misery on our heads if we don't release her."

"Even more reason to keep her safe!"

"She'll just leave herself," Theo agrees unhappily. "That's a lot of guilt for one person to bear. This would give her some control back."

"Seriously? You too, Theo?"

Shrugging, he retakes his seat. "She would be surrounded by a team of highly trained agents. Hell, we may even find this place quicker with Harlow there."

"I can't believe I'm hearing this."

"She isn't a kid, Enz."

"So you're ready to watch someone else get hurt?" I snarl at him. "You, of all people, Theo, know we can't take that risk."

"Enough," Hunter interrupts us. "This is our only shot. If we don't produce results soon, the SCU is going to halt funding and find someone else to take over the case."

That sobers everyone up.

"Who would they find to replace Sabre?" Kade frowns from his table. "We're the best around. Nobody else would stand a chance."

"So far, we've got jack shit to show for months of banging our heads against the wall," Hudson inserts. "Hunter's right; this is our only shot to make some progress."

"At the expense of Harlow's safety," I remind them angrily. "That isn't a price I'm willing to pay. She's going nowhere."

Stepping away from them, I retreat to the back of the room to cool off before I hit someone. The whiteboards reflect every second of our failure in taunting detail. So many lives have been taken.

We failed to protect these women. Not just us, but the whole damned world. Law enforcement. Families. Society. They were marginalised, made vulnerable by their social circumstances. Some have no family to visit their graves.

We have to do better than this.

But I won't sacrifice Harlow to do that.

In every single photograph staring back at me, I see her face. This is her legacy. It's a testament to all the excruciating pain and trauma she endured. I hate the thought of nobody being there to protect her.

Now that we've guaranteed her safety, Hunter wants to throw her back into the firing line. Endangering one life to save the potential many more that will end if we don't do this. It's an impossible calculation to make.

"Food for thought?" Brooklyn saunters up to me, leaving the others to continue talking.

"Something like that."

"Hunter has a good point, big guy. Sometimes the way forward is to go back. This is Harlow's past to unravel. She needs to be there."

"She isn't you, Brooke. The things she has suppressed, years of abuse and torture… pulling at those threads could break her. We'd be taking her straight back to her own personal hell."

"Maybe that's necessary," she murmurs, her eyes on a gruesome crime scene photo. "You helped me put myself back together, once upon a time."

"And it nearly killed you in the process. We had no choice but to tear your memories apart. Harlow doesn't need to be there when we hunt this bastard down."

Brooklyn's silver eyes pierce my skin. "She watched every single one of those women be brutally murdered in front of her eyes. This is her decision to make. You can't stop her from coming."

My forehead collides with the nearest whiteboard. "Dammit, wildfire. This is so fucked."

She rests a hand on my arm, causing her sweater sleeve to ride up. Brooklyn's body is more scar tissue than skin, but unlike Harlow's marks, it was entirely self-inflicted. If anyone knows what it's like to drown in their own demons, it's Brooklyn West.

"I can help her," she offers in a low voice. "She doesn't have to be alone when we go into this place. I'll do what I can to help."

"You'd do that?"

Her smile is crooked. "We owe Sabre a debt that can never be repaid. You didn't let me do this shit alone. I want to be there for Harlow now."

Pulling Brooklyn close, I ruffle her platinum hair while hugging her tightly into my side.

"You don't owe us shit. We're family."

"Then let's solve this case together, as a family," she replies. "Harlow is a part of that now. We can help her."

We seal the bargain with a bone-crunching hug. This angry, sarcastic slip of a woman has become an adoptive sister to us all. I know she'll take care of Harlow, in ways that we never could.

"Alright," I grumble into her hair. "I really fucking hate this plan, for the record."

Brooklyn snorts. "You hate any plan that doesn't involve sushi-rolling us in bubble wrap and killing anyone that gives us a second look."

"Is that a bad thing?"

She pats my back before releasing me. "Nah, it's not a bad thing."

Together, we return to the group. Hunter looks ready to declare his early retirement as Kade and Theo argue about the best route into the thick woodland.

Hudson's feet are propped up on the table as he happily smokes a cigarette in the chaos. Without Jude here to keep him in line, he's reverted back to his caveman ways. Typical.

"Harlow will come with us," I declare.

All eyes snap to me.

"What changed your mind?" Hunter asks.

"As much as I hate it, she has the right to choose. If we take that from her, we're no better than the people we're hunting."

He nods, checking with Theo, who also inclines his head in agreement. The three of us are the only family Harlow has right now. Her life is our responsibility.

"We'll bring in extra agents to beef up the perimeter," I add sternly. "I also want a helicopter in the air and drones surveying the surrounding land for any trouble. Nobody gets near her."

"And if the Michaels are in the church?" Theo replies.

I crack my scarred knuckles. "We rip those pieces of shit apart and let them rot in motherfucking hell, where they belong. I'll do it myself and let Harlow watch the damn show."

With the decision made, Theo sets his team to work mapping a suitable route to our location. This will be a huge logistical operation with lots of moving parts, and we're running short on time.

Dragging me into a quiet corner, Hunter yanks his hair tie out with a growl. Chestnut waves spill over his shoulders, and he takes a shuddering breath. If I didn't know him better, I'd say he's nervous.

"What if someone else is dead in there?"

I swallow hard. "We'd be leading Harlow into a bloodbath."

"Whitcomb's skeleton is a problem," Hunter worries. "This place could be the Grim fucking Reaper's lair. Not to mention the perps themselves."

"It's a huge risk."

His gaze is bleak. "We have no choice but to take it. If there's even a single hint of danger, I want you to grab her and get the fuck out of there. Don't worry about the rest of us."

"We have a safe house in Newcastle. That'll be our designated rendezvous if it all goes up shit's creek."

"Let's hope it doesn't come to that."

Hunter agreeing to this plan wouldn't have happened three months ago. Whether he realises it or not, Harlow's changed him. He never gives people the freedom to make their own decisions.

In our world, control and power come from the top. He's our commander-in-chief; we all follow his direction or suffer the consequences. That's exactly what's kept us alive for so long.

"Harlow's in therapy with Richards upstairs," he says, grabbing his phone from the table. "I'll speak to her."

"She'll need to meet everyone." I glance at the Cobra team, bantering amongst themselves. "They made it through, Hunt. It's possible. We can do the same for Harlow."

"I hope you're right. I'm not ready to lose her."

"Did you figure that out while your tongue was down her throat? Or after you took advantage of her on that damned trip?"

Hunter freezes on the spot.

"Yeah, I know all about that."

"She's a grown adult," he replies quietly. "It was fully consensual. I did not take advantage of her in any way."

"You'd just torn apart the basis of her whole existence, then took her to bed to make it all better. That's taking advantage in my books."

"Careful," he warns.

"How about your scoundrel brother? He's been fooling around with her too behind our backs."

Dragging me further out of earshot, Hunter curses up a storm. "All three of us, huh? I guess we should've seen that coming."

"She's admitted to having feelings for us all."

"Goddammit. I'm not looking to share Harlow with either of you stubborn assholes. We tried it before, and it didn't work."

My hands twitch with the urge to punch Hunter so hard, he regains his fucking hearing.

"Our relationship with Alyssa was not a failure," I whisper harshly. "How could you say that about what we had?"

His eyes stab into me. "Wasn't it? She's dead, and it's our fault. That's a failure in my eyes. Harlow deserves a hell of a lot better."

Before I can argue back, he storms off to head upstairs. There's no point following him or attempting to argue more. If he thinks I'm going to give up Harlow for him, he's sorely mistaken.

I know we're a broken family of hot-headed, unworthy idiots, and Harlow deserves to be with someone capable of loving her in a healthy, normal way, but that doesn't change how I feel.

I'm falling for her.

And I'll die to keep her safe.

Even from us.

CHAPTER 30

Harlow

Eyes On Fire - Blue Foundation

Sat opposite me in the comfortable interview room, Doctor Richards is taking meticulous notes. He's sporting another bright scarf, this one in an ugly shade of mustard yellow.

I enjoy his constant revolving door of crazy outfits. It gives me a distraction as he tortures my mind on a weekly basis. Given recent events, our sessions have been moved to HQ for the foreseeable future.

We've been at it for an hour, but he's resolutely ignoring the ticking clock. My throat aches from talking for so long and choking the emotions that want to overwhelm me.

"What happens next in your dream?" he prompts.

I anxiously pick at a loose thread in my sweater. "Mrs Michaels often hummed choir songs while cleaning up the basement. In my dream, I saw her dismantling a woman's body with a hacksaw. She was too heavy to carry out in one piece."

"What are you doing?"

"Nursing a broken wrist for refusing to help her cut apart my friend. I can still hear the sound of the woman's bones splintering. It felt so real, then I woke up."

"Use your senses. Describe it to me."

"Why?" I rub my tired eyes.

Richards places his pen down. "We have to open up all these tightly wrapped boxes, inspect the contents, and repackage them. It's the only way through."

My stomach hurts so much, I want to curl up in the corner of the room. These sessions are always intense. We've been wading through fragments of memories for a while, piecing together odd dreams and flashes of information that paint a harrowing picture.

The dream I had last night made me vomit when it startled me awake. I haven't eaten since. The sound of skin and bone being sliced keeps reverberating through my head like a broken record player.

"I don't want to talk anymore." I fiddle with my hair, battling the urge to pluck strands out in front of him.

"We still have fifteen minutes."

"Then we can sit in silence!" I snap back.

Lips pursed, Richards jots down some notes. I want to steal his notepad and throw it out of the window. He looks pointedly towards my leg. It's still sore, but the doctor said it's healing well. I was lucky to avoid any tissue damage.

"When confronted by your real family, you ran and placed yourself in danger. Does that seem like a healthy coping mechanism?"

"It was that or risk something worse," I say through clenched teeth. "I couldn't sit there for a second longer."

"Which is perfectly understandable," he combats. "But the way you chose to deal with it wasn't safe or constructive. That's why we're here. You can't keep running from what's going on."

"I'm not running."

"Perhaps you'd like to discuss your self-harming instead. Either way, we need to talk about what's going on. I'm not the kind of therapist that will sit here and let you spiral."

I gape at him. "My... s-s-self what?"

Richards removes his glasses to clean them. "Why don't you tell me?"

"I don't know what you're talking about."

"It may feel good in the short-term." He replaces his glasses and smiles reassuringly. "Using pain to cope with overwhelming feelings."

Linking my fingers, I ignore the screaming voice at the back of my mind. I know what he's talking about. The bald patch underneath my hair has grown bigger and more violent in the past week.

How he knows about it, I don't have to guess. One of the guys must've clocked what's going on and ratted me out. Shame slips over me, hot and clinging, until I want to crawl into a quiet corner to hide.

"It's nothing." I drop his gaze.

"Nobody is judging you, Harlow. It's normal to struggle with the trauma of what you've experienced. I want to help you."

"I don't need help."

"Is that why you're not sleeping or eating? And why you have started hurting yourself to cope? That doesn't seem like someone in control to me."

I close my eyes to hold the tears back. "Every time I sleep, I remember more about my past. The memories won't stop coming, and the more I remember, the worse it hurts."

He abandons note-taking and looks straight at me. Richards isn't a bad person. His job can't be easy, and he hasn't given up on me yet.

"I once treated a man that spent years of his life trapped in the mind of another." His smile is wistful. "Jude was forced to become a whole new person. He shut out the memories of his old life to ease the pain of losing himself."

"He couldn't remember? At all?"

Richards shakes his head. "It took a long time to piece those threads back together. We spent years working together."

"And it worked? He got better?"

"In a manner. Some things never leave us, Harlow. The size of our trauma doesn't shrink over time. With therapy, we learn to grow around it. Slowly but surely."

With a defeated sigh, I unclasp my fingers and make myself sit back in the chair. Richards smiles and picks his pen back up.

"I can remember the sound of her voice, and bits of what she looked like," I admit, squeezing my eyes shut. "It's all there, but it still feels out of reach."

"Then let's take a step closer. Listen to her voice, Harlow. Is it high? Soft? Loud? Quiet? Take in the smallest of details."

"She was crying." I wince, peering into the dark crevasses of my mind. "Her voice was kind of gravelly. She was older than the others."

"Zoom in a little further. Can you see her face?"

Taking a steadying breath, I walk myself back into my caged cell. Dank, dirty, the scent of spilled blood hangs in the air like smoke. Mrs Michaels' off-key humming wraps around me, broken by the awful crunching of the saw moving back and forth.

Pushing further, I follow the sound, returning to the sight that made me sick last night. Mrs Michaels lifts a stiff, blue arm to begin hacking it off, causing the corpse's head to slump and face me.

Empty, misted-over eyes meet mine. She's been dead for several hours. Her skin is grey, rubber-like, and purple around her neck where Pastor Michaels strangled her to death.

"Kiera," I breathe. "That's your name."

Her short hair is caked with dried blood, and her cracked lips once spread in warm, comforting smiles from between our cages. I think… she prayed with me, whispering for her personal God to save her.

"I recognise her," I say shakily. "She was maybe the second girl to arrive. One of the ones I'd forgotten until I saw her picture recently."

"Good," Richards encourages. "What else?"

"We prayed together. She was religious."

"She was?" he repeats, surprised.

"No… that doesn't make sense." Screwing my eyes shut, I try to keep my focus. "Why would he punish a woman of faith?"

"Go deeper. Visualise what happened."

"I'm scared," I admit.

"You're not alone, Harlow. I'm here and I promise that you're safe. These are just memories. They can't hurt you now."

My nails dig into my palms as I make myself go further, drinking in the scents and sounds. Rewinding the clock, I shove Mrs Michaels from the basement and return Kiera to her cell.

Dismembered limbs reattach themselves as her blood cascades back into her prone form. Colour returns as she begins to breathe again, her hands wrapped around the bars as we prayed together.

Our Father, who art in heaven.

Hallowed be thy name.

Pray with me, Harlow.

Here, like this. Shut your eyes.

"I can hardly hear her; there's a rainstorm outside. The basement is leaking. She's praying and her voice is shaking with each word."

"What else is she saying?" Richards croons.

Even after years of captivity, I was scared of the unknown. The women were terrifying to me at first, bringing death and violence into the basement.

It was a relief to have company at last and a harrowing sentence all in one. I could take my own beatings. They became routine, mundane even. But watching theirs was unbearable.

That man isn't your father, Harlow.

He's a monster.

I always knew he had the devil in him.

With a gasp, my eyes fly open. The warm lights of the interview room chase away the shadows that had infected my vision. I'm not in the basement. The past can't drag me back, kicking and screaming.

"I think… she knew him," I choke out on a sob. "Kiera told me that he wasn't my real father. I don't think I believed her."

Richards nods to keep going.

"When he killed her… she wouldn't stop screaming, begging him to spare her the Lord's mercy. He was angry, tearing her clothes off like an animal. It was so cruel, so violent."

I search the flimsy memory for anything else. It's like I'm digging around in an open chest cavity. Everything about this feels so wrong.

"She called him a… a… charlatan. What does that mean?"

Richards rubs his chin. "It sounds like she challenged him, and he didn't like it. Narcissists often don't."

"So she knew he wasn't a real pastor?"

"Potentially," he muses. "We know he gave himself a fake position of power to brutalise women under the guise of repentance. Self-deception cemented in violence."

"This makes no sense."

"Just take a deep breath for me, Harlow. You've achieved a lot here. Let's have a moment to close those boxes again."

Making myself relax, I unclench my hands and take a few deep, controlled breaths. My nails leave searing crescent marks in my skin. Even as Richards guides me through the breathing, I still feel like I'm teetering on a cliff's edge.

If Kiera holds a connection to Pastor Michaels that wasn't identified in the initial police investigation, the guys need to know. This could open a whole new field of enquiry.

"I have to go. Hunter needs to hear this."

Pulling my coat and scarf back on, I try to stand on trembling legs. Richards looks concerned as I try and fail to muster a thankful smile.

"Harlow, you need to stick to what we've discussed. Use your coping mechanisms and support system. These memories are traumatic. They will take some getting used to."

I offer a tight nod. "I will."

"Remember, you're growing around your trauma. Not erasing it. If you need to speak to me before our next session, I'm a call away."

"Thank you, doc."

He smiles back. "Go on, then."

Slipping out of the interview room, I head back to the foyer where I left Leighton scrolling on his phone an hour ago. The leather sofa is empty. He must've gone downstairs to the cafeteria to get food.

Waiting for the elevator to arrive so I can hunt him down, the doors slide open with a ding, revealing a frazzled occupant.

"Hunter?"

He looks up from his phone. "Harlow. I was just coming to get you. Leighton's doing something urgent for me."

"Is everything okay?"

Hair framing his face in disorderly waves, Hunter looks more agitated than when he left the house this morning. Everyone was heading into a big meeting when we arrived.

"I need to talk to you."

"Good timing." Grabbing his arm, I pull him towards a nearby office. "Something came up in therapy. You need to hear this."

Inside the office, Hunter extricates himself from my grip and shuts the door. I don't sit when he gestures towards an empty seat, pacing the small space instead.

Fire ants are eating at my skin, infecting me with doubt and worry. What if my mind is playing tricks again? I've unearthed these memories, but I don't know if I can trust them.

"Harlow?" Hunter asks with concern. "Talk to me, sweetheart. Tell me what you're thinking."

I stop pacing and bite my lip. "You know my bad dream last night? The one that made me sick?"

I scared him almost as much as myself when I woke up screaming like a banshee. He was asleep in the armchair as we'd been watching another black-and-white Christmas movie together.

"We unravelled it in therapy. It was about Kiera."

"Kiera James?" he answers grimly. "She was the second victim to be located. Particularly gruesome, if I recall correctly."

"They... um, dismembered her. That's what I was dreaming about. Mrs Michaels broke my wrist when I refused to help."

"Bloody hell, Harlow."

I wave off his sickened expression. "That's not the important bit. I think she knew him. She told me he wasn't my real father."

"You remembered that?"

"Yeah. She was religious too. He didn't like it when she insulted him, so he rushed through the ritual and strangled her instead."

Hunter takes a moment to process. "This doesn't fit his MO. The other victims were randomly selected for punishment."

"Because this wasn't about repentance and punishing her for sinning. It was some kind of revenge. He killed her out of hatred."

He shakes his head. "This is unbelievable. If he knew her, why was it missed in the previous police investigation?"

"You tell me."

With my news delivered, I feel shaken. Hunter approaches tentatively. When I'm pulled into his arms, I deflate. He rubs circles on my back, his beard tickling the top of my head.

"You're okay," he whispers.

"None of this is okay. He knew her and she was torn apart anyway. Why doesn't anyone else know this? Or am I just losing it?"

"I don't think you're losing it, sweetheart. Let me make some calls and check the records from the previous investigation. You did good."

"Too little, too late." I breathe in his spicy scent, even if I don't deserve to be comforted. "I can't bring her back."

Hunter guides my eyes up to his. "But you can stop anyone else from getting hurt. I have some news."

Panic spears me. "What is it?"

"The intelligence department has tracked down a potential location for where you were held."

"Did you find anything?" I rush out.

"Not that simple. It's deep in thick woodland and can only be accessed by foot. We have to go there and scout it out."

My heart pounds harder. "So we're leaving?"

His smile is tight and unhappy. "None of us like the idea of you being in danger. If Enzo had his way, you would never leave the house again."

"I've spent enough years locked away from the world."

"I know. Look, this is your decision to make, and we respect that. You're going to come with us and help track this place down. A deal's a deal."

He clutches my hands to stop them from shaking. The cold air of the basement is slipping beneath my skin, chilling my thawed heart back into an icy, impenetrable lump. I barely survived escaping.

Can I really go back there? Will I be able to cope with seeing it again? I honestly don't know. This seemed like a good idea, but the reality is another thing altogether.

"I have to do this," I say nervously. "You'll be there, right?"

"Of course." Hunter's fingers link with mine. "You'll have us and the Cobra team to support you. We'll triple security to make sure it's safe. I can't control what we may find inside though."

"You think… another prisoner?"

"Perhaps, if he snatched a girl immediately after dumping the last body for us to find. I don't want to rule it out."

Pastor Michaels has an intricate process, weeks of scheduled beatings and recited scripture to take the sinner from evil, soulless scum to a willing vessel for the Lord's divine retribution.

If there's someone else in there, she'll be knee-deep in her own blood. Nausea engulfs me as I realise what else could be waiting if they haven't bothered to move her yet.

"Laura," I whisper in horror.

Hunter's mouth is an uneasy slash. "She hasn't turned up. You need to be prepared. If we find this place, she might still be inside."

Swallowing the bubble of acid stinging the back of my throat, all I can do is nod. If I open my mouth, something else might slip out. A gnarly, twisted secret that could bring my whole world crashing down.

"We will be home for Christmas at the weekend," Hunter outlines. "We'll head out tomorrow on a private plane."

"Got it," I squeak.

Leaning close, his lips lock on to mine and swallow my silent screams of panic. I don't deserve the hidden sweetness behind Hunter's impenetrable façade, but his kiss pulls me back from the edge.

Pecking my lips again, he tucks me into his side. "Everyone's downstairs. We can go over introductions."

"Can you give me a minute? I need to splash my face and grab some painkillers. My head is killing me."

He scans my face with concern. "Go home and rest; it can wait until tomorrow. Leighton will have to drive you. We've got a lot of planning to do tonight."

"You're sure?"

"We need you rested and ready. Can you find your way to my office from here? There are some tablets in the desk drawer. The code is 041022."

"Got it, thanks."

Firing off a text to Leighton, he presses a kiss to my temple before heading back out to the elevator. The minute he disappears, I let my mask crumble.

If he knew how scared I was, I'd never be allowed to go. The thought of returning to Laura, my childhood and all the dark memories I've been pushing back is unthinkable.

I have no choice.

This could be our chance.

Steeling my spine, I make my way upstairs to Hunter's office. Inside, it's a disorganised mess. The last few weeks of chaos have clearly wreaked havoc on his tidy headspace.

Knocking back some pills, I glance over his cluttered desk. There's a smashed photo frame nestled amongst the stacks of paperwork. I dodge shards of broken glass to stroke my thumb over three familiar faces.

I've never seen Enzo, Hunter and Theo look so happy and content. Nestled between them, a pink-haired beauty grins at the camera. Her smile radiates so much warmth. Instinctively, I know it's Alyssa.

"I'll keep them safe," I whisper to the ghost.

"Hunter? You in here?"

Startled, I drop the frame so hard, it cracks against the desk. More shards of glass spill across the paperwork as someone enters the room.

"Harlow." Theo sounds surprised as he stops behind me. "Sorry, I didn't mean to scare you. Thought Hunter was up here."

"He's just gone back downstairs."

Theo's eyes land on the smashed frame. He visibly swallows before looking back up at me.

"He spoke to you?" he asks in a strained voice.

"I'm coming with you guys."

"You sure that's a good idea?"

"Do you not want me there?" I ask in return.

"I want you to be safe," he answers with a sigh. "But I actually vouched for this idea. I think it's important for you to be there."

I blink in surprise. "You do?"

He moves to lean against the wall, his glasses shielded by a loose curl. "I admire your strength. I'm not sure I'd do the same in your position."

Heat spreads across my cheeks. I have no idea what to say. Our late-night conversations are about books, theories, obscure ideas and observations about a world that scares us both to death.

Theo's very philosophical and painfully intelligent. It's an attractive, if not slightly awkward, quality to have. I've admired him for a while now. I didn't expect it to be returned though.

"Listen," he begins. "The thing is... well, um, it's a little bit complicated, you know?"

"Uh, I have no idea what you're talking about."

Sighing in frustration, he scrubs his eyes beneath his glasses. "I swear, I had it. Now all the words are jumbled up in my head."

Taking a tentative step closer, I rest a hand on his shoulder. "It's just me. You can tell me anything."

His pale-blue eyes scrape over me, assessing and afraid. I'm stunned as he takes my hand from his shoulder and holds it instead.

"I guess I wanted to apologise," he tries again. "The others have looked after you while I stayed away. I feel… shitty about that."

My eyebrows knit together. "Theo… you gave Laura back to me to say goodbye. You've kept the case going, working night after night. More than that, you've been a good friend."

"A friend?" he echoes.

"Well, I don't think strangers donate their entire library to random people or stay until the sun rises to discuss crazy book theories. That's what friends do."

His smile is a gentle evening breeze that warms the shell of my heart. Despite his awkward nature, Theo is a soothing presence. Quiet, reserved, observant. But beneath it all, fearsome in his own way.

"Are you friends with the others too?"

"What else would I be?" I answer softly.

For once, he doesn't hesitate or doubt himself.

"I've seen the way they all look at you."

His hand is still wrapped around mine, trembling slightly with each word. Anxiety runs over him like a static charge.

"I don't know what you want me to say."

"I… I… hell, me neither," he falters.

There's something in the loaded air that's sealing us in this room, letting everything else fall away. An emotion. I don't know what it is. The others don't look at me like Theo does.

"Can I just hug you?"

His request catches me off guard.

"You don't need to ask." I smile shyly. "But yeah, that'd be nice."

Offering his own tiny smile, he releases my hand and steps closer until his green flannel shirt is pressed up against my nose. His arms are surprisingly strong beneath the loose clothing he wears, wiry and muscular.

I breathe in his peppermint scent, spiked with the familiarity of parchment and antique books. It's like stepping into a library and being welcomed home into its warm, comfortable arms.

Where Leighton makes me laugh until I want to cry, Enzo treats me like I'm a precious artefact to be loved and protected. Hunter excites me, makes me feel beautiful and powerful.

But Theo… with him, I feel at home. Secure. Wrapped in soft blankets and soothing firelight, the pages of a book spread out on my lap. He's the welcoming arms of the family I always wanted.

His breath stirs my hair. "You feel good."

I tighten my arms around his narrow waist. "Do you live in a library or something? You always smell like books."

"Is that a bad thing?" He chuckles.

"Definitely not."

"My office is a bit of a lair." I feel his fingers stroke down the length of my spine. "I like books more than I like people."

"Seems fair."

Lapsing into silence, we hold each other tight. There's no pressure to separate or speak. I focus on the feel of Theo stroking my back, his breathing evening out as his anxiety fades.

When he releases me, it feels like an eternity has passed. The world has ended around us, succumbed to the ravages of time, and we're the last two humans left in this existence.

He looks at me… like I'm his whole world. That terrifies and excites me so much. I want to dive into his blue-eyed gaze and let myself be consumed by the oceanic waves.

"I haven't done that for a long time," he admits with an adorable blush. "Thank you for not being weirded out."

I can't help but laugh.

"Have you met me? I'm not sure weird is a strong enough label for the stuff going on up here." I gesture to my head. "If you need more hugs, you know where I am."

His eyes sparkle. "I may take you up on that. Listen, the others are waiting for me. I should head back down."

"I need to find Leighton. He's taking me home."

Nodding, Theo offers me his hand again, but it isn't shaking this time. There's a certainty to the way his fingers link with mine.

"Let's find him together."

CHAPTER 31

Harlow

Burning The Iron Age – Trade Wind

Bustled out of the black-tinted SUV, I throw my backpack over my shoulder. Rain is falling in thick curtains, soaking the smooth tarmac beneath my leather boots. The snow didn't last long.

The time has come.

We're going up north.

The sprawling airport is an unnerving sight. Huge aeroplanes are parked in neat rows, towering well above me like great steel beasts. Everything here is huge, from the miles of runway to the glistening glass buildings of the terminals behind us.

Enzo climbs out of the car and steals my backpack from me before I can protest. "Are you doing okay?"

"Yeah," I answer quickly.

"Are you sure?"

I haven't been able to eat or drink anything, including at dinner last night. It all tastes like ashes in my mouth. Sleep was also impossible, so I'm running on empty.

"Harlow?"

"I just need some space."

Enzo clears his throat. "Okay then."

He silently nods to the various agents standing in formation as we approach them. They're all dressed in black uniforms, packing visible gun holsters and schooled expressions.

"It's alright to be scared," he tries again as we cross the tarmac. "We're all here to help you get through the next couple of days."

I don't respond.

For once, I want Enzo to stay as far away from me as possible. He's too good at teasing the truth from me. If I'm going to keep it together, I need to hold every broken, ugly piece of myself inside.

One wrong move and it'll all crumble to ruin. My secrets are dangerously close to devouring me in a greedy, hellish furnace. Keeping them inside is going to take every ounce of control I have.

We're taking Sabre's private plane for the short flight up north. Their logo is even printed on the gleaming wing. Enzo gestures for me to go ahead, and I tentatively head up the narrow steps.

Inside, their wealth and power are spelled out in cream-coloured leather seats, dark-wood panels and a fully stocked bar lined with different liquors. Two rows of seats sandwich a wide, carpeted aisle.

At the back of the aeroplane, a gaggle of people are messing around with raised voices. I feel Enzo's hand on my lower back, gently guiding me towards them as my lungs seize up.

They fall quiet, and various eyes land on me with curiosity. I recognise a couple of the guys immediately. Becket and Ethan guarded my hospital room, and they offer me smiles of greeting.

The other two with them also wave with friendly smiles. They introduce themselves as Tara and Warner, the final members of the Anaconda team.

Enzo drops my backpack into an empty seat. "Harlow, you haven't officially met the Cobra team yet either. They helped in Devon too."

I manage an awkward nod. "Hi, everyone."

Squeezed into a window seat, a smiling, blonde-haired man waves at me. He's smartly dressed, his crisp, white shirt complementing his kind, hazel eyes.

"Hey, Harlow. We met while you were unconscious. I'm Kade." He gestures to the person next to him. "This is my brother, Hudson."

His brother doesn't speak, nodding instead. From the tattoos inked all the way up to his throat and multiple facial piercings beneath his messy, raven-coloured hair, he looks a little intimidating.

"Ignore this one." A female voice snickers. "He's a teddy bear really, beneath the emo exterior."

Standing up from her seat, the platinum-haired woman is looking at me expectantly. She looks around my age, but she's strong and sinewy like a trained marine. Her ripped jeans match the worn leather jacket wrapped around her shoulders.

"I'm Brooklyn." She tries for a smile, but it looks a little foreign on her mouth. "Enzo's told me a lot about you."

"He… did?" I reply anxiously.

"I knew this introduction was a bad idea," Enzo grumbles behind me. "Brooke, keep any embarrassing stories to yourself or find another job."

She smirks at him. "You're no fun. Come sit next to me, Harlow. I've got plenty of juicy stories to tell you about this lump of meat."

"M-Me?" I stutter.

Brooklyn pats the empty seat next to her. Taking a breath, I move my backpack and slide into the empty spot. Kade and Hudson are sitting behind us, leaving Enzo to move further up the plane.

I watch him go with a sigh of relief. Hunter, Leighton and Theo are piling on board with various bags of equipment, preparing for takeoff. They spot me with Brooklyn, and all seem to relax slightly. Clearly, they trust her implicitly.

"I hate flying," she admits quietly. "Although the bar is well stocked, I suppose. That's a bonus."

"I've never flown before."

"This is nicer than a commercial flight, so you're in luck. Better to sit with us than Captain Cockblock over there."

I choke on a breath. "Excuse me?"

"He said not to embarrass him." Kade sticks his head between the seats with a knowing grin.

"So?" she snarks back.

"I'm not standing between you and Enzo when he comes to break your legs for telling that story. I'd like to keep my face intact."

"Dammit," Brooklyn curses. "Why should I marry you if you won't defend me from leg-breaking assholes?"

He ruffles her shoulder-length hair. "Because I'm a catch, love. Don't complain. We'll defend your honour against anyone but him."

Kade disappears back between the seats, and I can't resist a glance. He has a laptop balanced on his lap as he resumes working. Next to him, Hudson is frowning at the men swarming over the tarmac.

Danger seems to cling to him, shrouding his entire stony persona in a threatening cloud. When he catches me staring, I'm knocked off-kilter by the tiny, reassuring smile he gives me.

"You ready for this, Harlow?"

"I, uh… I hope so."

Hudson cocks his head to the side. "None of us are going to let anyone hurt you. Stick by us. You'll be alright."

"He's right," Brooklyn says beside me. "You're not going into those woods alone. You've got every single one of us by your side."

Turning back to face her, I wring my sweaty hands together. These people don't know me, but they're putting their lives at risk to keep me safe. If anything happens to them, it's on me.

"He's dangerous," I squeeze out. "Pastor Michaels will hurt you to get to me. You don't know the things he's done."

"We don't hurt all that easily." Brooklyn's shoulder bumps mine. "This asshat isn't the first monster we've faced."

In her eyes, something dark and sinister shines. I can see the demons pulling the strings behind her strained smile. Somehow, she has control over them.

Everything about her is calm and assured, with an air of self-awareness. But crackling through that, the threat of violence is palpable. In a weird way, I do feel safe by her side.

"Harlow." She sticks out her hand, palm up. "You're doing the right thing by coming. I think it's brave. If we find the suspect, we'll make him pay for everything he's done."

Biting my lip, I put my hand in hers. Her palm is warm and dry, contrasting my clammy skin. She holds me tight before releasing.

"Promise?" I say under my breath.

Her smile is shark like. "Pinkie swear."

As the final equipment is loaded and the doors shut, the hum of the engine begins to rumble beneath us. My throat closes up as I fasten my seatbelt and fight to remain calm.

Brooklyn pulls out her phone and plugs in a pair of headphones. When she offers one to me, I gingerly accept.

"Takeoff isn't so bad," she whispers conspiratorially. "Shut your eyes and focus on the music."

Slipping it into my ear, she cranks the rock music up loud, props her booted feet up and closes her eyes. I copy her every move and let the aeroplane fall away.

†

"Circle around everyone."

Outside several black support vans, the car park roped off with police tape lit by flashing blue lights, our group gathers. Eight police officers and a well-sized army of Sabre agents stand at the edge of the forest, holding the perimeter and ready to move in if we need them at any time.

There's a helicopter humming in the air above us in case of an emergency, and the buzz of these little black devices, resembling big, metal cicadas, surrounds the perimeter. Theo calls them drones, whatever that means.

Hunter zips the bulletproof vest over his raincoat. "We're going to split into three teams to cover more ground. Myself, Brooklyn, Enzo and Harlow will take the central path with Fox on comms."

Inspecting several wickedly sharp knives before securing them inside his jacket, Hudson gives me a nod. Brooklyn is already armed, her vest bulging with two guns and an array of knives.

"Ethan, Tara, Kade and Theo will take the eastern route," Hunter continues. "You'll be supported by Rayna on comms."

Seeing Theo suited and booted like the others is a strange sight. His usual flannel shirt and faded jeans have gone, replaced with guns and steely determination. He smiles when our eyes connect.

"Last up, the western path. Becket, Hudson, Leighton and Warner, with Liam on comms. Each team has a trained first aider, and the medical team will be on standby with the local police."

Enzo steps forward as everyone shuffles into their teams. He's terrifying in work mode, roaring at various agents to get equipment organised and cordons set up.

"We've got air support keeping infrared surveillance on the whole forest," he adds. "Communicate, keep your eyes open and shoot to kill."

"We want the perps alive," Hunter corrects him with a sharp glare. "They have a hell of a lot to answer for. No lethal force."

Enzo grumbles, but reluctantly agrees. With the rules laid out, maps distributed and earpieces fitted, everyone prepares to set off. There's ten miles to cover and about six hours of daylight left.

We're racing against the clock. The foreboding forest surrounding us is dripping with malice, cloaked in darkness and mist. Nobody wants to be in there when the sun surrenders.

Before we set off, Theo approaches me. He looks startlingly lethal as he tucks a handgun into his covered holster.

"Be safe, alright?" he says quietly. "We still need to discuss *Jane Eyre* tonight. Make sure you come back in one piece."

"You too." I pull him into a fast hug, careful not to disturb his weapons. "Look after each other."

Behind him, Leighton waits his turn. He crushes me against his chest so hard, I squeak in shock. There's no sign of his usual playful smiles or jokes today.

"I hate this," he murmurs against my hair. "Hunter and Enzo will keep you safe. Just... don't take any risks, alright?"

"I've got it, Leigh."

"I mean it."

Releasing me, he ignores everyone and presses his lips against mine. I freeze, panicked, but he keeps it short and sweet.

"Sorry," he says under his breath. "I had to do that."

Sauntering away, Leighton ignores the death glares being sent his way from Hunter and Enzo. Theo looks more startled, and perhaps a little bit intrigued. They quickly rejoin their respective teams.

Clearing my throat, I find the others at the edge of the forest. Brooklyn double-checks my bulletproof vest, making sure the other two aren't looking as she slides a knife into the pocket.

"Just in case." She winks.

"Thank you."

"Know how to use it?"

I return her small smile. "Well enough."

"Well, alrighty then. Let's get this show on the road. Gentlemen?"

Both checking their earpieces are online, Enzo and Hunter sandwich us between them. We set off in synchronisation with the other two teams, plunging into the silent woodland.

The moss beneath our boots swallows every footstep. Tall trees stretch up into the heavens, casting shadows across thick shrubbery, slippery rocks and layers of thicket.

After walking a little way in, I duck down to stroke my fingers over the uneven ground. The phantom pain of rocks slicing my bare feet flashes through my mind with the earthy scent of the forest.

This place is spookily familiar.

I can feel myself sprinting through it.

"Harlow?" Hunter stops by my side. "All good?"

Straightening, I tighten my grip on the backpack of medical supplies I'm carrying. It's the lightest, and the only one that Enzo was willing to let me shoulder while my leg is still tender.

He's further ahead, walking in lockstep with Brooklyn as they talk. She seems to be a lot closer to him than the others.

"Yeah." I swallow hard. "This place feels familiar. I recognise the trees. They're different from the ones back home."

Hunter falls into step beside me. "Sitka spruce. My dad used to take us hiking when we were kids. He knows all the species."

"Do you get on well with your dad?" I ask randomly.

Climbing up a steep incline, he offers me a hand over the wet, moss-covered rocks.

"Sometimes," Hunter answers. "He's always had very exacting standards. I thrive under that kind of pressure, but it was really rough on Leighton. I didn't like that."

"Enzo said he struggled when he was younger."

"Leighton's always found family hard. Our folks haven't seen him since he left prison. It's breaking my mum's heart, but they can't force him to see them."

"Any idea why?" I clamber over a fallen branch.

"He doesn't want to deal with their disappointment. In his mind, they hate him. In reality, my parents just want their son back. Regardless of whatever he's done. It doesn't matter to them."

Enzo shouts from ahead and gestures towards a narrow path on the left. Tucking his map away, they lead the way as we follow.

"Do you think I'm a bad person for refusing to see Giana again?" I blurt out.

Hunter checks behind us before walking some more. "No, Harlow. That's a different situation. You're entitled to take things at your own pace. She'll still be there when you're ready."

"It isn't different, though, is it? Leighton is afraid your parents won't love him anymore. With Giana… I'm afraid of not being the person she once knew. And what that means for my future."

"Your future is yours to decide," he responds. "Regardless of what Giana wants. Leighton has to do the same. I know you'll both be okay though."

Pausing to scrape gelatinous mud off my walking boots, I look up at Hunter's impassive face.

"How?"

He sends me a crooked smile. "Because you've got us. If you think me, Enzo or Theo are letting either of you off the hook, you've got us all wrong. We're a family. We support each other."

Emotion envelops me. Even with the abject terror of our unknown surroundings, I can't help but feel at home in Hunter's presence. He doesn't scare me anymore. I feel whole around him.

"I'm not sure I deserve a family," I say thickly.

He sticks his hand out for me to take. "Everyone deserves a family, Harlow. Even fucked up people like us. Maybe we deserve it even more for that reason."

Letting his hand engulf mine, I accept his help over another rocky obstacle in the path. Hunter doesn't let me go after. The forest is a green blur around us, but he's the anchor stopping the fear from overcoming me.

A couple of hours into our search, we stop to drink some water and raid the energy bars in Brooklyn's backpack. She checks in with Hudson and Kade through our comms, gnawing her lip until she hears they're safe.

We pour over our map, marking the section we've scoured with a pen. The chapel was abandoned so long ago, nobody knows exactly where it is anymore. The others haven't reported a sighting yet either.

"Let's try further east, in this section here." Hunter points to a different patch of woods. "I read a land survey from the late 1800s that mentioned Mary Magdalene Chapel being further over."

Enzo's frown deepens. "It's off course. Harder for backup to reach us if we need it. They'll need to approach from the other side."

Nodding, Hunter tightens the laces on his boots. "I just have a gut feeling. It's too overgrown where we are. These trees are old, they would've been cleared for building materials to be transported during construction."

"Alright." Enzo sighs. "Brooke?"

She studies the map for a second longer. "Hudson's group is coming at it from another angle. Between us, we can clear that whole section."

They all look to me next. I nod in agreement, itching to set off again. Every second, I'm glancing around me, searching for Pastor Michaels' savage smile. This place is spine chilling.

Plunging deeper into the forest, we climb across a series of small streams. The sound of rushing water slices through my brain, bringing with it more disjointed flashes.

I slipped and slid that day, wading through water and mud, cutting my hands as I fought to escape. The memories are becoming clearer. Hobbling through a forest with broken bones was excruciating.

Another two hours and we're fighting against the sinking sun. Enzo has snarled at the map several times, checking the compass attached to his backpack and shouting down the earpiece at Fox.

As Hunter and Brooklyn stop to dig out their water bottles, I stroke my fingers on the gnarly bark of the closest tree. They seem to be thinning out a little, even though we're miles into the unknown.

Another stream runs parallel to the route we're taking through thorny bushes and tall trees. Jumping down into the stream, I turn and begin to walk down, following the flow of water instead of going inland.

"Harlow!" Enzo barks. "Wait for us."

But I'm enchanted by the fast flow of the water, breaking over rocks and the odd fallen branch. Something about the trees and slightly lighter moss is calling out to me.

I continue walking down the centre of the stream while the others stumble to keep up with me. It's cold and slippery, but I keep wading through, even as it gets deep enough to reach my ankles.

There's a splash as Enzo joins me. "Come out of there, little one.

You'll catch hypothermia at this rate."

"No, we need to keep going."

"It'll be dark in an hour. We're going to turn back and regroup on the southern edge of the forest with Theo's team."

He huffs in annoyance as I ignore him completely. My feet are aching from the cold water seeping into my boots, but it's setting off an alarm bell. Something is calling out to me in sinister whispers.

"The basement flooded a lot," I reveal to him. "Whenever it rained really hard, water gradually pooled on the floor. It seemed to seep in from beneath us."

"Nearby water source?" Enzo guesses.

My footsteps begin to quicken. "Late at night, I could hear it. Trickling away, loud enough to reach me. They brought me bowls of water and changed the bucket in my cell a few times a week."

"Which… would require water," he catches on. "Not something you'd find running in an abandoned property."

The other two seem to realise we've hit upon something and jump down into the water to join us. The further we walk, the deeper the stream becomes. It nearly reaches our calves now.

"On your knees, Harlow," I recite as we plunge into darkness. "If I can't hear your prayers, the Lord Almighty certainly can't."

Enzo stares at me with concern. "Huh?"

The temperature drops when the sun disappears. Mist is rising, coating each leaf and bramble in droplets of moisture. Gushing water accompanies my whispered prayers.

When I spot the first stone brick, the last three months vanish in an instant. Every laugh, smile, kiss and cuddle are gone. Stolen away with silent cruelty. God is laughing at me all over again.

I'm back.

Harlow's come home.

"Holy fuck," Brooklyn curses behind us. "Are you guys seeing this too?"

"Yeah," Hunter says grimly.

Grabbing a thick tree root, I yank myself up the steep bank. It takes several rolls through the dirt to clamber to my feet. The healing wound on my leg is screaming with pain. The trees have thinned even more, forming a narrow clearing.

Climbing out, Enzo walks a few metres before crouching to study the ground. "Tyre tracks. They're old."

He hoists Brooklyn out next, setting her back on her feet. Hunter follows, his face paling as he spots the crumbling stone structure ahead of us.

"How did they get a car through here?" Brooklyn wonders aloud.

Hunter points deeper into the clearing. "There. Something small could make it through."

As I begin to walk ahead, drawn closer by an invisible thread wrapped around my pounding heart, Enzo bars an arm across my chest.

"You've done enough," he says roughly. "Let us go in."

I push his arm aside. "This is my home."

His eyes widen, clouded by worry. Walking on, my boots sink into the mud-covered ground with each step. I can still feel it squelching between my bare toes from my escape months ago.

The chapel is exactly as I remember it. An isolated slice of antiquity wrapped in an earthly tomb. The stone bricks are crumbling, falling into ruin, and I can see the smashed stained-glass window on the side of the building.

"There." I point at it, marvelling at the height. "It's no wonder I broke my arm jumping out of there, really."

Enzo's chest rumbles with an enraged roar. "That's where you jumped from?"

"The door was locked and bolted all over. There was no other way out. I wasn't going to sit and wait for them to come back."

Pausing, all three of them draw guns. Enzo taps his comms over and over, but the signal has finally cut out. We're lost in the wilderness and far from the Lord's light in this intimate circle of hell.

"What should we do?" he asks Hunter.

Studying the chapel, Hunter rolls back his shoulders. "Let's check it out. There's no vehicle parked. We can handle whatever's inside."

"Can we?"

"Yes," Brooklyn answers, shifting closer to me. "I've got Harlow. We're going to be fine. Let's move."

With a nod, I extract the knife she stashed in my pocket and hold it tight. Enzo purses his lips and plunges forward, pulling a small torch from his vest pocket.

The closer we inch, the quieter it becomes. Even the sound of the stream drains away. Evil clings to each vine-covered brick. It's an oozing pyroclastic cloud that consumes us all.

Gun raised, Hunter moves to the left, beneath the shattered window high above us. Shards of glass are still buried in the rotten leaves slowly putrefying beneath our feet.

Raw slabs of carved stone mark the entrance. Creeping up the small incline, I almost run into Enzo's back. They've both halted, staring ahead in silent concentration.

"What is it?" Brooklyn hushes.

Hunter cocks his gun. "Door's open."

"So?"

He moves aside so we can see what's painted on the slab of wood. I recognise the Holy Trinity instantly. It's dried and flaked in places over time, but the dark-brown liquid can only be one thing. I know blood when I see it.

Stooping to duck past the macabre welcome sign, Enzo leads the way into Pastor Michaels' hunting grounds. Hunter keeps casting me apprehensive looks, but I ignore him and step inside the chapel.

"Oh," is all I can muster.

It's been methodically and catastrophically trashed. All the remaining furniture and stained-glass windows are destroyed. Not even the altar stands anymore. It looks like a bulldozer passed through here, intent on obliteration.

After sweeping through the empty living quarters and main worship room, Enzo declares the place clear. Hunter and Brooklyn don't lower their guns. It's pitch-black in here. The darkness can hide malevolent intentions.

Pulling my own torch out, I follow the path my bloodstained feet took. Every now and then, a red smear marks the stone floor. I can just make out the print of my own toes.

"Harlow," Hunter calls out. "Not alone. Show us where it is."

I point the light ahead, through an arched doorway with nothing but clinging shadows beyond.

"Follow me."

Sticking in a close formation, I somehow find myself leading the pack. Dread and nausea have melted into numb acceptance. I was always meant to end up back here. This basement and I have unfinished business.

With the narrow staircase in sight, the first waves of a stomach-churning stench hit us. It's ripe, rancid, so thick you can taste the individual notes of death on the tip of your tongue.

"Motherfucker," Enzo swears. "That's a body."

Muscling his way to the front, Hunter steps in front of me. "I know you have to go down there, but I'm going first. No arguments."

I gesture for him to go ahead. Swallowing hard, he takes a final breath of semi-clean air and plunges into the basement. With every inch, the smell grows. Demons are festering down here in the dark.

The steps groan beneath my feet, underscoring Hunter's silence as he reaches the bottom. He doesn't move another inch.

"Hunt?" Enzo calls urgently.

"Yeah," he responds in a flat voice. "It's… um, clear. He's not here."

But something is, the devil whispers.

Hunter steps aside to let the rest of us down. The slanted beam of light from his torch cuts through the bleak nothingness. It takes my eyes a moment to adjust. The outside world has spoiled me with all its freely available light.

"Harlow," Hunter warns. "Don't look."

It's too late. My feet move without being told, guiding me back to the cage where I spent thirteen years of my life. It's smaller than I remember it. This entire basement is. My home has shrunk, or I've grown.

But this cell doesn't belong to me anymore. Its new inhabitant swings from a rough hunk of rope tied into the perfect noose around her skeletal neck.

Skin, fat and muscle have melted into a black, foul-smelling sludge that clings to a soulless skeleton. Standing outside the broken cell door, I spot the gold wedding band that's fallen from her finger and hit the ground.

"Do not be deceived," I whisper into the dead silence. "God is not to be mocked; for whatever one sows, that will he reap."

"Is that Laura?" Hunter asks in a soft whisper.

Shaking my head, I point to the adjacent cage. Its door is still locked tight, holding another decaying skeleton prisoner. Several of the bones are missing, broken by my cage door, while another has been sent home for burial.

Stepping inside my cage, I pick through the blackened goo to reach the hanging remains. Scraps of floral fabric are fossilised in decaying bodily fluids.

Bending down, I extricate the wedding ring and hold it in the centre of my palm. It cut into my skin enough times when Mrs Michaels beat the devil out of me.

My voice comes out devoid, lifeless, drained.

"Hello, Mother."

EPILOGUE

Theo

Corpse Roads – Keaton Henson

Sitting in the light of the twinkling Christmas tree, I watch Harlow fitfully sleep on the sofa opposite. I finally managed to convince her to swallow a couple of sleeping pills an hour or so ago.

She winces, crying out in her sleep and grappling her neck, like someone invisible is choking her. I rush over, giving her a gentle shake to startle her from the dream.

Harlow sucks in a deep breath before dropping back off. Rather than returning to the sofa, I sink down to the carpet in front of her, staying within touching distance for when the next one hits.

My eyes grow heavy after a while, coaxed shut by the crackling flames of the fire, but my phone vibrating soon snaps me back. I step into the corner to answer.

"Hunt?"

"Yeah," he grunts without a greeting. "Listen, we're wrapping things up here. Forensics have extracted the bodies. We'll be flying back with them tomorrow."

"Okay, good." I rest my forehead on the wall. "Harlow finally went to sleep. I'm taking turns to keep watch with Leighton."

"How's she doing?"

"Not good." My voice thickens with emotion. "She was catatonic on the flight down. Wouldn't speak to anyone. Not even Brooklyn could coax her out of it."

He swears colourfully. "This whole thing is a mess. I'll call Richards and get him to make an emergency visit."

"You think it'll help?"

"I don't know what else to suggest."

Harlow lets out a strangled sob behind me and I race back to the sofa, quickly shushing her again. Her hand fists my t-shirt.

"That her?" Hunter asks fearfully.

"Yeah, she's fighting being asleep. The night terrors look pretty bad. Maybe sedating her was a bad idea."

"Stay with her," he orders.

"Obviously," I snap back. "Sorry, I'm exhausted. Brooklyn said she's going to bring Jude around in the morning. He might be able to help Harlow."

"Good call. We should be back by the afternoon. The superintendent has called a meeting. She's demanding an update."

"What did you tell her?"

Hunter scoffs, sounding as exhausted as I feel. "That we have two more dead bodies and no perp. She's going to steamroll us."

I sigh heavily. "Remind her who got her that fucking job in the first place. She owes us. We need more time and funding to see this through."

"What if he can't be found?"

The resignation in Hunter's voice is an unfamiliar gut punch. I haven't heard that defeat in a long time. Not since we waited for the results from his auditory test and got word that he couldn't hear a thing anymore without the aid he despises so much. Even now, he could still go fully deaf.

"We cannot give up, Hunt. Not now, not ever. Harlow needs us to see this through. It's her life we're talking about."

"I know," he replies tersely. "We will always protect her, but this bastard just slaughtered his own wife."

"What?" I gasp.

"The positioning of the noose was all wrong. Too high, and it was knotted from the back. Pastor Michaels hung his own wife."

"Fucking hell."

"Yeah, exactly. He could be in bloody Timbuktu by now."

"Then… we have to hunt his sadistic ass down and drag him back here face punishment for his crimes. We owe Harlow that much."

Hunter remains silent.

"Do you love her?" I ask him.

"What?"

"Do you love her?"

He hesitates before answering. "So much it scares me."

"What about Enzo? Leighton?"

"I don't fucking know, Theo. We would all do anything to keep her in our lives, no matter what it takes. What about you?"

With the phone pressed to my ear, I stare at Harlow's slack face. Her hair is splayed across the sofa cushions, showing a hint of the growing bald patch beneath the layers.

I gently run a finger over her sore, swollen scalp. She's stopped trying to hide it entirely now. The flight home was heartbreaking, watching the pile of hair in her lap grow.

Powerlessness is an old friend that I never wanted to be reacquainted with. I couldn't offer her any sliver of comfort that would be more appealing than the pain she was craving.

"I care about her," I answer his question. "More than I thought possible after Alyssa. I want her to be okay. I want to be the one to make her happy, whatever form that takes."

Hunter breathes down the line. "Then I guess it's settled. This isn't a dead end in the investigation. It's only the beginning."

"Well, there's one more thing."

"What is it?"

I clutch the phone tighter. "Harlow was mumbling a bit when we carried her on to the plane. She said that... she killed Laura. Strangled her so she wouldn't suffer and die slowly."

Hunter inhales sharply. "That can't be right."

"That's all I know."

"I'm sure she was just out of it and triggered by going back there. We can figure it out when the rest of us get home. Sounds like a meaningless ramble to me."

"Alright, I'll keep an eye on her anyway. Stay in touch."

We wrap up the phone call quickly. Hunter's dealing with local police and a media circus that have caught wind of our huge presence up north. He'll fly back with Enzo in the morning.

Hearing the shower flick off upstairs, I tighten the blanket around Harlow's shoulders and pad into the kitchen to heat up the lasagne Brooklyn dropped off for us this morning.

As I'm poking in the fridge for condiments, the security system in the entrance hall goes haywire. The glass bottle of salad dressing in my hand smashes against the tiled floor as I sprint for the door.

"Shit, shit, shit."

The emergency alert has been triggered. Someone's tried to punch in the wrong passcode several times and messed up the retinal scan.

Leighton's footsteps skip over several stairs as he bounds down.

"What's happening?" he shouts.

"Intruder at the front gate." I quickly unlock the system and check the camera. "Someone's out there. Can't see a face though."

"Shit. What do we do?"

"Stay here. I'll check it out."

"No, Theo!"

"Stay here," I repeat in a raised voice.

Snatching the gun that Hunter keeps stashed in the bottom drawer of the console—one of many around the house—I slip outside into the falling rain. The lights are all on, illuminating the empty driveway.

There's a shadow slumped just outside the gate, shivering after giving up on breaking through. With the gun raised high, I tentatively approach.

"Who the fuck are you?" I call out.

Nothing.

"Get up or I'll shoot. You're trespassing on private property."

If it's a journalist, I'll kneecap them for the damn thrill of it. I wouldn't be surprised if Sally Moore sent one of her bloodless cronies to fish for an update.

The figure finally stirs, using the gate to wrench himself upright. He's staggering, clearly inebriated, and dressed in threadbare clothing that wouldn't look amiss on a homeless person. Every inch of him is shaking with exertion.

"State your business!" I yell at him.

When there's no response, I cock the gun in warning. He takes one look at me and collapses into an unconscious heap. I'm a split second from shooting when hurried footsteps slap through the rain behind me.

"Theo, wait!"

Harlow stumbles down the slick driveway, soaked and wild-eyed as she escapes Leighton's embrace. I grab her around the waist before she can run past me, yanking her off her feet.

"Get back in the fucking house!" I shout at her.

"No, no," she screams back. "You can't shoot him!"

Jamming her elbow into my stomach, she wriggles free from my arms and lands on her feet. I come to my senses quick enough to stop her from stealing the gun in my hands.

"Harlow, stop!"

"Don't shoot!" She turns to look at the collapsed stranger, timid and uncertain. "I think he's my real father."

To be continued in
Skeletal Hearts (Sabre Security #2)

Pre-Order: mybook.to/SkeletalHearts

PLAYLIST

White Noise – Badflower

Holding Out For A Hero – Nothing But Thieves

Natural Born Killer – Highly Suspect

The Raging Sea - Broadside

Dead Letter & The Infinite Yes – Wintersleep

Even In The Dark – jxdn

New Eyes – Echos

Conversations – Juice WRLD

Heart-Shaped Box – Ashton Irwin

Come Undone – My Darkest Days

Speaking Off The Record – Hotel Mira

Without You – PLTS

Manic Memories – Des Rocs

Scavengers (Acoustic) – Thrice

.haunted. – Dead Poet Society

The Madness – Foreign Air

(if) you are the ocean (then) I would like to drown – VIOLET NIGHT

Someone Somewhere Somehow – Super Whatevr

Midnight Demon Club – Highly Suspect

Bad Place – The Hunna

The Search – NF

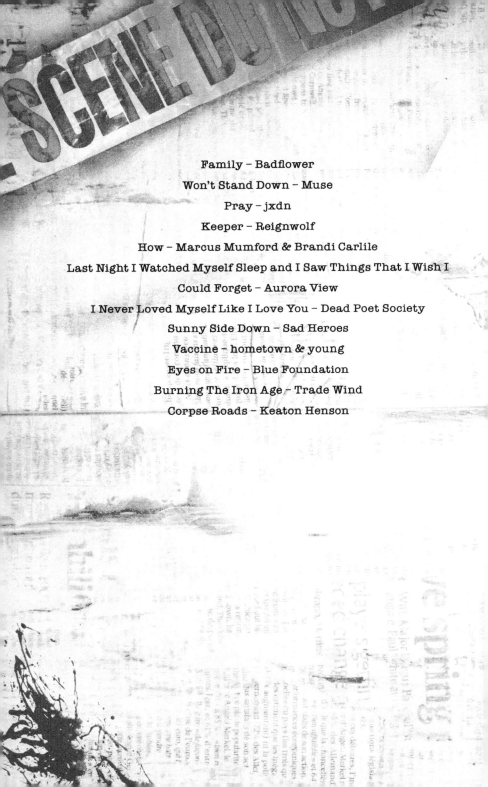

Family – Badflower

Won't Stand Down – Muse

Pray – jxdn

Keeper – Reignwolf

How – Marcus Mumford & Brandi Carlile

Last Night I Watched Myself Sleep and I Saw Things That I Wish I
Could Forget – Aurora View

I Never Loved Myself Like I Love You – Dead Poet Society

Sunny Side Down – Sad Heroes

Vaccine – hometown & young

Eyes on Fire – Blue Foundation

Burning The Iron Age – Trade Wind

Corpse Roads – Keaton Henson

WANT MORE FROM THIS SHARED UNIVERSE?

If you loved Brooklyn and her merry band of psychopaths, check out their completed story in the Blackwood Institute trilogy—a dark, why choose romance set in an experimental psychiatric institute where monsters walk among us and nothing is quite what it seems.

Twisted Heathens: mybook.to/TwistedHeathens

Sacrificial Sinners: mybook.to/SacrificialSinners

Desecrated Saints: mybook.to/DesecratedSaints

ACKNOWLEDGEMENTS

Harlow's story came to me in a fever dream well over a year ago. I was at a time in my life when I needed to know there are good people out there. Not heroes, but people capable of taking something intrinsically broken and piecing it back together.

Hunter, Theo, Enzo and Leighton were born of that wild hope.

I wrote this book for everyone who feels broken from time to time. Hey, there's no judgement here. I've come to believe that we're all just a little bit fucked up. Life would be boring if we were all sane and healthy, right?

Settle in and join the fucked up club.

We have t-shirts.

Thank you to every single person on my team who has helped me to keep my broken pieces together while I tear myself apart every time I sit down to write a book. This career is a constant process of destruction and rebirth, I swear.

I don't give him enough recognition, so Eddie, this book is for you. Thank you for being my rock and constant source of stability. I can't wait to be your wife, even though it took you seven years to ask me. Here's to forever, baby.

Kristen, you keep me going every single day. Every time I publish a book, I say the same thing here because it's true. I wouldn't be sane and still writing without you being my monkey master. I love you, wife.

To the fabulous people on my team – my PA, Julia, who is a superwoman and keeps my chaos in line. My amazing editor, Mackenzie, who never fails to build me up. Lauren, my proofreader, beautiful friend and all-round superstar, who deserves a medal for putting up with me. All of my dedicated street and ARC team members need a huge round of applause too.

Thank you to Lilith for being the most amazing friend a girl could ask for. I don't know how I'd cope without semi-psychotically voice-noting you on a daily basis. I love you, Excel Freak.

Lola, you deserve a special mention for holding my hand through nightmares (literally, and I'm still very sorry by the way) and for coming on crazy, drunken, tear-filled American adventures with me. Thank you for the beautiful memories.

And finally, I need to say a massive thank you to everyone else who supports and inspires me in the crazy world of author-land. Dani, Rosa, Emma, Zoe, Sam… you've all been there for me while I drove myself insane writing this book. Damn, I have amazing friends.

Our community truly is beautiful. I feel privileged to be a part of it.

Until next time,

Stay wild. I'll see you soon for Skeletal Hearts.

J Rose x

ABOUT THE AUTHOR

J Rose is an independent dark romance author from the United Kingdom. She writes challenging, plot-driven stories packed full of angst, heartbreak and broken characters fighting for their happily ever afters.

She's an introverted bookworm at heart, with a caffeine addiction, penchant for cursing and an unhealthy attachment to fictional characters.

Feel free to reach out on social media, J Rose loves talking to her readers!

For exclusive insights, updates and general mayhem, join J Rose's Bleeding Thorns on Facebook.

Business enquiries: j_roseauthor@yahoo.com

Come join the chaos. Stalk J Rose here…

www.jroseauthor.com/socials

NEWSLETTER

Want more madness? Sign up to J Rose's newsletter for monthly announcements, exclusive content, sneak peeks, giveaways and more! www.jroseauthor.com/newsletter

ALSO BY J ROSE

www.jroseauthor.com/books

Blackwood Institute
Twisted Heathens
Sacrificial Sinners
Desecrated Saints

Standalones
Departed Whispers
Forever Ago
Drown in You

Sabre Security
Corpse Roads
Skeletal Hearts